THE SWEETEST THING

MAYA HUGHES

Cover Design: Najla Qamber

1

SABRINA

Triple-checking the address, I snagged a parking spot around the corner from my destination. The tree-lined streets and brownstone townhouses on my way here hadn't helped alleviate my concerns that Barbara had given me the wrong address.

I checked my phone again. This was the place. I was relieved to be here, and I didn't want to fight more city traffic to find the right place if there had been a typo.

Not that I could be a chooser, what with me being a beggar and all. I'd needed a last-minute place to stay after my apartment had an infestation I couldn't get rid of—an infestation of my ex, whom I'd vowed to purge from my mind with a few bottles of tequila as soon as I could spare the money to buy them.

When Barbara offered up a free bedroom in the Center City condo where her grandson was living, I hadn't been expecting the ten-story white stone exterior of the deco-style building. The grandson part had also been a shock. That little detail had been sent after I'd thanked her for being so generous.

Hunter Saxton. The pictures she'd sent of him would've made my panties melt if I weren't on a strict no-man plan for the rest of the year. Sure, he had gorgeous blue eyes. Yes, the black t-shirt and jeans looked like they had been painted onto his fit physique in the shot where he was smiling with Barbara at her eightieth birthday party. And, of course, when I'd Googled him, the social media articles with photos of him in a suit that had been tailored to perfection told me everything I needed to know. Playboy. Man whore. Trouble. But whose bed he jumped into was between him and them, and he wouldn't be jumping into mine, so we'd maintain a friendly, aloof roommate situation for a few months until I'd saved up enough for a place of my own.

Using the designated app on my phone, I paid for the meter. I had an hour. Depending on how many hallways I had to trudge down, I might just make it without needing to spend more. It had taken me over three hours to get all my things into the car the day before yesterday, but that had involved a flight of stairs for each trip. This building certainly didn't have external staircases leading from each floor.

I checked the address again. It was definitely the right place.

Glancing into my back seat stuffed with half of everything I owned, the rest crammed in the trunk, I tried not to deflate. I'd needed to move quickly before my ex got back to the apartment we'd been sharing. I'd found out it had all been a sham—the kind that made my stomach curdle and made sleeping sitting up in my car for the last two nights a better alternative than spending another night in the apartment with him. My arms still burned thinking about lugging all this inside after packing it all up a couple days ago.

I slung my backpack on and grabbed my purse from the seat beside me. My essentials locked and loaded on my arms, I got out.

Taxis and cars zipped through the city streets. There was no going back. Not that there was anything to go back to, and not like I had a choice of where to go at this point. Pickings were slim and my money situation precarious. Grandma Georgina was much better at making friends than I was, and I owed her for Barbara's generous offer to stay as long as I needed.

Might as well get the heavy things over with quickly. No use in waiting and trying to lug them when I was tired. I'd bite the bullet and carry the biggest and bulkiest stuff first.

With all my rearranging, I'd already lost ten minutes off the meter. *Shit! Let's go.*

I bumped the back passenger door closed with my hip and stared up at the imposing stained wood and brass doors. It felt more like I was standing in front of the United Nations rather than my new apartment.

Balancing my rolling suitcase on top of the laundry hamper of gear, I half-stumbled, half-fell toward the doors. The wheels from my carry-on dug into my arms.

Before I could set my entire life in a plastic basket down to open the door, a man in a suit with gold accents along the lapel and sleeves and white gloves held it open.

The guy didn't look much older than me. He had dark brown hair and kind eyes—the type of kind eyes I needed right now. "Can I help you, miss?"

Being called *miss* felt weird coming from a guy who looked my age. I hoped this wasn't a portal into a *Shining*-esque building where I'd find an old typewriter and start slowly going insane.

I blew the hair out of my face. "Yes, that would be amazing."

"Are you moving in?" He wrangled the carry-on suitcase off the top of my hip-high laundry hamper and picked that up like it didn't weigh a million pounds.

"To 1001."

He tripped a little. "*You're* moving into the Saxton Penthouse."

I didn't even have time to be insulted, I was just as shocked as he was. The Saxton freaking Penthouse. *Thanks for the heads-up, Barbara.* If she'd have warned me, I'd have picked up a flapper outfit and feather headband on the ride over. "I didn't realize it had a name, but if that's 1001, then that's where I'm going."

His gaze swept over me a bit more shrewdly than before. Not mean, but unconvinced.

What? He didn't often get late-twenties women in sweatpants moving in with an assortment of bags and baskets like they were on their way to the world's worst bazaar?

"What was your name?"

"Sabrina Mason. Barbara Saxton sent me the address and said she'd have a key made for me and have it waiting for me downstairs." I'd thought downstairs was a mailbox or mat with a key tucked under it, but I hadn't expected a white-gloved doorman and a lobby that could've fit ten of my old apartments in it. In the group text with Grandma Georgina, she'd sent the address, details about when to arrive, pictures of Hunter, but had left out how palatial the building was.

My footsteps echoed in the lobby.

"One second." He jogged over to the concierge desk. "Let me find it for you."

I dropped my head back, staring at the thirty-foot ceilings. Everything was marble and granite, gold accents and statues. Old Hollywood called and wanted their set for *The Great Gatsby* back. Flower arrangements taller than me sat on a shelf that was more like a ledge in front of a twenty-foot mirror. A luggage trolley—brass, of course—sat in the corner. This felt more like a 1920s hotel than an apartment building.

"Ms. Mason—"

"You can call me Sabrina."

He smiled and nodded. "I'm Ian." He held out his hand.

I hesitated, not wanting to dirty those white gloves. Brushing my hand against my pants, I cringed at how sweaty it was before shaking his hand.

"Sorry, they're a little clammy."

"No problem. I have your key. Usually the movers come in through the freight elevator in the back. I'm happy to help with the rest of your luggage as well."

Not needing to carry all my stuff by myself? I almost hugged him. But I was also already screwing up being in this fancy place. Of course most people who moved in didn't look like they were showing up to a dorm room. "I could use the help. My car is parked around the corner. It's the mint green Mazda. I can move it and use that other elevator if you show me where it is." The last thing they had to want was me schlepping my crap through this pristine lobby.

"If you give me the key, I can load everything up and bring it to you. The freight elevator is much bigger, so there won't be a need for multiple trips."

"Are you sure?"

"Absolutely." His friendly smile was exactly what I needed right now. Maybe this would all turn out for the best.

"Thank you. Like, a million times, thank you." I fished my car key out of my pocket and handed it over.

Another doorman appeared and opened the door for someone else entering the lobby. An older woman in her seventies looking like Coco Chanel herself strode through the space like she expected cars to stop for her. And from the look of her, they probably would.

The other doorman crossed the lobby to the woman. "Mrs. Winters, the package you were waiting for has arrived."

Everyone was going to figure out I didn't belong. I needed to escape to the safety of the apartment. It would be harder to kick me out once I unpacked. Surely once I changed into my good leggings, they'd all realize how well I fit in here. Or maybe they'd all form a human chain across the lobby to bar me from the building. The basket scraped against the marble floor with a grinding, gritty sound. "I'll take these things up and be back to get the rest."

"Really, Sabrina, I can bring it up." Ian jogged back toward the front desk.

"O-okay, I'll head up then," I called out, wanting to unload my things like I was staking my claim before the hand-linking in the lobby began.

Jamming my finger into the elevator button, I prayed it wasn't the rickety, rumbling kind that took hours to arrive. I didn't want to ride up with Ms. Old-School Fashion Winters. Just what I'd need, some of my grimy peasant belongings brushing against her cream linen pants.

The elevator door opened, and I flung myself inside, pressing the 10 button. Doing the dance of impatience, I jammed my finger into the close-door button.

The doors sprung to life, closing, but before I could be

the least bit relieved, a dainty hand broke the plane of the space and the doors slid open.

I backed into the corner, pressing myself against the wood wall with the metal railing digging into my spine. I gripped the edge of the laundry hamper, and tried to pretend I was invisible. Maybe I should jump out before it closed like in *The Devil Wears Prada*.

"Moving in?" She turned to me with a small box in the palm of her hand. The doors closed, and she didn't push another button.

"Yes. To 1001."

Her eyes widened the smallest hint. "Looks like we'll be new neighbors. I didn't know Hunter was dating anyone."

My head shook furiously. "No, Barbara Saxton, his grandmother, offered up one of the bedrooms when I ran into housing issues. She said Hunter was away for the weekend, so I'm moving in now."

With a lip quirk, she looked me up and down.

A visceral urge to crawl into the basket hit me.

Her gaze wasn't mean or judging, more like assessing.

The doors opened onto the tenth floor. "It was a delight to meet you..."

"Sabrina."

"I'm Millicent, your new neighbor, but you can call me Millie."

"Nice to meet you, Millie."

"Did you need any help?" She looked down at all my things piled around me like I was a packrat on the move.

"No, it's okay. I actually forgot a bag downstairs, so I'll ride down and get it." I pressed the 7 button and went back to my corner.

"Let me know if you need anything. Hunter can be quite a handful." This time it was more than a lip quirk—it was a full, lip-parting laugh, which she quickly stifled, and straightened her face.

That didn't sound ominous at all. *What the hell have I gotten myself into?*

The doors closed, and I went down to 7 before coming back up to 10. Peering out of the opened doors, I checked to make sure the coast was clear. Palpable relief rolled through me, as did a few beads of sweat down my back.

I dragged my things out of the elevator and down the hallway. It felt like steam was rising from under the collar of my t-shirt and curling the hairs on the back of my neck. My arms hurt already. At least I was here. Using the key Ian had handed me, I stuck it in the apartment door and pushed it open.

Letting my purse drop off my shoulder, I collapsed against the wall. My backpack slid down my noodle arms. I still needed to help bring up the rest of my things. It was a dick move to leave it all to Ian. At least I'd sent off the first part of my product photography deliverables to my client before the bomb dropped on my life. Trying to make that deadline while I moved in would've been impossible.

The door swung shut behind me, but didn't fully close. I hoped the apartment had a bath. After today I'd want to soak until I was pruney and the water turned cold. Maybe I could finally come down from the frantic panic I'd been living in for the past few days.

While the building outside felt older, inside there was a modern but classic feel. Some clashes seemed to work. Old stained glass and lead lamps on dark wood polished tables stood out against the new wood floors.

Barbara hadn't mentioned when Hunter would be back. At least I'd have some time to settle in before he arrived and get my things unpacked and out of his way.

Maybe I could grocery shop a bit to make him a thank-you, I-swear-I-won't-be-a-shitty-roommate dinner whenever he got back.

There was a noise farther inside the apartment.

My pulse skyrocketed. I looked around me and pulled a pipe from the basket used for my lighting rigs. Creeping closer, I raised it above my head.

A shadow. A man. A Hunter. He rounded the corner with a spoon dangling from his mouth and a jar of Nutella in one hand. The words were muffled behind the spoon but came through loud and clear. "Who the fuck are you?"

His gray sweatpants were slung so low on his hips the Adonis belt of muscles leading straight to his package was slap-me-in-the-face evident.

The pipe fell from my grip, clattering to the floor. I was dick-dumbstruck for a second.

The ratty t-shirt with holes in it looked like it had been expertly distressed for the perfect vintage look.

His bleary, blue-eyed, piercing gaze snapped to the pipe I'd thought of bludgeoning him with and he slipped the spoon out of his mouth and shoved it into the jar. Jaw tight, lips pinched, muscles taut, he glared.

He had the look of a guy who used to be the cutest little boy on the playground, who girls had fawned over, and instead of losing all that childhood adorableness, it had morphed into killer looks with the faintest hint of boyishness to make you drop your guard—and panties—immediately.

The door behind me swung open.

"Sabrina, I'll have to make two trips to get everything up. If it's okay with you, I can move your car into the parking spot for this apartment so you don't have to worry about the meter." Ian rumbled in behind me. "Hey, Hunter. Thanks again for getting that scotch for my dad. I swear, he teared up when he opened the box."

My back pressed against the entryway hall. My head whipped back and forth from Ian to Hunter.

"What the hell, Ian? You're just letting this random woman into my apartment?" His voice boomed all kinds of pissed.

Ian froze, staring at me like I had all the answers to why my new roommate had flipped out. "She's on the list."

I shot Ian an apologetic look. Maybe Hunter had been expecting me later today?

"Hi, sorry about the pipe." I caught it with my foot and slid it behind me and extended my hand with a smile. "I'm Sabrina. Your new roommate."

He scoffed, trying to fold his arms, but the oversize jar of Nutella got in the way. "Says who?"

I dropped my hand. So much for making friends.

"Barb. Barbara Saxton. Your grandmother. She said I could stay here and left a key for me downstairs." I jangled the two-key-laden key ring.

His gaze darted to the key and to my gear before his face cycled through five emotions before settling on *hell no*. "We'll see about that."

Disappearing through a doorway with his tub of Nutella, he stomped away leaving Ian and I in the hall alone.

Ian cleared his throat. "Should I move your car and get the rest of your things, or..."

There wasn't anywhere else for me to go. Barb owned the place and she'd said I could stay, so stay it was. This looked like a big place. I was sure we could coexist without any issues.

Putting on the everything-is-fine smile I'd perfected over

the past few days, I turned to Ian. "That would be so helpful. I'll come down and you can show me my parking space."

His face spelled out how much of a chance there was that I'd have time to fully unpack before I was booted. But he didn't know about my secret weapon. Granny Power. At least I hoped it worked that way, and I'd lean into it hard if that was what it took to tough it out over the next four months until I saved up enough to get a place of my own.

Piling everything up in the corner of the first room, which looked like the living room, I tried not to eavesdrop on Hunter. The silky-smooth baritone was enough to make me forget I had sworn off men for the foreseeable future.

A door down the hallway cracked open. He leaned out with his phone jammed against his ear. "Don't get comfortable!"

I spun on my heel and marched out. Out of the frying pan and into the fire...

2

HUNTER

"Why didn't you tell me, GiGi?" The pipe-wielding intruder had looked every bit as shocked to see me as I had her. Maybe more so. The brunette with the brown-sugar-colored eyes and curves had made my Nutella-stuffed mouth water. But she was also in my space.

I had strict rules about who I let into my space, and now certainly wasn't the time to have a new roommate, especially one I had no idea about. I'd practically lived alone since I was fifteen and I liked my space.

Now there was a woman barging in with five tons of heavy equipment, if the continuous bumping and banging was any indication.

"You said you were out of town this weekend. Somehow you're in the apartment and have access to your phone. It's a minor miracle. Your Himalayan trek to Mount Everest ended so quickly."

"I told you I was planning a camping trip in the Poconos, not hiring a Sherpa to watch me suffocate to death on the side of a mountain."

"Well, I misunderstood, but I don't know why you're getting so worked up about Sabrina moving into the spare bedroom."

"I like my space, GiGi." The Nutella jar sat on the edge of the desk in the office. Sabrina had seen me stuffing my face with it, bleary-eyed and in need of a sugar spike, eating from a jar in my rattiest college t-shirt and sweatpants. There was no coming back from this.

"I worry about you bumping around in my place all on your own. Sabrina will be good for you."

"She's a stranger."

"She's Georgina's granddaughter, who needed a place to stay."

"That's what hotels are for. I can find her the perfect room. A view of the river, discounted price. Probably free." I had a laundry list of contacts.

"Oh no you don't. I don't want her staying by herself. She's had a rough time and needs someone to look out for her."

"My job does not lend itself to looking after anyone." My work on the New Year's Eve concert in four months would take all my time and attention and every spare ounce of energy I could muster, especially given how off my sleep schedule had been.

"Least of all yourself."

"She'd be more comfortable—"

"In the apartment, where she'll have access to everything she needs. And a wonderful new guide to show her around the city."

I didn't have time to play tour guide. "GiGi, I have a lot of big clients with events—"

"You mean parties to attend. I swear, you're half a month from becoming nocturnal."

I'd have to sleep at all to be nocturnal. "Please let me find her—"

"Young man." The warning tone in her voice brooked no arguments. "Sabrina will be staying in the guest room. You will be a gracious and generous host. You will make sure she's comfortable. You will not try to run her off. Do you understand me?"

There was no mistaking that she'd fly up here to kick my ass if I didn't make Sabrina comfortable. My eyes felt like dried-out mothballs. The chocolate in the jar had helped with my throat, which was raw after shooting up in my bed, screaming and covered in sweat.

A new roommate? How the hell was this going to work? Did she like being awoken in the middle of the night by a guy being revisited by ghosts of his past? Reliving my greatest-hits album of childhood trauma? If so, then this was the apartment for her. But I couldn't tell my grandmother that. She'd get worried, probably try to fly back up here to see if there was any way she could help. I'd have to deal with the roommate situation myself. "Yes, GiGi."

"That's what I like to hear. It'll be great for both of you. And thank you for the Slip 'N Slide. Everyone can't believe you arranged it for all the residents."

"You said you always wanted to try one."

"You know I thought I was way past my prime to give it a shot, but the little seat they buckled us into while we slid, and the wind rushing through my hair... It was exhilarating, Hunter. Everyone had so much fun."

"I'm glad you liked it." A contact had been looking to showcase their senior fun activities that went beyond shuffleboard. The safety-focused nostalgic activities for those with limited mobility had been a stretch to sell to a lot of retirement communities. After checking into the safety measures, I'd persuaded GiGi to have them come to her enclave in Florida. As anyone who knew her knew, once she set her sights on something, there was no deterring her. For better or worse.

"I love you, Hunter."

"Love you too."

"Good, now go be a good host and help Sabrina get settled."

"I will." Feeling like I was eight all over again, I ended the call and flung my phone down and dropped into my office chair. Yes, I was grumpy. Grumpy and fortifying myself to be a gracious and accommodating host for my new interloper. I steepled my fingers, tapping the tips together and trying to figure my way out of this.

Shooting up from my chair, I snatched my phone off the desk and left the office.

I skidded to a stop outside my doorway. At the end of the hallway, Sabrina walked across to the chest-high pile of her stuff stacked up along the wall.

She wrestled with a black box that looked like an equipment case. "Hi." She smiled before blowing a few strands of hair from in front of her face. Her skin was ruddy, and she was glowy with sweat and slightly out of breath.

I couldn't stop thinking about what other activities would have her looking the same way. Hands shoved into my sweatpants pockets, I warded off thoughts of Sabrina as anything other than someone horning in on my private space. Now was not the time for me to be horning out. If someone could let my dick know, that would be awesome.

Walking to the end of the hallway, I kept my face stony.

The front door creaked. "That's everything. It was nice meeting you, Sabrina," Ian called out from the front door.

His gaze was firmly locked on to Sabrina's ample, made-for-riding ass.

I shook my head.

"Bye, Ian," I called to him.

His gaze darted to mine, at least looking somewhat embarrassed. "Oh, bye, Hunter." He closed the door behind him.

I'd been living in this place for four years. A pretty girl shows up and all his loyalty, secured with vintage whiskey, disappeared with a bat of her dark lashes.

Finished fiddling with her Jenga tower, she stood and faced me. "Sorry to dump all this here, but you ran off without telling me which room was mine, so..."

Biting back a growl, I spun on my heel and walked back down the hall. I made it five steps before I realized she wasn't following. "Are you coming or what?"

She gave a small yelp and rushed forward.

I turned the knob on the first doorway and pushed it open. "This is your room." I added the "for now" in a mumble she didn't seem to notice. Arm extended, I sucked in a breath when she brushed past me, her shoulder grazing against my chest. A blooming warmth spread across my skin, even through my t-shirt. Her floral, sweet smell filled my nostrils, and I locked my knees. My head was playing tricks on me. That was what less than a couple hours sleep did. It fucked with your head and made you see and feel things that weren't really there.

"Wow, it's gorgeous." Her eyes lit up, and she looked around, taking it all in. "A queen-size bed. That's perfect." She clapped her fingertips together and tapped her two pointer fingers against her lips.

Her cheeks were still flushed. A sprinkle of freckles dotted her skin across the tops of her cheeks and across the bridge of her nose. "And I have my own bathroom." She rushed toward it, her shoulders dipping a little with a barely audible "aw."

"What's wrong?"

Spinning, she shook her head. "Nothing. It's perfect."

"Stop doing that. My grandmother's not here. And I'm not into playing the good, nice-girl game. Say what you're thinking." The bark had more bite than I'd intended, and I immediately felt like a dick.

She jumped before her expression shifted to narrow gazed, lip locked, pissed off. "Sorry for not complaining like an asshole about the free place I've been given to live in with only a couple days' notice. Some people work hard not to be jerks and never put people out."

"Listen, I don't want you here." I gritted my teeth. "But it's not my choice to make. It's my grandmother's place, so she sets the rules. The apartment is big enough for both of us. We can stay out of each other's way." Having her in my space had me on edge. My throat was still raw from last night's attempt at sleeping. I'd hoped to get a few hours today before I left for the night. Now it was looking less and less likely. Relaxing would be impossible with her here.

"When you put it that way, it makes me wonder how good you are at keeping this"—she circled her finger in my direction—"version of yourself from your grandmother, because I'm trying to figure out where the kind, good-natured, would-do-anything-for-anyone, exceedingly hand-some version of that guy is. I mean..." She folded her arms across her chest, pushing her breasts up with a jiggle under her shirt. "You've certainly got the handsome part nailed. I can't even lie about that, but man, you've got those asshole tendencies sharpened to a fine point." Leaning in, she stage-whispered with her hand beside her mouth. "Was that enough of me saying what I was thinking, or would you prefer I be more blunt?"

Feisty. And I couldn't say I didn't deserve it. I shoved my hand into my hair. Damn, I was tired and when I got tired, I got cranky, but I was usually able to work through that on my own. Now I had a roommate. I dropped back into the hallway and walked away without checking to see if she followed. "I'll show you the rest of the apartment."

Her footsteps trailed behind me, close enough to clip my heels like a fourth grader. *Was she doing this on purpose?*

I glanced over my shoulder.

She glanced around at the ceiling like crown molding had never been more interesting.

"This is my office." I pointed at the open door showing the desk with the jar of chocolate spread taunting me.

"Do you mean the office?" Peeking her head inside, she scanned the room.

The nervous, twitchy energy raced across my skin.

"And this is my room."

She shoved her head inside before I could close the door. "Oh, you have—"

"I have what?" My sheets were ripped off my bed, still probably sweaty, soggy. I pulled the door closed, nearly squashing her head.

"A...a wonderful view."

"Both rooms are off-limits." I needed to clean all my sheets before the sweaty stench took over the whole apartment and Sabrina started to wonder if she was living in a gym locker room. Although that wouldn't be the worst way to get her to not want to stay. Decisions, decisions.

"Always the gentleman," she grumbled under her breath.

Turning, careful not to brush against her, I walked back

down the hallway to the living room with the sixty-five-inch TV. The green and gray couch was so comfortable I'd fallen asleep there and woken before rolling off and nearly cracking my head on the edge of the coffee table. The knitted blue afghan draped over the back called to me now to put my head down on it and close my eyes.

I snapped them both open.

We walked through the formal dining room, which I'd barely used outside of "board meetings" for work, the breakfast nook with an eat-in four-seater table, and the galley kitchen with a six-burner Viking range and Shaker cabinets where I'd stocked an obscene number of coffee beans, not to mention the ones in the freezer. At this point, I wouldn't be surprised if I turned on the faucet and beans spilled out into the farmhouse sink. Sometimes it felt like the only thing I drank.

"This kitchen is beautiful." She wandered closer to the cabinets.

My heart rate spiked. So much coffee and Red Bull filled the cabinets.

She'd think I was a psycho.

"Do you like to cook?" She pulled one open.

I rushed across the room and slammed it shut with my flattened palm. "That one down there can be yours." The skinny cabinet beside the stove wasn't filled with anything more than expired spices.

"There's that unrivaled hospitality I've been told about."

"You're the one invading my space, remember? Do you need more kitchen space than that?"

She jolted.

Once again, my bite was sharper and more exacting than I'd meant it to be.

"Am I allowed to use the sink or fridge or will I have to

drink out of my bathroom sink and store my food out on the balcony during winter?"

"Why don't you worry about moving your stuff into your room?"

Her gaze swept up and down me.

My stomach curdled like week-old milk in the summer sun.

"Yeah, I will. Nice meeting you, Hunter. May our paths not cross more than they need to." She stormed out of the kitchen, and my shoulders and chest deflated like a balloon.

Whipping open the cabinets, I scanned them and grabbed a trash bag from under the kitchen sink.

If she was here, the thirty-seven bags of coffee and case of energy drinks could not be here. It was one thing to go a little overboard when I was all on my own. It was another to have her start prodding.

In the hall, she bumped and banged, getting her things together to get settled into the never-used guest room—her room.

I collected the blanket and pillow I'd passed out on in the living room church-mouse quietly. I picked up all the abandoned coffee and espresso cups and stuck them in the dishwasher. The blankets strewn around the apartment were folded and put back in their places.

Maybe this was a blessing in disguise. I couldn't pace the apartment at all hours with her here. Maybe I could train myself to sleep earlier. Sleep longer. Sleep at all.

A blessing, but it didn't mean I couldn't be pissed as hell about it. This apartment had been my sanctuary. The place where I could enjoy the peace and quiet that wasn't often part of my life, and recently where I could pace late into the night and wake up screaming all on my own.

Now it was being taken over by a doe-eyed invader.

After working in my office for hours listening to the bumping and thumping in the hallway and not getting a damn thing done, I gave up.

In my bedroom I decided to take the offensive position, not be on defense with her, thrown off guard by Sabrina's arrival.

I took a quick shower, trying to wake myself up, jerked open my closet door, and flicked through my button-down shirts and creased pants. No need to go full blazer, but I needed to show her I wasn't the sweatpants-wearing mess crying into a jar of chocolate.

I was Hunter Fucking Saxton.

I was the man everyone came to with whatever anyone needed, and who never let them down. The one who had beautiful women buying *him* drinks when he went out at night.

I slipped on my shirt and grabbed some cuff links.

There were a few invitations sitting in my inbox. I hadn't said yes to any yet, but that was about to change. Scrolling through my phone, I found the biggest party of the evening and accepted. The invitation also came from some of the most annoying people on the planet, but sucking it up for a few hours wouldn't hurt. It wasn't even seven, and the party wouldn't kick off until midnight at the earliest. I'd have to find a way to keep myself occupied, which didn't include staring holes through my bedroom door wondering what was happening on the other side.

I left my bedroom, pulling the door closed behind me.

Sabrina had changed out of her t-shirt. A camisole clung to her, the thin straps along with her bra straps fighting the gravity of her way-more-than-a-handful breasts. They threatened to spill over the top of the stretchy fabric. She brushed the back of her hand across her forehead and looked up before glancing back down at herself.

Fucking busted.

She rolled her eyes and grabbed a flimsy box, lifting it. The side ripped, tearing the box almost in half, which knocked over another box.

Instinct took over and I rushed forward to help her. Out of both boxes tumbled sheets. A lot of sheets. Like, a boutique-hotel amount of sheets. Different colors and fabrics. Some were still in the packaging.

"It's okay. I've got it," she shouted, lunging for the sheets and kicking them into her room across the wood floor. "Don't worry about it." She snatched the package of Millesimo Egyptian cotton sheets from my hands. I'd seen them when doing a favor for a guy living in a Liberty One penthouse a couple months ago. That set was over a grand.

"You look nice. Going out?" Sweaty and panting, she braced her arms on the doorframe—her not-too-obvious attempt to keep me from seeing inside and what she'd unpacked, which also had the side effect of making her camisole ride up, rising over her belly button.

She dropped her arms to yank it down, which dipped it even lower at the top. The mint green of her bra peeked out and her cleavage threatened to spill over the top. Her growl of frustration did nothing to mask the howl of attraction racing through me at full force.

I peered over her shoulder. Inside, stacked against the wall, there were even more sheets. Sheets and camera equipment. What the hell was her deal? "Yeah, headed out to a club opening."

She blew some strands of hair out of her face and stepped into the hallway. "Wow, club opening. That sounds exciting. I'll have everything cleared out by the time you're back." Using her body like a border collie, she walked me toward the front door.

"I won't be back until late." Turning to hide the uncontrollable erection straining against my pants, I talked to her over my shoulder.

Her head bobbed eagerly. "Even better."

"We need to set a few ground rules."

She reached around me and opened the front door.

"Awesome idea. We can do that tomorrow." The door pressed against my shoulder.

"And figure out a schedule—"

"Tomorrow, we can hash it all out then. Have fun at your party. Be safe. Bye." The door slammed at my back.

I stood in the empty hallway, the silence ringing in my ears.

Why'd it feel like I'd been thrown out of my own apartment?

Probably because I had. I stared at my apartment door. Walking into the elevator, I grumbled and tamped down my frustration. A wave of exhaustion slammed into me. I rubbed my eyes, not wanting to do anything remotely close to partying, but I couldn't go back into the apartment now.

The pieces weren't adding up. Why the hell was a woman who had sheets that expensive bumming a free room in my grandmother's apartment? Whatever it was, I wasn't giving up. I needed her out of there, quickly.

I'd lived alone since high school, and there was no way I was letting her into my space lying down. A nice, soft bed to lie down on. My eyes slid shut.

The ding of the elevator doors opening woke me from my micro nap. I scrubbed my hands over my face. She needed to leave, and I needed my space. There was no way she was staying in my apartment.

3

SABRINA

I collapsed onto my new bed. The soft comforter clung to my sweaty skin. I groaned. As much as I wanted to pass out and wake up in a few days, showering was a top priority. Crawling into a freshly made bed sweaty and gross would leave me tossing and turning and hating myself, and I was already doing enough of that for two lifetimes.

Grabbing my backpack, I sat on the floor and rifled through my clothes. Seven boxes of sheets and three boxes of neatly organized lighting equipment and a backpack stuffed full of clothes. A girl had to have her priorities straight. Right now, mine were to get clean and fall into a blissful, dreamless sleep brought on by emotional duress and physical exhaustion. Didn't everyone want to be me?

It was dark outside, but it wasn't too late, which was weird. Hunter had mentioned going to a club opening. My red-carpet invitations were often lost in the mail, but that seemed like something that would happen later at night. But what the hell did I know? The last time I'd been up past eleven and out of my pajamas had been a year and a half ago, trying to drag Cat into a taxi on the streets of London in February.

My phone vibrated on my newly made bed. *Speak of the devil. Cat calls.*

Fifteen minutes into our phone call, I had shaken my head so much my neck hurt.

"I'm going to need a more in-depth description of the previously mentioned cock cleavage." Cat Wright, the world's most outstanding best friend, yawned on the other end of the line.

"It's three in the morning for you. Don't you have better things to be doing?"

"Like what?" The words were muffled behind another yawn.

"I don't know. Go to sleep so you don't start a diplomatic incident with a shoddy translation tomorrow."

"Tomorrow's Saturday."

"Oh yeah. Sleeping in my car tends to make the days blur together." Burning anger and crushing guilt took turns putting me in a stranglehold. I took a shaky breath to loosen their grip on my throat. I latched on to a topic change to help. "Wait, Saturday? When has the weekend ever stopped your bosses from calling you in to work?"

"Tell me about it. If the paycheck wasn't as insane as it is, I'd tell them to all go fuck themselves, but then I'd have to hire someone to bring in a squad of supermodels to peg them all on pillow-top mattresses covered in rose petals."

"What the hell did your job description look like?"

"It was long and detailed," she deadpanned.

"Back to you getting some sleep."

"You're right. I should. Who knows when one of them will call me. It'll probably be right when my Henry Cavill dream gets to the good part."

"Thank god my sleep has been dreamless after leaving you-know-who." I'd braced for nightmares, but I'd take the blissful void over the grip of fear any day.

"Fuckface Von Asshole doesn't get a name anymore?"

"I don't want to bring any more bad juju into this new apartment by uttering his name." Or bringing up any memories of him. It was too raw, too painful.

"How about I utter it for you? I can bellow it from the rooftops. Seth Howe, you are a C U Next Tuesday, and I hope demons pull your balls out through your asshole for hurting my friend."

I slapped my hand over my eyes, shoulders shaking with laughter. "That was a visual I didn't need."

"But it made you laugh," she teased. "My work here is done."

"Get some sleep. When are you back in town?"

She yawned again. "For Thanksgiving. Maybe we can do a Friendsgiving and I can check out your hunky new roommate."

"He's not *that* hot."

"Oh please, I could hear your drooling through the phone when you angrily described him. I see some intense hate-banging in your future."

I had a flash of him pressing me against the wall, rubbing that glass-cutting jaw against my cheek, before the reality of how that would really go barged into my brain. "Trust me, I'm not his type. He wears cuff links and goes to club openings."

"You could wear cuff links."

I laughed. "You know what I mean. I barely want to change out of pajamas most days."

"But you do from time to time, and you look adorable when you do. Do not stay confined to this new apartment like you did the last one. Go out and live a little. Give Hunter a run for his money."

Living a little was how I'd ended up with Seth. I should never have texted him back after he'd put the pressure on to get my number that night I'd gone out for happy hour almost two years ago. He'd laid the charm on thick. His pursuit had been relentless. Who didn't want a guy who only seemed to have eyes for them? Who didn't want to feel special?

"Once I get to work on the next deadline, then I can finally mail out all these sheets I've sold to pay for new samples. Then I'll think about it." Selling products sent to me by clients wasn't exactly straight out of the freelance handbook in how to make a good impression, but desperate times and all that...

"So never. You could just say never. No need to lie to my face."

"I'm not lying to your face. I'm lying to your voice. How about this deal? Once you're in town, then we can go out. A girl's night on the town complete with debauchery, too many drinks, and off-key singing in the back of a cab."

"Sounds like a Tuesday to me."

"Of that, I have no doubt. Have fun, be safe and don't cause any international incidents."

"You know me."

"That's exactly why I'm saying it."

She laughed. "Love you, Sab."

"Love you too." I ended the call, then folded the last of the boxes and slid it into my closet.

I gathered up my pajamas, body wash, and towel, then peeked into my bathroom. The modern shower contrasted with much of the more classic interior throughout the apartment. Everything else was crown molding, chair rails, and ornate light fixtures, but the bathroom was a stylish spa surprise. Only it didn't have a tub. I wanted a deep, luxurious bathtub where I could close my eyes, wash away my worries, and relax for a solid half hour.

My muscles ached from the work I'd done today. Tapping my finger against my lips, I spun on my heels.

Hunter's less-than-stellar apartment tour had given me one peek into his room and bathroom. The bathroom with a tub.

Tiptoeing out of my room, I glanced down the hallway and my heart skipped into overdrive. With at least ten glances over my shoulder in the ten feet to his bedroom door, I knocked on the partially opened door even though he'd been gone for hours already.

"Hunter..." I poked my head in and listened for any signs of life.

It was a bath. Not a huge deal, right? He'd said I couldn't come into his room, but not his bathroom. I was splitting hairs—okay, more ripping them out by the roots—but my shoulders and thighs were killing me right now.

I wasn't coming in to steal anything—well, other than some time in his bath.

Walking into his bathroom, I sighed. The peek I'd gotten of the tub didn't do it justice. I brushed away an imaginary tear, my muscles no longer screaming with fatigue, but with joy. A white, freestanding, wide-ledge soaking tub big enough for three people stood against one wall. The raised back on one end was perfect for lying back and resting sore muscles.

Barbara had excellent taste. A chandelier hung over the bath. The handles and shower attachment were modern and sleek brass. Dimmers around the bathroom gave *cozy* a whole new meaning. A glass enclosed rainforest shower on the right had all of Hunter's soaps inside. He'd probably never even used the bath. If anything, I was doing a service to Barbara to check on it and make sure it was in working order.

After a little trial and error, I figured out the stopper and turned on the water to my perfect temperature.

Peering out of the bathroom, I held my breath straining to hear the slightest sound over the running water and praying that Hunter the Party Guy wouldn't make this an early night. It wasn't even eleven yet. I'd have plenty of time. I added some lavender oil to the running water and got undressed.

Hopefully after my bath, I'd finally get a good night's rest. The bed had been so comfortable for the three seconds I'd laid on it. But what if he was a total manwhore who brought women home all the time and enjoyed loud, noisy late-night activities that would keep me up? Not that it was any of my business, but the last thing I needed was another asshole who couldn't keep it in his pants.

Hunter and I were roommates. Reluctant roommates at this point. Temporary roommates if I played my cards right over the next few months with the leveling up of my clients. The account I'd gotten had almost felt like a mistake and if they hadn't actually sent me the sheets to photograph, I'd have thought there was a typo in the email address, but I'd still need to prove myself and stand out to be selected for the international marketing campaign and the bonus that came with it.

I clipped my hair on top of my head and set out my body wash and loofah. The stresses of the day were hard to wash away without a bath. Tomorrow I'd check on any feedback for the first round I'd sent in and get to work on making the next batch of images even better.

I was failing miserably at this whole adult thing, and thirty was right around the corner. Moving to my parents' house in Arizona wasn't my idea of fun. Short of buying a ticket to Moscow and curling up on Cat's couch, I was running out of other options. A crack in the door was all I needed to get someone to look at my designs.

Less worrying and more relaxing. I slipped into the bath, moaning. The tub itself was heated, taking away from the first-touch shock. If I wasn't careful, I'd pass out in here and he'd have a big surprise when he came home.

With all the grumbling and mumbling he'd been doing to Barbara about me showing up, he'd probably dispose of my body down the trash chute, dusting his hands off and whistling on the way back to his apartment of solitude.

The warm, bordering-on-hot water melted away the soreness. Music pumped in from my phone, and I closed my eyes, sinking deeper into the most comfortable tub in existence.

In here, there was nothing to worry about except for the water temperature and my new roommate catching me naked in his bathroom. But right now, I couldn't even worry about that. Tension slowly ebbed from my body one muscle at a time.

When I was sufficiently pruney and clean, I flicked the stopper and climbed out of the tub while it drained behind me. Drying myself and the floor off, I stared into the still-wet tub.

My pajama sweats, T-shirt, and fluffy socks triggered my yawn cycle. It would be minutes before I fell onto the nearest flat surface and passed out.

Finding more towels in a closet in the hallway, I went to work drying down the inside of the tub. It was polite to clean up after myself and I also didn't want Hunter to have any idea I'd been here. What he didn't know wouldn't hurt him. I piled everything up beside my closet to take care of tomorrow.

In bed, I pulled the sheets up to my chin and snuggled down deep in the pillow-top mattress. The thread count was stellar for a guest bedroom, not that I was being choosy. A burlap sack on the floor would've been enough to put me to bed. But after two nights sleeping sitting up in my car, it was nice to stretch out and relax.

Whatever Hunter dished out, I could more than take. I wasn't moving out and running away again. Barbara had told me the invite was open for as long as I needed it. I'd plan my next steps wisely, never worrying about a place to live again.

In the morning I lay in bed for twenty minutes, straining to hear anything coming from the bedroom at the end of the hall. It felt even quieter after the rumble of music that had started sometime after two. Who felt the need to bring the club home with them? Hunter, it seemed. At least there hadn't been any rhythmic banging noises, not that I'd have been able to hear much over the noise from his end of the hall.

Now I didn't feel even the slightest bit of guilt for using his tub. He was lucky I hadn't left the floor wet enough for a slip-and-slide accident during his middle-of-the-night bedroom rave.

The music had gone off at some point before sunrise. I'd fallen into a fitful sleep with my pillow over my head, so I was already in a rip-roaring great mood. Now the apartment felt eerily silent—not a creaking floorboard, a rustle of blankets, or a cabinet closing. Either he'd left already, or he had come home, cranked up the volume, and left again last night. I wouldn't have put it past him to have put his stereo on a timer for maximum annoyance to me even when he wasn't here.

He was probably shacked up with a woman he'd met at the club. A woman who loved a surly attitude, striking eyes, and a sneering smirk. Women proposed to serial killers in jail, and I had no doubts Hunter mopped up in the ladies' department.

Coffee, then grocery shopping were in order, but my stomach threatened a small-scale revolt if I didn't eat immediately. Skipping dinner had a way of turning me into a gremlin. Hunter was lucky I hadn't scrambled up onto the countertops to tear through the cereal boxes with my teeth.

Of course, everything in his kitchen was exactly what I'd have expected from a guy like him. The jar of Nutella was nowhere to be found.

Healthy cereals less appetizing than the boxes they were stored in. At least those were all full. Bottled water in the fridge. Not even old takeout. And a shit-ton of coffee. So much coffee and energy drinks.

With this much caffeine in the apartment, I was surprised Hunter wasn't bouncing off the walls and clinging to the ceiling.

My stomach rumbled like a speed bag in a boxing gym.

Eating the coffee grounds would be my next step if there wasn't any milk. I triple-checked the expiration date on the barely-a-bowlful of milk then gave it a sniff test. I opened the other cabinets. The matching light green mugs were in a row with all their handles to the left. Was Hunter a little anal retentive?

I grabbed a mug from the cabinet and poured some of

the milk into my mug. After a cursory sip, I was ninety percent sure it was fine to drink.

I took out one of the five hundred bags of coffee. Using my rusty barista skills, I fired up the coffee machine and dumped a heaping scoop of coffee into the filter before closing the tray and waiting for my morning ambrosia.

I sprinkled the cereal into a bowl and poured the last of the milk over it and chucked the carton. Milk was on the top of my grocery-run list, along with anything that wasn't coffee. I mean, I loved coffee more than the next person—dark, rich, heavy enough to get me through hours chained to my desk—but I did need other sustenance.

The dire cereal situation wasn't making me more patient for my coffee. Stale shards of bran sliced my throat. I'd have been better off chomping on some tree bark outside.

I stood at the counter and grabbed my phone, checking my messages. There was a response from a portfolio I'd sent over for a few textile designs. My spoon dropped into my bowl.

"Yes!" I punctuated the celebration with a fist in the air. They wanted to see more. They wanted to see samples. Shit, I needed to make samples. Which would cost money. Selling the current products I'd just unpacked had never been more urgent.

If I didn't get any bites on these designs in the next few months, maybe it was a sign it wasn't going to happen, but this was a glimmer of hope. I'd given myself the year-end deadline to try to stop myself from pursuing another pipe dream.

I had four months to finally make a name for myself in the design world and stop mooching the free housing off Barbara, or I'd pack it all up and knuckle down with a real job where I wasn't living at the whim of bargain-hunting clients or the luck of the draw. If I sold a design, that could be a steady paycheck—or at least a big enough one to keep me on my feet for much longer than a couple months.

The pungent smell of coffee filled the kitchen. I breathed it in like I could siphon caffeine from the air.

I leaned against the counter and scrolled through my upcoming pitch and portfolio for another linen company. I read it on my phone after finishing it on my computer. It was the only way I could proofread, and I'd been burned by clicking send and then noticing a glaring typo one too many times for things to go out without proofreading. I'd respond to even more calls for proposals today. After grocery shopping.

The Harper Linens opportunity was the only reason I hadn't schlepped my ass back across the country to stay on the ancient futon at my parents' house. They'd moved into a retirement community after I'd left, and space was tight. Right now I had my temporary reprieve.

Today I'd check out the sunlight in the room and figure out the best times for filming, and set up my lighting and product displays and staging.

The coffee stopped dripping, and I grabbed my mug and filled it from the pot. Five heaps of sugar later and I warmed my hands around the mug. I needed to find the thermostat. If it was over sixty degrees in here, I'd be shocked. This was meat-locker territory, even though summer weather waned outside.

I turned on my music and choked down the remains of the cereal mush. Singing into my spoon, I did my best to shatter the cabinets with my high notes. I wasn't an honors choir reject for nothing. They didn't know what they'd missed back in high school, and I didn't hear a single dog howling.

With my notebook beside me, I scribbled down my grocery list. The staples and a few recipes that would keep for a week in the fridge. Batching was my life, and I used it in every place I could. Why clean the kitchen every day when I could destroy it in one day and then survive off leftovers?

A door swung open. Not the front door.

A bedroom door. Hunter's bedroom door.

My heart raced, and my cheeks boiled. I grabbed the box of cereal and shoved it into the cabinets. I rinsed out my bowl and spoon before sticking them where I'd gotten them from. Maybe we could start off today on a better foot. Maybe.

I skidded across the floor and focused on my notebook. There was no way I could make it back to my room with him already out of his.

His footsteps got closer like the T. Rex in *Jurassic Park*, rattling what was left in my coffee mug.

He strode into the kitchen.

I kept my head down and peered up at him.

Gone were his holey, worn sweats and tshirt from yesterday. Now he was in flannel sleep pants and a fitted short-sleeve t-shirt. It molded to his pecs and biceps. Stupid healthy-cereal-eating hotness, even in the morning. Traces of sandy stubble shadowed his cheeks and jaw.

He stomped over to the cabinet and jerked it open.

An avalanche of bran flakes poured down the front of his chest. "The fuck." His head swung around in my direction. "Did you do this?"

My notebook had never been more fascinating. "I don't know what you're talking about. But I can help you clean it up." Clean up the mess that was totally my fault. I peeked at him. There were a few bran flakes in his hair and stuck to his chest. The chest that went beyond toned, straight to chiseled. "If you tell me where the broom is." I clasped my hands in front of me. So much for starting off on a better foot today. My stomach was in knots, but I didn't know if it was due to proximity to Hunter or feeling like I was about to get sent to the principal's office.

He opened the cabinet with the bowls and pulled the top one out. The soaking-wet one. With flecks of bran cereal still stuck to it. He held it up in my direction. "Don't know what I'm talking about, huh?"

Deny. Deny. Deny.

I kept my mouth shut and opened the under-the-sink cabinet.

"Whatever," he grumbled under his breath. "I'll get some coffee."

He flung the fridge door open and checked around inside. The door closed slowly, and he flipped the lid on the trash can, fishing out the empty carton.

Mortification hit me like a bucket of ice water. I cringed. The other foot of today had officially been stomped on. The new leaf was sunburned and withered.

"I suppose this wasn't you either."

I kept my lips sealed.

He leaned against the counter, glaring, while I pretended he wasn't, while I looked diligently for the broom and dustpan, which I found in the small slat-covered door right before the breakfast nook area.

He grabbed a mug and poured himself some coffee, using half a spoon of sugar.

Of course the guy with the rock-hard body would eat tree bark and barely use sugar.

The cereal crunched under my bare feet, poking the bottoms of my soles. I bent to sweep up the mess.

Even though I didn't look up, I could tell the moment he took a sip. It was followed by a spew and cough, counter-slapping and wheezing.

My neck and back got soaked with mouth coffee. I shot up from the floor, wiping at the heated liquid covering my back.

Maybe I liked my coffee a little strong.

The front of his white t-shirt was stained with coffee. At least it didn't look like he'd done it on purpose. He didn't seem the type to want to stain his clothes.

"What the fuck is this?" He shoved the mug in my direction. Liquid spilled over the edges and splattered to the bran-covered floor.

"Coffee."

"Are you trying to kill me? This tastes like tar."

I cocked my head to the side and rested my hands on the top of the broom handle. "Can't handle a strong cup of coffee?"

"I can handle a strong cup of coffee. I can handle a triple shot of espresso. This"—he gestured to the dark liquid he poured down the sink—"is an abomination. Although maybe it would've been better if there were some milk." He glowered, gaze narrowed, laser precise.

I didn't have a comeback for that one, so I went with chipper obliviousness. "The grocery store was the next stop on my list for the day before I get some work done."

"You work on the weekends?"

I shrugged. "Sometimes. Is there anything you need from the grocery store? I planned on buying enough for both of us."

"I don't need you to buy groceries for me." His words were lost in a grumble that went from his chest straight to his stomach.

"Listen, I'm trying to be nice. Sorry about the coffee. And the milk. Let me buy you breakfast. Can you tell me where the grocery store is?"

"No."

My jaw dropped before I clamped it shut and flicked my gaze to the ceiling to gather every thread of my patience. "Maybe show me on the way. I can buy you breakfast."

"No."

New tactic. I could play oblivious idiot with the best of them. I'd been played for one for over a year. Smiling wide, I stepped closer to him. "How about we go together?" I looped my arm through his.

His body stiffened.

I didn't try to hide my grin. "Please."

He swung his narrowed gaze to meet my smiling eyes. "Under no circumstances am I going grocery shopping with you."

4

HUNTER

"**D**o you like spaghetti?" She threw a box of pasta into the cart. "I make a killer marinara sauce."

Every step was like a dance with her.

I still didn't know why the hell I was here. Maybe it was how she'd leaned against me when she'd looped her arm through mine and asked me to go grocery shopping with her. Or maybe it was her smell. Since I'd gotten home last night and gotten into the shower, I'd been smelling it. The lingering herby, floral scent. When she held on to my arm, it invaded my nostrils, bringing back thoughts of how I'd jerked off in the shower trying to figure out why the smell hung in the air after I'd taken my clothes off.

It hadn't been from the club. It was something else, and when I smelled it, everything else faded away.

Which was how I found myself strolling the aisles of the grocery store seven blocks from the apartment, trying to keep myself awake under the fluorescent lights hanging over our heads.

Last night I'd come home and sat up in a chair beside my window, afraid to go to sleep and wake up screaming again. I'd turned on the music, put on my noise-cancelling headphones, and read until I'd nodded off. I'd jolted awake with a yell. My book hit the floor with a muted thud, but I'd been afraid to close my eyes again. I was coasting on less than two hours of sleep.

The alluring scent of coffee had dragged me from my room and into the kitchen. Little had I known my new roommate was trying to poison me with sludge.

"Is that all you're getting?" Sabrina pointed to the couple of oranges and carrots in my half of the cart. Why the hell were we sharing a cart anyway?

"You should be happy I'm not trying to drain your bank account."

She picked up a carrot and mimed biting into it. "You don't look like a rabbit to me."

"What's that supposed to mean?" I squeezed the bridge of my nose.

She could push me back to the apartment in the cart when I fell asleep in the aisle.

My lids were weighted down like five-pound bags of flour.

"Nothing. I guess you're more of a sweets guy, not a pasta guy. The Nutella is a few rows over."

"I don't know what you're talking about." I'd resorted to a sugar rush after one too many espressos had made me jittery.

She dropped a few cans of crushed tomatoes and tomato puree into the cart and tilted her head, looking up at me. "Nutella. Like the kind you were eating yesterday. I figured you must be out since there wasn't any in the cabinets."

My fingers gripped the cart tighter. "It was an old jar someone left behind."

"People just rock up to your apartment with jars of

chocolate spread? Do you leave a donation bin out in the hallway?"

Hate was a strong word, but I was getting there with my new, soon-to-be-gone roommate. "Would you drop it? Can we finish this up? I've got shit to do today."

"Touchy this early in the morning. I figured you'd be less hangry after inhaling those French toast dippers." She swirled her finger at my chest.

At the spot where a couple of dried droplets of syrup stained the front of my shirt, even after I'd dabbed them with water.

"I didn't inhale them." I'd devoured them. The sugar hadn't helped and now my stomach wasn't happy with me. Add that to a foggy brain and I was screwed.

Her nod and *umhmm* told me she believed it as much as I did.

After skipping out on dinner last night, I'd been left with few options at the club other than cocktail garnishes. Drinking and an empty stomach didn't mix, so I hadn't even had a chance to get blitzed to stave off my hunger. Instead I'd broken down and grabbed a cheeseburger on the way home. I needed actual fresh food since I wasn't giving my body the sleep it needed.

She disappeared around the corner to the next aisle. The baking aisle.

"Do you have a favorite?" She pointed to the boxed cake and brownie mixes.

"No." My mom and I would bake a dessert every weekend. Cookies, cakes, brownies, whichever we were craving at the time. The flavor always reminded me of her. That was why I stuck to overcomplicated desserts with more syllables than ingredients—they never stirred those childhood memories, which were much closer to the surface than they'd been in a long time.

"Well, I do." She threw on a fake Southern accent and picked up a couple boxes of dark chocolate brownies and yellow cake mix.

I was so fucked.

"Not that you couldn't tell already." Her shoulders curled in a little.

"What's that mean?"

"Oh come on, Hunter." Her voice swayed, drawing out all the syllables. "Look at me." She gestured to herself with the boxes of cake mix.

My sleep addled brain was roaming to dangerous territory. "What am I looking at?" Other than her holding sweet treats and highlighting her glorious rack and hips that filled out her jeans in a way I didn't need to be noticing at nine in the morning in a grocery store where other people were present.

Her lips pursed and she tilted her head, narrowing her gaze, and for the first time I didn't feel it was in a playful way. She was trying to peel back a layer of me with her eyes.

"Fine, whatever." She chucked the boxes into the cart.

In the meat section, she grabbed a few packages of fresh fish, beef, and chicken. "Are you buying for a small army?"

More staples went into the cart, my few things swamped by her selections.

"Since you've so graciously"—an eye roll punctuated how much she believed that remark—"welcomed me into your apartment, I figured the least I could do was cook. Cooking for one always throws off recipes. I also hate needing to do this more than once every couple of weeks, so it's good you keep your fridge, freezer, and cabinets barren except for all that coffee so there'll be plenty of space for all this." She swept her arms over the contents of the cart I was still pushing.

In the freezer section, she picked up a few bags of frozen vegetables and fruit.

"There, I think that's everything, unless you had anything else you needed."

"No, let's get out of here. It's already late, and I need to get to the gym."

Her eyebrow punched up. "Of course you do. Gotta work off those French toast sticks to keep your svelte figure."

I gritted my teeth, willing my eyes open. "I work out. What's the big deal?"

"No big deal. Just an observation."

She guided the cart into a checkout aisle and started unloading.

"Is there a law against exercising now?"

Her head jerked, and she locked on to me with her assessing gaze once again. "No. Why are *you* making such a big deal about it? I made a joke. You're the one getting defensive."

"I'm not defensive." I stuck more things onto the conveyor belt.

"Said the most defensive guy ever," she grumbled at a volume telling me and the checkout cashier it was definitely meant to be overheard. "Is the gym in our building, or do you go somewhere else?"

"Why?"

"Because I want to burn it to the ground? Why do you think? I want to work out. What? I can't work out?" Her defensiveness caught me off guard.

"Who the hell said you can't work out?" I gritted my teeth. "Can we just get the groceries and go? We'll talk about this when we get back to the apartment."

After another squabble at the cashier, I paid for my own things. The rest of the trip was grumbles, glares, and grabbing the shopping bags to schlep them back to the apartment.

Sabrina shifted the bags, flexing her arms and wiggling her fingers after five blocks, the ten bags' worth of groceries hanging off her like an avant-garde fashion show. "Why didn't you remind me we didn't bring a car?"

"I thought us walking here would've been enough to stick in your mind about needing to walk back." My arms were fine, feather light even with the one bag of groceries I'd paid for. "I can help you."

"How many times do I have to tell you? I don't need your help." She speed walked in front of me with bags going all the way up her arms. The tear in one of the bags widened with each step. What had started as a small hole enlarged with each step of her bouncy gait. I might've noticed it while checking out her ass in those jeans, or maybe I was only a concerned roommate.

The white stone apartment building was in sight. As much as I hated her invading my space, carrying the bags like that, she was going to lose at least one before we got there.

She must've noticed how close we were too. Her steps quickened, and she bolted through the intersection with the blinking green walk guy.

I hustled to catch up.

Cars zipped down the street. Shifting from side to side to see between the trucks rumbling by, I could make out her power walking like she was in the Olympics down the block, almost to the front door when it happened. The bag ripped, and she stepped on the cans and went down. Feet in the air, back horizontal, she disappeared behind the cars whizzing past.

I winced and rushed through the intersection, dodging a car barreling through the red light. I scooped up a can of tomato puree that had rolled the twenty feet away from the building.

She cradled her arm against her chest. Gripping her fingers around it tightly, she clenched her teeth together.

Shit, she was hurt.

Ian had already gotten to her by the time I made it within earshot of her. "Are you okay? Do you need me to call a doctor? An ambulance?"

Sprinting down the sidewalk, I slammed on the brakes and my bag slammed into my legs. "I saw you fall." They both looked up at me. Way to point out the absolute obvious.

"Next time I'll bring cloth bags." She looked down at her hand. Her whole body curled around it to protect it.

The groceries were sprawled out all over the sidewalk, not only from the ripped bags but from the fall.

"Are you sure you don't need a doctor?" Ian hovered.

Taking a deep breath, she loosened her grip on her wrist and rotated it. "I can move it fine. It just hurts like a mother."

I dropped my bags and reached for it. "Stop doing that. We need to get some ice on it." Panic settled deep in my chest. I held on to her arm, running my fingers down the inside of the forearm.

She shuddered.

"Are you okay? Are you sure it's not broken? Maybe we should go get you an X-ray." I turned, tugging her toward the street, raising my arm for a taxi.

She didn't move.

I whipped back around.

Her feet were planted on the sidewalk.

Her forehead crinkled, and she pulled her wrist out of my hold. "It's probably just a sprain. Calm down."

The brass-and-wood door to the building swung open. Ian wheeled out the luggage trolley, barely sparing me a glance, focused solely on Sabrina. It irked me and got under my skin how in a little over twenty-four hours, he acted like he'd known her for years. "This is a lot of groceries, Sabrina." He fussed over her and the bags, and I didn't know why the hell it pissed me off.

I picked up the splayed food items and shoved them onto the cart.

Ian kept talking, and Sabrina soaked it up. "Why didn't you let me know you were going shopping? I could've called the town car if you were worried about parking."

Yeah, this wasn't going to be good.

Her eyebrows dipped. "Town car?"

"Yes, we have three available to residents 24-7."

If she'd had bottle in her hand, she'd have probably shattered it on the ground and jabbed me with it. "Is that so? And anyone can use the town car?"

"Of course. Hunter uses it all the time."

Her eyes were slits. Simmering rage shot out of them, directed straight at me. "Good to know, Ian. Thanks for being a *friend*."

His chest puffed out, and he stacked her bags on top of each other, taking care to hang the eggs from the brass poles at the top.

Ian disappeared back into the building with the cart.

She whirled on me, still holding her arm against her chest. "You asshole." Through clenched teeth, she was raining fire and brimstone. "Why didn't you tell me there was a car we could take?"

I internally grimaced but flipped things around to cover my guilt. This wasn't all my fault. "I didn't expect you to buy enough groceries to feed a marching band."

She took a few deep breaths and closed her eyes. "I was trying to be nice. Ever heard of it? Trying to make up for the milk and the cereal this morning."

"You admit it." I jabbed a finger in her direction, enjoying the small, petty victory after feeling like the world's biggest asshole.

Her eyes popped open, then narrowed to a blistering intensity. "Was this all some giant torture scenario to get me to confess? Of course it was me. Do you have cereal fairies I should know about?"

"No, and I didn't think about the car. Contrary to what Ian said, I don't use it much."

A noise rumbled from her throat that sounded like a sound before an animal struck.

"Let's get upstairs." I pulled the front door open. "You need to put ice on your wrist."

"Talk about emotional whiplash. One minute you're Hunter Saxton MD asking about X-rays. The next you're an asshole bitching about cereal. Then you're Mr. Concerned."

I let it slide rather than continuing this argument in the lobby. The last thing I needed was more attention drawn to us. "From the way you were sprawled out on the pavement, I figured you'd be eager to get inside."

"And back to asshole. Is this your plan? Run so hot and cold it freaks me out and I move?"

I kept my mouth shut on the walk to the elevator. It hadn't been my plan, but it was certainly getting under her skin. Maybe it would be easier than I'd thought to get her to move. In a few days I could throw out some other options for alternate housing arrangements I could find for her. She might jump at it with no extra prodding from me. GiGi couldn't hand my ass to me over that.

For some reason thinking about her leaving sent a disquieting flare of irritation scratching at the back of my mind. I'd slept just as horribly as ever last night after getting home, walking past her room, and taking a quick shower. A hint of the edge I normally had when I walked into my room had been shaved off—not enough for the nightmares to stop, but I'd gotten more sleep than I had in weeks, although that wasn't saying much. But that was no reason to roll out the welcome wagon. I could get a cat if having another living thing in the apartment made it easier for me to sleep. A cat wouldn't be nearly this annoying. I sure as hell hoped it didn't have to be Sabrina. Hell, maybe I was getting over my insomnia and nightmares. Maybe I'd finally made it to the other side and it had nothing at all to do with her. I shook my head, rejecting the thought of her staying outright.

A voice I wished I'd never become familiar with stabbed at my eardrums. "Hunter."

Every muscle tightened. "Keep walking."

"Who is that?" She peeked over my shoulder, but I shifted, blocking her view. A gentle *ding* signaled the arrival of the car, and the doors opened.

"None of your business. Get in the elevator."

Her grimace was set to ear steaming, but she got inside.

"If that's your plan, I want you to know, I've put up with way bigger assholes than you."

"Is that a challenge?"

"A warning."

5

SABRINA

Two weeks later and it was still a warning I'd yet to be able to follow up on. Having a bum arm hadn't helped things when it came to dealing with my new roommate and truly getting rowdy. Plus, I'd been pretending I was a lot tougher than I was. I'd never been too good at maintaining the façade of impenetrability, even when I didn't have a roof over my head due to sheer good will.

"Why didn't you tell me you had bags?" Hunter tried to snatch the bag from my non-injured arm.

"Are you angry with me because I'm not asking for your help?" I held on tighter, grimacing.

"Let me take it. Do you want to hurt yourself even more?" He snapped at me like this was all my fault.

"Like you care." I rolled my eyes and let go of the bag. Fine, if he wanted to carry my tampons, shampoo, and conditioner, that was on him. I released my grip on the bags and he stumbled back.

He recovered and picked up a bag that had fallen to the floor. "I didn't mean for you to get hurt."

"No, you were just trying to make things difficult enough that I'd pack up and leave." I leveled my gaze at him. Our truce had been uneasy to say the least.

His eyes softened a hair before he turned and walked toward my room. "You've got no place else to go? No friends, boyfriend, parents?"

"My best friend is living in Russia, no boyfriend." I was proud I kept from wincing. "And my parents are in Arizona, where they downsized to a smaller house. If I had other options, I wouldn't have taken Barbara up on her generosity. I don't make it a habit of taking things offered to me that I don't need."

"What did the doctor say?" He stopped in front of my bedroom door, his eyes not boring into mine with his barely contained annoyance, but searching.

I didn't like the fluttering in my stomach. It was hard to concentrate when his gaze was locked onto mine. There were lines I wasn't crossing, especially not with him. Everyone else seemed to think Hunter was the nicest guy ever, but I'd seen what he was like when he didn't get his way. I did not need to deal with another overgrown man-child and lose another place to live. "None of your business." I reached for my bags.

He jerked them back. "Are you sure I can't pay for the visit?" The soft, caring way he said it sent even more confused signals to my brain. He was only trying to cover his ass so Barbara didn't chew him out.

"I wouldn't want you to think I was taking advantage." I took the bags from his hand and slipped inside my bedroom, then closed the door behind me. "Don't worry, I'm not going to tattle on you to Barbara. Your secret is safe with me."

Insufferable asshole. Somehow, on the cusp of thirty, I'd

been transported back to college—no, high school—when dealing with Hunter.

His shadow under my door rocked back and forth before darting off toward his room.

When I walked down the hall, I expected to be hit in the back of the head by a spitball.

Music rumbled the walls, which made my recording even more difficult than usual. That and my sprained wrist.

"How's the wrist?" Cat's voice came in over the speaker-phone at full volume. Not that I needed to worry about disturbing Hunter since he wouldn't hear an explosion in the living room.

"It hurts less." With my arm in a sling, I fought with the mouse in my left hand, trying to edit my latest disaster of a video.

"You're sure it's a sprain?"

"That's what the doctor said." Paying for the visit out of pocket hadn't been first on my list of how to spend any of my savings, but it needed to be done when the swelling had taken a while to go down. He'd given me a brace and some ibuprofen, and I was kicking myself for not toughing it out.

"What's the music in the background?"

"Hunter said he needs to listen to the music for work." Who the hell needed to listen to music at floor-shaking volume for work?

Although the lighting in the room was great, the overall feel was boring. Not that bedding was overly exciting, but I was up against big agencies for this work and beating them at their own game was just going to end up with me getting my ass kicked. My angle was more natural, high production, but images and video that felt more like a friend recommending a product or taking pictures to share. It also came with a much lower price tag for the companies than other, more established companies. Sometimes it worked and I landed the jobs, but lately my inbox was a trickle of possible positive responses, but there was still a ways to go until a paycheck arrived.

The bundle of abandoned sheets sat on the floor.

Background noise on her end was low.

I couldn't tell if she was at home or outside.

"What does he do?"

"I have no freaking clue. For all I know, he's a male escort." His comings and goings were all over the place. Not that I cared or even noticed him aside from the brain-pounding music, stomping, and the pot of coffee that seemed to always be brewed. I got it. He hated the way I made coffee. And damnit if his brews weren't as close to heavenly as possible. I never had to go out for coffee, which was a good and bad thing. My time in the apartment bordered on hermitville with all the work I needed to get finished by the end of the week.

"It'd be super weird if he were a female escort."

"You're hilarious. Most of the time he's in and out at random times during the day or out late at night. He wears suits a lot, and the rest of the time he's in that business casual, rolled-sleeve, button-down-shirt look." The same look that made me think dirty thoughts, not the murderous ones I usually held for him.

She growled. "Oh, I know the one. How are his fore-arms? Does he flex a lot? Are they sinewy and muscly?"

God were they. Tightening and bunching with every move. It was mesmerizing. "They're okay."

"You're totally hot for those arms. That's the first thing

you mentioned about..." She clammed up, and her voice trailed off.

A pang hit me in the center of my chest, like it was being used as a punching bag.

"How are you doing? You know." She cleared her throat. "With the whole Seth situation."

"As good as can be expected. I blocked him on everything. There were lots of messages at first, but I checked the folder I dumped them into and they've petered out." Somehow that hurt more, and the guilt washed right in after the waves of pain washed away. I didn't want him coming after me. He never should've pursued me in the first place. But I guess a part of me hoped he'd be hung up on me for longer. I wanted the torture drawn out a bit more. Now it felt like I'd be replaced in a week.

"Maybe his wife found out and he's been kicked out and is roaming the streets, sleeping in his car."

I hugged my knees to my chest. My guilt soured my stomach. I should've seen the signs. I should've asked more questions. I should've been smarter. "He was good at hiding her from me. Maybe he'll be just as good at hiding me from her."

"Don't get that tone. You didn't know. How could you have known? He was a pilot. You two moved in together. He flew you to visit your parents over the summer."

"But I always know. I'm the one who calls other people on their bullshit, and I'm living this wonderful life with a guy I think I might marry. And oh, what was that? I'll take 'Who Has Been Banging a Married Guy' for $800, Alex." I'd been an idiot, so blinded by the sweet words and loving attention that I'd dismissed the gaps in time as him being focused on his career. Had I not wanted to see? Avoided asking too many questions because I was so wrapped up in being loved by someone?

"I'll say it again. How were you supposed to know? He met your friends. He met your family. You spent holidays together. No one suspected he was leading a double life."

"I should've suspected it." The dirty taint clung to me no matter how many times I showered. My amazing boyfriend had turned out to be someone else's husband. The guilt gnawed at my gut.

"And the second you caught a whiff of his lies, you left the same freaking night. You're not a bad person."

"I—" How could I not be? I'd slept with a married man. My stomach knotted and churned, so close to roiling like it had when he'd confessed. There was a hint of satisfaction that I'd painted his pants with puke that night.

"Repeat after me. 'I am not a bad person.'"

"Cat—" What would people think if they found out? How could I face my parents, who'd been happily married for thirty years? Imagining someone breaking those two apart... I shook my head, trying to burn away every memory of Seth I still had left in my brain.

"Nope! I don't want to hear it. Say it loud and say it proud over the pounding music in the background. Say it." A teasing chiding in her voice. She'd call back if I hung up, flood my inbox if I didn't respond, and possibly send over a singing telegram if I didn't give in.

"I'm not a bad person." I rush-mumbled through the declaration, wanting to believe it but not sure I could.

"No. Stand up. Puff up your chest and shout it."

"I'm not going—"

"I swear, I will call your mom and tell her you're the one who knocked over the lamp in third grade and burned through the carpet in the dining room if you don't."

"Way to jump twenty steps ahead on the threats." I shoved my chair back from the desk. My grandparents had given my mom that gift on her wedding day. She'd loved it and placed it beside the china cabinet in the dining room. Cat had been banned from our house for a whole summer when she took the fall for it.

See, I was totally a shitty person!

"You'd have had me on the phone for the next twenty minutes if I didn't."

Standing up, I glanced around, although the door was closed and the blinds were drawn.

"Hold the phone away from your mouth so you don't blow out my eardrum. I want to hear you scream it."

With the phone in front of me, I put her on speaker and repeated the line. The tightness in my chest ebbed away, and I could scream it louder, a barrier in my brain being pounded on by my voice. I could almost believe it.

"Louder!"

I repeated it again with more conviction. At least, after all of Hunter's late-night dance parties, I knew the neighbors weren't sticklers for volume.

"You can do better than that. I can still hear the music thumping in the background. Drown it out for me," she shouted even louder.

Throwing my head back, I screamed at the ceiling, "I am not a bad person." The breath I released after my declaration didn't feel so tight. A stifled laugh burst free from my lips, and I covered my mouth with my hand, shaking my head. This was why she was my oldest friend. The one who didn't stand for anyone being an asshole to her best friend, not even me.

"There, was that so hard?

"Actually, yes." I plopped back into my chair.

"I've got to go in a second. Let's get back to the new roommate. We're hating him, right? Are we *hating him* hating him or loving to hate him? Tell me more about the forearms."

"Would you stop?"

"He's totally hot, isn't he?"

"In a guy-who-can-get-any-woman-so-he-does-and-leaves-them-all-high-and-dry kind of way." In a he'd-proba-bly-slept-his-way-down-the-Eastern-Seaboard way. He was hot, I couldn't deny it, but that didn't mean I wanted anything to do with him. My burns were still raw and I didn't need to jump right back into the fire.

"I'm sure he's not leaving anyone dry, if you know what I mean," she purred.

"You haven't even seen him."

"From the level of eye roll in your voice, I can tell he's freaking gorgeous. High fives to Gma Georgina for hooking you up with a hottie roommate."

"We don't see much of each other."

"I'm sure you'd like to see more of him. A lot more." Ten bucks said her eyebrows were waggling.

"I'm hanging up."

"Wait. One more thing."

"I thought you said you needed to go."

"I do, but it's cool. My date doesn't mind. Our drinks haven't shown up yet."

"You're on a date right now? Like right this instant?" Out in public? In a crowded restaurant with flower arrange-ments sitting in the center of a linen-draped table? The background noise on her end was minimal. Maybe she'd snuck off into the bathroom.

"Yeah, but it's cool. When my bestie calls, I answer."

"Why didn't you tell me?"

"It's fine. I'll give my date a blow job in his car to make up for it."

I slapped my good hand against my forehead. "Is he actually sitting right in front of you?"

"Actually beside me. I'm giving him a handy right now."

My cheeks burned, and I was thousands of miles away. "Oh my God! Come on! I didn't need to know any of that."

"You always said I was a good multitasker."

"I'm hanging up now."

"Wait! One more thing. You mentioned how your wrist was out of service for a bit."

"If you bring up hand jobs..."

"No, I was going to suggest a model. For your Harper Linens deadline. Find a hot guy, maybe that new roommate of yours, and he can be some man candy in your pics. It might help get their attention, and then you can rest your wrist."

"That's...actually not a terrible idea." Not Hunter, of course, but maybe I could find someone else.

"See. Multitasking."

"You're an absolute nut."

"I know and it makes you love me even more."

"True. Bye, Cat. And bye to your date, sorry for ruining your date."

"Nothing's getting ruined except for this tablecloth. Bye, Sabrina." She ended the call.

I stared at it in stunned silence. She couldn't have really been doing that, could she? No. But knowing her, she totally was.

A knock at my door broke through the mental picture trying to form of her juggling so many balls at once—ha!

"One second." I kicked the pile of sheets out of the way. My foot got caught on the fitted sheet, and I pitched forward, hopping to untangle my foot, and caught myself on the wall beside the door.

Great going, Sabrina. Why don't I injure both my arms and end up putting the sheets on with my teeth?

A little out of breath, I cracked the door. "What do you want?"

"What are you doing?" He folded his arms across his chest and peered over my shoulder.

I squeezed my face in the opening of the door. "None of your business. What do you want?"

"Did I hear shouting a little while ago?"

"How could you hear anything over your brain-scrambling music?" My teeth clenched. I was screwed if I didn't get these videos edited and touched up in the next forty-eight hours, and it would take me twice as long to edit them with my bum hand thanks to the man standing in my doorway in linen pants and a polo.

The sound rumbled through the apartment even now.

"Do you have someone over?"

"Why's it any of your business if I do?"

He growled. "All I'm asking is if you've brought someone into my apartment."

"Don't you mean *our* apartment?" I slipped out through the door, closing it behind me.

Which caught Hunter off guard. His folded arms banged into me, smack dab into my breasts. A solid whack intensified by me shooting forward out of my room.

"What is wrong with you?" He stumbled back.

"Come on, they're not that big." With a grin of satisfaction at his apparent fear of breasts, I crossed my arms over my chest, giving them a nice strong shelf to sit on. My wrist wasn't happy with the weight, but in the brace I could deal.

"And what's wrong with me? You're the one blasting

music for hours on end. It's surprising no one's complained yet." In my old apartment a vigorous walk to the kitchen in the middle of the day would be met with pounding from the apartment below.

"The soundproofing on these apartments is great."

Unfortunately it wasn't too great between the rooms of the apartments.

"Plus, Millie's cool."

My optical nerves were almost severed by the muscle strength that went into stopping that eye roll. Hot guy flirts with older woman to get on her good side. Not even original. "You know who's not cool with it? Me, because I'm trying to work."

"So am I." He stepped closer.

I cocked my head to the side. "Are you testing hearing protection?"

"No, listening to bands for a New Year's Eve concert I'm putting together."

Did he have dimples? I couldn't tell. Not when he was flexing his jaw like that. "Have you ever heard of headphones?"

"Have you? Noise-cancelling ones would keep you in your own little bubble." He mimed slipping them onto his ears and swaying to imaginary music.

I clenched my teeth, trying not to let him see how much he was getting to me. Trying to sleep with his all-night dance party was no picnic.

"Or my jackhole of a roommate could be considerate and not blast his music for hours on end."

"You're the one who invaded my space."

"You know what? You're right. I have, and what does any good invader do? Stake their territory. I've been trying to be nice after you proved to me you weren't above putting me in harm's way with the grocery-store stunt."

"That was—"

I held up my good hand. "Oh no, Hunter. Don't backpedal now. I was happy to be the quiet roommate, seething with ill intentions." I opened my bedroom door and slipped inside. "But now I'm thinking I'll get a little bit rowdy."

His face blanched in the closing gap of the door.

Good. I was glad. It wasn't like I would trash Barbara's place, but I was ready to make myself much more at home here.

6

HUNTER

"Are you sure about this? This requires a massive amount of front-loading on expenses if we take this on." Jameson adjusted his glasses and stared at me over his computer screen.

I twirled my pen, flipping it along the backs of my fingers from my pointer to my pinkie. Concentrating on the movement and pattern helped keep me focused and awake. I hadn't done a big event since we'd started the company just over a year ago. SWANK was an event planning company launched in the conference room when all of us were probably having a quarter life crisis. Leo had left his career as a pro football player behind with not much money to show for it. Apparently, not everyone pulls in insane paychecks. He'd taken over the business from his uncle's partner and we'd all jumped on board.

The company name was a combination of all our last names: Hunter Saxton, Leo Wilder, Jameson Asher, August Niles, and Everest van Konig. It had also been pointed out to us that the letters could be rearranged into WANKS, but we decided SWANK had a much better ring to it.

Leo had landed a multinational hotel chain, securing a steady funnel of corporate business. Everest worked with all the sports teams in the city for events tied to the games, which was always hilarious whenever he turned up in the office in a team jersey and a five-figure watch and Italian leather shoes. August had more wedding features in *Vogue* than some supermodels. Then there was me. Opening a couple clubs every few months, planning a record launch or two. I needed something big. I needed to start bringing in more high profile events.

The New Year's Eve stadium concert was the perfect opportunity.

"Do we have the cash flow?" Everyone else had been pulling their weight. How long until they turned to look at me, wondering what the hell I was even doing here?

Jameson was our guy in the chair, keeping the ship sailing straight and charming our grumpy inherited secretary. Everyone had secured a vital revenue stream for their niche except for me.

"How many other chances would we get to be at the forefront of an event like this? Finally make a splash in the music world."

"Did you ever think the reason Easton Events backed out and took the hit at doing it so late is because they knew it was an albatross?"

"Easton Events was on its last legs even before we siphoned off their best clients." Leo's fiancée—for real this time—had worked for them, and they'd treated her like garbage. Taking their clients had been a pleasure after the stunts they'd pulled with her. With my connections in the music production and nightlife scene, I could get this done. "They also didn't have me at the helm. Five thousand screaming music fans. Some of the biggest up-and-coming bands in the world if I play my cards right." And I always did, or had a plan with back-up plans to make sure I did. "We could have a surprise showstopper to make this a festival people are talking about for years."

"We can put it to a vote at the next board meeting."

"I know, but I need to know you're on my side, Jameson. Everyone looks to you when it comes to weighing out the risks. You've got my back, right?" I held out my fist. "When have I ever not come through for you guys?"

His face switched from guarded to wide open. "I'm not doubting you, Hunter." He squeezed the bridge of his nose under his glasses. "If you say you can get it done, I believe you." He knocked his fist into mine.

They trusted me to pull this off. The relief was swift. A lot of times I felt like they were all waiting on me to screw up, to finally not be the guy who could get anything. To fail and be shown the door. I'd already said goodbye to enough people in my life and I couldn't not have these guys in mine.

"But wrapping up this much of our cash flow into one event...it's a risk."

"One I am fully aware of and don't take lightly. I've already got ten bands lined up who can take the spots of the four who dropped out once Audio International said they were cancelling."

"Sounds like you've got a plan." Jameson gave his nod of approval.

"Always."

He checked his watch. "I've got to pick up Teresa from Girl Scouts. My mom's working a double."

"Tell Rachel I said hi."

He glared and disconnected his laptop. "No, I won't."

I sighed and shook my head. "I didn't mean it like that, just normal friend of her son 'hi'."

His glaring continued.

"Will you get over it already? I've seen your mom naked exactly once, and it was an accident."

He shot up, jamming his glasses back up his nose, and threw on his blazer, although we were a strictly business-casual office unless working an event required anything more. "I don't want to talk about it." He searched his desk and gathered a few more things before sliding everything into his bag. "Teresa's birthday is coming up, and you know she wants us to make her cake again."

"I'll get her a great present. What's she into this year?"

"Teresa doesn't want presents. She wants everyone there to celebrate with her."

Exactly, which was why I did not want to get caught in the cake catastrophe that had happened for the past two years. "I can get her a cut-the-line pass at Sesame Place. She'll be walking down Sesame Street hand in hand with Big Bird and Elmo."

"You're coming—early enough to help."

"Fine, but I'm strictly on cake-eating duty. Make sure the face isn't looking at me this time. Thomas looked like he rode through the night stealing children's souls." I shuddered. Last year's attempt at Thomas the Tank Engine had been a horror movie jump scare.

"Oh no." He rounded the desk. For all his mild-mannered-reporter look, he was still an inch and a half taller than me, and I wasn't exactly short. "You're on baking duty just like the rest of us. Better start brushing up on those skills." His hand clamped down and patted my shoulder on our way out of his office.

"Can't we just buy her one?"

"Stop trying to wriggle out of this. We're doing it. End of discussion."

Leo walked out of his office and shoved his blazer on. The fabric looked a thread away from ripping.

"I thought you were supposed to get smaller after you left the pros."

He stopped mid-button. "I refuse to turn into a flabby former player, but the volume of hay bales I was lifting all summer getting these company retreats put together was enough to kick my ass more than any linebacker. I'll never forgive myself for making cozy, s'more-filled company team building adventures a thing." He dragged his fingers through his hair and turned to leave. "I've got a meeting, then I'm headed straight home after I'm finished."

Jameson stepped forward. "I added Teresa's birthday to your calendar."

Leo's shoulders sagged. "Can't we buy her a cake and take her go-carting or something instead? Hunter could probably get her a starring role in Cirque du Soleil or her own pony if she wanted."

I opened my mouth.

"She wants us all there. It's all she wants."

Leo's lips pressed together. "You know we can't say no to her." He checked his watch. "I'm out of here. See you guys tomorrow." With a half salute he disappeared through the double doors and took the stairs instead of the elevator.

A voice shot through the open-plan space in the center of the office where the assistants and coordinators sat. "And you're the biggest asshole I've ever met!" A shower of paper and folders flew into the air.

August stood feet away from the desk with both hands behind his back.

His most-likely-no-longer-working-for-us assistant telegraphed all kinds of red-flag-waving behavior.

"I told him not to hire a guy." Jameson pinched the bridge of his nose.

The entire office had ground to a halt, everyone waiting for the eventual eruption.

"At least I'm good at what I do, unlike you." August's crisp cool voice was a stark contrast to the fuming happening feet from him.

I dropped my head, exhaling from the bottom of my lungs.

The guy lunged, fist flying through the air straight for August's face.

Like he was a superhero in his own movie, August side-stepped him and grabbed his arm, twisting it behind his back. "Now you're fired. Thanks for making it easy on me. The paperwork can be a real bitch."

The guy struggled. I hadn't even had time to learn this one's name.

Wrestling against August's hold, our ex-employee didn't stand a chance.

August marched his new ex-assistant right past us, out the front doors of the office and down the stairs. At least it was only three flights down.

Jameson shook his head and rubbed the bridge of his nose under his glasses. "Severance packages are going to have to be included in our bridal fees if he keeps this up."

"How many is that so far this year?"

"Eight." Jameson stared after the now-closed glass doors leading to the elevator. "I don't know why I bother putting out ads. At this point I could pull someone off the street and they'd probably last as long as the seasoned professionals he's chewing through."

"At least he's not this big of an asshole to clients."

"He charms them in his own way."

August stepped off the elevator with two cups of coffee like he'd just gone down for a stroll, not to throw someone out of the building.

He set one of the cups on Phylis's desk. She preened, patting his hand, and he pecked her on her cheek before walking back into the office.

Everyone else around us snapped back to their work the second he crossed the threshold.

"Do you have to run off every assistant we hire?" Jameson's grip tightened on his bag.

August walked past us with his arms spread wide. "Do I have to keep working weddings?"

"You're practically booked into the next century and obviously you do great work."

He charged forward, jabbing a finger on the hand holding the coffee toward us both. "You said this was temporary. I'd do weddings to get the business off the ground, and then I'd have an out."

"Do you think any of us know how to do what you do?"

"Why don't you plan a wedding, get left at the altar like a lovesick fucking puppy, then you can take over for me?" He glared at us both.

I pushed his finger back around his coffee. "Look, it's not ideal. We all know this. Do you think Everest wants to be doing sports? The jerseys probably give him hives, but we've all had to make sacrifices."

He scoffed. "Yes, hanging out in clubs and concerts is seriously the most taxing job any of us have—well, other than Jameson, who's about to leave and it's not even three yet."

Jameson rocked back like August had taken a swing.

I stepped between them and glared at August. "Even you know that was low."

August's eyes widened, and he dropped his head.

"Shit," he huffed under his breath. "James, I didn't mean that. I'm pissed off. I'll have double the workload now that Nathan's left the company." His jaw clenched, and he looked out the office doors.

Jameson nodded, his look nothing close to understanding. "Like clockwork. Maybe when the anniversary of your would-be wedding day comes up, you should head off to a deserted island so no one else has to be around you. Times like these I don't have to wonder why the hell you're the grumpy asshole all alone." He checked his watch. "I've got to go. I'll see you all tomorrow. Or maybe I won't show at all since I'm apparently completely ornamental around here." Marching off, he didn't look back. I was torn between running after Jameson and laying into August, but Jameson had to get to Teresa. There wasn't any time to kiss and make up. I'd shoot him a message later.

"What the hell, man?" I gritted my teeth, rounded on him and shoved his shoulder.

August stumbled back and caught himself. "I'm sorry." His jaw clenched, and without all the bluster, the pain was there, too close to the surface and raw. He stepped back and shook his head before slinking away into his office.

I followed him, closing the door behind me. "All the staff got an excellent after-lunch show." Trying to keep it light, I sat in the chair next to his desk. I hated when the group fought. Leo and Everest were the powder kegs of the group. We didn't need August turning into a third fuse. Keeping friends—real friends—was hard enough, but too much friction and our new business venture wouldn't make it past year two.

"Why are you in my office?"

"Is your goal to run everyone off today?"

"Yes." He sipped from his coffee and looked down at the portfolio on his desk.

"Wedding date coming up soon?"

Tension rippled through every muscle. He took a stilted drink from his cup. "It's tomorrow."

I sucked in a breath through my clenched teeth. "Sucks, man. Do you want to talk about it?"

His head lifted glacially slowly. "Does it look like I want to talk about it?"

"Trying to be a good friend."

His jaw popped. "No, I don't want to talk about it. Right now I need to go through the stack of résumés from the last round of interviews and find a new assistant who can start by tomorrow."

"Do you want me to help sort through them? Maybe come up with a short list?" This I could do. Reading people was my forte. I delved deep into what they truly wanted, got it for them, and kept them on the line for a favor I might need in the future.

August thought he wanted a competent assistant. What he needed was someone who wouldn't be scared off by all the glowering and grumbling, someone who'd push him and keep him in line at the same time. Not an easy combo.

He slouched back into his seat. "Sure, why the hell not? No guys, please. A slap across the face is par for the course, but I'd prefer not to have to dodge punches in my office. Plus, it helps with bride duty."

Three hundred applications and four hours later, August had his short list. There were three candidates who'd probably last a little over a month and one wild card I had a special feeling about. I'd learned over the years to go with that feeling.

"Don't burn through these four all at once. I'm putting a moratorium on vetting until next year."

August smirked and braced his hands behind his head. "What'll this cost me?"

"You know favors for friends are gratis."

"Lucky I'm in the inner circle then." He laughed.

Lucky indeed. I left his office and headed to my apartment. I could catch a few hours of sleep before I left for the meeting with one of the acts to persuade them to sign on for New Year's Eve.

7

SABRINA

I slipped the brace back on and paced my room. At least I could think with Hunter gone. My head shot up.

Cat's suggestion of some hunky muscle...maybe it wasn't so insane after all.

I bolted from the apartment, skidding my hundred-yard-dash run to the elevator when Millie's door opened.

"Sabrina, so nice to see you." She smiled and closed her door. "Headed out?"

"Not exactly. I needed to check down at the front desk about a favor." A favor I had no idea how to ask for. Maybe bribes of pasta and cookies would work? I had that level of cooking down to a tee.

"Accepting a delivery? You know they'll bring them up for you. They can even accept jewelry. They have a safe."

Oh, Millie. What a life she must have led.

Most of my jewelry was from Claire's, and here she was getting hers locked away in a safe. Probably delivered with an armored truck.

She linked her arm in mine, and we walked toward the

elevator. Her delicate, polished outside didn't exactly go with my t-shirt-and-yoga-pants look. I was surprised she hadn't had the building managers send out a notice about dress code, but Millie didn't seem to mind.

"It's not a delivery. I needed to ask a question. Do you know if Ian's on duty now?"

Her eyes widened. "Oh, Ian, is it? I'd have thought it would be Hunter." She pressed the down button.

"No!" My denial jolted us both, and now my cheeks were flamethrower-hot. "It's not either of them. Ian's been super helpful, so I wanted to ask him a question, and Hunter... well, Hunter's certainly been a person."

The doors to the elevator opened, and Millie stepped inside. "My, it sounds as if you two are off to an interesting start."

A start? I was tempted to check the front doorknob with the back of my hand whenever I returned to the apartment to make sure Hunter hadn't decided to *Home Alone* the place to keep me out. "We're still working on the whole living-together thing. Lobby?"

She nodded and I pressed the button, needing to steer the conversation from where her interested eyes and tone seemed to be trying to lead me. Hunter and I wouldn't be starting anything other than a semi-hostile roommate-ship until the end of December. "What are you looking forward to most before the end of the year, Millie? Any big plans?"

"Why, I don't think anyone's asked me that in a long time."

"Really?"

Her gaze darted toward the ceiling like she was cataloging her past interactions. "Where am I going? Or what do I need? When I'll be visiting? But not my plans." Another pause where she seemed to be assessing herself. "I'm thinking about getting a dog. The apartment is very big now without Gus. He was my husband. It's been three years and still feels like yesterday. Maybe I should move to Florida like Barbara." A wistfulness entered her voice.

Why'd I have to go and open my big mouth? Stick to the small talk. I was worried about my roommate problem, and Millie had been through a monumental change and was now all on her own. "She and Grandma Georgina are having a ball down there."

"Oh, I know. I'm in the group chat."

"They've got you in a group chat too?"

"I don't know how their fingers haven't fallen off with all the messages flying back and forth."

At least I wasn't the only one subjected to the glowing red notification of doom with numbers climbing like we were on an express elevator ready to launch us into space.

The doors opened, letting us both out into the lobby. Millie went outside, and I went in search of my potential new sheet model.

"You want me to help you make the bed?" Ian held the sheets in his hands with his head cocked to the side. "And record it?" He'd been getting off his shift, which was perfect timing. Already changed out of his uniform, he wore mesh shorts and an Iron Man t-shirt. He'd followed me up to the apartment as if he expected camera crews to pop out of any alcove and tell him he'd been punked.

"Yes. Well, I want you to make it."

"For your job?" His eyebrows dipped, gaze darting between the ironed sheet set, unmade bed, and me.

"Yes!"

"Seriously? You want to video me and take pictures of me with the sheets?" Skepticism was etched all over his face.

Maybe I could figure out another option. But it would be more of the same. I wouldn't stand out in what had to be at least twenty other people who'd gotten a shot to submit their work. I could try stop-motion. My wrist ached at the idea of all the time at the computer to attempt that. I also didn't want to weird out Ian. He was my only friend in the whole building other than Millie. "If you're not up for it..." I reached for the sheets.

He tugged them back. "No, I can do it. I just never thought of sheets as being someone's kink."

My neck and cheeks were match strike hot with embarrassment. "Not like that! Product photography. You know, those pictures on a website that show off different parts of a product. That's what I do. Before I moved, I scored a chance for a big campaign. I made it to the next round and I want to wow them with my final pitch. If they like them, then I get the year-long campaign and it'll be enough to live off for a year at least."

I went to my page and clicked on the first video.

Ian stood beside me watching one of my last jobs for toilet bowl cleaner. Not exactly glamorous, but it had paid some of the bills. But I'd put all my eggs into the sheet basket and hadn't won another job since.

In another, I'd tried my hand at being my own model.

On the screen, I was like a different person. Happy, confident, unbothered by anything. She was a hell of a lot more put together than me. It helped that no one could see me from the elbows down. They'd liked my videos and photos but preferred the ones without me in them. Go figure.

"Wow, you seem different."

"From my forearms." I laughed. "Yes, I can do a hand flourish with the best of them and seem prim and proper and not the least bit like a sweatpant mess."

"I didn't mean—I only meant it felt bright and light in the video."

"It's called acting." I bowed with a flourish, hoping my cheeks weren't fluorescent at this point. "It won't take long. I can pay you too. It wouldn't be much until I know if I've won the whole campaign."

He shook his head. "Don't worry about it. I can help you out."

Relief rushed through me. "I'll pay you back, I swear. And I've never used a model before, so bear with me."

He held the sheets to his chest and widened his eyes. "I'll be your first?"

I grabbed a pillow and whacked him. "That's one way to put it."

Ian took a seat at my desk off camera, and I set everything up, checking the angles and lighting.

"I'm ready and remember, we can do this a hundred times, if we need to. Just relax and be natural." My smile of reassurance didn't do much to wash the steel, rigid tightness from his body. Maybe this wasn't a great idea. I'd never been a director before. But he was here and so that was it. It was the best I could do right now. The novelty factor might be enough to cover over the fact that I'd assembled a human-like man robot to assist me today.

I shot the same motions over and over from different angles, wanting to get every single image and video clip I might need for the final submission. Working on a movie set or a full-fledged commercial needed a thousand times the attention to detail that photography did, and that was part of the reason I hadn't gone that way after graduating. Plus, I couldn't work as an unpaid intern just to get my foot in the door.

Textile design was a hell of a lot less stressful. Going in to fix an issue with my stylus was a piece of cake compared to dealing with all the moving pieces of this work.

I grabbed the camera for a slow pan of the perfectly made bed. With it set back on the tripod, Ian and I high-fived and flopped onto the bed after the final shot.

He turned to me, sitting up. "That's it?"

"Yes, it should be enough. Thank you. I can't tell you how much you helped me out today." I slid off the bed. "If you'll help me pull all this off, I can get it packed away."

He stripped the bed, and I adjusted my wrist brace.

"No problem. The whole way up here, I was worried you were trying to proposition me."

I jerked, my brace nearly flying out of my hand, and the Velcro rip sliced through the silence. "What?" Whirling around, I stared at Ian, who squeezed the back of his neck. "You thought I was asking you up here for sex?"

"Come on!" He threw his hands up in the air. "You wouldn't be the first tenant to ask for a little extra help in the bedroom."

"Are you serious? What's the dirt? Is it Millie? Saucy minx." I growled.

"No, not Millie! They don't live here anymore, but it was...awkward to say the least."

"Did they have you make the bed afterward?"

"I didn't do it," he hissed with incredulous wide eyes.

"Sure, Ian," I teased. "Don't worry about me proposi-tioning you. It's not my style." Abject humiliation? I liked to keep it to a minimum. Asking a guy for sex and having him turn me down wasn't my idea of a great time. Seth had been one of the first guys to ever make a move on me. Maybe that should've been my first clue that something was up. "I'm not exactly a wolf-whistle kind of girl. Let me load everything onto my computer."

Not that I was interested in Ian. He was cute and sweet, but I'd certainly gotten the friend vibe more than anything else.

Grabbing the memory card from the camera, I walked over to my desk.

"I'm not saying you're not ho—cute. You are. But every word out of your mouth sounds just like my sister." He shuddered.

I chuckled and slipped the memory card into the computer and the footage downloaded. That was one I hadn't heard before. *You've got a cute face. You're more of a guy's girl.* Or the worst kind, *I'm not into fat chicks.* Thanks, dicks, I'm not into face-melting assholes.

"It's cool, don't worry about it." I got the footage loaded, and it all looked fine. Editing would be interesting. "And everything looks good, thank you again. I'll make it up to you. How about I provide bodyguard services for any unwanted solicitations from other tenants?"

He laughed. "My sister's a ballbuster too. If everything looks good, I'll head to the gym."

I walked him to the door. "Ball busting is what I do best. You've gotta grab those balls"—the door opened—"and give them a firm, warm squeeze for all they're worth." My words trailed off.

Hunter's eyebrows furrowed like two perfectly mani-cured caterpillars readying for a duel.

Ian laughed again. "Hey, Hunter." He turned back to me. "Do you want me to see if there are any other guys at the gym who might be available, if I'm working? I don't want you stuck in a bind."

My gaze darted to Hunter. "That would be awesome. And we can work out a deal for money or gift cards or something as payment."

"Perfect." He sidestepped Hunter, who'd frozen just inside the doorway.

"Bye, Hunter. Bye, Sabrina." The door closed gently behind Ian.

"Hey, Hunter." I spun and walked into the kitchen.

"Why was Ian here out of uniform?" He followed me, his bag thumping on the counter in the galley kitchen.

I opened the cabinet, searching for my chocolate iced cupcake box. Going up on my tiptoes, I found it and used my fingertips to pull out a double cupcake gold mine. How the hell had it gotten so far in the back? "Because he's not working."

"Why's he here when he's not working?"

I closed the cabinet. "Why do you care?" The wrapper crinkled in my hands. Self-consciousness went out the door when it came to Hunter. At this point I didn't give a fuck if he thought I was a fatty who ate cupcakes, because guess what? I was. Fine, not fat. Curvy, voluptuous, whatever. I wasn't running a marathon anytime soon. My jeans gapped like a mofo at the waist to fit my butt and thighs, and I was fine with that.

He wasn't thinking I'd gotten this way by eating kale and salad. Every so often I needed a chocolate icing sugar rush.

"What was he talking about, other guys?"

I took a bite from the cupcake, dodging the vanilla cream center. "It's help for a project."

"What kind of project?" His gaze drifted to the cupcake with a strange look on his face.

The cupcake didn't taste nearly as good anymore. It was

probably stuck all over my teeth. And I looked like a slob, but I couldn't let him see me crack.

"Why are you grilling me?" I ate the creamy center and licked the cream from my thumb.

His jaw clenched. "I don't want random people in my apartment." The blue of his eyes flickered with an unnamed emotion, moving from the still-uneaten cupcake in my hand back to my eyes.

Embarrassment tickled its way up my neck. Okay, maybe I didn't need to be stuffing my face in front of a guy who probably spent enough time in the gym for it to constitute a full-time job.

"They won't be random people. They're Ian's friends, who'll be supervised by me the whole time." I marched toward him, trying to get to the hall and away from his exacting gaze.

"They're people you don't know and I don't know."

"Do you know anyone? Do you have friends?" Other than the one time his work friends had come over, he hadn't brought anyone into the apartment. Maybe he didn't want them to see him in his comfy clothes or to move a coaster out of place. I'd been prepared for him to bring back legions of women, but maybe they were scared off by his driving late-night music preferences.

His head cocked to the side. "Of course I have friends."

"Acting the way you do, I can't imagine they're happy to have you around for long." I needed more sugar for this conversation. I unwrapped the last cupcake and leaned to my left, brushing against Hunter to dump the wrapper in the trash.

He jolted and jerked back.

I rolled my eyes and straightened. "Easy, just throwing

the wrapper away." I took another bite. Screw ladylike, he was pissing me off. "What boundary am I crossing?"

"Personal space for one."

"You came in here after me. All I was doing was getting a snack."

"Without a plate or napkin."

Glaring, I shoved the rest of the cupcake into my mouth. "There, are you happy now?" My muffled words didn't seem to amuse him. *Go figure.* "For someone who works with clubs and music acts, you're sure uptight." I grabbed the lapels of his blazer, stunning us both. My knuckles brushed against his firm chest. The butterflies returned, and they'd brought a few hummingbird friends along. Recovering, I cleared my throat. No backing down. "Lighten up, Hunter. Can I go now?"

He didn't move. His gaze flicked to my mouth. "No."

Shit, were my lips covered in icing? I licked them and folded my arms across my chest and sighed. "Fine. Lay the lecture on me."

"You can't just barge in and take over."

"Take over? I haven't taken over anything. Other than food in the cabinets, what have I taken over?"

His nostrils flared.

"Do I have shit all over the apartment? Do I make a mess? Do I leave plates in the sink or make tons of noise?" I leveled my gaze at him. "No. Most people would call that a perfect roommate."

"I can't...I don't like having people in my space."

"Tough shit, dude. You're an adult. Deal with it. And I won't be here forever. Barbara is helping me out. That's all. Me moving in here wasn't some huge plot to systematically dismantle your life. Sorry you can't jerk off in the living room with me around. I'm sure you can handle the disappointment for a few more months." Without waiting for him to move, I barged straight into him, took the gap that opened to his left, and went straight to my room, locking the door.

He banged on the door. "We're not finished talking."

"Oh yes, we are." I clicked on my playlist and turned up the volume. "Two can play at this game." Right about now was when I could use a cupcake. Damn him for spoiling my sugar high. But I didn't hate how peeved he'd been by me inviting Ian into the apartment.

Taking Hunter's advice, I cranked up my music and gave him a taste of his own medicine, while editing the pictures. They weren't bad. They were actually pretty good.

Maybe I'd take Ian up on the offer of gym friends to help me with different product shots. And why the third degree about having him over in the first place? Was Hunter against having the "help" around if they weren't working? What a pretentious, sanctimonious asshole. If Hunter wanted to treat me like a bad roommate, I'd give him something to bitch about.

8

HUNTER

The taxi ride back to the apartment had me more on edge than normal. Maybe due to how hard it was to keep my eyes open. Maybe due to the two hours of sleep I'd gotten last night. Maybe due to my new roommate.

Sabrina had been lying when it came to her promise of getting rowdy. I'd expected a crazy party or two, trashing the place a little. But she hadn't done that.

She'd been slow and methodical with her invasion of my space. Muffled voices on the other side of the door, just enough so I couldn't pretend I was living alone anymore.

Plus, the lack of sleep was brutal.

Coffee wasn't cutting it anymore. Even espresso made me jittery, but I still wasn't functioning better than a half-dead zombie. If I could crank the music and pass out, maybe she wouldn't hear me when I woke up—or shot up screaming, which seemed to be my MO for the past few months.

I flung the door to the apartment open. My steps rattled the lamps in the hallway.

The door to Sabrina's room opened. Out walked a six-two guy who looked like he lived at the gym and her, sweaty and flushed with her wrist still in a brace.

A pang of guilt hit me hard. I should've called the town car or at least helped her with the bags even when she refused. Fortunately, her wrist wasn't broken.

"Thanks for all the help, Ramsey." Her rosy cheeks were full and tempting.

Not what I needed right now. I slammed the front door shut.

They both jolted, turning to stare at me.

Without another word, I brushed past Sabrina, whose scent had bored itself into my brain so every time I smelled it, the blood rushed from my head straight to my treacherous dick.

Torturing myself thinking about her with yet another guy wasn't what I needed after the fucked-to-hell day I'd had.

This was how she waged her war.

The pair said their goodbyes at the door.

The parade had begun as a trickle but now felt like a state university marching band. Anytime I left the apartment, I'd come back to hushed voices behind Sabrina's door. Hers and a deeper one. Male. Always.

I'd come back from work during the day, and she'd be there.

Today was the first day she hadn't closed her door all the way.

Lights were set up. A tripod stood in front of the window facing straight at the bed. Everything centered on the bed. What the hell?

Balled-up sheets sat in a pile on the floor. So many sheets. How many was she going through?

On her computer screen, the white, now-rumpled, sheet-covered bed was the focus of the lens.

"Are you—"

Before I could say anything else, she swooped under my arm, the wafting scent of lavender coming right along with her. She stood in the doorway to her room, pushing me back out into the hallway.

"None of your business." She slammed the door in my face. Was that the only way she knew how to end a conversation?

I lurched forward, the question nearly escaping, *Are you shooting porn in my grandmother's apartment?* But I clawed it back, not sure I wanted to have confirmation and increase her invasion into the near-hallucinatory half dreams where I swore I could smell her. Instead of asking a question that might wreck me, I went for self-preservation. "Keep the noise down."

"Same to you." She taunted from the other side of the wood. "Now go away, Hunter. Don't you have a party to get to?"

I braced my hands on the doorway. "Don't forget who lived here first."

"I'm not responding anymore, but you can sit out there all you like. I've got some videos to edit."

I pushed away from the door, seething all the way to my room. Pacing the floor, I got undressed. Was she seriously recording porn in my grandmother's guest room? Was she inviting guys into my apartment to have sex with them on film? Who were these guys? GiGi had said Sabrina was new to the area. Were these strangers? Was she being safe?

Would she get us both murdered by her sex-romp adventures?

But once I was undressed, I couldn't stop thinking

about her with other guys. I could still smell her. Her lavender scent invaded my nostrils everywhere I went, like she'd implanted it into my olfactory system with a few whiffs.

I cranked up my music and headed into the shower, trying to focus on work and the prize at the end of the tunnel. But every time I closed my eyes, I saw Sabrina, hot and flushed over me with her chestnut hair falling around her face like a curtain, cutting us off from everyone else while she rode me, tight and wet, to completion.

It was an embarrassingly short fantasy under the cold spray from the showerhead.

This woman was going to straight-up kill me.

"Now she's got guys coming in and out of the apartment all the time. Between that and the fact that she never seems to leave the house, she's driving me nuts. Not to mention the smell." It lingered everywhere, all the time, and my stiff-dick response was nearly Pavlovian and embarrassing as hell. "Is she running through the house spraying her perfume on everything?" I drummed my fingers along the side of my highball glass.

The insistent thump of the bass didn't totally drown out conversation in the VIP area of the Highland Club.

"And why does she have to eat all her food by picking it apart and licking it off her fingers?" It made me want to grab her wrists and lick it off myself. Would it taste even sweeter off her skin? "She's a pain in the ass, but I'm not going to let her ruin my night. I'm not going to think about her anymore."

The brunette with the off-the-shoulder top and

deadpan expression on the plush sofa beside me uncrossed her legs. "You've been talking about her for thirty-two minutes."

I rocked back in my seat.

She waved her glowing screen with the lightning-fast tenths of a second ticking away. "I'm not one hundred percent sure. I didn't start the timer until you'd already been talking for a few minutes."

My jaw dropped before I snapped it shut. A burn traveled to the tips of my ears and I grimaced. Tonight was about getting away from my new roommate. And I wouldn't think about her anymore.

She stood from her seat, smoothing out the shimmery skirt strangling her from mid-thigh. "Good luck with not thinking about her at all." Bending at the waist, she patted me on the cheek. "Here's a word of advice. No woman wants to listen to a guy talk about how much he wants to bang another woman."

My hand shot up, spilling whisky onto the back of my hand. "Whoa, I don't—"

"Oh yeah you do." She nodded and scrunched her nose up in a silent laugh. "Big-time." Spinning, she walked off to the other side of the VIP area.

We'd all had terrible roommates we bitched about. Well, I hadn't. I'd finessed a single every year of college and had lived alone since I'd graduated. But tons of people complained about people they lived with. That's all it was when it came to Sabrina.

Had I wondered what she wore to bed? Possibly.

Had I thought about licking icing off Sabrina's fingers? Sure.

Had I wanted to know what she was doing behind closed doors and had to catch myself from leaning into her smell whenever she was around? Yes, but I was chalking it up to temporary insanity.

She drove me batshit crazy, and I hated her in my space. Having her so close meant I never felt like I could relax. The moments of stolen sleep were even harder to manage when worries mounted in my head about what would happen once I drifted off.

A shadow fell over me. "Well, that was embarrassing. For you, not for me. For me it was hilarious." Everest slid into the previously occupied seat beside me. He unbuttoned his jacket and rested his arm on the back of the couch, looking like he was ready for his interview on *The Tonight Show*. Right now his smoothness made me want to punch him. While I always felt like I was faking it, Everest exuded a high-class, don't-give-a-fuck attitude.

"Hilarious like when you saw Maddy last." I bit out and took a sip from my glass.

His head snapped in my direction.

The booze curdled in my stomach, guilt souring the alcohol.

"Fuck, sorry. That was a low blow." The backstage run-in with his ex had left him silent and pissed off for at least a week afterward. She was on our list of two things we didn't bring up. Maddy and Milwaukee. The forbidden Ms.

He grunted and went back to his old-fashioned, scanning the crowd. "I didn't have to come out, you know?"

"I know." I scrubbed my hands over my face. My bleary eyes felt like someone had sandblasted them. The noise-cancelling headphones covered with the blasting music hadn't been working for more than a few hours of sleep. "The stress is getting to me."

"About the music festival?"

"How'd you—"

"Jameson," we both answered at the same time.

"I told him to let me bring it up at the next meeting." I didn't need him going to bat for me and convincing everyone I could pull this off.

"He's doing what he can to help you succeed. Trying to butter us up before we're all together at once, grilling you."

Of course they would. It was a big risk. One I hadn't taken on lightly, but one I needed to go for. "The opportunity won't come up again."

"Not every opportunity is worth the cost." He continued to stare out over the crowd like he was looking for someone.

He was, but she wasn't here.

"The only way to know is to go for it." I leaned forward and set my glass on the table, bracing myself for what I was about to do. I ducked my head, clasping my hands in front of me. "I was going to try to talk to Maddy." I turned, looking at him over my shoulder.

If I hadn't known him since junior year of college, I might not have picked up on it.

The nearly imperceptible locking of his muscles. The jump in his left eyelid. The reach for the lighter in his pocket, although he'd never smoked.

Jameson and August would be much better at seeing the signs than me, since they'd known him longer, but after working together for the past two years, the tells were easier to pick up on.

His head tilted, but he didn't look at me. "You want Without Grey to play the festival."

"It would raise the profile of the event tenfold." And make a name for the company on a national scale. Getting Without Grey involved would turn all the spotlights onto that night, especially since they were being so secretive while recording their new album, but that also meant more eyes on the concert, and having it fail would paint us as amateurs. It would paint me as an amateur, and risk the reputation of the rest of the guys.

"They're one of the biggest bands in the world." He said it like sawdust was being shoved down his throat.

"Will you be okay if I do?" His history with Maddy was as complicated as it got, and I wouldn't do this if I didn't have his blessing. He was one of my best friends, and if he wasn't cool with it, I'd find another way to take the night to the next level.

"If it'll help the event be a success... It's not like I have to see her. I'm not going to lose my shit, if that's what you're worried about." He looked to me with practiced relaxation. Tension still ran through him like a riptide.

"I don't have to—"

"Do it. It's been years. Not a big deal. She's moved on and so have I."

That was the least convincing sentence ever spoken, but tonight wasn't the time to bring it up. "She'll probably say no. Then it'll be a moot point." I shrugged, trying to keep it nonchalant, although I'd been working up the right angle for approaching her for over a week now. That was where people often screwed up. They went for the quick and easy ask, but often it was the finesse, the right phrasing and positioning that made what I did happen.

"You know she'll say yes." His gaze locked onto mine. "After you wrangled her the extension on her management consulting course senior year, she promised you our firstborn." His throat worked up and down like he was gasping for air. "So I'm sure getting her band, who will be in town anyway, to play a show wouldn't be too much of an ask." His mirthless laugh hurt my ears. It sounded like chewing glass while raking nails against a chalkboard.

"We'll see." I wished there'd been a different way to go about this. One where Everest didn't look like he was moments from clawing his way out of his own skin. Maybe this could be the chance for them to finally hash everything out and go their separate ways without this tether between them that spanned a decade and the thousands of miles they'd tried to put between each other.

Everest set down his glass. "I'm heading out. I've got an early meeting with the corporate management team at the rink tomorrow."

"Don't forget to bring your coat. Are you going to put on skates this time? Take a spin out on the ice?"

He stood and buttoned his blazer. "Fuck off."

"I'd have thought after all this time, you'd be a hockey fan by now."

Mr. Silver Spoon had probably gotten the biggest shock, being stuck with testosterone-fueled, liniment-covered, sweaty locker rooms. But working with upper management for all the major sports teams in the city allowed him to flex those old-money muscles and get us gigs we'd otherwise have been passed over.

Everest left and I sat back, checking the time, wondering what the hell I was still doing here. Ah, yes, avoiding my apartment. Sabrina had to be asleep by now. No bumping and thumping coming from her bedroom. No late-night visitors.

For all the new traffic through the apartment, she seemed to subscribe to the same rules I did when it came to no one sleeping over, but I doubted it was for the same reasons.

I got in a taxi and headed home. Tonight had done at least one thing—marked a band off the list. They'd been absolute assholes, taking the stage almost an hour late and being blitzed out of their minds. A band could function with one out-of-control member, but all four? That wasn't happening.

The concert needed to run smoothly. And the band and their manager couldn't be a clusterfuck or they'd be more of a headache than it was worth to have them play.

That was another plus in the Maddy column. Her issues with Everest aside, she was professional and made sure Without Grey were always where they needed to be.

The ride was short, traffic light at almost one a.m. A new doorman opened the door for me. They must've hired some new guys.

"Hunter." An all-too-familiar voice rang through the apartment lobby, but I kept walking.

"Hunter, I know you can hear me."

Sure, I could. It didn't mean I had to listen.

I turned to the doorman standing in front of Ryder. "You're new?"

"Yes, sir." His gaze darted from me to the insistent intruder to my right. "My name's Dean. Is he your visitor? I called up to the apartment, and the person who answered said she was on her way down."

My jaw clenched teeth-shatteringly hard. "Dean, he's not welcome here. The previous shift should've let you know."

His eyes widened.

Without turning around, I gritted out the words, "You can leave now, Ryder."

"Hunter! All I want to do is talk."

I glanced over my shoulder.

Dean had his hand on Ryder's chest and looked between the two of us.

The similarities were there. Blue eyes, light brown hair, similar jawline, but so much of that was my dad. So when I saw Ryder, I didn't just see him, but the man who'd betrayed my family. The same man I saw when I looked at myself in the mirror, and I fucking hated it.

The elevator doors pinged and opened. Sabrina stepped out with bedhead, navy sweatpants, and a gray T-shirt. With no bra on—kill me now. Why the hell had she agreed to come down here in the middle of the night for a stranger?

"There's nothing we need to say to each other." I marched toward her to get her back into the elevator and get us both out of here.

"This is how you treat your own brother?" The strained, angry voice snapped me out of the sweatpants stupor Sabrina had put on me.

My shoes squeaked on the polished marble floor.

Sabrina's eyes widened and bounced between me and Ryder.

I spun and charged back toward him. "I got this, Dean."

He hesitated before letting go and walking back toward the front desk.

I grabbed Ryder's arm and pulled him toward the front door. "Let's get one thing straight. We are not, and will never be brothers."

His gaze narrowed with the blustering anger only an eighteen-year-old could perfect. Blustering and ineffective. "We have the same dad."

"We had the same sperm donor and he's dead now, so any link that might've been there is gone. It was gone the second he cheated on my mom and decided to leave her while she had *cancer* to run off and start a new family with you and your mom. Why the hell are you even here in the middle of the damn night? Aren't you still in high school?"

There were times I could pretend I was over it. I could pretend saying *fuck you* to my dad and meaning it would erase the year of hell he'd rained down on me and my mom, and the two years of being in limbo after, but it didn't. Having Ryder show up here only brought back memories I'd rather leave behind. The ones where I had a dad.

"Why do you care if I'm out in the middle of the night? If it helps, he was no better to me or my mom."

"It doesn't." I turned around and marched off toward the elevators. "Don't come back here again, Ryder."

I grabbed Sabrina's arm and pulled her along with me.

She struggled, looking over her shoulder. "What— Who—"

"We're not talking about it."

She jumped, startled by the sharpness in my tone.

Stepping inside the elevator, I spared a glance at the sullen eighteen-year-old with his head drooped and fingers gripping the straps of his backpack tightly in each fist. Whatever he hoped to get out of showing up here wasn't coming from me. "Do you need an invitation or what?"

Looking over her shoulder, she glanced between us before stepping inside, worry furrowing her forehead.

"If you're going to be staying in the apartment, we need to have a talk."

Her gaze narrowed, but she didn't say a word. I was acutely aware of her sleepy eyes even though they glittered with promises of payback in pajamas.

I swallowed, trying to keep my gaze off her statue-stiff figure with locked arms and bedhead hair. The warm wood smells and five-hundred-dollar perfume lingering in the elevator hit me, and it felt like I was powering down. Like that last block to your house when you really had to pee and your body had given up on maintaining its control, only this was with sleep. I fought back a yawn, hoping I didn't fall asleep inside and leave Sabrina to drag me into the apartment. Or maybe she'd leave me to ride up and down all night. "Tomorrow. We can talk about it tomorrow."

The doors to the elevator opened.

"I can't wait." She marched off toward the front door, and I followed behind her, trying to figure out how I was supposed to get through the indeterminate amount of time we had left in the apartment with my sanity intact.

9

HUNTER

I jolted awake with a yell muffled by the music filling my room and shot up from the wingback chair in the corner. I must've nodded off at some point, since I was still in my clothes from last night. A groan ripped from my lips, and my hand flew to the side of my neck. The tweaked muscle sent shooting pain radiating down my back.

The sun hung low against the horizon. I checked the time: barely seven in the morning.

Straining to make out any noises in the rest of the apartment, I rubbed my eyes, which felt like they were filled with sawdust. All was quiet and it sounded like Sabrina was still asleep. The fact that my door hadn't burst open while I crashed meant I hadn't ripped her from sleep in the dead of night. At least that was one thing going for me.

My sleep had been close to nonexistent since she'd arrived, and I'd start seeing things if I didn't get a few minutes of shut-eye, but first I needed to talk to her.

I staggered into the bathroom and cranked on the shower. Once again I was bombarded with the gentle lavender scent that reminded me of Sabrina. I'd never been angrier at my dick, but it didn't stop me from closing my eyes and picturing her beneath me, crushing my lips against hers as I sank into her soft and supple flesh.

I came so hard the tweak in my neck wrenched even tighter and my knees nearly gave way. My hand slammed into the glass. Delirium had obviously taken hold. Sabrina and I needed to figure out a schedule. One where she was out of the apartment for a set amount of time, where I could sleep.

After cleaning up and toweling off, I got dressed. My armor of choice: pressed pants and a button-down shirt. At least I felt like I was a normal human, not a zombie.

I knocked on her door. "Sabrina, are you in there?" No stirring or movement. I knocked again. "Sabrina."

Trying the doorknob, I turned it all the way. The latch released, and the door swung open. She wasn't here, but once again I had a better view of her room now that she'd settled in, and I was even more confused than before.

The lights. The tripod. The cables running to outlets. The camera equipment. The neatly folded sets of sheets along the wall under the window, along with the boxes with new sheet sets sitting inside.

I gingerly stepped into the room like I might spring a booby trap and be hit with a blow dart in my neck. With the not-so-gentle throb there, it wouldn't be completely unwelcome.

My leg bumped into her desk, jostling her mouse, and the computer screen sprang to life.

On it, Sabrina stood at the foot of her bed with a smile, but it wasn't her I was looking at. It was the guy behind her, standing beside the bed, a couple feet from her with his shirt off.

I turned to the bed, staring at the rumpled tangle of sheets, then back to the screen.

She was editing a video. A video of her with a shirtless guy in her bedroom.

My blood pressure spiked, racing through my veins, screaming through my cells.

The front door opened quietly. The latch caught, and even footsteps padded down the hallway.

I tore my gaze from the computer and rushed from the room just as Sabrina rounded the corner.

Her arms full of groceries, she yelped when she spotted me in the doorway to her room. Her hands clenched, crushing her coffee cup and spraying hot coffee all over her hand and arm. Steam rose from the spilled liquid.

Shit, I hadn't meant to scare her. I was still in shock, stunned.

She screamed. The bags dropped to the floor. Cartons and a bag of oranges rolled through the doorway.

Rushing into the kitchen, I jumped over the spilled groceries. The spray of water and her hiss of pain ripped me out of my shell-shocked state.

"I'll get some ice." I yanked open the freezer door and grabbed a kitchen towel.

"What the hell were you doing in my room?" She glared at me with eyes filled with suspicion and under the glower was a hint of pain.

I bit back a wince. "Looking for you."

"From inside my room." She ran her hand under the steady stream of cold water.

"There was a noise. A thump. I thought you fell." That was me floundering and flapping around like a fish flung onto a dock.

Her eyes cut to mine.

Divert! "I'll make a paste out of baking soda and water. It'll keep it from blistering." Rummaging through the cabinets, I found the baking soda and stole some water, mixing it together to form a paste. "Here, let me put this on it."

Her gaze narrowed, wary, but the pain overshadowed most of it. "Why are you helping me?"

My shoulders sagged, and I shook my head. We'd not gotten off on the right foot. Hell, at this point both feet had been amputated. I was the helpful guy. When in crisis, I was the one everyone turned to, but she met any offer with suspicion. I couldn't even blame her. "I don't want to fight with you right now, Sabrina. That's part of the reason I came to your room."

"To snoop."

"Not to snoop. To talk." The paste thickened. I held out my hand for hers. "It's ready."

She turned off the water with her non-burned hand and moved closer to me, guarded like she expected me to fling the mixture in her face and run away.

But all the commotion hadn't wiped away the flood of feelings about what Sabrina was doing doors down from me. Equal parts furious and fascinated. Possessive and pained. Intrigued and irate.

She placed her hand into mine. Her warm, smooth skin slid against my fingers.

A pulse rushed down my arm. Shaking my head, I focused on her red skin, tender and close to blistering. I scooped the mixture from the cup and smoothed it over the inflamed spot. A glimmer of relief followed that I'd be able to help mend a little of what I'd done.

She hissed and her muscles tightened under my grip.

"Sorry," I mumbled and continued applying the salve until every spot of red had been smothered. "I'll get some gauze. I can tape it together to keep the paste from falling off until it's dry."

"It feels better already. How'd you learn this?" Her head tilted, and she peered up at me.

Without answering, I grabbed the first-aid kit from the far cabinet and wrapped up her arm. Tearing the last bit of tape, I pressed it against her skin, letting my fingers linger longer than I should have.

As much as I'd tried to blot out the images in my head of her on her bed, I couldn't get them out. What I did want to block out was the idea of her with another guy. The setup in her room didn't seem like it was for her own personal consumption unless she was into high-definition at-home viewing.

Did she need the money? Was that why she was here?

"Shit," she cursed under her breath before leaving the kitchen.

Rustling and banging came from the hallway.

She walked back in with some of the bags in her good hand. Goop dripped from one of the bags.

"That would be my eggs."

"I'll help." I rushed forward to grab the rest of the bags and put some distance between us.

She called out after me. "One of them has ice cream in it."

I grabbed the squishy pint of cookie dough ice cream. "Is this the only one?"

She hurried over with hands outstretched, totally forgetting about the cracked-egg mess.

Her sneakers slipped on the runny puddle, and she slammed into me. Her arms and legs went flying and her face smashed into my stomach.

I dropped the ice cream and shot my hands out to steady

her, but my shift sent my foot into the slick mess. Contact with the tiles was a distant memory and I went reeling backward.

We both pitched toward the floor.

I wrapped my arm around Sabrina, and my back slammed into the tile, pain radiating out from all the vertebrae of my spine.

But none of that compared to her body pressed against mine. Her hips were flush against mine, and the instant shift in blood flow from my extremities that having her on top of me brought on was the worst possible thing if I didn't want to add *perv* to the list of her strikes against me.

Our eyes shot open, and we spoke at the same time. "Are you okay?"

"No, are you okay?"

Her lips twitched before turning to a wince. She pushed herself up from between my legs, jerking her arm away and half falling back onto me.

"Oof."

Her elbow landed precariously close to my balls.

"Shit, sorry." She rolled off to the side, cradling her arm, which she'd only had out of a brace for a week or so, against her chest. Scooting away, she rested against the bottom cabinets.

The backs of my legs and fronts of hers were coated in eggs. "How many eggs did you buy?" I pushed myself up into a seated position.

"Two dozen."

"Are you prepping for an Iron Man triathlon?" I leaned against the dishwasher.

She was disheveled, arms and legs glistening with runny yolks and whites. Her hair had slid part of the way out of her ponytail, and she dropped her head back and smiled. "Maybe."

A thump of need slammed into me. To touch her again, run my fingers through her hair, and taste the lips that had been less than an inch from mine only a few minutes ago.

"None of this"—she waved her hands toward the coated floors, her bandaged arm, and our wet, stained clothes— "would be a problem if you hadn't been snooping in my room and scared the shit out of me."

"I wasn't snooping." I was totally snooping, but she didn't sound as angry as before. Maybe we were turning a corner.

She cocked her head and raised her eyebrows. Maybe not. "Let's have that boundaries conversation you were talking about. No stealing my food."

Of all the things, that was first on her list? One or two cupcakes when I needed an extra boost so I didn't get caffeine jittery. Okay, maybe more than a couple. My grocery list had always been only the basics, but hers were filled with temptations I hadn't faced before. A lot like her. But admitting it would make me a liar, and she'd never believe my lie about being in her room. Not that she believed it at all, but I'd try to ride this out to not double down on the dick moves. "I'm not stealing anything."

"Really? Some of the things I've bought have disappeared then."

The wrappers to the treats she'd brought into the apartment might be sitting in my bathroom trash can after I devoured the treats as a can't-sleep late-night snack, but that wasn't important. "I don't know what you're talking about. Can we have a serious conversation?"

She rolled her eyes and waved her hands in front of her. "By all means."

I folded my arms across my chest. "Visitors."

She jumped in. "Must leave before six p.m."

"I was going to say none at all, especially not that kid from the lobby from last night."

Her lips pursed before she tapped her finger against her full bottom one, dragging it down slightly.

My pulse throbbed, centering on my crotch, the distraction reaching near comical levels.

"Why would you think I'd invite some random stranger into the apartment?"

I tilted my head in her direction.

She sighed and rolled her eyes. "Who was he? And why can't he come in?"

"None of your business." I braced for more questions. She wasn't the type to roll over and take a bullshit answer, but I didn't need to go into my history with Ryder right now. Scratch that, ever again as long as he stopped showing up.

"Okay, warden. But I happen to remember some of your friends stopping by before."

"That was for work."

"Awesome, perfect. Work visitors are allowed." Her chin jutted out with a smug smirk.

"They're also my friends."

"So we're allowed coworkers and friends, according to you. Why are visitors at the top of your list?"

"Why wouldn't it be? It's more about the activity of those visitors." Images of her sprawled out on some guy's chest flashed before me—only they weren't covered in egg, but sweat. I shook my head to knock the thoughts loose.

Her eyebrows dipped. "Has anyone I've brought in broken anything? Tracked in mud? Made a mess? No, we go straight to my room. They use my bathroom. Then they leave. I haven't even had a meal with anyone else in here."

My fingers tightened against my thighs, gripping the muscle. "Are you seriously not seeing how what you're doing could make this living situation weird?"

She shook her head and stared at me like I'd grown a second one. "How is what I do behind closed doors making this living situation weird?" She looked at me like she was genuinely bewildered by how her having a parade of guys marching through my grandmother's apartment to have sex with her might make things the slightest bit awkward. "It's my job."

I shot up from the floor, banging my head against the upper cabinet handle. Wincing, I rubbed the throbbing spot. "Why?"

"Why not? It's not hurting anyone. It's okay money, but I have a lot more to shoot so I can level up."

I fisted my hands at my sides. More videos. More guys. More sex. "And you don't think I might not want it going on under my roof?"

"I'm not doing anything illegal. Plus I'll only be here for a few more months. It's not like I'm blasting music through the walls at all hours of the day and night." Her chin jutted out, eyes shooting daggers in my direction.

"Music and what you're doing are two different things. My grandmother might not think too kindly about what you're doing."

She stared back at me with a mix of confused irritation.

Join the club.

"Barbara is doing me a huge favor by letting me stay here. The last thing I want to do is abuse that generosity. Plus, she's seen my work, and she loves it. Even put in a few special requests of her own."

My mouth opened, but no words came out. GiGi knew. GiGi watched. GiGi put in requests. What the hell had

Florida done to her? It felt like the top of my head was being lifted off with a crowbar. "You're showing my grandmother porn?"

Sabrina's eyes widened, her lips parted, and her head jerked left, then right. "Porn."

"I'm not stupid, Sabrina. You didn't think I'd figure it out? The lights. Camera. Sheets. Guys you have coming in and out of here all the time."

Silence roared through the room. No noises other than our breathing and my heartbeat hammering in my eardrums.

Her shocked expression gave way to a sly smile. She lifted her hands and tapped her fingers to the center of her palm like the world's most patronizing golf clap. "You're right, Hunter. I don't know how I could've thought it would make it past you." She shrugged and held both hands palm up.

My jaw clenched. Why'd it feel like she was turning this all into one big joke?

"That keen sense of observation is unmistakable. Now that the cat's out of the bag, what should we do?" She pouted, making her full lips even bigger. "Are you trying to tell me I can't do my work?"

Her work. Her work having sex with other guys a few doors down from mine. Her work I'd been scouring the Internet for, if only to replace the vivid mental images that crept into the moments of sleep I'd managed lately. If ever there was a reason to wish I could get a good night's sleep to experience them more in-depth, here was another. That and not waking up hoarse and soaked in the middle of the night.

"I didn't say that." I wanted to tell her hell no, she couldn't. It wasn't safe. She might get hurt. Had these guys been vetted? Had they been tested? They had no right to put their hands on her. My muscles tightened, every cell screaming for me to put an end to this.

She wasn't mine. The streak of possessiveness blindsided me and told me now more than ever we needed some space between each other. Maybe it was because she was my first roommate. Maybe it was because she didn't look the type but was somehow totally mine. Maybe it was because her smell felt like it followed me everywhere and made it possible for me to sleep for more than a couple hours at a time.

Either way, we could share this space without me being driven to the brink of insanity. The New Year's Eve concert would take up a lot of my time. Between the office, scouting acts, and parties, I could stay away from her until she left.

"Then what would you like me to do, Hunter?" The syrupy sweetness of her voice sent a shudder down my spine. There were a lot of things I'd like her to do. None of which we should. Was she screwing with me? Batting her eyelashes and keeping her face wide-eyed and innocent.

"Nothing, just keep the noise and new people to a minimum." A few more months. In the meantime I'd have calluses on my palms from all my thoughts about what she was doing behind closed doors. I darted out of the kitchen.

"I'll do my best, Hunter." Her teasing voice followed me down the hallway. Why'd she have to say my name like that? Halfway between a growl and a purr. How she might say it while raking her nails down my back while I thrust into her. "But you know how *hard* it can be."

Fuck me.

No, that was precisely the problem. I was the only one in this apartment not fucking anyone at all.

10

SABRINA

Now that my wrist was no longer sore from the grocery store fall and didn't ache after hours of photo and video editing, I was still nursing a bit of tenderness on my hand from the coffee incident.

Freaking Hunter.

I swear, the man was a walking injury waiting to happen. If he weren't so shocked and apologetic after, I'd have thought he was using it to get rid of me. Much like his "boundaries talk" a few days ago. And what an enlightening talk it had been.

Porn! He honest-to-god thought I was shooting porn in my bedroom. Me of all people. I've heard there's porn out there for all tastes, but a curvy—okay, chubby—textile designer freelancing in product photography would be so many levels of weirdness.

But I had to admit, if felt good to see him so flustered and outraged, which had emboldened me to screw with him and withhold the clarification of his assumption.

Let him think I was picking up hard-bodied gym hunks

for hanging-from-the-ceiling sex marathon sessions. It was a few notches—maybe a few floors—above my current life status as a struggling freelancer trying to eventually make it as a creative. Not exactly original.

I made sure to bang against the walls and moan every so often when he was home. Just for my own amusement.

Now I could finally relax. I'd sent off my finals to Harper Linens. The respite only lasted for as long as it took to turn off my computer. Next came the inevitable wait for rejection. At least it meant my editing program could rest up for the next week. I grabbed my stylus and tablet and pulled up my neglected design portfolio, which had to feel abandoned after the weeks it had been since I'd opened it.

The thumbnails were filled with whimsical colors and shapes, more understated, classic patterns. A lot of different ideas without a hint of cohesion. Ah yes, now I remembered why I hadn't opened this.

For a long time I'd been holding back. After one 'no' too many, I'd given up for a while. The wallowing and feeling that I'd never have my designs seen had hit hard. But the tide was finally turning. After leaving my old apartment and old life behind and being in Barbara's apartment, more ideas flooded in.

Bouncing the ideas off my sheet models, I had been throwing around a whole new set of designs to add to my portfolio.

I dumped all my old designs in a folder and started fresh.

Textile design wasn't a job most people thought about. What even was it? But I loved thinking up new patterns and designs for everything from pillowcases to sheets to carpets. A fully coordinated look anyone would love to have in their house or apartment. The types of accents I'd want in a house when I finally got a place of my own. Who wouldn't want to see a section in Target with matching everything covered in a design they dreamt up. It wasn't high fashion, and others out there would probably roll their eyes at how excited a toothbrush holder with my designs on it would make me, but screw it, it was my dream and I wouldn't apologize for it.

My stomach rumbling and a pinch in my neck alerted me to how long I'd been hunched over my desk, scribbling away with design after new design flowing from the end of my stylus. Three hours had zipped by.

Sitting up, I cracked my back, wriggled my fingers and stared at the screen. Excitement bubbled up. I needed to send them to Cat now. She was always my biggest cheerleader but wouldn't hesitate to tell me something sucked in that perfectly abrasive way of hers. I sent off the link to the folder and a note to do her worst with the feedback.

My phone rang.

I picked it up and laughed. "You've seen them already? What do you think?"

"Hey, love. I've missed you."

Not the voice I'd been expecting. *His* voice.

It was a freezing fire-hose blast straight to the face. "Why are you calling me?"

"I'd have thought it was obvious. It's killing me being apart from you." The velvety baritone had once turned me to putty in his hands. But that was before he turned me into the other woman. Now it turned my stomach.

"You're calling me from another number?" I pulled the phone away from my ear and blocked it so the next time he called it wouldn't go through. Panic welled in my chest and guilt soured my gut like I was horrible for even hearing his voice on the other end of the line. Then Cat's voice rang in my ears and angry coals sparked before burning bright. Why couldn't he just leave me alone?

"When you blocked all my others, what was I supposed to do?" A petulant tone seeped into his voice. I had once mistaken it for a need to be with me, but I'd come to learn it was all selfishness wrapped up in deception.

"I don't know, take the hint and not ever try to contact me again? I fled our apartment. How much more did I need to do to show you we're over?"

"How can you say that?" He said it like it was an impossibility. Like me finding out was a blip on our road to relationship bliss. "You left. I came home and you were gone. I can't just let you go."

My anger grew, brewing deep in my stomach and burning bright in my chest. "Of course you can. You can very easily do that."

"We were together for over a year and you want to just throw that away? You act like it meant nothing."

My teeth clenched and I seethed. The betrayal stabbed me through the heart all over again. How quickly I'd locked up those old feelings and pretended they didn't exist. "You were married the whole time. Of course it was nothing."

"Don't say that. We're on the outs." The sulky tone grated on my nerves, shredding at the last fibers of my restraint. "We're getting a divorce."

More lies and excuses. "I don't care. If you'd cared about me, you wouldn't have made me the other woman."

"It wasn't like that." That whine in his voice, the same one I'd thought was endearing when he wanted me to stay home with him instead of going out. The one he used to keep me home so there wasn't a chance of running into his wife.

I jumped up from my seat and shouted into the phone. "How was it? You lied. Taking extra shifts. Visits to your grandparents. All lies to cover more lies and deception."

"She was never as good to me as you were."

"And I was a fucking fool. Don't ever call me again." I jammed the end button so hard pain shot down my finger.

Standing in the center of my room, my chest heaved, my stomach roiled, and I tried to catch my breath, my feelings chasing after each one like a stack of papers being stolen away by the wind.

My phone, still gripped in my hand, vibrated. I stared down at it and answered, ready to go to battle again.

"What?"

A pause on the other end of the line. "Is this a bad time? It's Ian. Is everything okay?"

I jammed the heel of my hand into my forehead. My muscles loosened, no longer prepared for the invisible threat on the other end of the line. "Hey, Ian, sorry about that. What's going on?"

"There's a delivery here for you, and I wanted to know if you wanted me to bring it up."

"I can come get it."

"It's no imposition, really."

Leaving the apartment was a good idea, even if it was only for a few minutes. Clear the air. Clear away the conversation. Clear Seth from my mind completely.

"Seriously, I need to get out of the apartment and stretch my legs for a little bit, even if it's just an elevator ride. I'll be down in a few minutes."

A thirty-second phone call from him had thrown my life

here from quiet and calm into a raging mess. All those old feelings came rushing back. The shame clobbered me hardest and made it feel like the elevator was shooting down to the center of the Earth.

He'd tainted my new room and new space with his voice. All the things I'd once thought were endearing now shone the spotlight on how stupid I'd been. I bristled at his invasion and tried to calm myself. No sense in leaving the apartment if all I was going to do was drag Seth right along with me. He was gone. He'd been blocked, and I'd keep blocking him until he got the message.

The ride down was too short. I took a few breaths, and the doors opened. The familiar smells and new floral arrangement beside the door helped me focus on normal human interactions where there were polite smiles and questions for everyone, and no one wanted to deal with anyone's actual problems.

Ian was waiting in front of the desk with the trolley loaded up with the boxes. More sheets. I swear, after shooting these videos and pictures, I was going to fall asleep on the bare mattress rather than make it again. Wait, why'd they send me more?

I grabbed my phone and checked my email.

A new message had come through. I'd made it to the final round. A half bark, yelp escaped my mouth. I slapped my hand over it and locked my muscles to keep from doing a freeze-frame jump in the middle of the lobby. The brief on what they needed was extensive. Shit! Okay, I could handle this. I hoped.

Ian stared at me like he didn't know if he should call an ambulance for my minor freak out. "Are you sure you don't want me to push this for you?"

Grinning so widely that he could probably see my molars, I wrapped my fingers around the brass trolley bars. "I've got it. I'm sure you've got better things to do." As much as I could use the company on the way back to the apartment to tell him why I was smiling like the joker and to celebrate, the desk was busy. It usually was on Fridays, with arranging airport drop-offs, reservations, and tenants using the town cars.

"If you're sure." He released it.

The trolley and I would have to come to an understanding. It didn't run over my toes, and I didn't bang it into every wall on the way to the apartment.

The elevator doors opened, and Millie breezed out into the lobby. I wanted to be her when I grew up, but I'd never have enough money or understated class. And even if I somehow got the money and figured out the class situation, I'd always feel like I was pretending and others would see through me. That was why I wouldn't try to pretend to be anyone other than me. Better to face the disappointment head-on than wait for them to find out. Not to say it hadn't been entertaining playing up all of Hunter's preconceptions about me. Better those than the alternative. Loner, loser who didn't have a place to live and has a big dream that's being shot down daily.

"Sabrina."

"Hi, Millie."

"So nice to see you out and about and without your brace."

I looked down at my arm. "I retired it a while ago."

"I'm glad you're on the mend."

"Where are you headed?"

"A little shopping for the grandchildren. I swear, it gets harder and harder to find them things."

"How old are they?"

"My oldest grandchildren are about your age, but my youngest ones are all under five."

"How many do you have?"

"Grandchildren?"

I nodded.

"Twelve."

"Wow, how many kids do you have?"

"Four. They've all been busy." She smirked.

The corner of my mouth twitched.

That was exactly the kind of sly dirty joke I'd expect a woman like Millie to subtly let loose. It was much different than one Cat might've thrown out there. Her pride and happiness at having such a large family shone through.

"If you don't find what you're looking for and need help picking out presents, I'm happy to help."

Her smile lit up her whole face. The edges of her eyes crinkled in a way that only made her look more beautiful. Did I have a crush on a seventy-year-old woman? Turns out I did. "Thank you, Sabrina."

"Bye, Millie." I wheeled the cart toward the elevator, determined not to ding it on the first try while Millie glided out the front door.

The wrestling match was on, and I was losing. How the hell did Ian make this look so easy? I was probably going to take out one of the side tables with fresh flower arrangements at this rate.

"You're not allowed in the building."

I glanced over my shoulder.

Ian barred his arm across the main entrance doorway.

I peered around Ian at the mini-version of Hunter. The urge to dig into the story of these two had been killing me since a few nights ago when I'd been called down in the middle of the night for an emergency visitor.

"Ryder, is it?"

He jolted hearing his name—or maybe it was the elevator ding. "How'd you know my name? Has Hunter mentioned me?" The kid's eyes lit up but turned wary. His skittish gaze darted back and forth.

He was a kid. A kid who looked like he could use someone to talk to, and it just so happened I'd love to deal with someone else's problems at the moment. It's not like I'd let him race through the apartment breaking things. Maybe it would be the push Hunter needed to actually speak with him. It didn't feel like that was something they'd done. And one thing I'd learned was not to string out disappointment. Rip it off like duct tape off your mouth when escaping a hostage situation. "Ian, let him in."

"Hunter has given express instructions for him to not be allowed in the building."

"But if he's a guest of a tenant, he's allowed in."

Ian checked over his shoulder.

"I take full responsibility. Please, Ian."

The kid's gaze darted from me to Ian.

I left the cart and touched the back of Ian's shoulder.

The fight seeped out of him, and his lips pressed into a grimace. "Okay, but if Hunter comes down on me, I'm throwing you under the bus."

"You won't need to. I'll jump in front of it for you. I'm serious. This is on me."

He dropped his arm and stepped back, giving Ryder enough room to slide through the door under Ian's disapproving glare.

"Come on. Maybe you can help me with this?"

Ryder eyed me like he expected a trick. Or maybe a hook

to shoot out of nowhere and fling him back outside. "Sure." He slipped into the elevator on the other side of the trolley.

I jabbed the up button. "I'm Sabrina. And you're Ryder."

"So he has mentioned me?"

My heart ached at the hopefulness in his voice. "No, he hasn't. I heard him say it when you were here a few nights ago." We pushed the trolley into the elevator, and I pressed 10.

He nodded. "You were the reason they even let me in the front door last time."

"Hunter's your brother?" From how chummy Hunter seemed to be with his work friends and how much he prided himself on being Mr. Nightlife, it seemed weird he refused to speak to his brother. Sizing the kid up, I couldn't believe he could do much damage. But my jerk radar hadn't been working properly for the past year or so, so what did I know?

"Half-brother, like he loves to remind me."

I drummed my fingers along the shiny brass. "He can be a real jerk sometimes."

Ryder smiled and laughed. "Yeah, he can."

The doors opened on our floor. "Tell me all about it."

We pushed the trolley down the hall to the front door.

Hunter's brother walked into the apartment like he was preparing for a tackle at any moment, hands shoved into his pockets, head down, gaze wary.

Seemed I wasn't the only one Hunter could be an asshole to. It sucked it was his own brother. I don't know if that made me feel better or worse.

Ryder helped me unpack everything and stack the boxes in my room. I ran the cart back downstairs and came into the apartment thankful Hunter hadn't shown up in the lobby while I'd been down.

Now that I had Ryder here, I wasn't exactly sure what to do.

Other than knowing he looked like he could use someone to talk to and also wanting to stick it to Hunter a little, I didn't have any grand plans for entertaining. Hell, other than the product shoots, I hadn't even had anyone else over. So I leaned on an old favorite. Food. Whenever I felt down, there was always something yummy to cheer me up. I could do the same for Ryder.

"Are you hungry?"

He shrugged. "I could eat."

"Do you want to eat? I'm not a chef or anything, but I could make a grilled cheese? Or turkey and cheese sandwich?"

His eyes lit up. "Grilled turkey and cheese, please?"

So polite.

"No problem."

"Thanks." He rocked back on his heels.

"Come into the kitchen and let me know what cheese you like."

He followed me into the kitchen.

I grabbed the food out of the fridge and a pan from the cabinets. My small talk was met with short, polite answers. He was a senior at Archer High, turned eighteen a few weeks ago, played piano, ran long distance, took the train into the city to see Hunter often.

It wasn't until halfway into grilling the second side of the bread, slathered with butter, that he asked his first question.

"Are you Hunter's girlfriend?"

I laughed, shaking my head. "No, just his temporary roommate." The cheese oozed from the sides of the buttered bread and bubbled and browned in the pan. I slid the sandwich onto a plate. "Are you a square or triangle kind of kid?"

"I'm not a kid." His chest puffed up, eyes locked in on the sandwich.

"Squares it is." I brought the knife down.

"Triangles."

Hiding my smile, I cut his sandwich for him and made another for me.

He was wiping his plate with his finger by the time mine was finished.

"Did you want this one too?"

He looked to me before nodding eagerly.

When I slid the sandwich onto his plate, he glanced up at me. "What about you?"

"This pan has more than a two-sandwich maximum."

I made two more before I got one.

He was hungry. But I wasn't sure if it was eighteen-year-old-guy hungry or there-was-something-else-going-on-here hungry.

After wolfing down three sandwiches, he was more talkative and less skittish.

"Do you have homework to do? What time are you supposed to be home?"

He shrugged. "I finished my work in school, and I don't have a curfew."

"I figured after you showed up here at one in the morning. What was that about?"

Another shrug.

"Your mom wasn't worried?"

"My mom's got her own life." He parroted it like it was a phrase he'd heard more than once.

Poor kid. I pulled some chips out of the cabinet when he didn't seem the least bit ready to leave.

"Did you want to hang out here for a while?"

He sat up straight and his eyes lit up before he cleared

his throat and nodded. "Sure, I could for a little while, if you wanted me to."

Holding back my laugh, I smiled and nodded toward the living room. *Okay, kid, thanks for doing me a favor.*

I found a 500-piece puzzle in the closet off the living room along with some board games. "If you don't have to be home, how about you help me with this?" The pieces rattled in the box.

"Sure." He smiled, shot up, and wiped his hands on his jeans.

No eighteen-year-old guy was this excited about a puzzle. It had been almost a decade since I turned eighteen, but I couldn't remember a time when any of the guys I'd gone to high school with would've thought a grilled turkey and cheese and a puzzle were a fun afternoon.

I peered over at Ryder, who was riveted to the puzzle, swaying to the music from my phone, mouthing the words. Why was he here? Did he have friends?

We scooted our chairs in and got to work finding all the edge and corner pieces first.

I still didn't know why I'd invited him in. No, I did. He'd looked so sad at the front door. Teetering on the razor's edge of hope that maybe he might get a chance to talk to Hunter. How many times had he tried before? That kind of persistence was rare for a kid his age. If he was here already, maybe Hunter would finally hear what he had to say. It had to be important. I knew all about being let down by people you cared about, and hoped maybe he could be spared some of that disappointment.

My stomach clenched. Or Hunter would prove just how shitty some people could be. There was no kicking Ryder out now. I crossed my fingers and prayed for the best.

"How are things at school?"

"They're fine. I'm working on my college applications."

"Wow, I was working on them up until the deadlines." And I'd had to be reminded of the deadlines over and over by my parents and college counselor.

"I'm trying to get them in early."

"Where do you want to go?"

He ducked his head, getting extra close to the pieces, running his fingers over them. "Fulton U."

"I've heard that's a great school. What made you want to go there?"

His neck flushed and red splotches appeared along his skin.

"Is it where a girl from your school is going? Best friend?"

He looked up, face fully ruddy, eyes a little sad. "It's where Hunter went."

Holy crap did this kid need a hug. All he wanted was a connection with his brother. Any connection.

Why would Hunter be such a jerk to him?

An hour or so later, I cracked my back and surveyed our progress. The frame of the puzzle was finished along with some bigger blocks of the zoomed-in image of colored pencils lined up in color gradient order.

The front door opened. My bright idea didn't feel so bright anymore. We'd had the boundaries conversation only a few days ago, which had pretty much centered around Ryder, but Hunter had to see reason. The kid obviously needed help.

Thudding footsteps got closer. My stomach knotted. The water in our glasses rattled with each step like a T. Rex was about to rip the roof off the apartment and devour us whole.

Ryder straightened in his chair. His hand gripped a puzzle piece tightly.

It seemed I wasn't the only one anticipating a blowup.

Maybe I could've found a better way. Maybe Hunter would be reasonable. Maybe it wouldn't be so bad.

Hunter's shadow passed by the doorway of the dining room. And then the roar.

"What the hell is he doing here?"

Coming home was always a crapshoot as to what I'd be walking in on. Sabrina wandering around in a tank top and shorts that barely covered her ass. Sabrina walking out of her room hot and sweaty with a random guy. Sabrina watching TV with her legs propped up on the coffee table. All of it was bad and made focusing difficult, but nothing had stoked the flames of my anger like the scene I walked in on.

Sabrina and Ryder sitting at the table with snacks and a puzzle, making themselves at home—my home. After I'd explicitly told her not to let him in here.

"Out, now." I clenched my teeth so hard it felt like I'd been chewing concrete on the way up.

Sabrina shot up and walked around the table. "Hunter—"

"I said, get the hell out of my house." My voice boomed so loudly they both jumped. I whipped my arm out, pointing to the front door, barely able to stomach the domestic scene I'd walked in on. My heart pounded so fast it felt like it was skipping beats.

"Hunter—"

"Now." The word came out half growl, half bark.

Ryder jumped up and grabbed the half a sandwich left on his plate. With a mumbled, "Thanks, Sabrina," he walked through the kitchen to avoid me and out the front door. Nice to know he'd acquainted himself with my house.

The door slammed, leaving me and Sabrina. Alone.

She stood and gathered up the plates with a look of glaring disappointment on her face.

It felt like a pair of knuckles were pressed into my sternum.

None of this was my fault.

She'd gone directly against my wishes, almost like she was testing me on purpose. I was too tired for this shit.

I headed her off and blocked her path to the kitchen.

With two plates in her hands, she peered up at me, her lips pressed in a grim line.

"What did we talk about a few days ago?"

She tilted her head. "How grumpy you are in the morning?"

"I told you I didn't want him here."

"What was I supposed to do when he showed up?" She shrugged like she'd been forced to bring him up here at gunpoint.

"Tell him to leave just like I do."

"Have you wondered why he keeps coming here?"

"I don't care."

"Maybe you should. He's your brother—"

"He's *not* my brother," I snapped.

She jumped and one of the crusts on the plate fell to the floor. "You have the same dad. That makes you brothers."

"Half-brothers at best, and our dad's dead, so why

pretend we have a connection?" My jaw clenched, frustration rising. This conversation was pointless. It was the same one I'd had with Ryder. With Leo, Everest, Jameson, and August. Why was everyone so dead set on me pretending he was anything more to me than what he was? A stranger.

Her shoulders dropped, her whole body shifting from high alert to something softer. "I didn't know your dad died. How long ago?"

I looked over her shoulder, staring off into the distance, trying to rein in the avalanche of rage that filled me whenever I thought about him. "A few months ago." Right around the time the nightmares came back. "It's not a big deal. I hadn't seen him in almost fifteen years, and I didn't plan on seeing him ever again. He's been dead to me a long time."

"Well, he hadn't been for Ryder." She licked her lips and searched my face. "Maybe that's the reason he's here. He's looking for someone to be there for him. An older brother who knows what he's going through."

"Then he needs to find another apartment to haunt because that's not me. He has no idea what I went through when my dad left me and my mom. So no, I don't want to be his shoulder to cry on while he tells me how much he misses the dad who fucked me and my mom over. I'll never forgive my dad for not being there when she died." My chest burned, breath singed, and I hated how close to the surface all this felt. Sleeping had become my nightmare, and it was screwing with my head. Why else would I be here, spilling my guts to Sabrina instead of leaving?

She turned around and set the plates on the table. "I'm sorry you lost your mom too." Her voice was gentle, quiet, soothing. "How long ago did your mom die?"

My tight jaw loosened. Now it was hard to speak, not

because of the clench of my teeth but from the emotions clogging my throat. I tried to clear the tightness, but it wouldn't budge. All the memories of her tinged with a sadness that would never go away. "Fifteen years ago."

Her eyes widened. "He'd have been three, Hunter. And I'm sure he's sorry about your mom too."

I leaned in, trying and failing to hold the rising tide of anguish threatening to swamp me. "I don't care. My dad was cheating on my mom for over three years and left when she got cancer. Ryder's mom showed up at our house with him while my dad was putting all his things in the back of the car and telling me it was all too much for him."

"How old were you?" she whispered.

"Thirteen. So I was there for her while my dad ran off and played house with the new family he'd started already."

Her face was filled with both shock and sadness. She stepped forward and reached out to me in jerky movements, like she was telling herself not to the whole time. Lavender invaded my nose even more strongly than it did whenever my thoughts drifted to her.

Her hand touched just above my elbow before sliding down in equally stilted movements.

The touch of her fingers on my arm even through my sleeves sent pulses along my skin. Deep, welling feelings picked up speed and turned into a greedy need.

I wanted to grab her. Hold onto both her arms and slam my lips against hers. Instead I locked my body.

Her gentle skim met my skin. My wrists under my cuffs and then the heel of my hand before my palm. Her fingers slid against my palm, her thumb settling on the back of my hand. "I can't imagine how that felt, and I'm sorry you were on your own. Where was Barbara?"

The tightness in my throat made it hard to breathe. "Australia with my grandfather." I swallowed, trying to dislodge the lump to get the words out. "He'd had a stroke while they were on vacation. It took a long time to get him stable enough to fly him back."

Her fingers tightened around my hand. "Did she get to see your mom?"

My pulse thundered against her hold. I cleared my throat. "Every other week. She flew back as much as she could." GiGi had been dead on her feet most of the time she'd visited. Trying to take care of two family members a world apart had come at a price to her. It was part of the reason she couldn't come back to this apartment. It held too many memories of her and Grandpa, but she couldn't bring herself to let it go. The renovations that had taken place over the years under the guise of selling it had been for my benefit.

"How long did she do that?"

"Until my mom died. She was at stage four when they discovered the cancer. She only made it through one round of chemo. Eight weeks from diagnosis to her death." I struggled to keep my voice even, not letting through a single crack. It had all happened so quickly, too quickly for me to process then. Too quickly even now. No matter how old I was, the second-guessing was always there. And the worry lingered for anyone close to me. Two months. Two weeks. Two seconds. Anyone could be snatched away.

Sabrina gasped.

These words kept spilling out of my mouth. I needed to leave before I said more.

Breathing in her lavender smell had lulled me into a false sense of comfort and masked the reason we were having this conversation in the first place. I snatched my hand out of her hold. "Now you see why I'm not going to be a big brother to Ryder. I'm trying to put everything to do with my father behind me, and now that he's dead, it's even easier."

I backed into the kitchen, my only path of escape.

"He's a kid, Hunter."

Turning, I stalked away. "So was I."

Jameson pivoted on his right foot, sneaker squeaking on the lacquered hardwood floor, and sunk the shot. The basketball swooshed through the net and bounced against the painted cinderblock wall of the gym. "Nothing but net." He held his shooting hand in the release pose for extra emphasis.

Leo jogged over to me, practically falling into my shoulder. "What's up with you, man?"

I shook him off. "Nothing," I ground out, stalking to the bleachers.

Around us, sneakers squeaked and the thud of basketballs filled the gym. Smells of ancient paint, wood, and sweat brought back all the memories of us getting our asses kicked in five on five back in college. Back during the first game when they'd needed another player on the court and I'd been hanging around after a workout.

Leo tossed me my water bottle. "Sounds like something."

I caught it and drained it, spilling water down my chin, mixing the freezing liquid with the steaming rivulets of sweat pouring down my neck. "It's nothing."

Silence. The kind that told me they weren't going to let me off the hook that easily.

"Ryder came to the apartment again."

Jameson pushed his glasses up his nose. "As in your brother Ryder?"

"He's not my brother," I bit out.

His jaw clenched. He'd made his feelings about the Ryder situation known. Teresa was his little sister. His big-brother instincts had been amped up after his dad died, but this wasn't the same. Not by a long shot. He loved Teresa. Hell, we all did, which was why in a week we'd go to his house to bake another monstrosity of a cake for her sixth birthday.

I didn't know Ryder, and he sure as hell didn't know me. "It's not the same, Jameson."

He gulped down his water, shaking his head.

Anger spiked through me. "How is it that I'm the bad guy? I'm the only one in the situation who hasn't done a damn thing wrong. My dad was the lowest piece of trash imaginable, but I'm wrong for being happy he's dead. My dad's son, who he had while cheating on my mom, shows up, and I'm supposed to open my arms to him. To the new family my dad left us for. And Sabrina just lets him in after I specifically told her not to. The same one shooting porn in my grandmother's apartment. But I'm the fucking asshole?" My voice boomed in the gym. All sneaker squeaks and dribbles ceased, leaving only the stomach-curdling silence.

Leo stood and cupped his hand on my shoulder. "Come on, everyone. Let's call this meeting officially over."

In muted movements, we packed up our things and headed to the showers. The trip to The Griffin bar didn't take long, but wedged between Jameson and Everest in the backseat, I felt seconds from jumping out of the moving car. My heart pounded like I hadn't left the court and had instead been forced to run sprints.

I still had the gym sweats even though I'd showered and changed. Running on less than three hours of sleep each night was getting to me. Stepping out of the car, I breathed deeply, trying to wake myself up and calm myself down at the same time.

We sat in our booth with the RESERVED note stuck to the top of a metal stand.

August stood beside the booth, letting Jameson scoot into the middle. I took the opposite end, and Leo and Everest took the chairs in front of the table. "Barry threatened to give our table away if we don't get at least five orders of wings. Everyone up for it?"

Barry, the grizzled owner and bartender who seemed pissed that his no-frills bar was slowly becoming a trendy favorite, had a lot more bark than bite, but none of us wanted to push our luck.

A grumble of approval rippled through the table. I could shove the wing sauce under my nose like smelling salts to keep my head from hitting the table. I couldn't deal with a late night, especially not after playing, but the thought of trying to sleep ratcheted up the anxiety.

A round of beers arrived. Leo slid them across the table. The cold, wet condensation glided against my palm.

They jumped into conversation again. Leo, the de facto leader, went over his newest client. In addition to Waverly Hotel Group, he'd secured a city-wide contract for events for corporate groups using the convention center.

Everest, no matter how much he professed to hate it, had cleaned up with all the sports teams in the city. Upper management loved him. Having a name like his opened doors, even in the sports world. It looked like he'd be wearing those oversize jerseys for even longer.

August kept up his bitter grousing over it being wedding season year-round now that he'd opened his services for international clients and locations. Cry me a river—the private jet his last client had booked to get him to Geneva had to have been a real hardship.

Jameson had his notebook out, making notes of what everyone had failed to let him know. Working his ass off to secure the contract for the fan zone coordination for the football national championship happening in two years in the city. Half the time the madness surrounding the playoffs was an excuse to party, but who were we to complain when we were the ones running the show and collecting the checks when it was all said and done?

I stayed fixated on the Yuengling label with the tear, poking and prodding it. Scraping my finger against it. In the din of the bar crowd, all voices and noises melded into a droning hum. The guys talked over the rest of the fall and winter plans, juggling clients. My eyes drooped.

"Hunter, do you need any help with the New Year's Eve concert?" August leaned in, eyes intent on mine.

I shot up, snapping my eyes open and sucking in a breath. "No, I have it handled."

"Are you okay?" Jameson bent forward, his blue eyes scanning my face over the thick black rims of his glasses.

"I'm good. Actually I'm going to head home." I didn't need them thinking I wasn't up for it and would drop the ball. I'd get home and come up with a game plan for sleep. A cartoon-sized mallet or a fifth of vodka were always options.

"Is that when the next scheduled show begins?" Everest had his arm draped over the back of his chair.

I gritted my teeth, sorry I ever even showed them Sabrina's room and started the conversation about what she was doing in my apartment. Kicking my foot against the leg of his chair, I pressed on the back of it, sending Everest flying. "I'll get a front-row seat."

Leo grabbed him, and Everest grabbed the edge of the table to keep himself from falling. Both shouted after me.

I needed to get to my apartment. The windows were down during my taxi ride. Falling asleep wasn't an option.

By the time I made it to the apartment, I was fighting sleep but also the terror that came with it. The chest-tightening, wake-you-up-covered-in-sweat fear of what would happen when I closed my eyes in bed.

There wasn't any noise from Sabrina's room. The puzzle she'd been working on with Ryder a few days ago was still on the table. Sometimes she sat there and found a few more pieces while picking apart her food and taunting me with her lips, teeth, and tongue.

I slammed my bedroom door and stared at my bed, trying not to feel the deep sense of betrayal that I couldn't lay in there without waking up in an overheated sweat, like I'd been running a marathon in my sleep. I turned on the music, cranking it up to just below floor rumbling. The soundproofing made it possible. Millie wouldn't be disturbed, and the apartment below mine was empty except for a few weeks in winter every year.

I'd be over this by then, or they'd be woken by my screams in the dead of night. Their choice.

In the bathroom I sat on the bench beside the tub. The sweet, calming smell filled my nose, and I dropped my head back, leaning against the wall. My eyes drifted closed. I just needed a few minutes here before I tried to get some sleep. A quiet settled over me. One without the beeping monitors, medical detergent, and smell of saline that had turned every dream into a nightmare for the past three months.

I breathed deeply and let myself drift off. Only for a few minutes, and didn't try to think too hard about why I wanted to crawl into bed with Sabrina and why I thought it would make any of this easier.

It wouldn't, and I'd learned that a long time ago.

12

SABRINA

The apartment was quiet and the smell of coffee lingered from the pot that had been warming since the early morning.

I didn't mind hours-old coffee. I got my mug and refilled it until the pot was empty around noon. After starting a new pot, I took a sip and grimaced.

Hunter hadn't been wrong. I sucked at making coffee. With my potently-caffeinated sludge, I went back to my room and hunkered down for a long haul of editing. The ache in my muscles intensified as the hours ticked by.

Sitting straight, I groaned and the muscles in my back ached. I slipped the headphones off and closed the video-editing program.

I needed to find a better desk. Once January got here and I hopefully got that big check, maybe I could. Blinking, I tried to banish the spots dancing in front of my eyes. That was it. Time to step away from the computer.

My neck cracked, and the muscles screamed for relief. The kind of relief I might get from a bath.

I'd tried to stick to our deal about respecting each other's spaces, but he wasn't here. At least I didn't think he was.

Hunter had left while I was grabbing a midafternoon snack from the kitchen an hour ago. But my noise-cancelling headphones blocked out all background noise, which would've masked his return.

I peeked into the hallway. "Hunter? Are you here?"

Not a sound.

"Hunter? I'm thinking of inviting ten guys over for a gang-bang scene and shooting it in the living room. You cool with that?" I walked down the hallway, not keeping my steps light. Knocking on Hunter's bedroom door, I turned the knob at the same time and poked my head inside. "Did you want to hold the mic?"

I looked around his room. His bed was made, no clothes on the floor, everything in its place.

One thing I'd say for living with Hunter, I never had to pick up after him. Dishes were washed, and laundry never sat in the washer or dryer, which was better than I ever pulled off. It was nothing like it had been living with Seth.

I'd taken care of everything. Laundry, cooking, cleaning. It probably had something to do with him having a whole other house to take care of. The pang hit my chest, but now it didn't feel like a blistering iron pressed against my rib cage.

It hadn't been my fault. And I'd left as soon as I found out. I wasn't a bad person. I repeated the mantra and walked back to my room to grab my bath stuff. You never really knew who someone was. We were all wearing masks, and no one ever wanted to let theirs down.

My track record with relationships didn't point at me being a good judge of character in the least bit. A string of failed ones, which ended with me getting my heart broken.

How much of it had to do with my terrible instincts when it came to sizing people up?

Walking into Hunter's bedroom, I had to admit, okay, maybe I was a little bit of a bad person for sneaking in, but he'd made my life stressful enough. I deserved at least a little relaxation. My toes sank into the carpet without a hint of a creak or groan.

This was probably the nicest place I'd ever live. Always cool and cozy, even when it had been blazing hot only a few weeks ago in August. Now, with things cooling down, my feet never got cold like they had in the old apartment.

On the way to the bathroom, I stopped short. On Hunter's sleek wood nightstand with the stained-glass lamp beside it was *The Prisoner of Azkaban*. The dust jacket was off, but the gold lettering along the spine didn't lie.

A Harry Potter fan? You didn't start with *Azkaban*. How many almost-thirty-year-old guys picked it up for the first time? Scrutinizing his space with new eyes, I looked for clues.

He kept the place too neat.

I'd have to search the bookshelves for the rest of the books.

I braced for the cold tile feel in the bathroom out of habit, but the underfloor heating meant the transition from carpet to tile wasn't the usual shock. I set my things on the counter.

My bath oil bottle rolled off the stack and fell into the bathroom trash can. I fished it out, but it didn't come up alone. Stuck to the outside of the bottle was a wrapper. A Tastykakes butterscotch krimpet wrapper.

That snake.

Here I was feeling the slightest bit guilty about using his bath and he'd been stealing my food and maybe trying to gaslight me with "the big girl can't remember how much she's eating" while laughing his way into carb and sugar-loaded heaven.

My fingers curled around my bath oil bottle, and my gaze narrowed. Grumbling under my breath, I jerked my towel from the stack and set it on the towel warmer. Turning on the water, I swore retribution. I didn't know how or when, but I would.

A few drops was all I needed for the bath, and the calming lavender scent derailed my thoughts of payback—at least for now. After getting undressed, I slipped into the warm water and rested my head against the back of the tub.

His confession in the dining room a few days ago had helped make sense of his intense dislike for Ryder. Dealing with his mom being so sick so quickly, his dad leaving, and finding out he had a whole new family couldn't have been easy.

After what happened with Seth, I couldn't imagine driving up to his house and staring his wife and kids in the eye. My stomach knotted into a bile-churning mess thinking about it. To be a teenager handling all that—adults couldn't handle it.

But Ryder had nothing to do with his dad's infidelity. And it didn't seem like his mom was a peach either. He was searching for someone to connect to. Someone like his big brother, who couldn't say more than a few growly words to him.

I closed my eyes and let the relaxation of the warm water wash away the knots and aches from a day hunched over my computer. I'd think of a way to solve the Ryder-Hunter problem, even if it was letting Ryder know he could come to me since his brother was determined to ignore him.

Forty minutes later I was sufficiently pruney, calm and

clean. Pulling the plug from the tub, I hopped out onto the towel I'd set on the floor so I wouldn't leave wet footprints on the bath mat.

I grabbed my other towel and dried off. Halfway through drying the tub, the front door opened.

My heart rate spiked, feeling like it was seconds from shooting through the top of my skull.

Hunter's unmistakable footfall echoed through the apartment.

"Sabrina? Are you home?" he called out from the front door.

Suddenly all that tension that had been washed away by my soak snapped right back into place. What was he up to? Had he brought someone home? Would they start boning in his bedroom? Talk about awkward. A flare of jealousy sparked in my stomach, which was idiotic—he didn't belong to me any more than the communal bowl of sugar beside the coffeepot.

"Shit. Shit. Shit." I finished with the tub and gathered up the towels.

"She's not here—for once."

I slapped my hand over my own mouth and shot back, pressing against the wall, and tucked a little behind the door clutching the two towels to my chest. I was a damp, naked, trespasser.

"You'd think someone in her line of work would be all about the nightlife and partying, but I don't even know if she drinks. I've never seen her leave except to get groceries."

If it weren't for the minor heart attack I was having, I might laugh at him still thinking I was a porn star.

"She's meticulous about cleaning, probably so the sex smells don't suffocate us both."

His voice got closer. If he walked in, I was toast.

"Maybe she went out to get some food?"

My head jerked back and banged into the wall. My body seized, and I rubbed the back of my head. What the hell was that supposed to mean? Peeking from my hiding spot, my stomach plummeted. My clothes were perched on the edge of the counter beside the sink. My heart pounded in my throat.

A door opened, and his voice got more distant. "What am I supposed to do? Ask her for her porn name? We've been over this." His voice sounded farther away but still in the room. "You don't think I've checked? Yes, I checked that too. There's nothing."

I leaned in closer to not miss a word.

He'd been trying to find my nonexistent porn? Why the hell would he do that? I looked down at my naked body. I wasn't *Sports Illustrated* material, but I didn't hate myself either. Getting to this point had taken a while.

"No, I'm meeting with Andrew about the lighting rigs next week." Back to work talk. "Hold on, I've got the details in my bag."

He left the bedroom.

Now was my chance. I darted for my pajamas and froze. There was no time to put my pajamas on and risk him coming back in. I bolted out of the room and down the hallway, keeping my steps whisper quiet and grateful the floor didn't give me away. Twenty more feet and I'd make it to freedom.

His voice got closer. "I know. He can be an asshole, but he's the biggest supplier in the area. If we don't go with him, it'll cost three times as much. I know how to handle him."

My head whipped back and forth, and I lunged for the laundry room door. Ducking inside, I dropped the towels and pressed my palm against the wood to slow the close.

With choppy breaths and my pulse drumming in my veins, I released the knob as gingerly as I could, cringing at the gentle click that felt like a bomb drop. I stepped back.

Fumbling in the dark, I snagged my shorts off the floor and shoved my legs into them.

Hunter's voice stopped moving. His feet blocked out some of the light peeking through the gap at the bottom of the door. "I need to run to the dry cleaners. I don't think I have any shirts left." The knob jiggled. "Please let me order her a cake. She never has to know."

There was nowhere to go. I backed up. My heart rate spiked, pounding in my ears. My fingers wouldn't cooperate. Weren't people supposed to get more coordinated during adrenaline rushes?

I fumbled around on the floor and found my shirt. Keeping one eye on the door, I pulled my shirt on over my head, skipping the bra for now. I bent to scoop up my damp towels and clothes.

The handle turned, and light from the hallway bathed the laundry room.

Yelping, I snapped up with my things clutched against my chest.

Hunter shouted and flung his phone in my direction. It smacked into me right below my neck and dropped into my shirt. "What the hell are you doing here?" He braced one hand on the doorway, eyes wide, and the other fist pressed against the center of his chest like he was trying to keep his heart from bursting through his sternum.

Welcome to the party, pal.

"Hello." My heartbeat rivaled the distant, tinny voice that called out from under my clothes. "Hunter, you still there?"

"Laundry." A half yelp/half yip. I fished his phone from

my cleavage and held it out, hoping my reedy smile didn't look as brittle and panicked as I felt.

He stepped into the laundry room, his face etched with skepticism. The blue button-down shirt matched his eyes, which were focused on me. "You were doing laundry in the dark?"

"Couldn't find the light switch?" My weak laugh wasn't making a believer out of him.

Leaning out of the room, he flicked the switch on the wall outside. "You've lived here for over a month and didn't know where the light switch was?"

The small voice came from the phone. "I hear people talking. Hello, can you hear me?"

My spit lodged in my throat, making me feel like there was a ten-pound rock shoved in there. "Nope, thanks for the help." I shook his phone in his direction, my arm wavering.

He didn't budge. His gaze skirted over me before assessing the laundry room like I'd been caught at the scene of a shattered jewelry case and missing diamonds. "Why didn't you answer when I called your name?"

"You did? Wow, so weird. I didn't hear a thing. Your friend's still on the phone." I shoved it into his chest and let it go, using his momentary distraction to my advantage. I rushed past him and into my room, flinging the door closed behind me.

All my loose and relaxed muscles were now wound so tightly I paced my room for a solid half hour, waiting for Hunter's big gotcha moment of figuring out where I'd been. But it never came. Slowly my pacing eased, and I lay down, trying not to think of what might've happened if he had found me naked in his bedroom. Those were thoughts that would stay only in my dreams.

13

HUNTER

I jerked awake, my scream blasting into the music pounding through my speakers. Covered in sweat, I shot up from my chair, fisting my hands in my hair. My copy of *The Order of the Phoenix* fell off my lap, landing corner-down on the top of my foot.

Throwing my head back, I shouted and hopped on one foot. It had been over a month since I'd had a full night's sleep, three months since I'd started waking up screaming. Frustration and irritation were waging a war with my brain, turning me into a Grade-A asshole.

My sanity was fraying, my eyelids were heavy like cement blocks, and my eyes were dry like someone had thrown gravel into them.

The clock beside my bed blared an angry 3:15 a.m. Limping to the bathroom, I pulled off my sweat-soaked clothes and stepped into the shower. Resting my back against the cool glass, I let the warm water pour over me. When I'd fallen asleep in the bathroom that one time, I hadn't woken up screaming, although I'd slid off my seat and smacked my head into the wall.

My thoughts drifted to Sabrina. That smell. Her smell.

Relaxation worked its way down my body like the stream of the shower until I almost fell asleep inside.

Getting out, I grabbed my towel, and the smell was even stronger. Not having any better ideas, I grabbed my blanket and pillow off my bed. Back in the bathroom, I closed the door and let the music run in my bedroom in case this didn't work.

I don't know what made me more afraid, that it would or that it wouldn't. After folding the blanket and arranging the pillow, I turned off the bathroom light and climbed into the bathtub. The thing was big enough for two, which meant it wasn't as tight of a fit as I'd have imagined. Inside, the smell was even stronger, and the calm intensified, blanketing me in a quiet I hadn't found in months.

Closing my eyes, I willed myself into a dreamless sleep where I wasn't drowning in the pain of my past.

I woke to the smell of coffee and a sunlight-warmed bathroom, not panting sweats and a throat raw from screaming. I stared up at the ceiling and banged my head against the tub, hoping to knock a screw loose, or maybe knock it back into place.

A couple minutes of thumping later, I climbed out of the tub and left the bathroom, dragging my comforter behind me like a *Peanuts* reject. I flipped off the stereo and made my bed.

Although I'd caught a few hours of continuous sleep, the most I'd had in a long time, coffee was still imperative before I left for the office.

I got changed, feeling less like a zombie. Opening my

bedroom door, the wall of dark, rich, aromatic scents drew me toward the kitchen by my nostrils.

Inside the kitchen, cabinets opened and closed, silverware rattled. Her music spilled out into the hallway, along with her low whisper of a sing-along. She moved into the dining room, probably poring over her puzzle.

The gentle coo of her voice over the Harry Styles song remixed in the clubs all through the summer was adorable. I smiled and leaned against the wall before shaking it off.

Never forget what she is. Intruder. Interloper. Invader.

One who was getting laid a hell of a lot more than I was.

I gnashed my teeth. I wouldn't think about her with other guys. Why torture myself? Especially after the night of sleep I'd gotten. Today would be a good day.

Shoving off the wall, I grabbed onto the steely restraint not to let myself think about Sabrina. I couldn't help but think of how horrendous her coffee skills were, though, while I filled my travel mug with coffee, and grabbed the creamer and sugar. She'd gotten to the coffee maker first, which meant the first sip would taste like I'd snorted a line of coffee grounds.

I needed more than coffee this morning.

Quietly I opened her snack cabinet and grabbed a package of the coffee cake cupcakes with the cream in the center, keeping the crinkling to a minimum. Not that she could hear me over the music and singing. At least I hoped she couldn't. I glanced over my shoulder and slipped the coffee cake into my pocket.

"Hunter, is that you?"

I gritted my teeth. "Who else would it be? Unless you've given away copies of my keys to all your friends."

She popped into the doorway, still in pajama pants and a tank top, and licked her thumb, her lips wrapping around the digit and a bit of her pink tongue peeking out between her lips.

Her perpetual torment.

At least she was wearing a bra, so I didn't strain my ocular nerves by trying not to look at her nipples pressed against the taut fabric. "You're hilarious."

"So I've been told." I popped the lid onto my coffee mug. "I'm heading out."

"Good. I've got a really busy day. I'll be putting in a lot of work and wouldn't want to bother you with all the noise." She crossed to the cabinet I'd closed earlier, opened it, and reached inside. "I swore—" She turned to me. "Have you seen my coffee cakes? I swore I had another one left."

"I can't keep track of all your food." I shifted from one foot to the other, and the package in my pocket crinkled. The sides of my neck heated. "Who knows where it went. I've got to go." I rushed from the kitchen and took off down the hallway to the elevator, a pang of guilt about stealing her food stabbing at me. I shook my head, telling myself it was a fair trade for all the space in my head she'd been stealing lately.

The worst part about my SWANK responsibilities was that I always felt like I was working a split shift—a split shift where my apartment was filled with a woman who'd taken over the moments of deep sleep I managed.

Going into the office was better than pacing in my apartment, waiting for her to invite over a new play friend. Not to mention that sleeping late during the day, while impossible given how my nights had been going, meant cramming all my work related to non-nightlife business into only a few hours. Showing up to the office during normal business hours but also needing to go out at night meant that sometimes my afternoons hit a dead zone where sitting around the office didn't make sense.

I didn't know why I'd taken to coming home instead of going to the gym or taking extra-long lunches since Sabrina had moved in. Maybe I was a glutton for punishment.

"It's a tight fit, but you can work it in."

I stood outside Sabrina's door, my heart trying to abandon ship straight out of my mouth.

"Enough, Sabrina." I flung the door open and froze. Deer-in-headlights froze. Crash-test-dummy froze.

She was on all fours on the bed, eyes wide, looking over her shoulder at me.

Ryder was in front of her on the other side of the bed.

"Hunter." She scrambled off the bed and rushed toward me.

"With my brother." A crazy, panicked feeling wrapped tight around my throat, choking me. My heart jackhammered, tripping and skipping beats, trying to send a signal to my brain to move.

"You called me your brother." Ryder's shocked words barely penetrated the thundering pulse in my ears.

"Now is not the time," I growled at Ryder, trying to decide if I should call his mom or beat the shit out of him.

"It's not what you think." She grabbed on to my arm, digging in her heels to stop my retreat.

I whipped around, glaring. "You're not in here with my brother talking about tight fits?"

"I am, but it's not anything like you're thinking." She held her hands out in front of her, pleading.

"Thanks for the cash, Sabrina. I'll let you two hash this out." Ryder bolted, not fast enough.

My breath rushed out in sharp pants. My vision, tunneling to a pinpoint, centered on her face.

"What the hell is it then?" How long had they been doing this? Was there porn of my brother floating out there on the Internet?

"Let me show you." She pulled me toward the computer set up on the dark wood desk by the door. "Don't move." Hesitating, her fingers tightened on my arm before releasing me and pulling up a file folder on the screen.

Irrationality slammed into me. I wanted to rip her computer in half and fling it across the room. As much as I'd searched for her online, there was an eruption of relief each time I came up empty-handed. I didn't want to see her with anyone else.

Instead of typing in any number of websites I'd definitely never checked out, she selected the first video file.

She jammed her finger into the enter key, and the video viewer popped up.

The name of the sheets she'd been receiving by the case popped up at the beginning of the clip in a classic, stylized font. Signature Hemmed Sheet Set. She pressed play.

In the video, the guy rubbed the sheet against his cheek and sighed.

"It's one hundred percent organic cotton. It's simple, but I wish you could feel this. It's so soft, I swear, if a cloud could be turned into a sheet, this is what it would be."

Confusion rocketed through my head, my brain muddled by a metric ton of confusion. "What the hell is this?"

She ducked her head but peered back up at me with blazing red cheeks. "My job."

I stared at the screen, waiting for the sweaty, nude part

of the video. The part I'd been envisioning in my head, only it wasn't some asshole with her, it was me.

The guy on the screen lifted the sheet before it flowed down onto the bed, and he smoothed it out, pulling the scrunched edge around the corner of the mattress.

"You invited a guy into your apartment to make your bed?" A sound jumped out of my throat, mind still whirring. In some crazy corner of the internet were guys jerking off to Sabrina and some guy making beds? Did they make the beds, then have sex in them? I cocked my head to the side.

"I'm a product photographer." Her lips twisted at the chagrined confession. "I was looking for a different angle to win the job, so I thought"—she shrugged—"having guys be my models would make me stand out, and it did."

My gaze shot back to the screen.

The guy on screen smiled for the camera as he made her fucking bed. Hospital corners and all. There were flawless transitions between the different cuts. Him smoothing out the wrinkles in the fabric. And the only fluffing going on was to the pillows after he slipped on the cases before he fell backward onto the bed with a shot from above.

"Are you serious with this?" I pointed to the laptop like it had just made an offending remark about my mother.

She shrugged, for once not having a snappy comeback. "Not sure what else to tell you. I'm a product photographer."

"This is your job?" The questions mounted, but one point rang louder in my ears until it became undeniable.

"I landed this project a week or so before I moved in. I owe them the finals at the end of this week, and then I find out if I won the job, and if I do then I get paid, which means I can finally move out. I had one more shot I absolutely needed, so I brought in Ryder for some last-minute help." She closed her laptop.

I dropped onto the partially made bed, shock still reverberating through my body. "You let me believe you were in here making porn." The adrenaline injection was no longer swinging me from anger to jealousy. Now it had plopped me squarely at the corner of confused shock.

A nervous chuckle. "I know."

I looked up at her, unable to keep the baffled tone from my voice. "Why?"

Her lips pulled to one side like they'd been tugged by an invisible string and she shrugged. "It was better than the alternative. I've never had someone think I could be a porn star. That part was fun. There was also the bonus of it making you insanely uncomfortable, so I just didn't correct your assumptions."

"Sabrina..." It came out in a warning, chiding tone.

"Hunter..." She matched my tone.

"Do you know what it's been doing to me thinking of you here with other guys?" The words tumbled out. I clenched my teeth together and gripped the edge of the bed. The one where she hadn't been entertaining multiple guys every week, but simply making the bed to showcase the high-thread-count sheets.

"Offended you? Disgusted you?" She shifted forward, her hands on her hips, looming over me with her knees so close they nearly brushed mine. The brush felt like it scorched my skin, searing it with a desire I'd kept contained until this moment.

Snapping the gap closed between us, I shot up and slid my arms under hers.

Her eyes widened and she backed up, but I followed until the wall was at her back and I caged her between my arms. "Made me more jealous than I've ever been in my entire life."

She gasped, eyes wide and lips parted. Her gaze skittered over mine, surprise scrawled all over her face. "What?"

I brought my lips crashing down on hers and held on to the sides of her face, fingers tangled in her hair. I breathed all my frustration into her, gulping down her taste and inhaling every bit of her.

Her muscles stiffened before she gave in to the onslaught I couldn't contain with a moan. Her fingers fisted my shirt, tugging me closer. She tasted better than I could've imagined. Her body rocked against mine.

I'd wanted this since the second she stepped through the door. Everything I'd done was to stop myself, but right now I couldn't remember why. Not when she felt this good against me. Not when she responded to me like this.

My blood pounded in my veins, rushing toward my cock. My erection strained after seconds of pressing against the softness of her stomach. I flattened her against the wall, trying to get closer.

A throat clearing behind us was the only reason either of us came up for air. "I forgot my backpack. Don't mind me." Ryder shot past us, yanked his bag off the floor, and raced out of the room. The front door slammed shut, signaling his departure and snapping me back to reality, and to all the reasons I knew this wasn't a good idea. The temporary living situation, the mountain of work I was drowning under, and the fact that I hadn't been able to sleep through the night once since she arrived—not that I'd been doing any better before that.

Sabrina and I both stared at the empty doorway, then looked back at one another.

I cleared my throat, taking a step away when every part of me wanted to pin her against the wall—this time without any clothes between us—but I was also acutely aware of how I'd pounced on her. "Sorry." My head dropped, fighting against every instinct telling me to continue what we'd started.

"For which part?" She pushed off the wall with her arms crossed, teasing me with her glorious rack mouthwateringly close.

"All of it."

"All of it? How about ruining my video and scaring off my helper for the day? Snooping in my room, and stealing snacks?"

My head jerked back.

"Stealing your snacks?"

"Don't deny it. I saw the wrappers in your bathroom trash can." She marched forward.

"What were you doing in my bathroom?"

The fire in her eyes was doused.

"Why were you in my bathroom? You accuse me of snooping when you've been doing the same." She could've found me sleeping in the tub. What kind of explanation would I offer up? This reinforced why I needed to stop things before they started. Would I fall asleep with her in my arms and then slink off to the bath to get a good night's rest that didn't end with me flailing in my sleep and drenched in sweat.

"I haven't been snooping." Her lips pinched together. "I was taking a bath. You've got the only bath in the apartment, so I use it. Sometimes."

Another visual assaulted me, doing nothing to quell the insistent erection trying to make itself known. Sabrina wet and naked in my bathtub, soaping herself up. Resting her head against the high edge with her breasts peeking from under the waterline. Damn it.

Then it hit me with lightbulb clarity. "You've been using your lavender stuff in my bathroom."

"I use a bath oil." Confusion filled every word and her gaze.

"You've been mind-fucking me with your bath oil bullshit."

She jerked back. "No, I haven't. Taking a bath is hardly mind-fucking someone."

"The smell. When I walk in there, it's all I can smell. It's invaded my nasal cavity and my brain, rotting it from the inside out." One mystery was solved. The smell hadn't been me about to have a stroke from insomnia, but the complication made it that much worse. Was it Sabrina or was it the lavender? She'd been driving me out of my mind, but there was relief that a cause had been found. It could be the smell alone. I'd go out and buy a gallon of lavender oil if that's what it took. But something told me it wouldn't be that easy.

"I clean up every time, making sure I don't leave anything behind. Making sure you'll never even know I've been there."

"I thought I was going insane."

"So did I when all my treats were disappearing." She jumped forward, jabbing an accusatory finger toward me.

"It's not the same. Not even a little bit. Every night I've been drea—" I stopped myself from blurting out how pathetic my fixation had become.

She'd invaded my room and my mind. Her taste still lingered on my lips.

I needed to rein in my control and get a good night's sleep. Once I solved that situation, maybe my brain wouldn't be filled with a staticky fog that made it hard to focus on anything other than her whenever she was close. A panicked punch slammed into my chest. I couldn't let anyone else get close. "My bathroom is off-limits."

"How about a compromise?" She went big-eyed, softening like she was a second from melting into me.

I gripped the sides of my legs so I didn't grab her again. "No compromise. Good night." Running away wasn't exactly what I'd call what I did—more like striding with purpose.

Changing into sweats, I could still taste her on my lips. Her sweet, soft lips and heavenly curves that were pressed against me.

No! I wasn't exactly a prize. An insomniac who might be out of a job in a few months if I screwed up this New Year's Eve concert. It was better this way, safer. If I could finally get some damn sleep, keep Sabrina at a distance, pull off the concert, then maybe there could be something more between us, but right now I was a fucking mess. No matter how much I wanted her, I couldn't have her. Not yet.

I grabbed the book off my nightstand and flipped it open, trying to keep my mind off her, and closing it when I got to the pages I'd ripped out years ago. I'd awoken from the couch we'd put in the room beside my mom's bed. Her hands were folded on top of the book pressed against her stomach. They were the pages I'd tried to read right after they took my mom away to the funeral home. The ones I hadn't wanted to cry over, not when my tear ducts had felt like they were filled with sandpaper. The ones that had proven to me that even in fiction death wasn't visited on the people who deserved it, but stole people from us when we needed them most.

Sitting on the edge of my bed, I stared at the open door to my dark bathroom. The tub was framed in the doorway. The only place I'd been able to sleep without nightmares. The place that smelled like her.

I flipped on my stereo, not cranking the music as loud as I normally would. Dragging my pillow and blanket off the bed, I walked toward the bathroom. Maybe tomorrow I could buy some lavender candles or an air freshener and see if it did the trick. In the meantime I needed to keep my distance from Sabrina. I was an unholy mess right now, and I didn't think she'd enjoy sleeping in the tub with me so I didn't wake up in sweating, flailing chaos.

14

SABRINA

I paced in front of my desk beside the glow of my phone, squeezed the last of the water out of my hair, and tossed the towel into the hamper. Now that I didn't need to stop by the gym a few blocks away for model specimens, I'd finally decided to work out in the gym in the apartment building. Maybe by the end of the year I could achieve my goal of running up a set of stairs without feeling like my lungs were going to collapse.

Working out to be a size 2 wasn't in the cards for me, but I could sure as hell boost my stamina. And I'd kept my daydreams of getting all sweaty with Hunter to a minimum. They'd accompanied less than half of my workout. Okay, maybe 75 percent.

Finishing up the last submission to Harper Linens meant more time for designing. I'd been wandering around the city looking for inspiration and even taken some from the design details in the apartment. I had at least a hundred different designs to sort through and decide which I wanted to add to my portfolio.

"He kissed you!" Cat's voice blared from my phone on my desk. My door was cracked.

Thank God, Hunter had left a couple hours ago, bypassing me in the kitchen and rushing straight out the front door like I might pounce on him at any minute.

I mean, the kiss had been fine. Maybe a little more than fine. Serviceable. Serviceable like a rabbit with new batteries, hot breaths fanning my face that I swore I could still feel.

Okay, I hadn't been able to get the kiss out of my mind since the moment his lips had landed their blistering sear on mine. But now we were back to the avoidance game.

Not that we'd been making much progress before the kiss. One step forward and a giant leap back. This was just par for the course. Maybe his goal was to avoid me from now on. At least his music hadn't been blasting last night.

I didn't mind being avoided. The last thing I needed was to have to flee another apartment at a moment's notice because of another set of guy problems.

I grabbed the shipping labels off my printer and double-checked my list to ensure I hadn't mixed up the packages. I'd finished up all my shooting, and unless I planned on making an apartment-wide blanket fort there wasn't much I could do with them now. The extra cash would go to the sample-making I'd planned to do for my designs and would pay the grocery bill for the next month. "Shout it a little bit louder. I don't think they heard you in Siberia."

She inhaled and shouted at the top of her lungs. "Sabrina's hot-as-fuck roommate kissed her."

Even with the phone a few feet from me, I still shrank away from the earsplitting sound.

"Where are you?"

"In my office."

The papers fell out of my hand. "You screamed that in your office?"

"The door's closed. It's no big deal."

"You're at a whole different level, Cat." I shook my head, going back to sorting and labeling the sheets I needed to mail today.

"Trust me, I know. But you don't manage to get all five of these jackholes out of as many scrapes as I have and not get a little leeway."

"Like screaming 'fuck' in the middle of the workday in your office."

"It's the little things that make life worth living. Speaking of little things, did you cop a feel when he was ravishing you?"

I laughed and shook my head, trying to banish the fluttering swarm in my stomach, the electric tingle that ran across my skin whenever I thought about it and where I'd have liked things to go. Stupid celibacy.

He thought I was in here riding dick into the sunset, but I had barely more interaction than a handshake since the first day I'd moved in. "Not little at all."

"Yes! Sabrina's going to get some. Sabrina's going to get some."

"Did you not hear the part where he ran away after? Pretty much sprinted away. Maybe his relief over not living with a porn star got the better of him."

"Nope, it was that delectable ass of yours."

I rolled my eyes and smoothed down another label. "Let's not get carried away."

"Come on, during junior year? You're going to pretend you don't remember."

I covered my face with my hand. "Can we not bring that up?"

"They need to bronze those shorts and put them under glass in the president's office."

"In my defense, I was very drunk."

"No defense needed. They're probably still talking about the dance-off even after all this time."

"God, I hope not." Back in college, with confidence levels at an all-time high, I might've let my liquid courage fling me up onto stage for a dance contest I'd had no business entering. College Me had a fearlessness I could only look back on in awe, not believing we were the same person. But she hadn't been hit with the dings I'd faced since walking across the graduation stage, pumping my hands overhead.

"It might be a slight exaggeration, but there's certainly some ass fans out there. The bounce. The curve. The way you could bounce—"

"Can we please stop talking about fans of my ass?" I jumped up, snatching my phone off my desk chair and shouting back so I didn't have to hear anymore.

Life had changed a lot in six years, but I could always count on Cat to not let me forget that once I'd been fearless.

That was why she got the first dibs on sheets after I was finished with them. Not that she needed them with the size of her paychecks, but it made me feel better to show her how much I missed her.

Right at that moment, movement from the corner of my eye sent me down the plummeting embarrassment carnival ride.

Hunter stood in the hallway, frozen, staring straight at me.

Rushing forward, I closed the door and banged my head against the wood. I snatched my phone off my desk and took Cat off speakerphone. "Hunter heard you," I hissed.

"Trust me, he doesn't need to be told what he already knows."

"I hate you."

"You love me."

"No, I hate you." Now he was going to think after one kiss I couldn't stop thinking about him and I was telling my friends all about what happened—which was precisely what was happening, but he didn't need to know that.

"I love it when you talk dirty to me."

Unable to contain my laughter, I shook my head. "I'm hanging up now."

"Wait! When are you coming to visit me?"

"I have no clue. Every cent I have is going into producing the design samples. And anything left over goes to my moving out fund. Maybe after New Year's."

"That's so far away."

"Ms. Fancy Pants Translator, you could always come visit me."

"As if they'd give me more than twelve hours off. I swear, this place would collapse if I took a full week off."

"The curse of doing your job well."

"You're telling me. But I promise when you visit, I'll take a couple days off."

"Don't make promises you can't keep."

"Half days."

"The last time I visited, you had me sitting in your office all day and I felt like I was with my mom at Bring Your Kid To Work Day. All I was missing was a juice box and coloring book."

"I'll make sure I have both this time you visit."

"You're hilarious."

"I bet I didn't feel like your mom when I took you out that night."

"My shoes never turned up?"

"Nope, neither did my dress."

"That poor taxi driver."

"Don't worry, he had his fun. That night is why I always wear boy shorts and have a camisole in my clutch."

"You've lost your clothes since then?"

"Once or twice."

"Be safe, Cat."

"You know me."

"I know, that's why I'm saying, 'Be safe.'"

"I'll do my best. They're calling to wrangle a client. Got to go. Love you."

"Love you too."

I ended the call and finished up my shipping bonanza, taking extra care with the packaging to avoid leaving my room. Not like I had a roommate I'd kissed, who was wandering around out there, who'd heard me gossiping about him. Not at all.

I stacked all the packages together. Developing the ability to teleport to the lobby without Hunter seeing me would be handy right now, but both his office and bedroom doors were closed and the rest of the apartment was quiet, unlike what I dealt with every single night. Why couldn't he be this courteous when I was trying to get some damn sleep. Maybe I'd become nocturnal.

After dropping off the packages, I was starving, and the linguine shrimp scampi wasn't going to make itself.

Music drifted from Hunter's room like always—but not at earsplitting levels. Not the type of level meant to drown out the existence of other people. Was it that hard to be alone with himself that he always needed the music playing? At least he wasn't lying in wait for me to leave my room, or maybe he was hiding from me, afraid he'd made out with a Stage 5 Clinger. Either way, I needed to eat, and I'd have to face him at some point. I glanced over my shoulder and then down at myself. Maybe I should change. Put on something a little less "changed into my PJs directly after a shower and worked for three hours before tearing into the kitchen for food" and a little more "person who intends to leave the house at some point this week." But why pretend to be someone I wasn't?

Hunter had seen me before. There was no genie going back in the bottle on this one.

I turned on my boy band playlist and gathered up my ingredients and set the pot down on the stove. Every noise sent my gaze darting down the hall.

My goal in life was to have enough money for a house with a kitchen half as nice as this and a stove with a pot-filler spout. A door closed and I jolted. Was that his bathroom door?

I filled the pot and cranked up the heat, adding a little bit of oil and a lot of salt to the water. More than I meant to when I jumped at a sound behind me before spotting that one of the oranges had rolled off the shelf. There might have been a little nervousness about seeing Hunter again.

After seasoning the shrimp, I melted the butter and garlic in the copper pan I'd been afraid to use for my first few weeks here. The heavenly scent of sautéing garlic in butter was one of my favorites. I added the shrimp and waited for them to pink up, tossing them in the pan.

This recipe felt decadent, but it only took a few minutes. That was my kind of luxury.

The water boiled, and I slipped the fresh linguine inside. Less than ten minutes later I had a plate of steaming seafood deliciousness topped with enough parmesan that my lips would burn, but I kept eating.

After a three-minute debate with myself about eating in my room or watching TV, the living room won out. I wasn't hiding from him. We'd have to see each other eventually and hiding would mean I was embarrassed about what Cat had said. I preferred to pretend it hadn't happened is all. Let him think it was all in his head. *I* wasn't going to be the one to make this weird.

I took my plate out into the living room along with my drink and set both on the table beside the couch. The one with the lamp I'd been afraid I'd break by trying to turn it on when I'd first moved in.

I grabbed the remote from the neat row of remotes on the coffee table. Crossing my legs under me, I balanced my plate on my lap and scooped up a forkful of creamy, buttery pasta and shrimp and shoved it into my mouth.

My infinite scroll stopped on a Sandra Bullock rom-com. Only she could make being a ticket taker on the Chicago metro system look glamorous. I settled in with my food.

"Sabrina, what—"

I whipped my head around to Hunter, tugging the pasta off my fork so that it dropped onto my chin. Brushing my finger under my bottom lip, I wiped away the mess and grabbed my napkin.

"Yeah?" I covered my mouth with the back of my hand.

He stood in the doorway, frozen for a moment.

Did I need a reminder of how not graceful I was? "Did you need something?" I snapped, my embarrassment flustering me.

"Your food smelled good. I just wanted to know where you ordered it from." He stepped into the room, looking ready for a night out.

A jealous streak shot through me. Not my business. We kissed once. Not exactly a declaration of love.

The tips of my ears were burning. Please call the fire department. "It's not takeout. I made it myself."

"It smells good." He stood beside the arm of the couch, right in front of the table where my drink sat, and tilted his head, peering down at my plate.

"With garlic, butter, and parmesan cheese there's not a lot that can go wrong." I chuckled and stuffed another forkful of food into my mouth. It was so good, and if I wasn't careful, I'd eat the whole damn thing tonight instead of saving half for tomorrow. Not exactly what my hips needed right now. "There's more in the kitchen if you want some." I gulped down my mouthful to cover my uneasiness. Why had I offered it to him? What if he hated it? What if I ate a pound of pasta on my own? Better Mr. Chiseled ate some rather than being alone and left to my own devices.

His eyes widened, and he shook his head. "I'm headed out." His gaze stayed trained on my plate.

"I didn't say sit down for a four-course meal. Have a bite and see if you like it." I used my plate hand to motion to the kitchen.

He looked from the doorway back to me. "Maybe later."

I speared a shrimp and dragged it through the sauce. "There's no guarantee there will be any later."

"What was that?"

"What? Nothing." I snapped my mouth shut. "Here. Try it." I held out my fork toward him. "If you like it, I'll set some aside for you."

His nostrils flared, and only then did I realize how intimate my offer felt. Food I'd made. From my plate. On my fork.

Instead of backing up and once again telling me he had to go, he crouched down. His knee brushed against my calf. His gaze was no longer trained on my fork. It was trained on me, zeroed in so sharply I was happy I was wearing a thicker bra so I didn't give him a full-high-beams situation.

"Sure, I'll try it." He didn't take the shrimp off my fork. He didn't take the fork from my hand. He wrapped his fingers around my wrist and brought the fork toward his mouth.

Hold the freaking phone. When did we jump from ignoring me to straight seduction?

My stomach, which was now filled with pasta and seafood, was doing a minor acrobatics performance complete with backflips and a trapeze. My pulse jumped wildly beneath his grip.

He plucked the shrimp off the fork and chewed it slowly, keeping his eyes locked on to mine.

He groaned and his eyes drifted closed like he knew exactly what he was doing. His lips curved, shiny with butter. Bastard.

A furious level of flustered rocked me. Was it too late to swap positions with the shrimp?

His eyes shot open, and he released his hold on me like he'd been burned.

I nearly fell off the couch, shooting my arms out to stop myself from falling over. Only then did I realize I'd been leaning forward, about to take us both out in a pile on the floor.

He walked backward like I'd pounce on him if he turned his back "Night, Sabrina."

I wasn't the one doing sexy food tastings like I was trying out for soft-core porn.

My gaze narrowed, fixating on his retreating figure, and my jaw dropped.

Had I been played? Was this his plan to screw with me after I'd screwed with him by not confessing I wasn't shooting porn in my bedroom? Or was it something else? Something I was afraid to think about because I didn't know if I was capable of a fling right now.

Hunter didn't exactly scream *relationship guy,* and being in a relationship wasn't what I needed right now. I needed to focus on my designs, pitch them to potential buyers, and branch out on my own, where I wasn't reliant on anyone but me. If there was one thing I'd learned, it was that no one was ever what they seemed and my trust in them would come to bite me in the ass.

So, no, Hunter Saxton wasn't an option. The risk was too great. But damn if my inner vixen wasn't throwing the bitch fit to end all bitch fits, professing that we could play it cool and have a little fun before we moved out in a couple months.

Only a little fun, although with Hunter I had a feeling it was big. Very big. Everything about him screamed Big Dick Energy. Whether I'd find out or not would depend on just how much of my sanity I was willing to risk. And right now, after a couple months flying solo with nothing more than my rabbit, it was probably more than I should...

15

HUNTER

I closed the apartment door and walked to the elevator, slamming the heel of my hand against my forehead. What the hell was I thinking? This wasn't how I got her out of my head.

The shrimp had been heavenly, but the way she'd looked at me was nothing but sin. The kind that made me want to taste her all over again.

Focus!

Tonight could make or break the concert. Maddy had finally responded to me. Announcing Without Grey when tickets went on sale in November would ensure a sold-out night. It would also skyrocket the coverage of the event. For good or bad. If they said yes, I'd have millions of eyes on my work.

I arrived at the studio and paced instead of sitting where the receptionist had motioned for me to wait. Before, it would've been because I hadn't had a good night's sleep and didn't want to nod off in the chair; now it was because anticipation buzzed in my veins and I didn't think I could sit even if I'd wanted to.

"You're finally here." Maddy's tone was unmistakable. Slightly snarky but smooth all at once. The perfect combination of biting and persuasive required when managing one of the biggest bands in the world. At a few inches over five feet, her voice had been known to clear hallways and bring record execs to their knees at the negotiating table.

"Am I late?" I opened my arms.

"Sorry, no, just used to dealing with musicians and their own concepts of time." She rolled her eyes but let me envelop her. "How's everyone?"

"Everest's a bit of a grumpy bastard, but that's to be expected—"

"I didn't ask about Everest." She jumped back. Her voice went shrill and slightly panicked.

"Maybe not, but—"

Her hands rested on her hips. "Do you want to see the guys or not?"

I drew my fingers across my mouth like an imaginary zip.

"That's what I thought. You have ten minutes before the guys kick you out. They don't like to be disturbed when they're recording, but they're finishing up eating, so they'll be less angry."

"Can't you work your feminine wiles on them?"

Her gaze narrowed, and she reached out. A sharp pinch radiated down my side.

"Ow! What was that for?" I rubbed the spot.

"Feminine wiles. I'm sure I know exactly who that comment came from. Do you want to talk to them or not? Because right now it seems like you want to talk your way out of a shot to speak with them."

"Nope, sorry. Backing off." We walked toward the door beside the reception desk.

"How's he going to react when you tell him you came down here?" She turned and walked toward the frosted glass door, swiping a card in front of the lock, which turned green.

My mouth opened and closed, not sure if this was a trap or not. Hadn't we just said we weren't going to talk about Everest? But the expectant look on her face told me she did want an actual response. Proceeding cautiously, I answered her question. "He gave me his blessing."

Her fingers slipped off the handle. She grabbed it again and tugged the door open. "If you say so."

"He did. I told him how much it could raise the profile of the company and how the tickets would sell out on the first day, and he was on board."

"That I believe. Money and attention have always been Everest's first loves."

"There was another."

She shot me a glare and marched toward me until my back hit the wall. "You can leave right now."

"Sorry for the overstep. I won't do it again." I held up my hands, palms out.

"You'd better not." Turning, she grumbled under her breath about how ungrateful I was and how she never should've agreed to this.

The hall was filled with a muted silence. Not even the sounds of our footsteps carried in the soft carpet. The silence was eerie and artificial, created from the massive amounts of soundproofing to keep music from bleeding from one studio to another.

"They're in here. There might be a little breakfast left if they haven't devoured it all." She swiped beside the door with a silver number 5 on the outside.

"Breakfast? It's almost eleven at night."

She pushed the door open, and laughter and music burst through the doorway. "Does anyone want to tell our guest why you're all eating breakfast at 10:48 p.m.?"

One hand shot high in the air. The hand of the six-foot-three drummer in a Rolling Stones T-shirt and black jeans with closely cropped black hair strained bouncing up and down like he was sitting in the first row of second period English class.

Maddy pointed to him. "Austin."

"Because it's breakfast for us since Maddy dragged us all out of bed an hour ago."

"You woke up at nine?" And I'd thought my sleeping patterns were fucked.

"I'd have slept until noon tomorrow." Lockwood, the rhythm guitarist, took a bite of bacon.

"Would you like yet another album where we have to bring someone in to play your part? I can have that girl from Chicago on a plane by tomorrow. At least it would be one less piss-poor attitude I'd have to deal with."

Lockwood threw down his bacon and glared at Maddy before hopping up and storming out of the room.

"Maddy," Camden, the lead singer, warned.

"What? I'm the bad guy. It's what I do. Do you want to act like you didn't ask me to get him out of bed?"

"No. Guys..." He looked to Elias, who played bass, and Vale on the keyboards and jutted his chin toward the door Lockwood had stormed out of. They headed out after Lockwood with Austin, leaving Maddy, Camden, and me behind in the studio.

"If this is a bad time..."

Camden grabbed a chair and sat on it backward, facing me. "That's just Lock doing what he does best." His jaw clenched. "Causing trouble. And we're having breakfast now because we were up all night writing. When the muse arrives, you can't stop the flow. So we're all paying for it today." He rubbed his eyes. "Maddy told us all about the show."

She offered me a bottle of orange juice.

"Thanks, Maddy." I took it, if only to occupy my hands. "I can give you more details. I don't know how much you've been told about it already." I looked between them.

Camden rested his elbow on the back of the chair and propped his chin up on his fist. "Why do you want us there?"

"Do you want me to blow smoke or would you like the real answer?"

His lips twitched. "Contrary to popular opinions, I'm not a huge fan of smoke. It wreaks havoc on the voice." He tapped his throat.

"You're one of the biggest names in the world. Adding you guys to the bill raises the profile of the event and ensures a sellout. My company had this dropped into our lap. No one else wanted to touch it, but there's a lot of potential to make this a tent pole event in the city. Maybe make sure the city shows up on the map, instead of just being a yawning gap between DC and New York. Plus, it's my chance to show my friends who I run the company with that I can pull my weight."

"I can respect wanting to make your mark." His tone was understanding. "These friends of his include your ex." He didn't look to me but Maddy.

Her chin jerked in a sharp nod.

"And you're cool with us working with him?" He flicked his fingers in my direction.

"Hunter and I go way back. I owe him. The situation with Everest"—the words came out strangled—"has nothing to do with this request."

Camden scrutinized her and looked back to me with the muscles of his jaw clenched.

Long-shot odds were looking more distant by the second.

The door to the hall opened. A young guy, probably an intern, poked his head in. "Maddy, we sent the car for Alistar, but they're having trouble finding him. Do you have another contact number?"

She growled and shot up from her leaning position against the mixing console to grab her tablet and phone. "This is what I get for working with fucking musicians."

The door closed behind her, and Camden and I were left alone.

"I understand if the past between Everest and Maddy is your no. Same with you guys being busy. I get it, and there's no hard feelings." If Without Grey said no, the concert would be doable, but the hustle would have to be a hell of a lot harder to get the kind of buzz needed around an event that had been painted as doomed.

"Do you know how many requests we get to perform at one-off events?"

"Probably a few hundred a week."

He shrugged. "Possibly, but the amount she brings to us" —his chin jerked in the direction of the door—"is less than a handful. Only non-tour performances she thinks will help the band level up. Headlining major festivals, televised events, things like that, except for this one. She didn't give us the hard sell, but she did bring it to the group conversation." He stared at the closed door with a contemplative look. "I'll agree to this under one condition."

I shot up straighter in my chair, leaning forward. "What do you need? Anything." Calling in every favor I had would be worth it for this.

"Help me figure out how to get Maddy and her ex, Everest, in a room together. She pretends like whatever happened between them is in the past, but none of us believe her."

My mouth hung open. Of all the things I'd anticipated that wasn't it. "You think she's going to go for that?"

Camden laughed, his eyes glittering in the dim studio lights. "Hell no, she'd rip my balls off and feed them to us for brunch if she knew. But that's my condition."

I licked my lips, not believing I was so close. "You don't need to talk it over with the rest of the band?"

"No, they're in full agreement with me on this. You help me get them in a room for as long as they need to finally hash all this shit out and we're in." He extended his hand. His trust in me at pulling this off and getting them together was all that stood between me and three months of hell. A conversation between Everest and Maddy seemed less unthinkable against that—barely.

I clasped it, pumping it twice. "You've got a deal."

Everyone returned to the studio, and after signing an NDA, which Maddy had at the ready like a gunslinger, they let me listen to one of the new songs they'd been working on.

A little after midnight, I got back to the apartment.

I gingerly unlocked the door, prepared to quietly get to my room without disturbing Sabrina, when music flooded through the open door. Her love of boy bands knew no bounds and the songs were on repeat so often that I could probably sing a whole damn concert's worth of them. Not that I ever would. There were a lot of things I could pull off, but singing sure as hell wasn't one of them.

On alert, I followed the sound. It wasn't coming from Sabrina's room but the dining room.

I poked my head in the door and stopped in the doorway.

She sat in the far chair on her knees, leaned over a new unfinished puzzle spread out on the table. One arm was braced under her breasts, pushing them up even higher under her long-sleeve t-shirt. She had a puzzle piece in her hand and scanned up and down one edge of the unfinished picture. Her hair was down, falling over her shoulders, every shade of brown highlighted in the bright overhead light.

I should go to my room and not disturb her. Hadn't I just made a pact with myself to not get involved with her?

She caught her bottom lip between her teeth, plumping it up even more. The pink fullness glistened when she released it and let out a breath, going back to the top of the puzzle and starting her scan all over again.

"Can't find it?"

She yelped and pitched backward.

I shot around the table and caught her in full flail, locking one arm around her. "We have to stop meeting this way."

Her eyes widened, and heavy breaths shook her chest. Her fingers clung to my shirt. "Yeah, we do. If you weren't always so stealthy it wouldn't be a problem. I swear, you're a hazard waiting to happen."

"I'll try marching into the room next time." I wanted to hold her chin between my fingers and crush my lips to hers again. To explore every inch of her. My fingers tensed against her ribs, right under the curve of her breast. A soft brush was enough to send my blood into overdrive.

"Thanks for catching me," she whispered.

"It's only fair since I made you fall in the first place."

"True." The corner of her mouth quirked up.

I cleared my throat and shifted myself to right her in the chair. "You're up late."

"It seems I've gotten used to sleeping with a full concert going on in the room next to me, so I couldn't fall asleep."

That hit like a mallet to my chest.

She smiled and released her grip on me, righting herself in her chair and putting both feet on the floor. "Looks like we've been screwing with each other's heads all along." Pushing her hair behind her ear, she peered up at me.

Her gaze mesmerized me, shoving me headlong into a fast and furious recounting of how responsive she'd been against me earlier this week.

Leave, Hunter. Say good night and walk into your bedroom, close the door, crank up the music, and crawl into your tub that smells less and less like her every night and try to get some sleep.

I ripped my gaze from hers and focused on the puzzle pieces on the table. Picking up one of the pieces lined up along the side, I flipped it over. I spotted the matching pattern, analyzing the partially formed image as much as I'd been riveted to Sabrina, and slid the piece into place.

"No way!" She shot forward, leaning against the table. "I've been looking for spots for those for the past hour!" Her body sagged back into her chair. "I swore those pieces were going to kill me. But I can't not finish it. I'm a completist." She glared at the puzzle. This time I wasn't on the receiving end of the withering look.

The music shifted. A ballad. Damn Harry Styles and his insightful lyrics about turning into someone you swore you'd never be, falling whether in love or in a freefall after it goes south and fears of never being with the person he truly cared about. In the same room with her, his words hit me harder than ever. "Would you like some help?"

She sighed, sat back in her chair, and waved me off. "You

don't have to. It's late and I don't want to infect you with my obsessive hatred for this thing."

"It's been years since I've done one. And it's not that late." I took my jacket off and set it on the back of the chair.

"Was this puzzle yours?" She stared at the puzzle with flickering glances toward me.

"My mom and I spent a lot of time doing them once she got sick. I got a light-weight card-playing table that would fit over her hospital bed. I'd sit with her for hours while she got her treatments." I spun the piece between my fingers. Those were bittersweet times. Happiness clouded by the shooting pain of loss.

"That must've been hard."

"It wasn't easy. But GiGi hired the best care she could find. Nurses, home aids, transportation to and from the hospital and doctor's appointments."

"Still—you were a kid. That had to be rough on you."

"Not as rough as it was on her." I dropped a three-piece combo into their spot along the edge of the puzzle. The impressionist watercolor painting came more into focus. "But I did what I could to help. I tried to surprise her and make her smile." Sadness tinged the memories of coming home from school to her and spending hours together watching movies, working on puzzles, or going out on the days she felt up to it.

"What kind of things did you do?"

"You know, the usual. I'd bake cookies for her, get her flowers, acquire a half ounce of pot, arrange for carolers to stop by the house for Christmas."

Out of the corner of my eye, I saw her mouth hanging open.

"Did you say you got your mom pot?"

I shrugged, trying to keep my laughter contained. "How else was she going to eat the cookies?"

"At fourteen!" Her voice carried over the music. "I don't even think I'd know where to get pot right now. How'd you pull that off back then?"

"A magician never reveals his tricks." I waved my hands in front of my face before setting the piece I held down in place.

Her head tilted to the side, and her gaze bored into mine.

"Okay, just this once. There was a guy in my woodshop class who everyone said was a stoner. I figured he'd know where I could get some. He did. I visited his dealer, struck a deal, and got the pot for my mom. She'd sit out on the back porch and smoke wrapped up in blankets, then come inside and we'd eat and laugh like everything was okay."

"What deal did you strike with the dealer?"

"He had a younger sister who was trying to take an entrance exam to a private school that had generous scholarships. He needed a tutor to help her. I had a friend who wanted some street cred. He got to hang out with the stoner, the dealer gave him some extra on his next couple orders, the sister got a tutor, and I got my mom what she needed."

The puzzle piece dropped out from between her fingers, and she stared at me with Bambi-wide eyes.

I laughed, unable to contain it this time, and touched her chin. An electric pulse traveled up my arm. With a gentle hold, I closed her mouth, keeping myself from brushing my thumb against her lip.

"And it worked?"

"For as long as it needed to. The sister got into the private school. I think she's a doctor now, maybe finishing up her residency. The dealer went legit too. He moved out to Colorado to sell legally out there."

She sat back in her chair. "Wow. I was too scared to steal a sip of booze from my parent's liquor cabinet, and you were cozying up to drug dealers. And you continued your wheeling-and-dealing lifestyle after?"

I shrugged. "I became known as the guy who could get things. Students, teachers, parents. It wasn't all nefarious or drug-based, but somehow I figured it out." All it took was recognizing what someone needed, even if it wasn't what they thought they needed.

She let out an amused puff. "I'm sure you did."

"What's that supposed to mean?"

Her gaze swung to mine, and a flickering smile tugged at her full lips. "I have no doubt you're a rock star when it comes to peeling back the layers of people's brains to get what you want."

"Why'd that sound like an insult?"

She shrugged, but her eyes were intent on mine like she was trying to peel back some layers of her own.

"What do you want, Sabrina?"

Her lips parted, and her breath hitched in a way that sent a shot of awareness coursing through my veins. The closeness of her pinkie mid–piece-placement to the side of my hand. The way her chest rose and fell, her breasts taunting me. The brush of her foot against mine under the table.

She shot up from her seat. "Another drink. I'll get you one too."

It was stupid for me to stay, but damned if I could make myself go.

16

SABRINA

A quiet evening at home with Hunter working on a puzzle wasn't what I'd thought was in the cards for me, but here we were. The conversation flowed when we weren't at each other's throats. He was easy to talk to, which was frustrating on so many levels. Why couldn't we have had these sorts of interactions from the beginning without him being a territorial asshole?

He got up to refill my glass for a second time.

I leaned over the back of my chair and called out to him in the kitchen. "But how did you get the pro tennis player to do private lessons?"

Metal on glass clinked from the other room. "That was easy. A donation to his charity was all it took. When money's involved, it makes things a lot easier, but sometimes money can't buy what you need. That's where the research and finesse comes in." He walked out with my drink and a beer for himself.

I took a sip of the blackberry bramble Hunter had mixed up. It was a step up from my normal vodka cranberry and was dangerously delicious. "Wow, you weren't lying about being a guy who could get anything."

"Not anything. There are limits." He grinned looking like a man who could absolutely find a way around every 'no'.

"I have no doubt if you put your mind to it, you could figure it out." I spotted another picture match and pumped my arms overhead, simulating a crowd roar.

"Finally found it?"

"The drinks are making this puzzle a lot easier."

He laughed and pulled out the piece I'd just tried to ram into one spot and flipped it around, smoothing it into place. "It does when you cram the pieces in wherever you want."

My cheeks heated. "I was close."

"You were." He peered over at me, and my stomach did the equivalent of trying to get a queen-size sheet on a California king—so much tension.

For over an hour we'd worked on the puzzle. I'd had two blueberry brambles, and the buzz was strong.

"Where'd you go tonight? Usually you get back later than this."

"Keeping tabs on me?" He sipped from his beer.

"It's hard not to know about your comings and goings when your music blasts down the hall like a drum line is using this as a practice space." I dropped my head to find the straw in my drink and ended up chasing it around the rim of my glass with my mouth. My seduction technique was flawless. I snorted and snagged the straw.

Hunter's gaze intensified. Reaching out, he steadied my straw, and I wrapped my lips around it, brushing against his fingers.

After another fortifying gulp of my drink, I slipped my tongue out and licked his thumb.

He sucked in a breath but didn't move.

Maybe it was the booze flowing through my veins. Maybe it was that this was our first civil conversation that had lasted longer than ten minutes. Maybe it was because now I could see why everyone else thought Hunter was such a great guy, but I nudged the straw out of the way and wrapped my lips around his thumb, drawing it into my mouth. It tasted like a hint of barley and hops from his beer.

His eyes widened before his lids lowered and his gaze hooded. The depths of them pooled with desire.

The volleying in my stomach intensified.

His fingers curled around my cheeks and jaw, brushing against the front of my neck.

Goose bumps rose all over my body, and once again the thick fabric of my bra kept my stiff peaks under wraps.

I held onto the back of his hand and let his finger fall free from my lips. "Hunter..." My mouth opened, but I didn't know what to say. Here I'd been fellating his thumb. It wasn't exactly easy to slide back into *whoops* or *sorry about that* territory, especially when I still had his hand in mine. A hand he hadn't tried to pull back.

This zing between us wasn't lessening. It had been building, previously covered by anger and animosity. Now that the barriers were down, it was harder to fight like I had been since I'd walked in on him in his sweats with a jar of Nutella. The thrum pulsing along my skin became a throb between my thighs.

"Yeah." His voice was deep and gravelly.

A tingling crept up my spine, making me light-headed—or maybe it was the drinks, but I one hundred percent believed Hunter would have this effect on any woman.

"Why'd you come back early tonight?" It was a stupid question. What the hell did it matter why he'd come back early? But the thought of another woman twisted my gut. Had someone else touched these lips tonight?

His other hand skimmed along the inside of my outstretched arm. The sensation stirred even more previously suppressed feelings. "I was ready."

"And now?" I ran my fingers over the pulse point on his wrist. It jumped wildly under my fingers.

His pupils dilated, the blue encroached upon by the black, before I was tugged out of my seat. His arm wrapped around my waist, fingers sinking into my flesh, and I made the short journey from my chair to my new seat.

Once again, his body was pressed against mine, but this time I was in his lap.

My previous swimming thoughts zeroed in on our new seating arrangement. I squirmed to get off him, not wanting to crush him. I hadn't sat on anyone's lap since Santa in the fourth grade.

Instead of sinking into him, I shot up, and flushed, embarrassment heating my cheeks. I dropped my eyes.

Hunter's chair slid across the hardwood floor. "Sorry," he mumbled under his breath.

My head shot up. "No, I'm sorry. I wasn't expecting that. The drinks must've gone to my head." My humorless laugh didn't make this any less awkward.

His lips turned down. "You're right. Sorry if I took advantage."

"What? No, I didn't mean that." Damn it! By covering my embarrassment, I'd convinced him he'd made an unwanted advance when it had most definitely been wanted—too wanted. And that was the problem. "I just meant—the shift made my head a little swimmy." *And I was freaking out about crushing you.*

He picked up his jacket from the back of the chair and

slung it over his shoulder, and just like that, our evening was over. "Thanks for letting me join in. I'm heading to bed." He hesitated before pushing his chair back in and walking out of the room.

"Anytime."

"And Sabrina?" He caught his hand on the doorway and looked over his shoulder.

"Yes." It came out breathlessly anticipatory.

"You can use my bathtub. It's not a big deal." His fingers drummed against the door.

I nodded instead of squeaking like a chipmunk on helium.

"Good night." He paused.

My heart skipped a beat, waiting, wishing, wanting.

After he disappeared down the hallway and his door closed, I slumped back against the table. "Good night, Hunter."

I scrubbed my hands down over my face and slapped my cheeks a few times. *What the hell were you thinking?* Wasn't this the exact opposite of what I was supposed to be doing? I'd broken up with Seth six weeks ago. Hunter at least didn't pretend to be a non-lady-killer. Getting involved with him would shred my heart and once again leave me without a place to live.

Don't do it, Sabrina. Don't even think about it.

In my bed, I tossed and turned, trying to get to sleep.

Hunter's music invaded my room just like he'd invaded my head.

But after all my protesting and promises to myself, I fell asleep thinking of his lips and hands on me and his body pressed against me.

～

"Tell me how that one fits. If it's too tight, I can go get you a new one." I leaned into the men's fitting room doorway.

A faint "okay" was the only response.

I peered over my shoulder, looking back at the department store racks and shelves. This wasn't how I'd expected to be spending my Tuesday afternoon, but as much as I longed for it, my life had been nothing near predictable for quite some time.

A phone call, an honest-to-God phone call from an eighteen-year-old had been enough for me to know something was up. He had an alumni interview for his Fulton U college application this evening, and I was who he'd turned to. My heart ached for this kid who didn't seem to have anyone.

I wandered close to the fitting room near the tie section.

He peeked out of the open doorway. "How's this?" The light shirt and black pants fit him well. Uncertainty and indecision were painted all over him.

I definitely didn't miss the old teenage insecurities. I'd now traded them for more adult ones, but at least I wasn't dealing with acne and raging, fluctuating hormones.

I felt like a big sister. Was this what being a big sister felt like? Should I give him a wedgie? Or ruffle his hair?

"Looks like I've still got it from my days working at the Gap."

He stared down at himself and looked back at me with skepticism in his eyes like I'd suggested wearing a Big Bird costume. "Are you sure this is fine?"

"You look great. Very professional. I think Hunter has the same outfit."

Ryder's eyes widened, and he jerked at the buttons angrily. "I'll choose something else."

I grabbed his arm. "Hey, what's that all about?"

"This is stupid. Why am I even going to this interview? I'm not going to get in. It was stupid to even apply. Hunter doesn't even care." He tried to spin away, but I held on, stunned by his shift in demeanor from nervousness to biting despondency.

"Ryder." But I didn't have words, and I didn't know how to make it right. That I was the only one he could turn to, a stranger who'd made him lunch once, told me a lot about how lost he felt.

He kept his head down, but I could feel his pain coming off him in waves. It weighted down the air around him like a blanket.

"Hunter's dealing with a lot of things right now. He..." Our talk last night had shed a lot of light on how much Hunter was still struggling with his mom's death and how his dad dying was probably making it even harder. He'd showed me a different side to him. He could be a good guy. "He'll come around. Don't give up on him yet. Plus..." I knocked my elbow into his arm and smiled. "Now you've got me on your side, so I'll help too. Do you need someone to read your essays? I was better at art, but I can at least make sure it's free from F bombs."

His eyebrows dipped. "Why the hell would I curse in my essays?" He laughed and shook his head.

At least I'd gotten a smile out of him. I held my hands out at my sides, palms up, and shrugged. "Let's grab some food before the interview. I'll wait with you until it's time."

His face lit up. "Really?" He sounded like a little kid being told they were getting the present they wanted for Christmas.

"Really. Now, let's get your clothes situation figured out, and then we can review the questions they sent over. We've still got three hours before your interview."

Ryder rushed back into the fitting room and tried on a few different options. In the end he chose the first one. The one I'd said looked a lot like Hunter's. A pang knocked into my heart for both of them. For Hunter, looking at Ryder was probably a reminder of their dad and the circumstances under which they became brothers. For Ryder, all he wanted was some attention and acceptance from a piece of family he had left, no matter how tenuous the connection.

Instead of going back to the apartment, we walked to campus and found a spot to grab a coffee and snack that wasn't too far from the alumni interviewer's brownstone.

I pushed the mug across the table to Ryder. "Do you think this would be a fun place to go to school?"

He looked around Uncommon Grounds, the coffee shop we'd stopped in. "I could, although it was super weird all those guys were lined up outside. And there's almost no one inside."

"I thought the same thing." I surveyed the place. Only a few of the booths were occupied. One had a girl sitting at a table all alone with a stack of notecards. Another had a guy who looked like a football player sitting with an older woman. Other than those two booths, half the ten tables inside had someone at them with a laptop propped open and covered in books. "But whatever they're waiting for must be important for them to be waiting in line."

Ryder shrugged. "Do you really think there's a chance Hunter will finally talk to me?" He stared into his coffee, rolling the mug between his hands.

I covered the back of his hand with mine. "I do. None of this is easy for either of you. People deal with their pain and sadness in their own way. Sometimes they don't know how much they're hurting the people around them. The people they care about." I wasn't sure if Hunter would come

around, but I wouldn't crush Ryder's hope. Being an innocent bystander during someone else's fuckups never felt
good, but at least there was a chance the two of them would
eventually talk and maybe connect like Ryder hoped.

He pulled his hands closer to his side of the table and
away from mine. "He doesn't care about me."

The pang in my chest hit harder. "He doesn't know you
yet, but we're not worried about that now. It'll come later.
Right now we're focusing on getting you into Fulton U. Now
let's go over the questions they sent you." I rubbed my hands
together like an over-the-top maniac, but it worked.

Ryder rolled his eyes and his cheeks worked to contain a
smile, but it still peeked out like the sun saying *hi* on an
otherwise rainy day. He sent me a message with the questions. "Okay, first question: What do you feel you can
contribute to the FU community?"

A *pfft* was barely stifled behind his lips. His mouth
curled up into a smile like he'd just cursed behind the principal's back.

"I'm just reading what you sent me." I held up the
phone. "Get it out of your system now." How the hell did
they expect eighteen-year-olds to keep a straight face with a
question like that? Killer beer pong skills. An overriding
urge to hit on classmates. Keg stand abilities.

He rubbed his hand under his chin. "Maybe it's a test."

"Most likely. And if it is, you're failing."

He schooled his features but seemed more relaxed. "I'll
bring my determination, adventurous spirit, and dashing
good looks to the Fulton U student body." He turned his
profile and plastered on a Prince Charming plastic smile,
complete with raised eyebrow.

I rolled my eyes. "You're a shoo-in."

He laughed and waved his hands in front of his face. "Okay, I'll be serious. Let's keep going."

We went over the questions a few times and came up with some questions for him to ask the interviewer.

With our cups drained, we headed back out into the chilly weather to the interviewer's house. The line outside the coffee shop had disappeared, so whatever had happened was over now.

Standing at the end of the block, I gave Ryder a thumbs-up as he rang the doorbell to the house. It hit me as I stood outside, rubbing my bare hands together against the brisk evening air, how far away college felt, but it also only seemed a couple years ago. Back in high school there had been the excitement of opening my inbox and scanning for subject lines that said, "Congratulations," or "You've been accepted." Now it was mainly spam emails, bill notices, or project rejections that were the difference between my bank account hitting $0 and maybe splurging on a happy hour every once in a while.

But this was about Ryder and his big plans for the future. Since there wasn't a helicopter parent around, I'd sure as hell be the biggest cheerleader in his corner.

My phone buzzed. Smiling, I answered the call. "What time zone are you in now?"

A familiar groggy voice responded, "No idea, but according to my phone it's one a.m."

"Barely bedtime."

"Exactly."

"What's up, Cat?"

"I'm going to be in DC in a few weeks. I checked and it's the same time as that expo you were talking about. Will you be coming down for it? We could meet up. Have some fun."

"You won't be working?" I was skeptical because no one I knew worked or partied harder than Cat, and I didn't have the same bounce-back I'd had at twenty-three, still enjoying the alcohol-tolerance booster only college could provide.

The last time we'd tried to hang out while she was on the clock, she'd left the key to her room with the front desk, and I'd been awoken at one a.m. by her popping a bottle of champagne before dragging me out to an after-hours poker game that lasted until six a.m. We'd stumbled back to her hotel room, where she'd rolled out of bed for a nine a.m. meeting after puking in the potted plant in her room.

"I'll make time for my best friend. Are you going to the Apparel & Textile Expo?"

Disappointment grabbed a shovel and dug deep in my chest. "They won't sell me a ticket. I've tried twenty different times, but they're not budging."

"That sucks. Do you want me to sick the Ivans on them?" Three of her five bosses were named Ivan, which was why they mainly went by their middle names.

"I don't think I need anyone thrown in a trunk over this."

Her scoff was swallowed by a yawn. "They don't do that anymore. Do you want me to ask?"

I didn't even call Cat on her office phone. It was probably being monitored by Interpol. The last thing I wanted was a favor from the Ivans and the NSA knocking on my door when their trunk-throwing ways returned someday. With Cat, I had no doubt she could talk her way in to and, more importantly, out of anything. But I wasn't thin enough to slip through the bars of any prison.

"No, but whether they accept my application or not, I can always come down to visit you."

"I can come up. I know cash is tight." Empathy radiated

through every word. Cat knew what it was like to scrimp and save, to double-check your accounts before you bought a candy bar, but she'd left that behind once she put those language skills into action and hadn't looked back. She had enough shit to deal with when it came to her family and her new healthy paychecks.

I wouldn't be another hand held out, expecting her to take care of things.

"The odds of you scoring a whole twenty-four hours off the clock seems unlikely. Plus, I don't know if this building has a helicopter pad for when you're called back by the Ivans like a homing pigeon." Sometimes it felt she worked for a much hotter version of Miranda Priestly from *The Devil Wears Prada*—with even worse boundaries.

"They're seriously not paying me enough for this shit." She said it like she'd repeated it to herself many times in her head already. "Either way, we'll see each other, yes?"

"Absolutely!" It had been over a year. I was ready to fling open my windows and scream with excitement, but I bundled it up, not wanting to get my hopes up. Her schedule changed at a moment's notice, and I didn't want her to feel bad if she couldn't make it.

She yawned again. "Awesome." It sounded more sleepy than enthusiastic. "I miss you."

"I miss you too."

"Where are you now? Out?" She woo'ed and I imagined her with her sleepy arms overhead like she was at a club or out at a bar. "Getting some much needed time on the dance floor?"

"Yes, I'm at a silent rave."

"Ohh, I went to one before—"

Of course she had.

"I'm out, but not like that." I broke in before she related yet another of her stories that made me feel like I'd never fit as much crazy in my life as she had in only one weekend.

"Where are you?"

"Waiting outside of a Philly brownstone for Hunter's little brother to finish a college alumni interview."

The pause was so long I checked to make sure the call hadn't dropped.

"Okay, I'll need to be fully awake for *that* conversation. But right now, I'm about to pass out." Another yawn. "Night, Sabrina."

"Sleep well. Turn your phone off as soon as we're finished talking."

"Son of a bitch," she growled. "Too late."

"What?"

"Ivan No. 2 just texted me. Maybe I can hide out in your apartment after I murder him."

"Please don't. Tickets to Russia are super expensive, and I'd prefer not to visit you in a prison there."

"Don't worry, we're in Norway. Their prisons are supposed to be super nice."

I couldn't be sure she was joking. Not wanting to take any chances, I blurted out, "Please don't kill your boss." Damn it, now I was probably on a list and they'd play this recording at her trial.

Her drowsy reply calmed my nerves—some. "I'll think about it. Love you. Bye!"

I stared at the glowing screen of my phone before looking up ticket prices to Norway. Damn, that was expensive. Please don't let her get arrested tonight.

My pacing and leg shakes to keep warm on the sidewalk drew a few sideways looks from people passing by. I waved, my cheeks no longer burning from the wind whipping around the corner.

The yellow door Ryder had stepped through earlier opened, lighting up the stairs. He wore a wide smile and seemed like he'd grown an inch since he'd walked inside. Turning on the doorstep, he extended his hand, shaking an older man's hand before stepping back off the stoop.

I walked toward him with small, measured steps, not wanting to make it to them before they'd finished saying goodbye.

The door closed. After checking over his shoulder, Ryder rushed forward, grinning so wide *my* cheeks hurt.

"It went well."

He grabbed me and hugged me tight before releasing me. "He's a former member of the admissions committee. He said I'd make a great addition to the incoming class and he'd make sure they knew."

I grabbed onto his coat sleeves and jumped up and down like an idiot, joy volleying back and forth between us. Someone needed to celebrate his win. "I knew you'd kick ass in there."

He sobered a bit and his head ducked. "Thanks for your help."

Grabbing his arm, I pulled him down the block. "I'm happy to help any time you need it."

After walking Ryder to the Speedline stop, I went back to the apartment, trying to think of ways to bridge the gulf between the two brothers. Inside, I dropped my things in my room before changing, grabbing some chicken tortilla soup with some chips, cheese and sour cream added on top and taking my place at the puzzle table.

The spoon clinked against the side of my bowl. There were five more rows of the picture completed. My head snapped to the empty doorway. Maybe there was some hope for us—him—yet. Definitely not us. There was no us, and there wouldn't be an us. But that didn't mean we couldn't get along and make the best of the next couple months.

With a slight smile, I dug into my soup and worked my way through the next set of pieces.

"Why would you make that deal?" Everest chucked a thick fabric sample book at my head.

It thumped open behind me, spraying swatches all over the floor. I rounded the table, trying to keep us at least a few feet apart.

His arm had gotten better after all his time hanging out with pro athletes, so I didn't want to give him an easy hit.

"I thought maybe it would be a chance for you two to hash it out. It's been years. The dance you two are doing... It might be better to just let it all out."

"And this has nothing to do with getting her band for your concert?" His voice rattled the windows of the conference room. Someone peered inside before wheeling right around and disappearing from view. A legal pad went sailing by my head. "You offered me up to lock down a band for your show."

"It's not just any band. It's Without Grey."

"I know who the fuck it is. You don't think I know who they are? They're the ones who stole her from me." His fingers tightened around the metal cup with whiteboard markers in it. He slammed the cup down and dropped into a chair.

"Stole her from you..." I walked around the table with my stomach plummeting and pulled out a chair beside him. "I thought you said you two agreed it wouldn't work when you met her after the Europe trip. You said it was mutual."

He took out one of the markers and rolled it under his flattened palm against the table. The cap beat out a rhythmic pattern. "I did say that, didn't I?" His lips twisted in a humorless smile.

My muscles locked. "She cheated on you? Why didn't you tell me? I'd have never asked her if I'd known that." Shock ricocheted through me—and guilt. Guilt that I'd even brought her up to him, and the jokes I'd thrown out over the years when it came to her. I'd walk away from the deal and figure out a different plan and make sure I didn't bring Maddy up to him again. Anger and bitterness burned in my chest at the thought that she was a fucking cheater.

"I never said she cheated." His words were rough and raw.

I rocked back in my chair. Some of the strain lessened. I hadn't been trying to force him to spend time with a woman who'd broken his trust and his heart, no matter how much he'd tried to pretend it wasn't the case. "So what the hell happened?"

He glanced at me. He fished the lighter that he always had with him out of his pocket, although he'd never smoked, and flicked the lid open and closed. The metallic scrape was the only sound in the conference room.

"It doesn't matter." He slammed the lid closed and spun it between his thumb and forefinger.

"Maybe it's why Camden made this part of the deal."

The lighter fell out of his grasp. "Camden wanted me to meet with her?" He stared at me like I'd told him aliens had beamed down and made the request.

"He said he wanted her to finally get some closure and for you two to finally talk things over."

His jaw clenched. "I'm sure he does want her to get closure. He wants her to move on so they can ride off into the sunset together." He snatched up the lighter and fisted it in his grip.

"It didn't feel like that—"

"She's still thinking about me." His eyes lit up with a hint of self-satisfaction and longing, which morphed into teeth-clenching bitterness. "The fucker needs me out of the way for good. The ghost of her past is haunting her even now." Shooting up from his chair, he turned to me. "I'll do it." He smiled, half-insane, half-longing, like even he wasn't a hundred percent sure how he felt about it.

And I wasn't going to be the one to push him over the edge.

"Ev, listen. I can find another way if you're not okay with this."

His jaw clenched, the muscles under his cheek bunching. "No, I want to do it."

I glanced around at the destroyed conference room littered with all the signs of how okay with this he was.

"Seriously, I can figure out—"

"Set it up." He'd mess up those perfect teeth with how hard he was grinding them, but I knew when to back off.

Maybe it would be good for both of them. Camden seemed to think so. Everest at least thought he thought so. Maddy...well, I wouldn't be asking for any other favors anytime soon.

"And don't forget we're on baking duty this weekend."

My mouth opened.

"You're not getting out of this. If I have to be there, you have to be there. Jameson will make all the funding for this project magically disappear if you screw with Teresa's big day."

I snapped my mouth closed and nodded. Jameson wasn't petty. He didn't do anything without a reason and wasn't one to be vindictive, except for when it came to his mom and little sister. He wouldn't pull funding, but he'd probably make me crawl over broken glass for the next year if I so much as put in a purchase order for extra pens.

Everest left the conference room, and I got to work cleaning up the mess. He was a whirlwind when he wanted to be.

Alone with my thoughts, I found myself right where I always was whenever I had a moment alone. My mind drifted to the only person who seemed to push through all the chaos happening up there.

Sabrina.

A sharpness stabbed at my thumb. I'd snapped a pencil, wanting to punch myself in the face over how things had gone down over the weekend.

I wanted to shove the broken wood from the pencil under my fingernails. I'd been too much of a coward to face her since our kiss.

Last night I'd slept on the floor of the bathroom, trying to upgrade myself from the bathtub. I'd woken and rapped my knuckles on the tub, flailing and feeling like my heart was trying to escape out of my throat. That had been all the confirmation I'd needed that I'd made the right choice, but I couldn't stop hating myself for not being strong enough to have slept next to her. Strong enough to wake up beside her and kiss her good morning before burying my face between her thighs to taste her until she cried out my name.

I slammed the notepads I'd gathered up on the conference table and stared at the whiteboard with all the plans I'd made and laid out for the guys—the ones that should be filling up my every waking moment. Instead it was her, and at this point I couldn't blame her for wanting nothing to do with me.

HUNTER

S abrina was becoming a temptation, and resisting only made it harder to walk away.

I'd slept in the bathtub again like a psycho. But the sleep hadn't been as sound. The lavender air freshener didn't smell like her. I hadn't woken up screaming, but I'd still been covered in sweat. This didn't feel like progress.

Work had to get done. Now that Without Grey was tentatively on board, it meant everything needed to be bigger.

"I'm arriving there now. We need all this rigging ASAP, and Trevor's the best deal I can get this close to New Year's Eve."

The flick of Everest's lighter carried through the earpiece. At least he was still talking to me. "We're still two months out."

"Unlike your events, which depend on which team wins, these things get planned a year in advance. I'm lucky I caught him, or we'd be paying double the price to have everything trucked in from Virginia."

"I like the sound of half the price."

"Me too."

I parked on the gravel lot outside the warehouse looming over me. The side door flew open, and Trevor, my contact, walked out in a pink polo with a popped collar and loafers with no socks. He rushed toward me like he didn't want to be associated with the warehouse on the industrial lot.

It had taken him twenty-four hours longer than expected to call me up after I "accidentally" tagged him in a social media post while out at a club with tables filled with bottle-service booze. I'd reached out to apologize, and he'd said we should catch up.

"I got to go, Everest. I talked it over with Maddy." A little white lie never hurt anyone. "She agreed to meet during the promo tour for the next album. It won't be until late next year. Are you good with that? If you are, then we can sign the contracts with Without Grey this week." Camden had come up with the idea of the promo tour. It would be a week, in a hotel where Maddy couldn't escape. "Ticket sales are going well, but this would push them over the top." In reality, the sales had been sluggish. Without Grey would skyrocket sales and save this event from the raging inferno it was threatening to turn into. Asking Everest for help knotted my stomach. I would not be the fuckup. No one else needed help aside from backup on the day of for bigger events, and usually we spent most of the time networking, not putting out fires. I wouldn't be the weak link, but I did need his help for this one.

"Fine, just put it on my calendar and I'll be there. Who knows, maybe she'll cancel, then we all win." His voice didn't make it sound like not meeting with her would be a win.

"Thanks, Everest, I owe you."

"And when I call in the favor, no matter what, I don't want any questions."

"None."

I ended the call and hopped out of the car. Trevor walked along the passenger side with his eyes locked onto the pristine paint job and whistled. "She's a beauty, Hunter."

"She certainly is." The Porsche Cayman wasn't mine. It was a short-term loan, a favor for a contact who needed to keep it on the road while he was in Australia for the year. Trevor was the classic silver-spoon type who was kept on a tight leash by his father. The multimedia company he'd started working at after graduation sold and rented tech to most major events in the area, but for now he was stuck in the lighting rentals department learning the ropes of the business.

The chip on his shoulder was so big sometimes I wondered if he wouldn't tip over.

I buttoned my jacket one-handed like I'd practiced for hours growing up with the suits my grandmother had given me back during my senior year of high school. Had I been the douche who wore suits to anything requiring a dress shirt back in high school and college? Maybe. But I knew it would get Trevor's attention.

His gaze snapped to my lapels and cuffs. "Nice suit. Where's it from?"

The charcoal-gray, mill-sourced Scottish wool came out when I needed to make a particular impression. "This?" I pulled at the edge of my jacket like I couldn't remember what suit I was wearing. "I'm pretty sure it was Common-wealth Proper, although it might've been Robbini Bespoke. The tailor came to my apartment, between a meeting I had with Without Grey and a dinner I had to get to at The Union

League and I was just needing to get it done, so we didn't have much time for small talk."

"I heard the waitlist is a few months long for both places." He rubbed his hand along his chin.

I cocked my head to the side. "Really? I didn't know. When I called them up, they gave me an appointment the same day." It helped that Everest worked with most pro athletes in the area, so they were always happy to give anyone at SWANK a spot.

Trevor reset and diverted his attention back to the car.

"When you said we should hang out, I thought you meant out-out, not just you swinging by my office."

"I was in the neighborhood and thought I'd stop by. I was out last night, we could've hung then, but I didn't hear from you."

He made a noise of displeasure. "My dad had us all at a corporate retreat. Just a bunch of guys sitting around talking about how to make sure everyone is happier and more productive at work. If they don't like it, they can leave."

Once he took over, his company would be paying through the nose in severance packages. I could see the talent bleed from a mile away.

He ran his hand along the midnight-blue spoiler fastened to the almost-nonexistent trunk. "I'd love to get one, but I need to prove to my dad I can be responsible with my money, which means I'm stuck with the Audi until my bonus comes in." He rolled his eyes like this was the most unfair stipulation put on the six-figure job that had been handed to him.

I'd known he'd like the car. It was why I'd brought it. "Things have been crazy. I've got a Siren Song event I'm putting together that's already twenty percent over capacity."

His head popped up. "At the Hale & Hue?"

"You know that place? The venue is so small getting any other bodies in there will be impossible, but I've got a VIP list a mile long and I'm turning people away. We physically can't get any more people into the place." I was laying the groundwork for my request for later, putting the pieces in place to pull off the huge ask.

"I haven't had time to check it out yet." He'd tried to get his name on the door list for the past five months.

"Maybe after Siren Song you could come by and it'll be less crazy."

He nodded absently, his gaze sweeping over the car. "Maybe..."

"Do you want to take it for a ride?"

His eyes lit up before his face dropped. "Yeah, but I can't open her up like I'd love to."

"I was planning on heading to the motorsports track after we caught up to see how hard I can push it. I can see if they could move up my time." I'd booked it for exactly this time.

He glanced back up at the building. "I told them in the office that I was meeting with a client?" A hint of sheepishness crept in. Maybe he wasn't one-hundred percent self-absorbed.

"We can have a meeting then. We can talk and drive, right? I could be a client." I dangled the key fob.

He strode around to my side of the car. "Hell, yeah. Let's go." He grabbed the key from my hand and jumped in, unable to contain his excitement.

We got to the test track in record time. I'd have to apologize to the car owner for the finger dent on the roof of his car.

During our break after two laps, I handed Trevor a bottle of water and went in for the ask, while his body was humming with endorphins after hitting 135 MPH on his last run.

"Did I tell you about the party I've got going on for New Year's?"

"No, where at?"

"Wells Fargo Center."

He gulped down the water. "Sounds like more than a party."

"It might be a little more than that. We've got some great bands. I took over the promotions and prep from Easton Events."

He snorted. "Those guys were absolute assholes."

"But their incompetence has put me in a bind. I need lighting rigs for my New Year's Eve concert."

He leaned back against the car like he owned it. "Are we providing the sound and stage?"

"No, that was already confirmed and paid for by another team before I signed on." All the avenues this conversation could go down had been mapped out in my head on the way over. It helped that Trevor wasn't a particularly imaginative kind of guy.

He winced and stared up at the sky. "My dad has this hard-on for package deals. He wants to lock in whole events just for us."

"I can understand that, and we'll definitely add your team to the top of all our future lists."

His brow creased, and his lips tightened.

"I haven't made the announcement yet, but I can tell you first." I glanced over my shoulder, selling the secret. "Without Grey's going to be performing. That's what my meeting with them was about." I'd spit shine Everest's shoes for a year, but I wasn't going to let this opportunity slip through my fingers when I was so close.

He shot up from the car, choking on his water. "No fucking way."

I grinned. "Yes, they'll be there and if you're providing the lighting rigs, then I'm sure I could get you a meet-and-greet with the band."

His demeanor shifted and became more subdued, disinterested. It seemed he'd learned a few things working with his father, but I could see the glint of how much he wanted this in his eye.

He shrugged. "That would be cool, but it would be a lot of hassle dealing with my dad over it." His fingers tightened on the bottle. Man, did I need to set up a poker game with him. I'd walk away with half his trust fund.

"I could sweeten the pot if you wanted. Tell me what you want."

He went full lean against the car with his ankles crossed and arms folded in smugness. "I want a spot on the guest list for two for Siren Song."

"Dude, that's impossible, I told you." What was almost impossible was keeping up this performance, but duty called.

"I guess you'll have to figure out which VIP is getting booted to make room for a bigger one. If you want the rigs, that is." He took a gulp from his water bottle.

Dealing with guys like him was easy. If he felt like he was putting someone in a tight spot, getting one over on people who rolled in his circles, and he got to make some money as well, it was a deal he couldn't walk away from.

I spent a couple minutes grimacing, staring at my phone and making fervent texts where I asked August about cake flavors and Leo about his skincare routine. Their replies blew up my phone, filled with even more questions and emojis used in ways I don't think the inventors intended. At one point I turned the phone sideways trying to figure out the coded message from August. He wanted me to put my eggplant where?

With a grimace, I turned to Trevor and shoved my hand into my pocket. "I'm going to have my ass handed to me over this, but I got you a spot. I can't even tell you who I had to kick off the list." I let out a long, deep breath and shook my head.

He rocked forward. "Who?"

"No, I can't tell you, but..." I dragged my hand through my hair. "Let's just say there's a pro football player out there who wants to punt my ass through the uprights right now."

His eyes widened, and so did his grin.

"We have a deal, right? You'll get me all the rigs at the price I need them."

He extended his hand. "Consider it done."

"Good." I wish there were an audience because I deserved a fucking standing ovation. Normally I'd have more time to work the angles to make this a trade in my favor, but with my ass to the flames, I'd take him feeling like we were even when he'd gotten me something I needed that would've cost an arm and a leg to source from elsewhere.

I drove us back to his warehouse office, no longer needing to put my life in Trevor's hands now that we had our deal, and headed back to the city. Back to my apartment. Back to Sabrina.

I'd kiss her again. Any thoughts I'd had about chalking the first time up to a fluke were blown out of the water when I couldn't keep myself from touching her.

Her comment about the drinks had made me feel like a dick. I wasn't someone who liquored a woman up and then went in for the pounce. She was a temptation beyond any I'd faced before. I'd never wanted anything as much as I wanted to feel her against me.

It rocked me to my core. My fingers gripped the wheel even tighter. This was about denial. We'd been doing the denial dance for so long, of course all I could do was think about her. She lived in my apartment.

I saw her every day and she was forbidden fruit.

There was only one way to keep myself from going off the deep end. Indulge, but not too much. Just enough to take the edge off. Satiate myself and her, then back away into normalcy.

My sleep wasn't as bad anymore. The tub situation wasn't ideal, but at least it helped me get my head on straight for long enough to sort through the wheelbarrows of paperwork I needed to complete.

Maybe the two of us could work out an agreement. She'd be here until the end of the year according to her. Two more months.

From the moment I stepped inside the apartment, I could tell she was here. I peeked into the dining room, but from the silence I knew she wasn't inside. The puzzle we'd worked on had a few more rows completed but there were still large chunks that didn't have any connection to the border yet.

Her door was open. I peeked into her bedroom. The computer hadn't gone to sleep yet. Her bathroom door was open.

My heart rate spiked, thinking back to our conversation yesterday.

"Sabrina," I called out for plausible deniability in attempting to alert her to my presence.

I checked the laundry room after and found it empty as

well. My blood hammered in my veins at the idea of where she was right now and what she was doing. My bedroom door at the end of the hallway was open wider than I'd left it.

All I was doing was going to my bedroom. Maybe getting myself ready for a shower after a long day at work.

The jingle of droplets hitting water sent all that blood rushing straight to my cock.

The bathroom door was open. Her gentle hum filled the silence of my bedroom. There was only one question filling my head.

What next?

My application to Apparel & Textile Expo had once again been rejected. Apparently having no revenue in my company I'd spent money to create on paper had been a flag for the organizers. There was still no word from Harper Linens, but I couldn't exactly eat the sheets they'd sent over and the grocery money would run out by the end of the month. The grind and rejection were getting to me, which meant relaxation was in order.

No longer needing to sneak into Hunter's room like I was a member of the *Mission: Impossible* team had taken some of the danger and excitement out of my life, but that had been replaced with the endless thoughts about him.

Sweet Hunter was harder to deal with than Asshole Hunter. He made me want things I'd vowed not to pursue until I had my life together. Or at least wasn't bumming a place to live off his Grandma.

I lifted my arm, letting the water drip off my fingertips. Resting my head against the tub, I closed my eyes, happy for the dimmer in the bathroom. I wished I could light a few candles to bring on the full spa experience.

But I didn't want to overstep. Hunter had given me his blessing, but that didn't mean I could start staking my claim on his space.

The sand under my feet continually shifted when it came to him. It felt like he was avoiding me, sometimes running away from me. Maybe I was less interesting when he thought no one wanted to watch me sleep with random guys. The kiss burned brightly in my mind, the ember of a memory that refused to be extinguished. Our puzzle night of fun hadn't done much to un-confuse me when it came to what exactly we were doing. But what he did do to me sure as hell felt good. I let my fingers drift down between my legs.

"Glad you're making yourself comfortable."

I shot forward, sloshing water close to the edge of the tub, and my arm shot across my chest before I sank back into the water. "Hunter! Hi! I—I didn't think to ask before I got in. I'm sorry, if you'll turn around, I'll get out of here. After sitting at my desk all my muscles felt like they'd seized up, so I thought I could get in and get out before you noticed. I didn't use the lavender oil."

He stood in the doorway with one arm propped up against the frame. His black-and-silver cuff links glittered in his double-cuff sleeves, and he held onto a charcoal jacket slung over his shoulder. Built in a way that looked natural, not from hours obsessing at the gym, he was a walking wet dream.

Good thing I was in the bath already.

"I said you could use it."

"Did you need to use it? I can hop out." And go into my room, crawl under the sheets, and die of embarrassment. Good thing he hadn't arrived five minutes later when I'd have been in the throes of a full-on Hunter-inspired masturbation session.

He set his blazer down on the counter and slipped off his cuff links. "You don't need to hop out."

Goose bumps rose on my whole body, tightening my flesh even in the warm bath. "I don't?"

"Only if you want to." He stared at me, and there was a flicker in his eyes like he'd made a decision.

My stomach flipped, straight into a back handspring. "I don't?"

The corner of his lips lifted. "Was that a question?" He rolled his sleeve from the cuff, folding the pressed white fabric higher up his arm, exposing the tanned and sinewy forearms. Veins, tendons, muscle.

"No. I just got in, but I wasn't expecting an audience." Had the heat kicked on? Because my skin not submerged in the water didn't feel the slightest bit chilled. It felt closer to super-heated as his gaze swept over me.

"You're driving me absolutely crazy."

Standing beside the tub, towering over me, he could see my body beneath the water.

A shiver skated along my skin.

"In a good way?" My body was on high alert, vibrating in a wanton way where the water teased and taunted body parts like I wanted his fingers to.

"In the worst way." He finished with his second sleeve, never taking his eyes off me. Eyes blazing with a carnal passion that sent shock waves through me. "Do you want me to leave?"

I fought the urge to squeeze my legs together. "No."

He walked behind me, disappearing from my view. But I could feel him. His heated gaze warmed the air around me. My shoulders, the back of my neck, flushing my skin without a single touch.

The rustle of fabric against fabric. The thump of hard-soled shoes and the thud of a leather wallet against the tiles.

My awareness of every movement and the anticipation of what came next made my breaths short and choppy.

"Good." The whispered word was against the back of my neck, so close his lips brushed the shell of my ear.

A tremble shot through me. My heart raced, galloping in my chest.

His fingers trailed down my shoulder. His stubble scraped against my cheek. His lips sought out mine.

One of his hands rolled my wet, stiff nipple between his fingers while the other hand fisted my hair and turned my head to the side until his mouth found its mark.

His lips were searing on mine. If our kiss in my bedroom had been a Fourth of July sparkler, this was a grand finale New Year's Eve fireworks extravaganza.

I felt the scrape of a shirt against my back as his fingers dipped lower, breaking the plane of the water as they slid down my body, turning the shivers into shudders.

I sank into the kiss. The back of my head resting against the back of the tub gave me no escape—not that I wanted one—from the engulfing power of Hunter's mouth.

Moaning and squirming, I held onto his arm. Water droplets from my fingers flowed down over my chest.

His fingers dipped between my legs, teasing my clit. The ministrations intensified when his finger pressed inside me. His thumb worked the electrified bundle of nerves while he pushed a second finger inside, followed by another. The strum of his thumb on me sent my back arching off the tub. An explosive orgasm ripped through me and made it feel like the bathwater around me should be sizzling.

I ripped my mouth away from his and cried out, clamping my thighs around his hand, trapping him against me. The water splashed and sloshed when I came down, still clinging to his arm.

Panting hard, I turned and shifted up onto my knees and placed both hands on the sides of his face to bring him closer.

Instead of pulling me out of the tub—still in his clothes like he was in a trance, unable to stop himself—he climbed in with me.

I yelped and tried to back up. The rough scrub of fabric, zippers and buttons sent aching, needy pulses shooting through my body.

The water spilled over the edge of the tub from the rapid displacement before settling at a height just under my breasts. The water licked at the undersides of them. I laughed. "I could've gotten out."

"I wanted to get in." His arms looped around me and pulled me against his chest with hands splayed across my back.

The rub of his wet clothes against me clashed with the sensations from the water and the smoothness of the tub.

"I can see that."

His hand squeezed and massaged my ass, grinding me against him. Bright blue eyes stared back at me, filled with mischief and desire. "Are you clean yet?" He picked up my loofah bobbing in the water and dragged it along my back.

A shiver shot through my body. My nipples rubbed against the sodden fabric clinging to his chest. "I can't quite remember."

"Maybe we should wash you up again to be sure." The loofah skimmed from my shoulders, down over the generous curve of my ass.

I fumbled with the wet buttons of his shirt and flung it open once all were undone. I shoved at the soggy edges and pushed it off his shoulders. "Most people undress before they get into the bath."

He grinned and traced his finger from my cheek down my collarbone. "What can I say? I was distracted."

Beads of water dripped from his fingers and rolled down my chest like he controlled the water to tease and caress me.

Feeling braver than I'd ever felt before, settled between his thighs, I leaned forward and stole another kiss.

He met my lips with a scalding intensity. His fingers sank into my hair pulling me tighter against him and stealing my breath.

Panting, I jerked back, trying to catch my breath under the spell of suffocating lust.

His chest rose and fell. His hands dropped to my ass, kneading and massaging.

I slid my fingers along his wet, bare torso down to the buttons and zipper of his pants. Sliding my hand inside, I stroked up and down his solid length. The water splashed with each stroke.

He sucked in a ragged breath. His hips jerked in response to my touch. "What you're doing is probably illegal in five states." His head banged back against the back of the tub.

A rush of power flowed through me at how tightly he gripped my hips and the clench of his jaw, like he was barely hanging onto his control.

The zipper bit into my skin, and I pulled his weighty length out of his pants. He hissed and tugged me forward now that I had more leverage.

"You have to stop, or I'm never even going to make it inside you."

I smirked. "Oh, is that where this is going?" I ran my thumb over the head of his cock.

His eyes snapped open, and his Adam's apple bobbed up and down. "You're dangerous."

The fire in his gaze sent an all-over shudder of anticipation rolling through me like an ocean wave.

"I've never heard that one before."

His fingers slipped between my legs, toying with my clit until sharp gasps shot from my lips. "It's absolutely true. You've got me on the brink of control with how good you feel."

A battle of the wills where we were both winners. My hips rocked against him, and his rolled with my touch. Our gazes stayed locked, transfixed on each other. The clear blue blazed with an unquenchable fire, which added to the pleasure flooding every nerve ending.

"I can't take anymore." He tugged me toward him, the head of his cock tapped against my clit, and my head dropped back.

I rocked forward.

He nudged at my opening.

"Shit, one second." He bit out and leaned over the edge of the tub and rumbled around before picking up his wallet. His muscled ass certainly improved the aesthetic of the bathroom. Out of his wallet, he produced a shiny metallic wrapper. He tore into it and rolled it on with a practiced efficiency I couldn't be jealous of right now.

I needed him inside me.

He sat on the wide edge of the tub with his back against the wall and beckoned me forward, positioning my legs on the outside of his.

His hands gripped my ass, tugging me closer. Releasing me with one hand, he cupped my cheek. "You're beautiful, Sabrina."

In a fluid motion I wouldn't have thought possible, he

lifted me and dropped me down on his lap, stretching me with each glorious inch. The pleasure danced with pain at the invasion, unlike any I'd felt before.

I grabbed his shoulders and gasped, sinking down onto him. With one thrust of his hips, our legs met again and I was fully seated, moaning and clinging to Hunter.

Although I was on top, I felt like I was along for the ride. Muscled thighs beneath mine worked in concert with his hands and arms to drive into me with an unmatched ferocity. Water splashed around our calves, sloshing around, masking some of the sounds we made.

He canted his hips, changing the angle, and intently rubbed against the spot I'd only been able to find on my own.

I clawed at his back, and my moan turned into a scream. I threw my head back and trusted him to keep me from falling. My orgasm hit swiftly, like slamming into a brick wall of pleasure. There was nowhere to go. There was only him.

Both his arms wrapped around my back, and he hugged me to him with his hips moving even faster and drawing out his pleasure as he expanded inside me, filling the condom and heightening the white-hot blaze of my own climax.

Shuddering and trying to catch my breath, I collapsed against him, resting my head against his shoulder.

"Wow." I laughed.

His hands tightened on my back. "You're not kidding." He chuckled, the sound reverberating against my chest.

Then his muscles tensed, and he ground out, "Fuck."

20

HUNTER

"What?"

Pain shot through my calf like the muscle was trying to be ripped from the bone.

"Are you okay?" Sabrina lifted herself off me.

We both groaned at the loss, but mine was augmented by the stabbing in my leg.

"Cramp." I slid off the edge of the bath, trying to straighten my leg. "Cramp in my calf."

Her gaze darted from my face to my leg, some of the tension easing from her stance. "Okay, let's get you out of the tub."

She bent to get my pants, soaking wet and trapped around my ankles, off. But the full-on nude view of her did nothing to help with the blood-flow imbalance in my legs.

I gritted my teeth to try to calm myself, when all I wanted to do was collapse onto the bathroom floor and not move until the pain went away.

"Hold onto me and we'll get you into bed." She handed me a towel and took my arm.

I looped my arm around her shoulder, wrapped the

towel around my waist and hobbled to the bed, trying not to shout.

Still dripping wet, she glowed like a sea enchantress and a torturer when she set my leg onto her nude lap and ground her fingers into my spasming calf muscle. "How's that?"

I gripped the bed and tried not to yell. "Don't stop. Push harder." Clenching my jaw, I stifled my shout when she leaned into it and applied more pressure.

Her fingers moved all around the muscle, kneading and massaging. The sharp pains loosened to no more than a dull ache, and I collapsed back onto the pillows against my headboard.

I was left sweaty and panting. I'd never had a cramp worked out quite like this, although I preferred our workout in the bathroom above anything else I'd ever done in the gym—or anywhere else, for that matter. Even now, her scent invaded my nostrils and relaxed me even more.

She smiled, crawled up the bed on her knees, and fell into my extended arm, which I wrapped around her.

Under my towel, my dick was ready to shake off that embarrassing display for another chance with Sabrina. I'd already had her once but couldn't stop myself from wanting her all over again. The lavender smell seemed ingrained in her skin, a lingering scent that could've been overpowering, but mixed with her own natural smell, it was heady.

Lying beside her, it would be easy to fall asleep. Quick and blissful until I was ripped from sleep in a cold sweat, swinging at ghosts from my past.

The bathtub worked on the worst of the nightmares. I could sleep. I didn't wake up screaming, but I did wake drenched. It was still too big of a risk to take, sleeping next to her.

I slid out of bed and went back into the bathroom. Looking around, I spotted her clothes and towel. I gathered it all up and brought it back with me into my room.

She was still on top of the blankets with a small smile playing on her lips. Stunning in every sense of the word and there was a rightness I felt in my chest at having her in my bed. But she couldn't stay there.

After setting her things on the edge of the bed, I shook out the towel and motioned her forward. Swallowing against the tightness in my throat as she crawled toward me, I shoved my hips against the edge of the bed so my erection couldn't spring up and cause even more trouble.

She sat in front of me on her knees. Full, heavy breasts I couldn't wait to lick and suck all over again swayed with every move.

I shook my head, trying to beat back those thoughts. If I fell into bed with her, there was no way I wasn't falling asleep with her in my arms, and that wasn't possible.

Gently lifting the ends of her hair, I blotted it with the towel to keep it from getting her pajamas wet.

"Well, this is a surprise." She cocked her head to the side and smiled.

My chest was tight, bracing for what came next. I lifted her shirt up and pulled it down over her head.

"And they say chivalry is dead." Her smile widened, and my heart ached. This was exactly why I'd been trying to avoid this situation.

"Not completely." The crank tightened between my ribs.

She popped her arms out of the sleeves, and I grabbed her pajama pants, kneeling on the floor and trapping my dick the best I could. I couldn't help myself and ran my hands up her legs before getting a grip and pulling her pajama bottoms on as well.

"We had fun tonight." I shoved down all the other ways I wanted to describe it. How I'd felt things with her I'd never felt with anyone else. How I'd felt things I'd vowed to never let myself feel.

"Yeah, a lot of fun. It was certainly the most vigorous bath I've ever taken." She laughed and lifted her hips off the bed to help me, and I was mouthwateringly tempted to drag them right back down and prop both her legs over my shoulders and feast on her until she ripped half my hair out and was hoarse with screaming my name.

Instead I held onto her waist, not letting my hands sink into her supple flesh like I wanted.

I cleared my throat, the tightness making it hard to breathe. Staring up at her, I was in awe.

She was the most beautiful woman I'd ever seen, from her breathtaking smile to the mischievous twinkle in her eyes to how she filled out her pajama top. All of me wanted all of her, and that was a huge fucking problem.

"Then we both agree. We had a fun time."

Her head tilted, and her lips parted. Her tongue darted out to lick them. Could she still taste me too? "We did. What are you trying to say?"

I bowed my head and got my dick under control before standing and kissing her. With the reins tightened on my desire, I kissed her but didn't let myself plunge headfirst into her taste.

"I'm saying, we don't need to make this more than it was. It was a mistake."

Her smile fell, and a soft gasp burst through her lips. She looked at me with stricken eyes.

"I don't want things to be weird because we're room-mates." I picked up her things and handed them to her. "I'm going to take a shower, so you can head back to your room. Night, Sabrina."

Rushing into the bathroom, I closed the door against every instinct I had, which wanted to dive back into the bed and take her with me.

Inside the bathroom, I rested my head against the door and closed my eyes. It didn't smell like her in here anymore. The scent didn't wrap itself around me with comfort. But I had to be strong enough not to get involved with her.

In the distance, a door slammed. Her door. I turned on the shower for plausible deniability and grabbed a few towels. With steam filling the bathroom, I went to work on drying the tub, every moment that I wasn't in bed with Sabrina with my arms wrapped around her a torture. The faint smell was stronger inside the tub, but coupled with all the memories of what we'd just done, it would be even harder to get to sleep, possibly even more impossible than it had felt only a week ago.

With everything dry, I grabbed my blanket and stared at the empty tub. Was this what it had come to? Would I spend the rest of my life hiding in a damn tub so I didn't wake up in a panic, feeling like my heart was trying to hammer its way through my sternum?

Sabrina most likely hated me, and I couldn't even blame her. I'd rather she hate me than pity me. Tonight was the last night I'd sleep in here. I needed to shake this off, whatever it was.

After lying in the tub for a half hour, unable to stop the flashes of how I'd taken her with water sluicing off our bodies and wanted to do even more, I went back into my bedroom and grabbed the book off my table.

Nothing like a little childhood nostalgia to kill the nonstop thoughts of how she'd tasted, smelled, and felt that refused to subside. I'd get some sleep, and tomorrow I'd sleep in my bed and white-knuckle my grip on my insomnia and nightmares and maybe find a way to get back into Sabrina's good graces.

Maybe.

21

SABRINA

I closed my computer and banged my head against my desk.

What had I been saying about wanting to keep my hands off Hunter? About how terrible an idea it would be to get involved with him? How he was probably a womanizing asshole?

Turned out, my instincts weren't shot to shit and I'd been absolutely right.

Now I was in the unfortunate situation I'd been trying to avoid in the first place. Living with a guy I had the hots for and also hated, without anywhere else to go.

There was the option of going home to Arizona and sleeping on the futon in my mom's sewing room. But the Apparel & Textile Expo was so close, if I could just get an invite. My design skills were good. I could create and print up a fake pass and wander in like I belonged and carpet bomb the place in my samples before security threw me out.

How long until Hunter decided the living situation was a bit too awkward and Barbara called me up and said it would be best if I moved out? I should soak all his underwear in bleach.

These were all mature ideas to help with my current life status.

A trip to the gym was what I needed. It wasn't like I could feel any worse about myself.

Forty-two seconds into my one hour—who was I kidding? Twenty-minute workout—my name was said, so close to my ear that I lost my footing. My feet flew out from under me. One second I was glaring at the red blinking treadmill display, and the next I was staring up at the ceiling of the apartment building's state-of-the-art gym.

"Sabrina?" There it was again.

No. No. No. I'd obviously died and this was my oxygen-deprived brain playing one last joke on me.

Hunter hovered over me. His bright blue eyes brimmed with concern.

"I'm okay." I closed my eyes, trying to keep my face from bursting into flames. This was exactly what I got for attempting to work out. *Message received, universe.* I wouldn't make this mistake again.

Strong hands gripped my shoulders.

My eyes popped open.

Hunter crouched beside me and stared intently. His worry sent a shot of anger flooding my veins. Where did he get off looking at me like that? Like he cared. Like he hadn't unceremoniously shoved me out his bedroom door minutes after the best sex of my life. Like he wasn't the world's biggest dickhead and I didn't want to punch him in the balls.

I shook his hands off. "I said I'm fine." At least there was no one else in the gym. My humiliation had been restricted to a man I'd already humiliated myself in front of. Thank God for small favors.

I pushed myself off the floor.

Hunter's hand pressed against my back.

"I don't—" I whipped around. That was a mistake. Dots swam in front of my eyes, and I swayed, grabbing the handrail of the treadmill.

"Sabrina, sit down." He held onto my hand with his other arm wrapped around my back and walked me to the polished wooden bench beside the water cooler with lemon slices floating inside.

"Seems I can't help but get banged up whenever you're around." I shrugged my shoulders to dislodge his arms from me, careful not to shake my head. My words came out sharper than I'd intended, and I'd only just caught myself from saying *hurt*. Being the wounded castoff wasn't how I wanted to live out the next two months in the apartment.

His gaze dropped, but he didn't back off.

Instead of leaving me to wallow in my embarrassment solo, he grabbed ice from the container on the other side of the cooler and wrapped it in a towel.

"Seriously, Hunter—"

He held the makeshift ice pack to my head, focusing on the towel like one shift of an ice cube might cause my brain to start leaking out my ears.

I swatted his hands away and kept the ice in place. "You can start your workout. I'll be fine. I just need a few minutes."

"That was a hard hit." He loosened his hold, but the arm he kept braced on the seat of the bench brushed against my back.

My stomach was overrun by an invasive butterfly species

that needed to be wiped out ASAP. The bump to the head hadn't knocked any sense into me.

"Thanks for the play-by-play. Go ahead with your workout."

"Let's get you up to the apartment."

"Why won't you just leave me alone like you asked to be left alone that night? Can't I get the same damn courtesy?" I shot up and immediately regretted it. Everything around me got woozy.

Hunter lunged forward and grabbed me, steadying me and stopping me from getting another hit to the head.

No face-saving for me. Nope, that would be way too much to ask. "Fine, let's go."

Begrudgingly, I walked back to the apartment with him hovering the whole way.

Once back in the apartment, Hunter typed furiously on his phone while I lay down on the couch. There was no nausea or any other concussion indicators I'd found through my rapid-fire Googling, although now I was pretty sure I had amoebic dysentery and possibly leprosy.

He left the room, and I stared at the ceiling. The crown molding was gorgeous. I closed my eyes and sketched out the patterns in my head and tried to think of ways to incorporate them into my newest design.

What was the point? I wasn't getting into the expo. No one wanted my designs. I'd never get even a baby toe in the door. And Harper Linens hadn't gotten back to me. My options were dwindling by the second, and so was the money in my bank account.

From the back of the apartment, Hunter's voice heightened in intensity. I guess he'd switched from texting to an actual call. There was a lot of bass and clipped, sharp responses.

"Do you want to get changed or go like you are?"

My eyes popped open. "Go where?"

"To see a doctor." He leaned over the back of the couch.

I swung my feet off the couch and sat up, waiting for any dizziness or weirdness, and there was nothing. That meant no concussion, right? The jury was still out on leprosy, but it meant I didn't have to spend any more money on a doctor. "I don't need to see a doctor." And I certainly didn't need the bill. At this point I'd camp out in DC outside the Apparel & Textile Expo and try to slip my samples into the conference goers' bags if that's what it took, so every penny counted.

"I'm taking care of it."

"Hunter..." I dragged my fingers through my hair and peered over at him. "Why are you doing this?"

"It's my fault you fell. The least I can do is make sure you're okay. The last thing I want to do is wake up in the morning and find out something happened to you because of me."

Why did he do this to me? The emotional whiplash was giving me more of a headache than the bump to the head. But it would make us both feel better to know everything was okay with me, plus the doctor would be able to discount the symptoms that, according to the internet, pointed to typhoid fever.

"I'll get changed." Standing, I took stock of how I felt, and it was more of the same. No dots, no lightheadedness or other issues. "Give me five minutes."

Hunter nodded and watched me with an intensity that flickered against my skin. Concern. That's all it was. Concern and nothing more. Who wanted to wake up with a dead woman in their apartment? Not Hunter.

I changed and waited by the front door.

He walked out after changing as well, with a small wrapped box under his arm.

"What's that?"

"It's for where we're going."

"You bring presents to your doctor?"

"Something like that." He opened the door and motioned for me to head out.

Our trip to his car was uneventful, and the drive took much longer than I'd imagined for his doctor, especially now that I felt fine. My head was a little achy, but there hadn't been any dizziness since we got to the apartment.

Maybe we should turn around now. No use wasting everyone's time when I was perfectly fine. I'd embarrassed myself enough already today.

We pulled up to the curb of a residential street, and I peered out the window at the houses on either side of the road.

"There's a doctor in here?" I laid the skepticism on nice and thick.

"There will be. I called a friend, and he said he'd stop by since today's his day off." He reached into the back seat and grabbed the blue-and-green wrapped box with the purple bow.

I leaned over in my seat and eyed the two-story house with painted shutters on the suburban street through Hunter's window. My stomach knots were loosening after we'd driven through the part of town where my old apartment had been—the one I'd shared with Seth. But fifteen more minutes away from there, I felt like I could breathe again. A quick glance down the empty street smoothed out the last bits of my frayed nerves, and I had room to be curious about what we were doing here.

Cars were parked in driveways and along the curb in both directions, but it was quiet. Maybe my knock to the head had me more paranoid than usual.

It wasn't like Seth and his wife would be wandering down the street hand in hand. I didn't even know where he really lived. Who the hell knew, maybe this was his neighborhood. My palms got clammy. Irrationality was taking hold. I flung the car door open, not wanting to be out in the open like this anymore.

I rounded the front of the car. "Where is this?"

"Jameson's mom's house."

"Why are we here? Is your friend Jameson a doctor?" I was pretty sure he worked at the event planning company with Hunter. The cars parked in front of this house were nicer than the rest along the street. A couple looked like one a doctor might drive, and one had a name I couldn't even pronounce in my head.

The front door flew open. "Hunter! Hunter! Hunter!" A little girl dressed in a Captain America helmet, Black Panther top, and Hulk pants barreled down the front steps and took five strides before flinging herself into Hunter's arms.

"We're here because it's this little munchkin's birthday." He turned to me with a sheepish grin.

He didn't seem the type to have elementary school friends—although on a maturity level, I wouldn't be surprised if they were on the same level.

"Happy birthday, Teresa."

"Teresa! Do I have to put the chain on the front door?" Jameson stood on the steps outside the front door in dark-rimmed glasses, a fitted t-shirt and jeans. He was the one who looked like a brown-haired Clark Kent—all he was missing was the curl against his forehead. He was a bit like the tech guy in a movie who still went through the same training regimen as the action hero.

"I didn't want Hunter to miss all the fun like last time." There was a hint of chiding in her tone.

I liked this kid already.

"I told Jameson I'd be here. Not even Sabrina giving herself a concussion could've stopped me from being here this time."

Well thanks for dragging me along. "I told him I was fine." I mumbled under my breath like I needed to justify the situation to the little girl.

Jameson flung a towel over his shoulder. "We've already got the first batch of cakes in the oven, but there's a lot more to do, so you're here just in time. Nice to see you again, Sabrina."

I flicked my wrist in a stiff wave and walked over to Hunter, who still had Teresa clinging to him. "We don't have to do this now. I can take a taxi back. I don't want to intrude." Fighting tooth and nail, I kept my bottom lip from between my teeth. Plus, going back across the bridge meant less of a chance of running into Seth. The whole state felt like a no-go zone now.

Hunter stared at me over his shoulder. "You're not. My doctor friend will be here in a little bit; then if you want, I can drive you to the apartment and come back for 'Happy Birthday.'"

"No! You have to help. It's what friends do. And it's all I wanted for my birthday." Teresa tightened her grip around Hunter's neck.

My paranoia and issues with Hunter weren't a justification for ruining Teresa's birthday. I could tough it out for a

couple hours. A checkup would stop my WebMD self-diagnosis wheels turning over the next week with every twinge
or bit of light-headedness. Other than a brief visit not too
long after I'd moved in, I didn't know them at all. Maybe
with more people around, those creeping feelings of
wanting to strangle or kiss him would be smothered and we
could move on from here and go back to ignoring one
another.

"If it's okay with the birthday girl, I'll stay so you don't
miss any fun."

Hunter bounced her in her arms. "What do you say,
Teresa? Is it okay if she stays?"

She peered over his shoulder and stared at me.

I waved, feeling lamely nervous that this little girl in a
Captain America helmet would serve up a thumbs-down
and banish me back to the car. Hunter deserved a mind-
game slow clap.

"Are you Hunter's girlfriend?"

Not expecting that line of questioning, I laughed. More
of a bark than an actual laugh, but I couldn't keep a straight
face. Laughter was better than letting the feelings I'd
tramped down since getting changed in the apartment make
all the doubts I had about myself come roaring back. "No,
not even a little bit."

Hunter's body went rigid, and his gaze darted to mine
with a flash of an unrecognizable emotion.

Teresa cocked her head to the side with her lips pressed
together. "That's what Zara said too." Leaning in, she
cupped her hands over Hunter's ear while keeping her eyes
on me.

He shook his head. "Let's get you inside." With the hand
holding the present pressed against her back, he swung
around to me, gesturing for me to go forward.

Jameson backed away from the door to let me enter and pushed his glasses up with the back of his hand. He wiggled his bright red fingers at me. "I'd shake your hand, but I don't want to permanently dye your skin. I'm still working out the kinks of working with fondant."

I laughed. His hands looked like one of the unfortunate images I'd scrolled through on my self-diagnosis rabbit hole, but I doubted he had a raging case of poison ivy all over them. "No problem."

Hunter closed the front door and set Teresa down, handing her the present. "For you."

She eyed it with her arms crossed. "But you're still staying, right?"

He smiled. "Of course."

Her tiny head bobbed and she took it from his hands, placed it down on the couch and whirled back around.

"Cake time." Teresa grabbed Hunter's and Jameson's hands and, using her full body weight, pulled them toward the kitchen. They smiled and let her drag them toward the door.

The kitchen door swung open, and another person jumped out of the way to let the steamroll of bodies past her.

Hunter called out over his shoulder, "Sabrina, you remember Zara, Leo's fiancée?" Then the door swung closed behind him.

Zara and I stared at each other for a second, still a little in shock at the strength of the little girl, and turned to each other.

"Good to see you again, Sabrina." The elevator ride conversation we'd had that one time the guys had all come to the apartment building had been short and she'd been on the way to pick her brother up from the airport, so we hadn't had much time to chat. "Thank god there's another woman here. Until Jameson and Teresa's mom, Rachel, gets off work, we're all we've got."

The kitchen door opened again.

"What about me?" Teresa jumped up and down beside Zara.

She crouched down beside the little girl. "How could we forget the birthday girl? Which Marvel movie are you on?"

"*Black Panther.*" She curled her fingers like claws.

"Do you want us to watch with you?"

Teresa pursed her lips with her head swinging from me to Zara. "No, it's okay. I'm sure you have grown-up things to talk about." And that was all before she scampered up the stairs.

"Ah, to have that much boundless energy." Her gaze swung from the stairs back to me and she sat on the couch. "How are things going rooming with Hunter?"

"They're going..." Instead of elaborating, I just left it there. The only thing more confusing than where the hell my life was going was how I'd get through the next couple months living under the same roof as Hunter. Kill or kiss. It was more of a debate than I'd have expected, with his stupid, sexy smile.

"It must be going well if he brought you here." A coy curiosity ran through her words, which she kept light, and her green eyes were primed to pump me for more info.

It was probably the shock of the century that he'd shown up with me. Hunter didn't exactly strike me as a guy who did relationships with his whole get-the-hell-out-of-my-bedroom routine after sex. I was surprised he didn't have an ejector seat or trapdoor installed in his room. It felt like something the building would probably install if he requested it.

"More like he tricked me into coming under the guise of a doctor's visit."

"He did?"

"It's a long story. Let's just say me and the treadmill won't be on speaking terms for quite some time after the fall I took." He was probably telling everyone it was why he brought me here in the first place, no sense in making a story up or being evasive. They seemed like a close-knit group.

I wished Cat were here. After leaving college I'd been mainly on my own until Seth. Maybe I was better on my own.

She sucked in her breath through her clenched teeth. "Sounds painful. That's why I refuse to work out. You don't want to invite injury like that into your life." Her laugh was infectious.

"It was more embarrassing than anything when Hunter found me sprawled out on the floor, but also painful. I was woozy, so he was adamant I see a doctor."

Her eyebrows scrunched down. "Is he going to have Jameson's mom check you out? She's a nurse."

"I'm not sure. He said a doctor friend, but maybe I misheard him." Had I missed the change of plans? He'd definitely said *doctor*. I was scratch-my-head confused at this point.

We sat on the couch and chatted a bit longer, trying to ignore the crashing and cursing coming from the kitchen.

Leaning forward, I stared at the kitchen door. "Should we go in there?"

"No, absolutely not. We can provide drink reinforcements in a little bit, but we're under strict orders from Teresa not to help." She shifted closer and whispered, "We'd be choked by testosterone in minutes or they'd try to foist the cake-making off on us, and I for one would prefer not to be picking icing out of my hair for the next week."

"A week?"

"I swear, Leo was sweating icing for a month after the last time."

I envisioned Hunter and I repeating our bathtub session after an inordinate amount of time spent licking icing off his skin. Flutters built in my stomach and between my thighs. "Must've made for some tasty fooling around." My eyes widened, and I slapped my hands over my mouth.

I jumped at her laugh. She peered over at me with tears shining in her eyes and clutching her stomach.

We both dissolved into laughter, which was heightened by the thudding and banging coming from the other room.

After a few deep breaths, I collapsed back onto the couch. Turns out I got an ab workout today after all. My stomach muscles ached from the laughing fit.

I hadn't realized how nice it was to have someone else to talk to. Someone who was easy to relax around. Someone who wasn't nine time zones away.

Zara leaned back. "Having you here adds even more fun to watching five grown men attempt to make a cake like they're building a homemade rocket. At least you'll be here next year, so I won't have to suffer alone."

That froze the last of my laughter in my chest, and I shook my head. "Hunter and I aren't a thing. I'm not just saying that to be coy. And we won't even be roommates after December. I have a new promotional campaign I'm shooting that pays out at the end of December. Then I'll finally have enough saved to find a place of my own." I turned back to her. "What do you do?"

"A boring job." From the way her eyes lit up, I could tell

she found it anything but. "I'm an interior designer for the Waverly Hotels Group."

My heartbeat skipped. A fellow designer. "Shut the front door! Are you serious?"

Zara laughed and looked at me like she wasn't quite sure if I was making fun of her or not. "Yes. Are you a big fan of interior design? Or Waverly Hotels?"

"Both." I held one hand to my chest. "Sorry, I'm having a fangirl moment. I'm a textile designer."

Her head cocked to the side. "Hunter said you were into product photography."

"That too, but I'm trying to move into textile designs, preferably in-house. Pitching and winning these smaller jobs is a grind, and I don't know how much longer I can keep up with it. That's why I've been trying to get my foot in the door somewhere with my design work. I even reached out to Waverly." My cheeks heated with embarrassment. I'd applied for their textile scholarship and had been rejected. Same with all the other applications I'd put in for various positions.

Zara's eyebrows shot up, and she leaned in closer. "Really? Are you going to the Apparel & Textile Expo? That's where so many deals and decisions are made." Her excitement was palpable.

I sank back into the couch, disappointment and sadness winding tightly in my stomach. The place where it all happened and I'd been shut out over and over. "I've tried a bunch of times, but I'm not a registered buyer or company, so...."

"Oh, I hadn't realized there were requirements to get a ticket." Her stunned look turned to one of pity.

Don't mind me, just a loser you're sharing a couch with. Don't worry. It's not contagious. At least I didn't think it was. *Let's shift this off me.*

"Are you going?"

She nodded and ran her thumb along her bottom lip. "I've gone for the past two years. It's nice it's so close this year. I was just planning on taking the train down." Her lips pinched with preoccupation.

"I thought so too, but every application I submit is rejected. I even spent money registering an LLC, but no dice. It's not a big deal. If I can't go, I can't go." I shrugged, trying to play it off like it wasn't the biggest deal in making the jump from product photographer to textile designer who actually got paid for her work that didn't just live in her makeshift studio.

Zara was probably trying to come up with a gracious way to exit this conversation.

Her head shot up. "Let me see what I can do. I know we get a ton of passes for the design and buying teams. Last year I'm sure there were extras. If I got you a ticket, do you think you'd be able to make it?"

My heart stopped for a second, and I nearly jumped out of my seat. Had she just asked what I thought she'd asked? Gripping the cushions beneath me, I nodded so hard the ache in the back of my head returned.

"I'd walk on the highway if I had to. Do you think they'll give a pass to me, even if I don't work for Waverly?"

"It's not a lock, but I'm pretty sure I can make it happen."

I'd flung myself at her, nearly knocking us both off the couch, before I could contain myself. "Zara, you're my new favorite person. Holy shit!"

She laughed and returned my hug. "It's not a done deal yet. I'll let you know on Monday."

Bouncing in my seat, I gripped the cushion so I didn't tackle her again.

Maybe coming here hadn't been a massive mistake after all.

22

HUNTER

Every surface in the kitchen was covered with baking tools and supplies. Tools that looked like torture devices were coated in red fondant, which wasn't helping with the crime-scene look Jameson had culti-vated in the overly full kitchen.

Cake flour, powdered sugar, blocks of butter, regular sugar, brown sugar, and enough eggs to make Rocky proud covered the counter. Five guys crammed into a domestic kitchen with more machinery than a small restaurant had ratcheted up the heat in here. I might've gone the tiniest bit overboard with the favor I'd put in for with a local restau-rant, Tavola, asking for some of their portable ovens and other supplies.

We each had a station. Leo was on vanilla cakes. Everest was on chocolate cakes, which were Teresa's favorites. August and I were handling chocolate and vanilla icing. Jameson had been stuck with the fondant and modeling chocolate. It was only fair.

"So Sabrina, huh?" Leo grinned at me while he locked the metal bowl under the stand mixer.

I added milk to the powdered sugar and butter whirring around in the mixing bowl, pointedly ignoring him.

Watching her fly through the air and slam into the floor had sent my heart rocketing into my throat. When she'd tried to push me away and got woozy, it cemented my commitment not to leave her alone.

"It's not a big deal that she's here." It was a huge deal. I'd never introduced a woman to the guys before.

She'd met them during a meeting we'd had in the apartment not long after she'd moved in, but even that made her the only woman I'd ever been attached to who'd met them. Everyone else had introduced someone they were dating for various reasons. Leo had brought Zara to Teresa's the first year after she gotten the engagement ring that belonged to neither of them stuck on her finger. I'd helped them out of that mess.

We'd all known Maddy back in college. She'd been closer to one of the guys than a girlfriend, though.

August and Carrie had been high school sweethearts, so they were a package deal from the beginning, but she was never one of us.

Jameson never had issues with bringing whoever he was dating around us, but never to the house to meet Teresa or his mom.

I'd been the lone one who never crossed the streams of my friends with who I was sleeping with at the time. Not that Sabrina fit that mold, since we weren't doing that anymore, no matter how much I wanted to.

My inner circle was complete. Adding another person, especially someone who was already living with me, would mean getting closer to her than I had in a long time, and I preferred the arm's-length way of handling things. It was easier and led to cleaner breaks. Less involved, there wasn't any confusion about what we were to each other.

With her lavender scent, big brown eyes, and ball busting, Sabrina had come closest to throwing off my equilibrium when dealing with the opposite sex. She left me unsteady and unsure, which unsettled me. I wanted to draw the lines that had always been so clear to me even deeper in the sand. But the pull was still there. Undeniable, alluring— and unattainable if I wanted to keep my focus sharp and not let distractions set my arm of the company up for failure.

Everest stuck a knife into the center of a cake in the oven. "You do know the last woman brought to this cake catastrophe is now wearing a real engagement ring, not the fake one you got her last time we did this."

"Let's change the subject." Now the question bombardment had begun, not that it was unexpected.

August cranked up the heat under the pot of cream on the stove. "Not everyone who introduces us to a woman intends to marry her, or even date her. Can we stop jumping to conclusions?" He grumbled and grabbed a giant bag of chocolate chips and poured them into a bowl.

Jameson pushed his glasses up with the back of his hand that was so red it looked like he'd sliced an artery. "Have you starred in any of her pictures or videos?"

"Product photography and videos. It's not exactly scandalous." What we'd done was much closer to what I'd imagined when I thought she was shooting porn, although she'd have needed an underwater camera for at least some of it.

I jammed my hips against the counter to hide how much the mental snapshots of our night together had affected me. *Deep breaths. Slow my heart rate down. Do not think of a glistening-wet Sabrina on her knees between my legs.* My dick stiffened and knocked into one of the metal hand pulls of the cabinet. Pain radiated down my shaft. I winced and clamped my jaw tight, choking back the groan.

"Don't kink shame." He laughed. "Perfectly lit beautiful products. Hand models make a shit ton of money. I'm sure someone out there gets off on it."

My head whipped around, and I glared at him. "Someone like you." Now more than ever I was happy she'd used other guys in her photos and videos and nothing more than her hand was in other shots. Not that it still didn't set me on edge to know there was probably a guy out there jerking off to her fingers and perfectly filed nails.

He folded over the fondant he'd been molding and grabbed a rolling pin. "Nope, definitely not my kink at all."

Leo, Everest, August, and I all exchanged looks. I spoke up first. "What exactly is your kink then, Jameson?"

His face went as red as the fondant he shaped into a disc with his hands. "You're all assholes."

August taunted, stirring the melting chocolate in a glass bowl on top of the double boiler. "Someone's keeping secrets."

"Like you don't all have secrets? Fine, I'll tell you all my bedroom secrets if you guys tell me about Milwaukee."

A stack of empty cake pans clattered off the stove. August spun around with wide eyes before crouching to pick up the scattered pans.

Everest knocked into the blast chiller, banging it into the wall.

Leo focused on the slowly mixing batter like shifting his gaze for a single second would send the whole thing up into flames.

Jameson slammed the towel he'd been keeping over his shoulder down onto the counter. "It's been years, guys. Just tell me what happened." He braced his hands on the sugar-coated laminate and stared at us.

There was no noise in the kitchen other than the hum of the appliances I'd arranged to have delivered after the last two disasters of birthday cake assembly duties.

Our trip after graduation to the city was a no-go topic in our circle. We didn't discuss what had happened in Milwaukee and preferred to forget it ever happened, although local law enforcement, the parks department, a bank, and the Milwaukee County Zoo probably wouldn't be so forgiving.

"Teresa and my mom had the flu and I couldn't go. Six years later you assholes are still holding out on me?"

Everest recovered and grabbed a bowl filled with choco-late batter. "You're lucky you weren't there."

"I swear, I won't tell anyone else." Jameson looked to Leo, who he'd been friends with since middle school. Then to August, who he'd roomed with freshman year, and Everest, who'd lived next door, and then to me, who'd been the last one tagged into the friend group. That none of them had told him yet drove home how much everyone wanted what had happened in Milwaukee to stay in Milwaukee, and also how I was the last one added to the group that had been solid before I'd shown up junior year of college. Hell, Maddy had probably been closer to most of them before the breakup than I was.

It sucked being on the outside, but I wasn't going to be the chink in the armor, not after everything Everest had put on the line to help extricate us from that situation.

August shook his head and walked over, dropping his hand onto Jameson's shoulder. "You don't want to know."

A phone timer went off, saving us from the Jameson-Milwaukee press.

"Let's get this cake made for Teresa."

The timer was silenced, and we got back to work. A quiet tension blanketed the overly crowded kitchen. It was a lot like how things had been in my apartment since Sabrina moved in. Either a rippling irritation or an unreliable tension, although the kind in this kitchen had nothing on the kind that kept me digging my fingers into my thighs when she was near so I didn't reach for her. So I didn't wind my fingers into her hair and breathe in her scent.

Jameson slapped a rolling pin against one of the multicolored fondant boulders. "Thanks for getting the stand mixers for us, Hunter. The last two years it's been a pain in the ass sharing one hand mixer."

Everest pulled a sheet pan of cake out of the oven and swung it around. "And the extra oven."

Jameson ducked out of the way of the blazing hot pan. "Everest! How many times have we said to warn us first?"

Everest stuck the pan into the chiller, which dropped the temperature to around forty degrees in a little over an hour. "How did we do this last year without the blast chiller?"

Leo poured his batter into two round pans. "What? You didn't have one of these in your Viking kitchen growing up, right next to the ice cream machine, double ovens, and wine fridge?"

"No, the chef took care of all that, and the wine cellar was on the far end of the house beside the movie theater, so I don't actually know. Maybe we did have one." While his voice was laced with sarcasm, none of us believed Everest had been joking about the type of house he'd grown up in.

Leo grumbled not so low under his breath and shoved the pans into the oven.

"How much more cake do we need?" I added the

powdered sugar into my bowl and flipped on the machine. A cloud of white sprayed me in the face.

Everyone froze before bursting into laughter.

I slowly opened my eyes and looked down at my shirt and pants. Literally caked in sugar, I spit bits of sugar out of my mouth and shook my head, throwing even more sugar into the air.

The guys all shouted.

"If I have to be covered, everyone's getting covered."

Jameson coughed and swatted at the dusty air. "You got off easy the first time we did this. Now it's time to pay the piper."

"Only because I was getting a three-carat diamond for Leo. That kind of rabbit-out-of-a-hat-pulling requires some time and finesse." It had required more than that, but I'd gotten it done in record time and came out of the trades without owing anyone anything.

That was the way I worked, especially when it came to my friends.

What did Sabrina want? What did she need? Was she anywhere near as hungry for me as I was for her? After our night together, she'd steered clear, not that I hadn't done the same, but I needed to know if she spent her nights staring up at the ceiling wishing she was beside me.

23

SABRINA

I dried my hands on the fluffy green towels in the bathroom and checked myself out in the mirror, taking my hair down and finger combing it. I cursed under my breath and rolled my eyes and whispered to myself, "What the hell are you doing, Sabrina? Who are you trying to impress?" I put my hair back up, shaking my head the whole time.

I jerked open the door, flicking off the light, and closed it behind me.

One step out of the bathroom and Hunter entered the narrow hallway.

"Are you okay?"

"Hunter, seriously. It's not like I'm going to sue you. No need to shoot into concern overdrive." I tried to scoot past him.

His arm shot out to block my path. The heel of his hand pressed against the wall and his shoulder almost touched the opposite one. His fingers were covered in icing.

What I wouldn't give to lick them clean.

I may have let out a low hiss-growl combo. *Get a damn*

grip and buy some new batteries for your vibrator, Sabrina. Cat would be disappointed in me right now. Good thing she wasn't here.

He ducked his head. "I'm not worried about you suing me. I'm worried about you." His gaze heated.

This wasn't fair. Being this close to him did a number on me every damn time. My skin heated where his hand was braced against the wall and brushed against my shoulder. What the hell was wrong with me?

Hunter was the human version of a faulty shower. One second you were being bathed in steamy, glorious heat massaging every muscle in your body, and the next it was a full ice-cube spray to the face.

"No need. I'm feeling good. Your doctor friend will be here soon, right?" I added extra pep to my voice.

See, you're not affecting me at all. My stomach wasn't flip-flopping, and my breathing wasn't shallower than the kiddie pool.

A knock at the front door broke the irresistible pulse between us.

Jameson called out from the living room. "Hunter, Sabrina, the doctor's here."

I stepped back and dropped my gaze to the floor, trying to get my heart rate under control.

That was exactly what I needed right now. The doctor taking my blood pressure and pulse and rushing me to the hospital thinking I was having a heart attack. No, it was just the kind of effect Hunter had on women.

Damn him.

Hunter hesitantly dropped his arm and stepped aside.

I scurried past.

Behind me, the water in the sink turned on. "I'll be right there. Just let me clean up."

I rushed into the room where others were present and I wasn't in danger of melting into Hunter's body under his avid gaze like I'd never been the focus of this much male attention in my life.

In the living room, an older man with black hair with salt-and-pepper streaks at the temples stood with his hands clasped behind his back. Was every guy Hunter knew hot? He gave off some serious Sean Connery in *Entrapment* vibes.

"And you must be Sabrina." The accent. Holy shit. He had a Scottish accent.

Over his shoulder, Zara's eyes widened and her mouth hung open. She mouthed the words, *holy hotness.* It appeared even the engaged woman noticed his stately-older-gentleman looks.

I slapped on a smile and extended my hand. "Yes, I'm Sabrina. So nice to meet you, Dr..."

Good thing he was holding on because I was almost on the ground.

He smiled. "Dr. Sean." He pumped my hand in a firm, but not too firm, grip and released it. "Hunter tells me you had a fall and were having some dizziness and nausea."

"Only a few minutes after I bit it. By the time we left the apartment, I was feeling fine, but he wanted to be sure." I glanced at Hunter, who'd emerged from the bathroom. Yes, I was wholeheartedly shifting the blame onto Hunter. But the joke was on me. My cheeks heated at the intensity of his gaze.

Dr. Sean chuckled, and the corners of his eyes creased. "With a lady like you on his arm, I can't blame him."

I opened my mouth to correct him but snapped it shut. No sense in explaining our now-complicated situation to a stranger.

Hunter didn't jump in to clarify either.

At least for once, we were on the same page.

"Are you okay with me checking you over out here?"

"You're not going to need me to get naked or anything?"

A laugh burst free from his lips, and he shook his head emphatically. "It's not that kind of exam."

"Then I'm good out here."

Zara hopped up and walked past me mouthing, *oh my god*, before going into the kitchen leaving me, Hunter and Dr. Sean in the living room.

Hunter perched on the arm of the couch beside the chair where I sat. His gaze was trained on me like I might spontaneously combust at any moment.

I hated how having his full attention made me feel. It annoyed me that he'd gone into full protection mode. And I hated how warm and fuzzy it made me to know he cared.

Dr. Sean sat on the coffee table beside his bag.

He checked my pulse, which had felt like the blood in my veins was trying to escape with each beat. Next was my blood pressure before he got out the blinding light tool and tracked the movements of my eyes.

I pressed my lips together, letting him do his work.

"Where was it you bumped your head?"

I reached back and touched the spot on the back of my head that was only slightly tender.

The doc leaned forward and felt around, looking up at the ceiling. He dropped his hand. "Right, everything here looks good. No signs of a concussion or other issues. If you start experiencing any nausea or dizziness, you should call me." He looked between me and Hunter.

"I will," Hunter blurted out from his spot on the edge of the seat.

The flustered flutters were back, the ones that happened when Hunter looked at me with an intensity that didn't make me feel like a piece of furniture in the apartment we shared or a person he kept around for pity. Those were dangerous feelings. "I'm sure it won't be necessary. It's been over an hour, and I'm feeling fine now."

The doctor nodded. "As long as it stays that way, you'll be just fine." He stood.

Hunter's hand shot out. "Thanks for coming out here, Sean."

Dr. Sean shook it. "No problem, especially after you got me those tee times. I swear, I've been trying for months."

"Always happy to help."

"How much do I owe you?" I winced, doing my mental tally. Every dollar counted, especially if Zara worked her magic for the expo.

Owing Hunter wasn't a game I wanted to play. Feeling indebted to him when I had nothing to offer in return—I'd been down that path before, which was how I'd ended up with my whole life packed into my car and sharing an apartment with him in the first place.

Dr. Sean made a noise halfway between dismissal and offense. "Nothing. Of course not."

"But you came all the way here." I refused to look at Hunter.

"It wasn't that far, plus it never hurts to be owed a favor by this guy." He jerked his thumb in Hunter's direction and winked, packing up his stethoscope into his bag.

The front door opened, and a harried woman rushed through.

She stopped short once it registered there were two people she obviously didn't know in her living room. Her head rocked back, and her eyes widened. "Sean?"

Okay, maybe it was just me then.

"Rachel?"

She set her keys down on the bench beside the front door. "What are you doing here?"

"Hunter had a friend who needed a once-over." He gestured vaguely in my direction.

She tucked her hair behind her ear with a playful smile. "Since when do you make house calls?"

"I make special exceptions for special people." He leaned in closer like he was letting her in on a secret.

Holy flirting. Was it getting hot in here or was that my not-concussion?

Hunter stepped forward. "I didn't know you two knew each other." He looked back and forth between the two of them.

Jameson's mom touched the side of her neck. "We work together."

Dr. Sean cleared his throat. "Sometimes I'm on her floor." The tension between these two was off the charts. Well, at least this diverted some of the heat and attention from the Hunter Situation. *Get some, Rachel.*

"Mom?" Jameson walked out of the kitchen with a bowl in hand, a towel over his shoulder, and colored flecks of fondant clinging to his hair. "Who's this?"

"This is Dr. Sean. He was here helping with Hunter's friend."

Jameson nodded with his jaw clenched and kept his eyes on the two. It seemed I wasn't the only one picking up on the connection between them. Although Jameson didn't exactly look happy about it. "Hunter and Sabrina, we could use your help with cake stacking."

"Sure thing." I rounded the chair I'd been sitting in, happy to be out of the flirting firing line.

"Mom, Teresa's upstairs. Are you heading up for a

shower and taking her to do the pizza? Or should I order it instead?"

"Go ahead in with Hunter and his friend. I'll walk Sean out and go get my shower." Her gaze didn't leave Dr. Sean's face, and his was locked onto hers too.

"Mom—"

Hunter grabbed Jameson and walked him back into the kitchen.

I followed and peered through the closing door in time to see Dr. Sean leaning in closer to Rachel. Well at least someone had a guy not afraid to show her he was into her.

Turning, I bumped into Hunter's back. I shimmied to the side, trying not to think of the tingles that radiated through me from the simple touch and how he'd been watching me throughout Dr. Sean's checkup.

The kitchen was filled with way too many bodies and a ridiculous amount of equipment.

Cables and power strips crisscrossed the floor in a trip hazardous maze. "Where did all this come from?"

"Hunter." Everyone answered in unison like the question should be obvious.

That seemed to be his forte. Hunter was the man who could get his hands on anything—including me.

Jameson pushed his glasses up and turned to everyone like a Sunday night quarterback prepping his team for the big game.

"We have five sheet cakes, five round cakes and what feels like three gallons of chocolate and vanilla icing. We need to stack the cakes, so we need everyone's help here." He locked eyes with everyone individually. "Stack. Ice. Carve. Ice. Decorate. Are we ready?"

All heads nodded, and he gave more instructions. I tried to keep up. As much as I appreciated not being shoved to the sidelines out in the living room, I was terrified of being the one who dropped all the guys' hard work on the floor and ruined Teresa's birthday.

A chilled sheet cake was laid across my outstretched arms.

Hunter stood beside me, balancing a double stack of circle cakes in each hand.

I talked out of the side of my mouth. "He takes his cake seriously."

The whir of machines and a mini-conference happening in the corner meant Hunter and I were the only ones on our side of the assembly island.

Hunter chuckled. "He does. When it comes to Teresa, he's serious about everything."

"Is his dad...gone?" There hadn't been any word of him stopping by, and he certainly wasn't crammed into the corner in the kitchen.

"Right before Teresa was born. It was a freak accident with a downed power line. After that, he stepped up for his mom and Teresa."

Metal on metal clashed and clanked.

"It's great he was there for them."

"It's great they had each other." His lips dipped in a sad smile.

My heart ached for teenaged Hunter, who'd lost his mom and his dad in such a short period of time. There had been no siblings to share that emotional load. And just like that, Hunter had once again jammed his foot into the door I'd been slamming shut in my heart. Between the doctor's house call and seeing him here with his friends, how could I not feel something for him?

Maybe I needed to have Dr. Sean look at my head again.

Get it together, Sabrina. No one said I was buying

matching heart necklaces for us to share. Plus, Cat would kill me if I went halfsies on one with anyone else. I could like him. It didn't mean I had to be in a relationship with him. It didn't mean we couldn't go to our beds at the end of the night after some insanely hot sex. Maybe this was the perfect situation to get me over the post-Seth slump.

I could bang a hot guy who'd already seen me in my pajamas with bedhead before I'd brushed my teeth. In less than two months, I'd move out and move on in more ways than one.

Why not let myself indulge? The way he looked at me wasn't uninterested. I hadn't been a pity fuck. If he had issues with intimacy and getting close to people, well, welcome to the party.

It was the perfect situation. Perfectly perfect. Better than perfect.

Standing beside him, our arms brushed against each other as we held our cakes in place while Jameson and Leo rushed around us, sizing up the shape and hammering in skewers and dowels into the growing mountain of cake.

After a team effort to stack, balance, and keep the cakes from falling over, we stepped back to evaluate the progress.

I tilted my head to the side and noticed everyone else was as well.

August, the one with the black hair and manicured scruff, tilted his head. "Is anyone else noting a little bit of a" —he held out his hands and shifted them so they were no longer level with one another—"lean."

Jameson crouched down. "Damn it. We need more cake."

Leo slapped down his offset spatula. "Who is eating all this cake once we're finished?"

Zara caught my eye from across the room and jerked her head toward the kitchen door.

I didn't need to be told twice to escape whatever impending cake-splosion might be coming.

"We should probably get them some liquid reinforcements. They've been at it for hours already." Zara walked farther into the house to a door, and cooler air blew through the gaps around it. She opened it and flicked on the light.

It was a garage, albeit neater than any I'd been in before. A set of bikes were hung up along the wall near the front. Plastic boxes with block lettering written across them were neatly stacked on shelves. Christmas decorations had been pulled out, including a large box labeled TREE.

There were seats toward the back, a carpet thrown down in the middle, and a desk with a blackened computer monitor.

"Jameson's hangout. Leo and August used to hide out here all the time when they were younger. Sometimes he works from here if his mom needs him to watch Teresa."

Clanking and clattering from the kitchen could be heard all the way out here.

Zara opened the fridge beside the door and pulled out a couple of bottles of beer and a container filled with ice from the freezer. She walked to a large cabinet and pulled open the doors revealing a hidden bar set up. Grabbing a few glasses, she scanned the shelves before pulling a few bottles down.

There were bar tools I'd never seen before and even a small sink tucked into the handcrafted cabinet. "Do you think they had this back when they were growing up?"

She laughed. "Probably not as nice as this. More like a couple bottles of warm beer and a stolen bottle of Bailey's." While it might've been where the guys hung out when they were younger, it was clearly a man space now, minus the family stuff near the front of the garage.

"Looks like Jameson certainly enjoys his cocktails."

"I think he likes to make them for everyone. He always wants to be prepared."

I certainly got that vibe from him. Hunter was the guy who could acquire anything. Jameson felt more like the one who had his bag stuffed to the gills for any eventuality you might run into. He'd probably been an Eagle Scout.

We mixed up the drinks and walked into the kitchen to hand them out. I attempted Hunter's bramble and held it out to him.

He lifted his icing and cake-covered hands.

"Aren't you supposed to be making the cake, not playing in it?"

"Somehow I got stuck on cake ball duty for all the leftover pieces from the carving Jameson's been doing. Teresa will take them in to her class." He glanced over his shoulder like Zara and I hadn't walked in with drinks for everyone and he needed to sneak. "But I could absolutely use a drink."

I lifted it to his lips, and he sipped with a grimace, keeping his gaze on mine over the rim of the glass.

"That's delicious."

"Liar," I teased.

His lips curled into a smile and brushed against the backs of my fingers. "Thanks, Sabrina."

Breathless and locking my knees so I didn't turn into a puddle, I nodded. "No problem."

A loud *bang* sliced through our moment. "Can someone clear some space on the counter? I have four cakes coming out of the oven." Everest swung around from the oven with his mitts on and an apron, searching frantically around the crowded space.

Leo jumped out of the way. "Hey, Richie Rich, this is the second time we're going through this today! Why didn't you let us clear the space before you took them out?" He dodged the fiery pans, nearly jumping up onto the counter.

The two of them continued their bicker-fest. I used it as my escape. What was it about a man in the kitchen that made it impossible to resist him?

Hunter covered in powdered sugar, smelling like vanilla —he was downright edible. *Down, girl.*

You help a guy out with a drink and his firm yet gentle lips brush against your skin and you're ready to pull him down onto the floor in an icing escapade that would send everyone else running from the room.

But their group was tight, and there wasn't a doubt in my mind that if things came down to doing a favor for me and her friendship with Hunter, Zara would choose him. The last thing I needed to do was rock the boat and have my possible expo invite rescinded.

At nearly six that evening, Teresa and Rachel came back with pizzas. Rachel had taken her shower and headed out with Teresa to make pizzas for everyone at the request of the birthday girl, and to spend some extra time with her on her special day after working a double the day before. The guys also emerged from the kitchen after a few more rounds of booze and time-outs when things got too heated.

Streaked with a rainbow of fondant and icing colors, the guys gingerly placed the five-tier cake with each layer highlighting a different superhero on the table. The superheroes all looked like toxic spill versions of themselves. But all the guys wore wide smiles and a sense of accomplishment rippled through the room.

Teresa stood on her chair and stared at the cake with wide-eyed wonder. Her giddy smile and laughter were infectious. It wasn't hard to see how they'd all been talked into doing this for her for years now.

Who didn't want a little kid to look at them like they were an actual superhero? Her face and excitement made me think of Ryder and how Hunter could be that superhero to him with just a conversation.

My smile faltered a bit.

Rachel popped open the metal lid on the cookie tin and instead of cookies inside there was a collection of candles. She pulled out a six and a pack of matches.

Everyone crowded around the bench-seating dining room table, bumping shoulders against one another. The room wasn't made for nine, but we wedged in.

I leaned in and whispered to Hunter, "That's the scariest cake I've ever seen in my life."

"This is an upgrade. You should've seen the one they did for her fourth birthday." He shuddered. "His creepy train eyes followed me in my nightmares for a week." His face paled, and he swallowed thickly. "The Sesame Street one last year for her fifth wasn't as unspeakable."

Apparently this one wasn't the only showstopper of horror.

"Maybe next year I'll have a Harry Potter cake." Teresa stood in her chair with both hands planted on the table, doing a little kid shimmy where you weren't sure if they had to pee or not.

The guys all groaned.

"But Jameson said I need to read all the books first even though he hasn't read them."

I looked to Hunter. The books had been sitting on his nightstand looking well-worn and read.

Not a peep from him. Of course, he wouldn't want to ruin his cred by admitting to liking and still reading Harry Potter, not even to his friends. He'd slipped his suit jacket back on after washing up since the cake had been assembled and decorated.

Always Mr. Put Together.

We sang "Happy Birthday" to Teresa—not Hunter, though. He very convincingly mouthed the words with his chest heaving like he was belting it out along with everyone else.

And then it hit me. I'd never even heard him so much as hum before with all the music he was constantly listening to, but I shook my head that he couldn't even sing the simple song around his closest friends. It looked like he was used to putting up walls with everyone, even those closest to him, so that somehow made what happened between us feel less personal. It wasn't me. It was him.

After the candles were blown out, we had cake before dinner, as was required on an occasion like this, and then ate the pizza Teresa and Rachel had made at their birthday-bonding cooking class—lopsided pizzas with way too much sauce, but they were delicious nonetheless.

Everyone was given a layer of cake to take with them. I wasn't complaining. As scary as the cake looked, it tasted damn good. I just had to make sure I closed my eyes so the bleeding icing colors and fondant mixture, which looked like a sickly pile of week-old food or a puddle of bile, didn't spoil the taste.

Hunter and I said goodbye to everyone, and I thanked Teresa for inviting me to her birthday. I met her request for me to show up next year with a noncommittal sound and a sprint to the front door.

We got back to the apartment, and although I hadn't

been on my feet nearly as long as Hunter had been, I was wiped. I hadn't been around so many people for hours on end in a while.

Once again, I kicked myself for letting Seth isolate me like he had. I'd thought his homebody nature had to do with flying all over the world. I figured when he was home, he just wanted to be with me, which had been romantic. Then I thought it was because of how I looked, and he'd played right into those insecurities because it meant he got his way for longer.

Gaslighting motherfucker. But my stamina for large groups and going out had been decimated over the past couple years. Not that I had cash to run around from bar to bar, club to club, or even felt like it anymore, but I hated the time I'd wasted on him.

Maybe thinking about Seth was my defense mechanism for Hunter. He was really good at wearing two different faces, even around the people who meant the most to him. I had no doubts that the holey T-shirt, stained sweats, and jar of Nutella would never make an entrance around anyone else ever again.

The reminder couldn't have come at a more perfect time.

We walked down the hall instead of walking toward my room, which would invite another at-the-door, lips-barely-brushing interaction. I plucked the container of cake from his hands.

"I'll put that away." I backed up toward the kitchen.

"I'm glad you're okay. And thanks for coming today."

I stepped back, banging my hip into the countertop. Wincing, I rubbed the spot.

His eyes widened, and his gaze dropped to where I was rubbing.

"It's fine. It's nothing. That's what I've got the extra

padding for." I slapped my hip and barely kept my cringe at bay. *Way to draw even more attention to your ass, Sabrina.* Like everyone wasn't completely aware of the size.

His head tilted, and his eyebrows furrowed.

"Thanks for calling Dr. Sean." I pulled open the fridge door, blocking my view of him. "I'm going to make a cup of hot chocolate. Good night, Hunter."

There was a long pause. I took as much time as possible putting away the leftovers and grabbing the milk from the fridge.

"Good night."

I let out my held breath and closed the door at his retreating footsteps. I wasn't going to add another *mistake* to my life right now.

24

HUNTER

Sabrina and I had fallen into a friendly roommate routine. Bumping into one another in the hallway or the kitchen during the day, we'd exchange a few words before my work or hers pulled one of us away. Her time spent scribbling on her tablet had gotten more intense and frequent over the past couple weeks. She'd sit in the living room or her bedroom or even on the kitchen counter, engrossed in whatever was on her screen.

Sabrina's brush-off after Teresa's birthday was exactly what I'd wanted, and still I hated it. I hated that I couldn't kiss her again, but she was the one being sensible here.

The light would be on under her door late into the nights when I'd get home from whatever event I'd been coordinating into the predawn hours of the morning.

One of the guys would stop by, which, now more than ever, sent bolts of jealousy streaking through me even worse than when I'd thought she was shooting porn.

It wasn't about touching her or having sex with her, it was about spending time with her. Being in her presence, which had been denied to me almost completely outside of those brief interactions.

Sabrina had thrown the shields up, and who could blame her? I'd been saying the same things to myself over and over again. Only it was getting harder to stay away from her. I couldn't stay away completely.

Some nights were different. In the dining room, sitting in chairs opposite one another, we'd work on a puzzle. The thousand-piece puzzles only took us a few days of daily dedication. Then we'd break it apart and start all over again with a new one. It felt like a metaphor for us. This new version of us was steady, even, easygoing, but the tug of resistance pulled at my gut every time I walked away from her. Every time I closed my bedroom door after she stepped into hers, I wanted nothing more than to barge in after her and bring her back to my bed.

Instead I settled for time with her before I left for the night, putting together a picture piece by piece and trying to make sense of where the pieces I had in my hands fit.

I'd get her a drink or two. She'd try remaking them, and we'd laugh at how terrible they were—almost as bad as her coffee. I breathed deeply every time she walked past me or I set a drink in front of her. These were the only times I'd allowed myself to get close to her for more than a handful of minutes.

But she hadn't been at the table when I got home from the office today. I hated how much I looked forward to talking, laughing and watching her hum and sing boyband songs other people would be embarrassed to admit they liked while working on the world's most frustrating puzzles. Somehow, they weren't nearly as annoying when I was with her.

My day had been filled with team meetings for the New

Year's Eve concert. Tonight I was headed to a venue to find a new opening band to kick off the concert—one without egos so big that they'd balk at playing to a mostly empty stadium. I slid my jacket on and slipped a cuff link through one double cuff. The flicker of the TV caught my eye through the living room doorway.

The nightmares weren't as sharp now, which meant I got some decent sleep, but my nights were still restless thinking about her.

Her smell clung to some of the towels, and I'd take the secret to my grave that I'd taken one or two and used them as a pillow to help me sleep. I needed to shake off her hold on me, but sometimes I wasn't sure if I wanted to.

Leaving the apartment hadn't been my top choice for tonight, but we'd finished our last puzzle a day ago and she hadn't brought out a new one. I made a note to order one tomorrow.

Part of the reason I was going out tonight was to drain my battery. After getting used to running on what felt like minutes sleep, the four to five hours a night I'd managed to get over the past couple weeks had my energy reserves close to maxed out.

Sitting in my bedroom, staring up at my ceiling, dissecting every bump and bang from Sabrina's room and trying to orchestrate casual run-ins in the hallway would drive me crazy.

The concert would be in full chaos mode when I got there, but arriving before eleven would mean waiting around for the band to finish up. There was no point in going if I wasn't maximizing my time there to buy a few rounds and socialize like it was my job because—well, it was my job. A job I'd dive headfirst into as long as it meant I wasn't pacing my bedroom listening for Sabrina's door to open.

Before long she'd be calling her friend Cat, whose stories filled half our puzzle time, to tell her the stalker was coming from inside the house.

I stopped short when I walked into the living room. The pungent smells of beef, chicken, and salt, sweet and spice mixed, overtook the whole space.

Sabrina was curled up on the couch in fuzzy socks, sweats, and a t-shirt. Her still-damp hair was pulled up into a ponytail tangle. She had a bowl of beef and broccoli and a beer—one of mine—on the coffee table in front of the couch.

Styrofoam containers of food were set out on the table on top of a kitchen towel. There were blue pen scribbles on top of each and a few plastic containers filled with a brown liquid and floating dumplings.

My chest tightened with longing. In my head she looked up at me and moved the bowl onto her lap and patted the couch cushion beside her. Once I sat, she'd lean in close and rest her head against my chest. I'd play with the strands of hair that dampened my shirt, and she'd rub her hand along my leg absently while we ate and fought over which show or movie to watch next.

Instead of the scene in my mind, her head jerked toward me. She swallowed her food and stuck two fingers in her mouth for a screeching wolf whistle. "Wow, quite the look you've got going on for a night on the town." She didn't make room and tried to keep her voice light although there was a hint of strain there. "Let's see the whole thing."

Not wanting to deny her and not hating the way she looked at me, I did a slow turn, letting her see the full ensemble. The suit was one of many lining my closet, tailored, dry-cleaned, and ready at a moment's notice. They were my shield against the world. Who didn't feel like they could handle anything in a custom suit that turned heads and made people notice?

"Someone's getting laid tonight in your super fancy outfit."

I rankled at her thinking I was sleeping with anyone tonight. But that had been the gist of what I'd said, hadn't it? That we were casual and fun and it didn't preclude having that same kind of casual fun with someone else. Cementing our relationship to roommates didn't spell out that I had no interest in anyone other than her. But I hated the idea of her thinking that about me. "Is that why you think I go out?"

Her smile teased. "Why else?"

I shrugged. "Have fun. Drink. Dance. See new people."

"I have all the fun I need right here. If I want to dance, I put on some music and jump around like an idiot to my heart's content, not worrying about how terrible I am. As for new people? That's what this magical glowing box is for." She waved her fingers in the direction of the screen.

"How about actual humans? Other than your male model friends, I don't think you talk to anyone else."

She shrugged and took another bite of her food. "I talk to Cat. And what are we doing right now?" She gestured with her fork from me to her. "I believe some might call this talking."

I sat on the arm of the couch. "I mean with other people."

"Other people suck sometimes. When's the last time you stayed in?"

"Going out is my job."

Her sauce-covered lips quirked up. "You mean to tell me, every single evening you go out, it's for work?"

"Most of the time."

She leveled her gaze at me.

"A lot of the time."

An eyebrow lift.

"Fine, a couple times a week."

She laughed and sank back into her seat. "You're way too easy to break. If you were a spy, I'd have all the national security secrets in a matter of minutes."

"Maybe you're just good at seeing through my bullshit." Maybe it was why she scared me so much. Getting close wasn't something I was good at anymore. It wasn't something I wanted to be good at. The risk of losing another person that I cared about banged in my chest. But it often felt like I didn't have a choice with her. Fighting this got harder with every passing day.

"It's only because I see you outside of the custom wool suits hand-woven on the rolling hills of New Zealand from sheep fed organic grass and given daily massages by the farmhands."

"Why would it matter if the sheep are fed organic grass? Isn't all grass organic?"

She shrugged. "That was the most outrageous part of what I said? You tell me. You're the one who ordered it."

"It's Scottish wool, not New Zealand wool."

"Well, soooorry."

"What did you order?" I stepped closer to her spread and lifted one of the lids with my finger.

She smacked the back of my hand.

"It's not yours."

"Whose beer is that?"

Her eyes widened, and her shoulders rose. "Hey, Hunter, can I have one of your beers?" She called out like she was asking me while I was still in my bedroom.

I cupped my hands around my mouth attempting to throw my voice. "Maybe, if you share some beef and broccoli with me."

She grumbled under her breath and nodded toward the plastic utensils in the bag still holding some of the containers.

"Did you invite someone else over? Why'd you order so much?"

"Nope, it's for me. They were running a two-for-one special, so I stocked up for the week."

"You do know this is packed with sodium."

She rolled her eyes. "I'll talk it over with Dr. Sean the next time I see him. I was sick of rice, beans, and grilled chicken, so sue me."

"I can go grocery shopping." I unbuttoned my jacket, shrugged it off, and draped it over the arm of the couch. I picked up the container, keeping it in the bag in case of leaks, and sat on the couch beside her.

On the screen a team of three were in a room traversing an obstacle course over a churning, bubbling floor of liquid that looked a lot like lava.

"Not the rocket. It tips," she shouted as a man jumped onto the slippery foam rocket and pitched forward into the churning lava water, complete with a slo-mo descent into the depths and screams from his teammates.

"What is this?"

She pointed to the screen as the remaining teammate made it to the buzzer and slapped it, screaming out the show name. "*The Floor Is Lava!*"

"I don't know why I'd have thought it was anything else."

"I'm getting another beer. Did you want one?" Sabrina stood and walked past me. The curves of her hips and thighs were right at eye level.

Straining my neck muscles to keep my gaze locked onto hers, I nodded and choked out a "sure."

I set down my food and ran my hands over my face. *Get a grip, Hunter. Five more minutes.* I'd stay and drink half my beer and then leave.

She came back in and handed over the beer just in time for the next episode to start.

"Oh, new room." She lifted the bottle to her lips. They wrapped around the opening, and her bottom lip glistened when she pulled the bottle away again and pressed her lips together.

Wisps of hair danced around her face, slowly drying. The world faded away. The TV, the cold glass sweating in my hand.

She sat beside me with her legs crossed and settled into the couch, her gaze riveted to the screen. The laughs and winces played out across her whole face. The amusement lit up her eyes and flushed her cheeks, making her look like she'd just walked in from the November air.

Her gaze flicked to mine and she smiled. It was like the one I'd envisioned when I walked in. Then she looked to the box sitting on the table. "Jerk! You ate all my beef and broccoli."

The captivation spell ended. I ripped my gaze away from her.

"Says the woman drinking all my beer."

"Not all your beer. There's still one or two left."

"You owe me." I'd have liked to collect the debt by taking her to my bedroom all over again. By peeling off her sweats, jerking her t-shirt up over her head, and crawling between her legs with her heels digging into my back while I sampled her like I hadn't had a chance to last time.

"How about I share one of my fortune cookies with you

and we call it even?" She dangled the cellophane-wrapped cookie in front of me like it was a crown jewel.

Not exactly what I had in mind. "Maybe."

She flung the cookie at me.

It hit me center chest.

Her yelp drew my attention. She cupped her nonexistent junk when a guy slipped and landed hard on a bar in the game, which seemed strategically placed for the exact perfect nut shot. I got secondhand nausea and hunched over a little.

Another episode ended.

"Do you need to go, or did you want another drink?"

I got up to block her move to the kitchen. "No, I've got time and I'll make the drinks to save the last of my beers from your grubby little paws."

"Your beer or your booze, I'm good with either." She laughed and leaned back with both arms propped behind her head.

My blood hammered in my veins. I wanted to dive onto the couch and climb on top of her, pin those arms above her head, and attack the spot on her neck where her hair brushed against her skin. I wanted to kiss the lips that had entranced me all night with her laughter and quips. I wanted her.

Shaking my head, I turned and walked into the kitchen.

After mixing us drinks, I walked back in.

"Were you juicing the blackberries yourself? Hurry up." She waved me forward.

And I nearly stumbled. "You waited for me?"

"Of course." She wiggled her fingers in my direction, grabbing for her glass. "These shows aren't nearly as fun to watch alone. Sit." She patted the spot beside her.

My chest tightened, and I sat beside her, barely making

it on numb legs. All of this with her—the nights poring over puzzles and talking, bothering her while she cooked dinner or her bothering me, hanging out and watching TV—this was the longest I'd ever spent with someone since the guys back in college.

I'd forgotten what it felt like to have someone around to laugh with, watch crappy TV with, be myself with.

Sabrina saw through me. From the first day when she'd walked in on me, she'd seen straight through me, which was the scariest thing I'd ever faced.

But sitting beside her watching men and women slip and slide into fake lava while drinking and cracking jokes was the most I'd felt like me in a long time. Not Hunter, who was the guy who could get what anyone wanted, or Hunter who knew someone who knew someone to get you into the hot club or concert or championship game. Just Hunter, the kind of jerk with a secret Nutella addiction who was slightly fucked in the head.

The fears of what it meant to get close to her faded in the afterglow of her ball-busting laughter.

One episode rolled into the next. We moved from one game show to another, watching contestants try and fail their best at cakes even the best chefs would have trouble recreating.

I handed Sabrina napkins when she spewed her drink out her nose at a reveal of a cake creation that put Teresa's Marvel superheroes cake attempt to shame. It was meant to be Superman, but it looked more like a poorly taxidermied raccoon.

"Is that a hunchback or is that supposed to be his arm? He's Superman's evil twin." She gasped for air and wiped tears from her eyes, averting her gaze from the TV. "You guys have got to go on that show."

I laughed and gulped from my glass. "We have enough on our plate."

Her back went straight, and her lips parted with a finger held up beside her face. "What about a Bake-Off between all five of you? I'd pay money to see that." She shoved her balled-up napkins into the empty container on the coffee table. Gripping her side, she finished the rest of her drink still chuckling. "I think I pulled a muscle."

"That's what you get for making fun of us. We're SWANK, we're the hottest new up-and-coming logistics and event coordinators on the East Coast and watch us make absolute fools of ourselves." I wiggled my fingers in her direction and sunk them into her sides, not missing the chance to touch her, even if it was under the cover of tickling.

She yelped, rocking up onto the arm of the couch and kicking her feet at me. "You're playing with fire! I'll kick you so hard you'll swear you're rooming with a horse."

Her foot connected with my chest.

My laugh came out as more like a wheeze. I stopped my advance and tried to fill my lungs with air.

"Sorry." She cringed. "I tried to warn you."

"Solid hit." I rubbed the sore spot on my left pec.

"Are you sure it's okay?" Her hand connected with my chest.

My heartbeat knocked against my ribs like it was breaking and entering. All the wants I'd been pushing aside for weeks came flooding back in.

Her lips. Her body. Her moans.

The way she calmed me and was the most comfortable person to be around other than the guys. Even they didn't see the sides of me she'd seen. This was everything I'd been trying to stop, but right now it felt inevitable, like the nightmares where I was running away but never moved, only this wasn't a nightmare. It was a dream denied.

She was all I could think about to the point of madness, and I didn't know how much longer I could fight this.

I shrank back, not wanting her to know how much her touch affected me.

She jerked her hand back and dropped her gaze. "Sorry." Swinging her legs down so her feet were flat on the floor, she busied herself with packing up the containers.

"Sabrina..."

"No, don't." It came out harsh and heavy. "I don't get you, Hunter. One minute you're into me and the next...." The plastic bags rustled as she closed the lids on the containers and gathered up the fortune cookies. "I get you liking your privacy and not wanting to get involved with someone you're living with, but then stop sending mixed signals. I'm tired of the push and pull."

"I—" My mouth snapped shut at her glare.

She was right. All the comfort and happiness of a few minutes ago had evaporated. It was like someone had flicked the lights on after last call at a bar and I was the sticky floor you hadn't noticed until that moment. I wanted her, and the tightrope I was walking was getting thinner every day. For some reason I'd thought I could have a taste, just enough to take the edge off and be okay, but balancing high in the air, falling for her felt scarier than ever. "You don't need to clean up. I can get all that before I head out."

Her lips turned down and pinched together. "Fine, have a great night, Hunter." She left and her door slammed shut.

I packed up all the dishes and food from our night in and then left. Instead of going to the afterparty for the concert, which was long over, I walked around the block. Each step cemented my resolve to change things between me and Sabrina. The denial was getting to both of us. Keeping her at arms' length wasn't working. My restraint was weakening with every second I spent with her.

On lap five around the block, it hit me. I sent out the messages and waited on the replies on how to fix what I'd spent the last two months making sure stayed broken.

25

SABRINA

Footsteps rumbled the floor and a sweaty, panting Hunter slammed into my doorway, bracing his hands on the doorjamb. His Adam's apple bobbed.

I shot up from my seat. "Is something wrong?"

He swallowed audibly. "I have a surprise for you."

My extended hand dropped to my side, and I cocked my head. "A surprise?"

"Yeah, what are you doing tonight?" His words were less breath-starved.

"Finishing up my pitch for a new promotional campaign. I've had another few inquiries." But still no word from Harper Linens. Every day the nail in that coffin was hammered a little deeper, so I'd take what I could get. Any interest was good. Not a deluge, but enough to set myself up with some much-needed cash.

He looked over my shoulder. "When's it due?"

"Next weekend."

His shoulders relaxed. "Perfect."

I looked over my shoulder and back at him. "What the hell is going on?"

"You'll see."

Someone knocked at the door.

"Perfect timing. Don't go anywhere." He disappeared back down the hallway.

"Where the hell does he expect me to go?" I walked closer to the door, praying he hadn't bought that One Direction cardboard cutout he'd threatened to buy last puzzle night.

Voices came from the front door. More than one. Okay, he hadn't ordered from that awesome Chinese food place and wanted me to stick around to share his egg foo young.

"We have three hours. Will that be enough time?" Hunter rounded the corner with three people. Two women and a man.

"She's adorable. That'll be more than enough time." The woman in all black who looked like she'd entered an Audrey Hepburn look-alike competition rested her hand under her chin.

"Enough time for what?"

The other woman tilted her head like a confused teacup poodle. "To get you ready?"

Each question spawned ten more.

"Get me ready for what? What in the world is going on?"

Hunter tapped his fingers against the doorjamb. "It's like I said before about getting you out of the house."

My hands whipped up to my hips. "Which part of the push and pull is this, huh?"

"Most definitely the pull." He ducked his head and backed up. "If you need anything, let me know." His chin lifted and his gaze lingered on me, leaving an electrifying trail tingling from the tips of my fingers to my toes. "Have fun, Sabrina."

"I'm Beth. Let's do this."

They walked past me with suitcases and a garment bag and full-on mobile clothing rack into my room like I wasn't even standing there. Spinning, I followed them inside. "What exactly are we doing?"

Zippers unzipped, case latches clicked, and an efficient cascade of beautifying products took over the desk where my computer and monitor were set up.

"Oh, check out this bathroom. I call dibs for hair in here." The other woman walked past me, gathering up her cases from my bedroom floor. On her way back, she stopped. "I'm Lina. With this exhaust fan and these outlets, the bathroom will be perfect for hair, okay?" She turned to walk back into the bathroom.

Shooting my hands out to my sides, I shouted, "What is going on?"

They all stopped what they were doing and snapped up straight.

Beth walked toward me. "Didn't Hunter tell you?"

"No, hence my complete and total confusion."

She set down the twenty makeup brushes in her hand and crossed the room to me. "Beth, Lina, and that's Franco. We're your hair and makeup team for the night. Hunter said you're going with him to Siren Song and wanted us to make sure you had everything you needed." She waved her hands in the direction of the team. My team.

"Oh." I stared at the gray carpet, trying to make sense of what was happening. Why was Hunter doing all this? He wanted me as his date tonight. He'd brought in three people to surprise me with a makeover and a night out on his arm. Maybe it meant something more. Or maybe he knew that I'd be here with nowhere to go and would make an easy and convenient date.

Either way, I was putting it in my fuck it bucket. I could do with some leg stretching, and who was I to turn down getting my hair and makeup done? Besides, the dresses on the rack were showstoppingly gorgeous. Most probably wouldn't fit me, but if nothing else, they made my fingers itch with inspiration.

She tried to catch my gaze. "Are we a go? Or did you want to talk it over with Hunter first?"

My head snapped up. "No, I'm good. Where do you want me?"

Nothing other than mascara had been on my face for over a month—okay, maybe a few months. August. It had been August since I'd worn makeup. I'd only realized it now. With Seth, I'd always felt like I needed to be done up, at least as much as I could. I'd thought it would change how much time he spent with me. But none of that had been because of me.

Once I'd moved out, there wasn't a need. I certainly hadn't been trying to impress Hunter, so it seemed pointless. But a bit of pampering and professionals doing their thing? Turning that down felt silly, even if I had no idea what the hell Hunter was planning.

For the next hour, I was at the mercy of the Glam Squad. Tweezing, plucking, and waxing all took place in the bathroom Lina had transformed into a mobile aesthetician's space. After a quick trim and roller setting, which seemed like a lot of work for them to put it all into intricate braids, I was handed off to Franco for wardrobe.

Shockingly, everything fit. I glanced at my closed door when the first dress zipped perfectly. How had he known my size? Also, how scary was it that he knew my size? That was generally a closely guarded secret, not that a number mattered when, you know, he had eyes, but it took away one of the many things that I always felt like I needed to keep under lock and key.

After five dresses, we finally found the perfect one. The light blue knee-length dress had a lower back than I'd normally wear, but since when was anything I was doing normal? With three-quarter-length sleeves and a high neckline, it didn't feel too over-the-top with detailing and beading all over the bodice and hem. This one didn't scratch or itch. Lavish, iridescent, and slimming, it was gorgeous and nothing like anything I'd ever had the balls to wear before.

"Off it goes until your hair and makeup are finished. Lina will get to work on your nails while Beth handles the makeup."

A director's chair appeared out of one of the suitcases, and I was set up, feeling like I was headed for an awards-show red carpet. Five minutes to the three-hour deadline Hunter had given them, I slipped my feet into the navy heels.

"Are you ready to see the whole look?" Beth held the floor-length mirror that had been relegated to the closet in her hands. They'd begun packing their supplies up and stacking them by the front door.

I looked down at myself and smoothed my hands over the dress, my fingers running against the tightly packed beading. "Ready as I'll ever be."

The three of them stood on either side of the mirror, and I squeezed my eyes shut. Chancing a peek through one eye, I prayed I didn't feel like a complete and total idiot. I caught sight of my reflection, and my chin lifted.

Beth held up the mirror. "What do you think?"

I opened my eyes and did a double take the second I looked into the mirror. "That's not me."

"It damn well is." Lina settled her hands on both my shoulders.

"Wow."

"You stole the words right out of my mouth."

I jolted and looked over my shoulder at the man in the reflection standing in the open doorway. Looking back at myself, I couldn't help the streak of self-consciousness slamming into me. I went to tuck my hair behind my ear, only to be blocked by the dangling earrings brushing the tops of my shoulders.

"Thank you. You clean up pretty nicely yourself." Hunter was the epitome of a man poured into a suit. It was fitted where it should fit and loose where it was meant to be loose. Just enough pull in certain spots to indicate what kind of body he had underneath. Not muscled but powerful. Capable of throwing you into bed. Capable of throwing me into bed. Those old memories came back to me, sending the sexy shivers tracing their way down my spine much like he had that night.

Taking a breath, I looked back at myself.

I cleaned up all right as well, if I did say so myself. I needed to remember that. I turned and checked out my profile, twisting the shoes to get a better look at my legs. The heels were gorgeous and probably cost as much as rent had been on my old apartment.

"We will let you two get on with your evening." The three of them rushed out of the room with furtive, smirking glances.

Silence reigned in the room.

"You didn't have to do all this if you needed a plus one for tonight. I swear, I could've pulled myself together if you'd given me a little notice." Glancing at my reflection in the mirror, the perfect hair and makeup staring back at me looked like me, but not me at all. "Okay, maybe not like this, but..."

"This had nothing to do with me not thinking you could pull it off."

"Then why?" I stared at him, trying to figure him out.

"I wanted tonight to be special." His eyes flickered with a promise that sent my stomach into butterfly barrage territory.

My body hummed with the intensity of his gaze. It would be so easy to get caught up in him and let myself forget we'd been doing this dance for months now. "Why?"

"You're full of questions tonight."

"You're full of secrets."

One eyebrow dropped, and his voice took on a coarse rumble. "You have no idea."

My skin dimpled with goose bumps, and my lips parted. I wanted to know all his secrets. Secrets that might explain who exactly he was and why I never felt like I could get my footing when I was around him.

He spun to my left and held out his hand. "Are you ready?"

I tilted my head and stepped forward, placing my hand in his. "As I'll ever be."

26

SABRINA

"It's a play on *A Midsummer Night's Dream*. In whatever incarnation people wanted to go with." Hunter pointed out at the floor-to-ceiling flower pillars. They swayed along with the aerialists in hoops wearing fairy wings above the partygoers below. It was as if the sprinkler system had been triggered, but instead of a shower of suspect water from years-old tanks, they'd sprouted white, pink, cream, and purple flowers. Floral waterfalls transformed the space to the point that I had no idea what it would look like in the light of day.

I glanced over at Hunter. Getting caught up in the moment was scary, but I didn't know how to stop myself. And couldn't bring myself not to soak it all up.

A woman walked by and offered me a crown of flowers like other women and some men walking around wore.

I looked to Hunter.

He smiled and leaned in closer. "It's the small touches our clients look for in making a memorable event."

The hairstyle the designers had done on my hair made perfect sense. Dipping my head, I let her put it on me and arrange the ribbons over my shoulder. The crown nestled on top of the perfectly imperfect messy braids, completing the half-up, half-down look.

"What do you think?"

People were dressed from every era of interpretation of the play. Some were more modern, others wore period costumes, some went with a beach version in sparkling floral bikinis. I was glad Hunter hadn't added one of those outfits to my options for the evening.

I couldn't stop staring at the room and the beautiful people in it. "I don't even know what to say. The first thing that comes to mind is gorgeous."

He bent, speaking directly into my ear. "You're absolutely right." The heat from his lips, which weren't even touching me, sent teasing tendrils racing across my skin.

I touched my chin to my shoulder and caught his eye. Why'd I feel like he wasn't talking about the beautiful party he'd put together tonight? Damn him and those freaking eyes.

Servers wove their way through the partygoers with flower-covered trays loaded with champagne flutes. The music rumbled and thumped, vibrating the floor.

"Let's go." He took my hand, pulling me toward the elevated areas around the perimeter of the room.

My heart was in my throat, unsure of what the night held in store for me. Whatever it was, it felt like it would change things between Hunter and me forever. And I still didn't know how I felt about this. Hunter was complicated in a way that made Seth feel like the maze on the back of a cereal box.

From the beginning I'd been drawn to Hunter, dumbfounded by him. The anger and us butting heads helped throw the brakes on and slow things down, but now the brake lines had been cut and I was powerless to stop the train barreling through my chest.

We walked to the white velvet rope, which was lifted without a word from Hunter. Inside, there were circular couches with columns from the center with tall flower arrangements that cascaded down like a floral weeping willow, creating a living curtain over whoever sat there.

Flickering lights sat inside frosted glass votive candle holders, covering the area in a warm glow. More servers came through with trays filled with food and drinks.

"You put all this together?"

The corner of his mouth quirked up. "With a team of other people. Designers, suppliers, the client. But I got everyone on the same page and made it happen." He stared out at the room, pride radiating in his gaze.

Design ideas hit me like a fire hose to the face. I grabbed my phone out of my clutch, needing to not forget all the different details I could use for inspiration. "Can I take pictures?"

"Of course. But try to keep the lens off the other VIP areas. People tend to get testy if they feel you're horning in on a private moment."

I nodded, not planning on taking pictures of any faces, although some of the outfits and costumes were stunning. Who wouldn't want another reason to wear their killer costumes outside of Halloween?

Hunter handed me a pink drink in a martini glass with a hibiscus flower floating in the center. "It's a Sakura Martini." His fingers brushed against mine and lingered. The air around us crackled with an anticipation that felt like it was always just under the surface, even if I tried to pretend it wasn't. "Sabrina—"

"Hunter!"

I caught myself from stumbling forward in anticipation of his next words and instead took a sip of my drink when a man in a white suit, white wig, and cane that made him look like seventeenth-century French aristocracy, walked over to Hunter and hugged him. "This is the best one yet." The man wrapped his arm around Hunter's shoulder and held up his cane arm, looking out at the sea of over-the-top beautiful costumes. "You've outdone yourself once again."

"Thanks, Mikal. I'm happy you're enjoying yourself."

"How could I not?"

"I wanted to introduce you to my date, Sabrina."

The man whirled, and his eyes widened. "A vision." He took one of my hands and kissed the back of it while bowing low, but kept his champagne-colored gaze on me.

Once again, I had to question whether Hunter had a hotness barometer he used to gauge whether or not he hung out with someone. First his grown-up boy band of friends and partners at SWANK and now this man. My stomach did a baby backflip, but nothing close to when Hunter touched me. This new addition wasn't trying to do anything more than flex his flirting muscles. He winked and wrapped his arm around the waist of the woman who followed him up the stairs in a similarly embroidered dress to the one I wore.

We introduced ourselves and admired each other's outfits. Normally, I'd have never felt like I wanted to be in the same room with her while all dressed up because the comparison would find me woefully lacking, but tonight was different. I didn't feel like I had to compare myself to her. I was me and she was her, both striking in our own ways, plus I got to go home tonight with Hunter, in whatever capacity that presented itself.

They left and a revolving door of partygoers came to see Hunter like he was holding court.

He introduced me to everyone else who stopped by to check in with him and congratulate him on topping himself. And I had to admit, I had no doubts. It was my first time seeing him in his element. He was charming, of course, and he knew the names of everyone who spoke to him or found them out quickly. The conversation was always about them and he pulled out a little tidbit from an offhand remark that made their eyes light up, and they left the conversation even happier than when it had started.

This was another side of him. The charmer. The showman. The Hunter Saxton.

Most of the people seemed to be business associates, which made sense. He was at work, after all. No wonder he thought I was slowly mummifying myself since I barely left the apartment. If this was what every night was like, I'd imagine staying home with me was boring as hell. Although he never seemed to act that way. He always made it feel like there wasn't any other place he'd rather be than doing puzzles, teasing me about my music choices or watching trash TV with me.

It moved something in me that I'd seen all sides of him. I'd seen him when he had his guard down, and those quiet moments in the apartment felt all the more special now after finally seeing him in his element.

Watching him in action, I had no doubts about how he pulled off feats of greatness. Anyone would find themselves entangled in his web of warmth, where they felt like he had their full attention throughout the conversation. But the glances he shot me or the way my drink never went dry or how he moved us to seats without a word from me when my toes started to pinch...

Although others diverted his focus over the hours, I had

no doubt I had his attention. It was unnerving and exhilarating all at once.

The steady flow of people meant we barely had a moment alone, except on the dance floor. Bodies bumped and jumped around us, but he held me in his arms, dancing to music that only existed in his head. It had a rhythm and a melody he painted across my body with his own, and then it ended. On our walk to the VIP area, the French aristocrat showed back up and needed Hunter.

"Do you want to go?"

My feet were begging for mercy. "I'm going to go sit down."

He leaned in, his lips brushing against my ear. "I have to go speak with someone, but I'll be back as soon as I can."

Now my stomach was in full-blown acrobatics. If I turned my head, we'd be kissing. I squeezed my thighs together, wanting to know what other plans he had for tonight. He was in perpetual pull mode with not a push in sight, and the magnet strengthened with every second spent with him.

I nodded and climbed the steps to the VIP area rope, which was lifted without me saying a word. It seemed some of Hunter's shine had rubbed off on me after all.

I spotted an empty couch along the wall, but I was intercepted before I could make it there. "Hello, gorgeous. We haven't had a chance to talk all night."

I pinched my lips together before turning and relaxing them. This was Hunter's friend—well, maybe not friend, but someone he worked with who had showed up earlier with a gorgeous woman. "Trevor, right?" I stopped my retreat to a gloriously padded seat when the guy stepped in front of me.

He lifted an eyebrow with a smirk. "Yes, and you're Sabrina."

"That I am." I rocked on my heels with my clutch in my hands and searched the twinkling and glittering dance floor for Hunter or any other friendly faces, which was crazy since I didn't know many people in the city. "You and Hunter work together, right?"

He laughed. "Not quite. He and I have done business together, but we don't work together. My father runs one of the largest sound production and rental companies on the East Coast."

I hated how he tried to get in a dig at Hunter or pretend working for Daddy's business somehow made him better than Hunter, who'd created his side of the business with not much else other than his hard work, charisma, and determination to succeed. Where would this asshat be without Daddy's money?

"That's awesome for your father."

The level of smugness and preening from this guy made every attractive part of his exterior wither, but I kept my tone light and reminded myself he was someone Hunter worked with.

"It will all be mine soon." He gulped from his glass with his gaze on me like he was waiting for me to start fanning myself and squealing with delight at being in his presence.

"That's great for you." I crossed one arm over my chest and sipped from my drink, scanning the dance floor where Hunter had disappeared.

"I've never seen you around with Hunter."

"Probably because I've never been out with Hunter before." I hoped Hunter would be back soon and kept my gaze pointedly away from Trevor. Where the hell was this Trevor's date? Not that I could begrudge her wanting to get as far away as possible. I also didn't want Hunter to come back with us standing so close and get the wrong idea.

Trevor's arm brushed against mine.

I glanced over my shoulder and jerked away facing forward, my skin crawling, but I tamped down the urge to shove him away. This was Hunter's work event. I needed to play nice. I took a half step to the side, trying not to be obvious in how much I didn't want to be near this guy.

He didn't take the hint and moved in closer, using the volume as an excuse to tell me all about how he'd be taking a trip to Bali soon before bringing things back to me and Hunter.

He was close like we were packed in at a concert, not in a VIP area with plenty of seats and tables for the other people enjoying their time in the space.

"Hunter has been known to enjoy the company of many different beautiful women. Maybe he's trying something different."

I wasn't sure how to take what he said. Granted, I'd been trying not to pay attention. "What Hunter did before he met me and what he'll do after me are none of my business."

"I could certainly find some entertaining options for you after Hunter's had his fun."

Ew! The balls. "I'm not a hooker or plaything, and one thing I know for sure..." Leaning in, I held his gaze, wanting him to know exactly how much I meant my next words. "Under no uncertain terms will whatever I do after Hunter be you, Trevor."

His nostrils flared, and his hand shot out, hooking my elbow before I could back off. "And why the fuck not? You should be happy I've even spared you a glance when there are gorgeous, thin, and classy women here tonight."

And playing nice just went out the window. Trying to jerk my arm from his grip, I spoke through clenched teeth. "Then why the hell don't you go bother them, asshole. Get your fucking hands off me." I tugged my arm again, but his grip tightened.

"Who the fuck do you think you're talking to, you fat bitch?"

"Don't you fucking talk to her like that." Hunter grabbed Trevor's hand, jerking it away from me, and from the noise Trevor made, Hunter wasn't holding back an ounce of the rage pouring off him in waves. His hand shot out, and he grabbed Trevor by the throat like he was going to carry him out by it.

Trevor grunted and stared at Hunter with wild eyes. "What the fuck are you doing?" he gurgled and flailed at Hunter, who had his fingers around Trevor's throat.

"Hunter, stop!" I shouted, grabbing his shoulder.

He looked from Trevor to me and released his grip.

Trevor stumbled back, his hand shooting to what had to be a sore throat. "What the fuck, Hunter? What's your problem? I tell a fat chick she's fat and you lose your fucking mind?" He stared at Hunter, bewildered, like he couldn't understand why anyone would kick up such a fuss over me. His acid gaze cut to me.

The delicious food and drinks I'd been indulging in all night curdled in my stomach. Bile churned, burning its way up my throat.

Hunter stepped in front of me, blocking Trevor from my view. "Get out of my fucking sight."

"You want to fuck her, fine. Have fun blowing your knees

out. And the deal for the rigs for New Year's is over. And that six-figure deposit—consider it gone."

Dread sank its claws deep into my chest. No, the concert was so important to Hunter and his business. Why'd I have to freak out? I'd put up with assholes before. I could've laughed it off and played dumb. This was a big deal for Hunter. And I'd ruined it for him.

"Leave, now," Hunter growled with a barely leashed fury.

Somewhere in Trevor's lizard brain, he must've realized how serious Hunter was. His face paled as security took him by the arm and led him away, but he wasn't done. Trying to jerk free from security and failing, he whipped around and jabbed a furious finger in Hunter's direction. "Good luck finding someone else within a thousand miles who'll work with you. I hope you've got extra money to get all your gear from Chicago from here on out."

Confused heads turned in our direction at the shouting drowning out some of the music.

Then Trevor was gone and it was only me and Hunter— and the twenty other people who'd been an audience to what just happened.

Hunter turned to me.

My stomach knotted, and my throat tightened. I didn't have the words.

Rage reverberated through his body, and he stared at me with his eyes still blazing. "Let's go." His voice was harsh and clipped.

I wanted to be anywhere but here. How had things gone so wrong? Tears prickled at the edges of my eyes, and I lifted my chin and blinked to keep them from spilling over.

Hunter turned me and placed his hand on the small of

my back, not so much pushing me toward the door, but more forcefully ushering.

Partygoers went back to laughing, dancing, and drinking with glances in our direction, trying to figure out what just happened. I was still in shock, not able to get a handle on it myself. But every step toward the door felt like a trip back to the real world and not the magical place this had been before it turned sour.

I opened my mouth, trying to find the words. "I'm—"

"No," he bit out.

My lips slammed shut.

A black town car idled by the curb, and he jerked the door open and got me inside without even asking if this was the right car. I slid across the leather seats and pressed my back against the door on my side, not sure who this Hunter was I was dealing with.

I'd fucked up his big deal. I knew how important the New Year's Eve concert was to him. Over our puzzles, he let me in on all the details and how much time and energy he had put into it. How much it meant to the business.

He had so much riding on it, and I hated that now a crucial part of it was in ruins. This was what I got for leaving the apartment. Why hadn't he let me stay in my bubble?

The stifling silence smothered the car ride back home. The whole time I kept running through how I'd screwed that up for him, how upset he was and how the whole evening had been ruined.

"I'm—"

Before I could get the sentence out, he cut me off. "Don't say another word." It came out as more of a bark than a shout, but I jumped all the same and tilted my head back, staring at the marked roof of the car.

I clammed up and tried not to cry, blinking back my burning tears.

The town car pulled up to the curb in front of the building. Hunter got out. I'd reached for the handle on my side when I saw he held out his hand to help me out.

Scooting across the town car, I took it and stepped out onto the curb beside him.

His nostrils flared, and his body was rigid.

"Head upstairs."

"You're not coming in?"

"I need to go for a walk." He shoved his hands into his pockets turned away from me.

It felt like a gut punch or like someone had shoved their hand into my chest and decided to explore for a bit. "Hunter, I'm sorry." I hated the pleading tone in my voice. My shoulders rolled forward, and I wrapped my arms around myself.

He leaned his head back, staring up at the night sky.

"I know this is a big deal for you—"

He whipped back around with eyes full of fury. "I swear, if you apologize for him and what happened back there again, I'm going to hunt him down and beat him unconscious."

I gasped, confusion slamming into me. The November air stung my teeth.

His hands were out of his pockets and he squeezed them in fists in front of his face. "I'm seconds away from rushing back across town and knocking every capped tooth out of his goddamn mouth, and you're here apologizing to me about it? For what he did?"

"I... It was my fau—"

He stepped closer so quickly I took a stumbling step back. He jammed his fist against his mouth like he was trying to hold back and shook his head, letting out a long, low breath that filled the air with steam.

Some of the tension in his body drained away, and he opened his arms to me.

Hesitantly I stepped forward.

One hand pressed against the center of my back, and the other traced down the side of my face. "This wasn't your fault. Don't for one second believe I've thought that. I knew he was an asshole. I just never thought he'd put his hands on you like that or say what he said to you. I'm sorry. But never think that I'd put New Year's Eve or anything else happening in my life above you or let someone treat you like that for a deal. *Never.*" The words came out forcefully, vehemently. "Tell me you understand."

I nodded, my throat clogged with emotion.

He wasn't upset with me. He was upset *for* me. More than upset. He was raging and ready to beat the crap out of someone for me.

I wasn't one to condone violence, but I had to lock my knees so I didn't turn into a puddle at his feet.

"Can I hear you say it?"

Right now he reminded me of Cat. It was good to have someone else in my life who I could count on.

"I understand. Now can we go upstairs?"

The corners of his mouth dipped. "I think I should still probably take a walk."

Wind whipped past, freeze burning my ears. I wanted him to be with me and didn't want him beating himself up about this any more than he'd admonished me not to.

"It's freezing. Come upstairs."

"I'm a little too amped up still, and after how I'd been thinking about you in this dress all night, I don't want to..." He tried to pull away.

"You don't want to what?" I locked my hand onto his, not allowing him to let go, and ducked my head to catch his gaze.

"Ruin tonight by losing my cool."

I let go of his hand, leaned in, and whispered, "If you losing your cool means tearing this dress off me and having sex on any available surface in the apartment, then I'm letting you know right now, I'm all for you losing every last bit of your cool." With my palms pressed against his chest, I explored his neck and the shell of his ear with my lips before nipping him.

His hold on me tightened and he shuddered.

If I hadn't been trying to keep up my cool, brave-girl front, I'd have pumped my hands overhead at his reaction.

Gripping my chin, he traced my bottom lip with his thumb before his lips crashed down onto mine. The chaotic chemistry spilled out onto the pavement. His insistent lips and sweeping tongue danced with mine and drew a gasp from me.

Cool was out the door as my body heated. I expected steam to rise from under his jacket, signaling just how intense the fiery feeling pooling in my belly had gotten.

"How was that?" he asked against my lips.

"Warmer." The cool-girl front was melting fast.

He guided me to the front door with his hand on the small of my back dipping maddeningly lower with each step. "Let's get you inside and out of these clothes."

The doorman opened the door, and we walked across the lobby.

I jammed my finger into the elevator button. "Let's."

27

HUNTER

The humming in my body shifted from rage to something much more dangerous the second my lips met Sabrina's. It was dangerous to more than my fists or my face; it threatened to wreck my heart. The fury dissolved like a winter's chill leeched from my body by the forced air in the lobby.

I'd wanted to tear Trevor apart when I saw his hand on Sabrina and what he said sent me into a wrath mode I hadn't experienced before. And for her to apologize to me...

It was only the plaintive look in her eyes and the apology that quelled the beast clawing inside of me. Trevor was garbage and I'd always known that, but he'd been useful garbage. A fool who could get what he wanted and I could get what I wanted, but when what he wanted became Sabrina and to disrespect her when she shot him down? All bets were off.

I'd spend all night letting her know that none of it was her fault and the vileness he'd spewed at her was as worthless as he was. If he couldn't see her beauty, then he didn't deserve it. There had never been another woman who'd gotten to me like Sabrina.

All I saw was her, and all I wanted was her. How I'd restrained myself this long was a minor miracle. But dancing with her, touching her, kissing her had driven home how our first night hadn't quenched half the thirst I had for her. I was crawling in the desert, and she was a glass of ice water under the shade.

Inside the hallway, we rushed to the front door to our apartment with matched steps of anticipation. Once the door closed, both our coats hit the floor and my hands were in her hair.

Hers were on my back, and I turned to press her against the wall before pitching forward into darkness. Twisting my body, I took the brunt of the fall.

She looked up at me with wide, twinkling eyes.

Shoes dug into my back, and above her head, coats swayed, jostled by our unceremonious plunge into the coat closet. A hanger flipped off the rod and whacked me in the center of my forehead. Real smooth.

"Was this where you meant for us to end up?" She didn't try to stifle her laughter.

I yanked at a boot that had been digging into my back and tossed it aside.

"Not exactly."

"Are you always this suave?" Her full-on grin banished the last gasps of the tumultuous feelings that had plagued me outside.

"I've been known to be smoother."

She crawled off me and sat on her haunches, watching me try to extricate myself from the tangle of dropped coats and hangers.

I tried to sit up but was jerked to the side, unable to move. Something was caught on my shirt.

"A little help?"

She crawled back over me with her knee settled between my legs and hips astride my thigh. Her fingers moved deftly by my collar. With a sharp tug, the tension eased and I was able to sit up.

Instead of pulling us both free, I gripped her hip and the back of her neck, meeting her lips with the hunger I'd restrained all night.

Her body jolted before she sank into me, like she'd melted from my touch.

I cupped the side of her neck, and the coats brushed the top of my head. A cashmere peacoat dropped over the top of us, blanketing us in darkness.

Sabrina broke the seal of our lips. Her melodic laughter tapped against my heart, pushing it close to bursting.

I was feeling things for her I'd vowed not to feel, not just for her but for anyone. She made me want things, wish for things I'd sworn would never be for me. Resting my forehead against hers, I tugged the coat off and let it drop to the floor.

I traced my thumb along her cheek. "Maybe we should get out of the closet."

"Good idea." She scooted off me once again and stood in the dimly lit hallway looking like an ethereal vision. The flower crown was gone, but little bits of baby's breath stayed nestled in her hair.

Looking up at her with the light creating a halo over her head, flowing dress dancing around her knees, and desire swimming in her eyes, I was overpowered by how much I wanted her.

I jumped up and wrapped my arms around her and scooped her up.

She yelped and pushed against my chest. "Hunter, put me down." With wide eyes she wiggled her body, pressing her full breasts even harder against me and driving the blood pumping through my veins even lower to the point of pain. Walking was difficult with my cock trapped against my inseam, but I couldn't be deterred from my objective, which was getting her into my bed again.

"Stop squirming." We made it down the hallway with her repeating the phrase the whole time.

The tender feelings were getting harder to ignore. Not the carnal pleasure still riding me hard, but all those feelings draped around our quiet moments together—sitting with her at the table scrutinizing every puzzle piece, listening to her rock out to One Direction, or sitting on the couch with her curled up beside me.

Finally in my bedroom, I loosened my arms and did as she asked.

She dropped onto the bed and shot a playful accusatory glare my way. "I told you to put me down."

"I did." I toed off my shoes.

She kicked hers off too. "I meant in the hallway."

"I meant in the bed." I unbuttoned my shirt.

"I'm too heavy to carry." She jerked down the zipper on the back of her dress.

"Obviously not, if I did it." My shirt dropped to the floor.

Her gaze narrowed, and she gathered the bottom of the dress and whipped it over her head. "Tell me you won't carry me again." Her glower was tinged with desire, and I didn't miss the way her gaze skimmed over my now-exposed skin.

My mouth watered. The light pink molded cups of her

bra pushed her breasts up, simulating the overflowing handful I'd experienced already. The black underwear wasn't lacy or skimpy, but my cock didn't mind, rising to the point the zipper of my pants bit into the head of my cock.

Her body called to me, striking a keen chord of yearning to be inside her all over again.

My belt jingled, and I kicked off my pants. "Not on your life."

"Hunter, be serious." She chucked the bundle of fabric straight at my face.

I let the dress fall and crawled onto the bed, dropping my hands on either side of her. My body skimmed along hers. Our lips were less than an inch apart. "I'm completely serious."

She gasped. Her breasts, still contained by her bra, pressed against my chest. "I don't want you to hurt yourself."

There were only two swaths of fabric between her and me. "I won't." I ran my fingers through her hair.

"But you might."

My lips were on her. Her mouth, her neck, the spot just below her ear that made goose bumps rise on her skin.

With one quick change in position, her legs were wrapped around my hips.

The heat of her nestled against my body, just above my dick, was torturous and exhilarating all at once.

Hungry and insatiable, I flicked the clasp on her bra and dragged my mouth from her lips to the stiff peaks I'd been waiting to sample for far too long.

Using my tongue, teeth, lips, and fingers, I teased her, switching from one nipple to the other.

My cock pressed into the soft bed, torturing me.

The heat of her pussy seared my skin, and her

squirming made it hard to focus. Every moan sharpened my drive and spurred me on.

Soon her fingers in my hair became less caresses and more clenches.

Wanting to make this an unforgettable night without a hint of a rain cloud, I shoved myself lower.

My dick rubbing against the bed was torture, but I was determined to taste her this time.

Tugging her underwear down by the waistband, I flung them across the room and settled myself between her legs.

The hair covering her folds glistened, and her clit peeked out from its hood, demanding attention.

Happy to comply, I circled the bundle of nerves with my thumb.

Her feet slammed against the mattress. "Oh, shit!"

My smirk was lost to the need to give her pleasure even though my cock was screaming for relief.

Taking my cues from her moans and cries, I lathed her opening with my tongue, wanting every drop of her. Every sound from her pushed me closer to my brink.

I dipped my fingers inside her pussy and her back arched off the bed. Rubbing them against her walls, I found the spot that earned me a heel to my back. The pain made the pleasure I was giving her that much sweeter.

My name burst free from her lips with a raspy moan.

Liquid fire felt like it had been poured into my veins.

Her legs tightened around my head, blocking out all sound other than the thundering of my pulse. She relaxed and I crawled up her body, triumphant at the dazed look in her hooded gaze.

My body was ablaze, ready and on the brink if I didn't have her soon.

With sex-hazy, glazed eyes, she grabbed me and pulled me on top of her.

"You're the most beautiful woman I've ever seen."

Even flushed from her orgasm, the redness in her skin deepened. "I could say the same about you, Hunter."

The barest of chuckles made it through the tightness in my throat.

Her fingers increased in urgency, pushing against my boxers. "I need you now."

For some reason I wanted this to last. I wanted to be here with her as long as I could, staying in this perfect moment where nothing else mattered except for the way she looked up at me.

A quick tug later there was nothing separating us. I dragged the head of my cock up and down her slickness, shuddering at the teeth-clenching pleasure rocketing down my spine.

Finally gathering enough sense, I grabbed a condom from the nightstand and rolled it on.

She hitched her legs higher on my hips, heels against my spine, opening herself up to me completely. "Stop teasing m—"

The last word was lost to a gasp when I plunged deep into her in one motion. Buried to the hilt, I gripped the sheets to keep my orgasm at bay.

Settling over her, I opened my eyes, and she stared up at me with a hooded, unfocused gaze. I rocked back before powering forward.

She gasped and tightened around me.

"Are you happy now?"

"Completely." Her body arched and her breasts rubbed against my chest, adding to the avalanche of sensations ripping through my body.

The tight, velvety grip of her around me, coupled with the spasms and ripples of her walls, nearly ended me. My jaw locked, and I ground out curses, trying to rein in the pleasure rocketing through me. The waves of pleasure rolled over me hard, threatening to kick me back up onto the shore like an inexperienced rookie.

Her fingers tightened against my back, digging into the muscle, and her body went rigid under me. She buried her head against my neck and clung to me like she was afraid she'd float away.

My hips snapped, racing toward the orgasm just out of reach. Letting myself loose, I pounded into her, and her gasps heightened until she screamed my name against my skin.

I plunged over the precipice of the chaotic storm of bliss, feeling it in my teeth, still clenched tight, and holding onto her.

My heart pounded, drumming in my chest at more than the pleasure hurtling down my spine. I wanted to hold her all night. I wanted to wake up beside her. A lurch jammed into my ribs that I'd be robbed of the peace of sleeping beside her. It was too risky, and I didn't want to risk hurting her in my nightmare state or the shame that would come along with this misery I'd been living with for months. But that was later and this was now. I'd soak up all of her for as long as I could.

Slowly her muscles relaxed, and she dropped back onto the bed. Her legs fell free from the lock around me, and I fell forward, bracing my weight above her but not wanting to separate just yet.

"That was..." Her words were sex-drunk slurred.

"It really was." Pulling myself free from her, I groaned and she moaned.

"I think you just made a new best friend." Her eyes drifted closed.

After disposing of the condom, I was back on the bed with her. "Really?"

She opened one eye and nodded. "Oh yeah."

"Does this mean I have permission to carry you whenever I want?" I grinned down at her, brushing the sweaty hair from her forehead.

She chuckled, her breasts jiggling as she swatted at me.

My cock, which had no business being ready for another round, stiffened against my leg.

Her fingers brushed against the center of my chest. "I'll think about it."

In the panting afterglow of sex, she groaned and rolled over, sliding out of the bed.

I propped myself up on my elbow and reached for her with my other hand. "Where are you going?"

She scrunched up her nose. "To my room." Like it was the most obvious answer ever.

"Why?"

"Hunter, let's not play games." She said it almost like she was let down.

"I'm not playing games. It's still early." It wasn't even midnight yet. Trevor had done one favor and gotten us back to the apartment earlier than I'd have normally left.

"You need your space. It's fine. I get it." She waved a placating hand in my direction.

"Sabri—" We still had time. I'd go pound an espresso if that's what it took to make sure I didn't nod off.

Her face filled with irritation and a sliver of sadness. "I won't make you kick me out again."

My throat tightened, and the words barely made it out. "I wasn't going to kick you out." Even to my own ears it was a lie. I wouldn't kick her out like the first time, but I'd have had to come up with a reason for her to go. Maybe taking her to her room and having her again before tucking her in again.

"Were you honestly going to ask me to stay?" She propped her hands on her hips, looking every bit as magnificent as she had in the dress.

My gaze dropped, unable to say the words or explain that I couldn't have her stay the night. My heart sank. It had been brimming with the possibly of the night and more time with her, and it was gone now.

She was out of my bed, ready to flee back to her own room, and I didn't even have the words to tell her I wanted her with me. I'd been under her spell since she moved in, but I had tamped it down, locking it away because I couldn't tell her what she wanted to hear. I couldn't ask her to stay.

"Exactly." Her shoulders dropped a fraction.

All the anger I'd been feeling earlier was now directed right at me. "Don't—"

"We're fine. Night, Hunter." She bent and kissed my cheek. "I'll see you in the morning."

At each of her gentle footsteps retreating down the hallway, the blows in my chest hit harder. Her door closed, not slammed. It hurt even more.

I wanted her to rage at me, throw things at me, tell me how much of an inconsiderate asshole I was. Instead she was understanding of an issue I hadn't even been able to put into words, which wasn't going away.

I grabbed a pillow and held it over my face and screamed into it.

With anger still warring in my chest, I got out of bed and closed my door. With a tap on my phone the speakers came to life, music spilling out into the dead silence of the room.

28

SABRINA

A sound woke me, but it wasn't the music rumbling through the walls. At this point, without the driving bass line, I probably couldn't sleep. I stared up at the ceiling, straining for what it might've been. Nothing.

My eyes drifted closed again.

The three-minute-long guitar solo shredded for the third time tonight. He could at least have put a few different albums on repeat. At this point I could probably pick up a Fender Strat and play it myself.

There were no sea legs for Hunter Saxton.

We'd had sex, not once but twice. He'd taken me to Jameson's, and I'd met all his friends. We'd even had a night in together, not that I hadn't woken up on the couch by myself with a crick in my neck, but there had also been a blanket draped over me. But tonight he had been sweeping me off my feet on an entirely different level, and unfortunately, literally. Playful and hot as hell, it was everything it felt like we were, but then came the inevitable moment when it all ended.

Leaving was a lot easier than being escorted out again, but the pang in my chest had still been there. A lump in my throat where I'd hoped maybe I'd been wrong and he'd drag me right back into bed with him, but I'd been right and he'd let me go. At least now I knew where I stood. I knew what we were and only hoped I'd be able to protect my heart against the charm rocket boosters Hunter flicked on at a moment's notice.

Fun and light, I could do that.

After tossing and turning through another two songs, I flung off my blankets and got out of bed. Maybe a night cap could get me back to sleep.

I opened my door, and my ears perked up at a noise between the breaks in the music. A voice talking, but the words were indistinct.

Following the sound, I stood outside Hunter's door. The music kicked in again. I strained to hear over the din of the song.

But his voice was there. It was three in the morning, who could he be talking to? Pressing my ear against the door, I leaned in.

Those weren't sounds of conversation. They were sounds of pain. Gut-wrenching, soul-splitting pain.

Without thinking, I flung the door open.

Tangled in his sheets, Hunter thrashed and flailed in his bed.

I rushed to him and grabbed his shoulders.

A hoarse cry came from his throat.

"Hunter, wake up." I shook him, but his eyes were closed and his thrashing intensified, nearly dropping me off the side of the bed. Were you supposed to wake someone from a nightmare?

The pain in his voice ripped from his throat, which sounded raw, scaring me.

"Hunter!" I shook him harder. "Hunter, it's me. Wake up."

He shot forward. His head almost collided with mine.

My hands moved from his shoulders to one between his pecs and against his back to steady him.

His heart thundered beneath my palm, pounding even faster than the shredding solo. He stared at me with unfocused eyes.

"Hunter..."

He jumped and his gaze shot to mine. One second I stared into his eyes, and the next, I was crushed against him. His arms locked around my back so tightly I struggled to breathe, and my face was buried in the side of his neck.

Sweat soaked through my shirt, plastering it to my body, but all I could focus on was the trembling Hunter holding me with a fear-and-desperation-laced grip.

I stumbled, trying to get my feet back under me, and swayed as much as I could in his grasp, my own heart rate spiking at finding him this way.

Shuddering breaths shook his body. His fingers clutched at my back.

"It's okay. I'm here." I wished my hands were free to try to calm him more. Instead I used my voice to soothe him, repeating the phrases over and over and rocked us together.

He buried his face deeper into the crook of my neck, inhaling so deeply it felt like a breeze was whooshing in through an open window.

We sat there, clinging to each other until his heart no longer beat so strongly I couldn't tell which was his and which was mine.

Tears prickled in my eyes, but I squeezed them tight.

This wasn't the time for me to freak out, but waking up to Hunter like this... I'd never been more scared in my life.

I rubbed my hands up and down his back with my restricted movement.

His grip loosened slowly and I could extricate my arms.

I wasn't sure if he was clinging to me now because he needed me or because he didn't want to face me. I dragged my fingers though his soaking hair.

"Why don't you take a shower and get changed? I'll make some hot chocolate."

He didn't say a word, but his arms released a bit more, no longer lung-restrictingly tight. His head dropped, and he finally let go completely.

I ran my fingers under his chin, lifting his head and not letting him evade my gaze.

"Grab a shower, and I'll get the hot chocolate. I'm not taking no for an answer. I'll be back in a few." Leaving, I didn't wait for his response.

I ducked into my room and changed my clothes, which were drenched. In my flannels, I popped into the kitchen and found a couple packets of marshmallow explosion hot chocolate. What was the point of hot chocolate without an absurd number of mini-marshmallows?

I searched through my stash and grabbed some chocolate chip cookie bars and a bottle of water. With the snacks and water shoved into my pockets, I walked down the hall to his bedroom.

Hunter sat on the edge of his bed with a towel wrapped around his waist. Water, not sweat, dripped from the tips of his hair and rolled down his neck.

"Here's the hot chocolate." I set the mug down on his nightstand and turned the handle toward him.

He stared straight into the dim light of the bathroom.

I fished the other supplies out of my pockets. "Why don't you get dressed? The hot chocolate is here for you."

He nodded without saying a word and walked into his closet.

I looked at his bed and darted back out of the room into the laundry room. Sheets for the bed were neatly folded on the shelf. Inside his room, I hugged the sheets against my chest.

A drawer closed in the closet, and I got to work, ripping the sheets off his bed, glad my skills could finally come in handy.

I was tucking the flat sheet under the mattress when Hunter walked out, shoving his arm into his t-shirt.

He stopped when he saw me. "You don't have to do that."

"I know." I smoothed out the sheet and grabbed the duvet, unbuttoning it and pulling the bulky material out. "Is this why you didn't want to sleep with me?" I peered up at him, hope burning brightly that I had been wrong for once, that all my instincts had been leading me astray.

His chin dropped in a grim nod.

Relief filled my lungs, and now all the feelings I had for him didn't feel so scary. I wasn't the only one trying to find my footing.

I shoved my arms into the new clean cover inside out, grabbed the edges of the duvet, and pulled it through, covering the whole thing in one solid shake.

"How the hell did you do that?"

"Magic." I wiggled my fingers with my arms wrapped around the bulky material. "It's also kind of my job. The hot chocolate will get cold. Why don't you have some?"

He walked around me and picked up the mug from the bedside table. "And you're sharing your snacks with me?"

"I thought you could use it more than I could." I finished with the duvet and grabbed the pillows.

"You really don't have to do that."

I peered over my shoulder. "I know, but it needed to be done."

He set down his mug and helped me with the pillows before walking me over to the seating area where he'd set up the food and drinks.

The chairs were so big I felt like I was a human-sized cat ready to curl up. Instead I picked up my mug and sipped from it, not sure where to look. The stilted silence made it hard to swallow.

Hunter drained his mug.

"I'll get you another cup." I set mine down, relieved for an escape. In the kitchen I tried to come up with a game plan. He didn't seem like he wanted to talk, but it didn't seem like what he'd had tonight was a run-of-the-mill nightmare. He'd been so scared, holding on so tightly and not wanting to let go. Was that how he woke most nights?

When I walked back in, I handed him the mug, but Hunter's hand hooked around my wrist before sliding to my waist, not letting me return to my chair.

Instead he pulled me down onto his lap and set down his drink.

I squirmed, trying to brace my weight on my legs.

Not letting me, he swung my thighs over his lap so I was fully seated on him. "Stop moving."

"Let me sit in my own seat then." I twisted, pulling away.

"You don't want to sit with me." His arms loosened from around my waist. He was giving me my opening to hop up and sit in my own seat. But the phrase felt like it held more meaning than sitting on his lap. Suddenly I was torn between my insecurities and what he seemed to need to feel better.

I looped my arms around his neck. "Of course I do. But you need to tell me when I get too heavy."

"Never." His arm wrapped back around me, and he grabbed my mug, handing it to me before he took his own.

"Do you want to talk about it?" I sipped from my hot now-lukewarm chocolate.

His head dropped against the back of the chair. "I guess that was inevitable, huh?"

"You know how much I love to get under your skin." I poked a finger into the center of his chest. The soft cotton was warm and dry. I rested my hand against him, letting his heart beat against my palm. "How long have you had the nightmares?"

"A few months." He took a gulp from his steaming mug and winced.

"What are they about?"

His muscles tightened under me. He stared out the window beside us. The seconds ticked by with nothing more than the twin sounds of our breaths and my heartbeat whooshing in my ears.

Taking a breath, I prepared to change the subject.

"Losing everyone I've ever cared about."

I set down my mug, feeling like my chest was being cracked open.

He'd dealt with a lot of loss already. My parents were still alive and healthy. My grandparents on both sides had died before I could remember. I'd never lost anyone else close to me. "These are new nightmares?"

He nodded. Damp strands of hair clung to the side of his face. "New now." His fingers tapped against the sides of his mug. "I've had them before." His head dipped, and his jaw muscles clenched. "When my mom died."

"And the new round started when your dad died?"

His body stiffened. "This has nothing to do with him. He just happened to die around the same date she did."

I opened my mouth and snapped it shut. Tonight wasn't the night to push it. "Do you have the nightmares every night?"

Another grim nod. He picked up one of the chocolate chip cookie bars and split it in two, handing me half. "Every night."

Taking a bite, I gave myself some time to find out more without pushing him too hard. "How are you getting any sleep?"

He tilted his chin, eyes boring into mine.

"Ah, you're not." I took another bite. "That explains the Mr. Grumpy Pants routine."

"When have I ever been Mr. Grumpy Pants?"

I leveled my gaze at him, wanting to inject a little playfulness into the night. A little less heaviness.

His gaze darted away, and he took a bite of his cookie. "Maybe a little." He grumbled with a half laugh, half huff.

Leaning against his chest, I sank into the cradle of his arm, and we stared out at the soft glow on the horizon. "You should call out of work today."

He set his mug down and scrubbed a hand down his face. "There's so much work to get done and less than four weeks to make it all happen. And after last night, I need to find a new supplier."

My stomach plummeted. Guilt gnawed at me. "I'm sorry."

His hands tightened on my hip. "I wasn't blaming you. I was blaming myself for signing with him in the first place."

"But now you've got a mountain more work do to. I know how much the concert means to you."

"I'd do it again without a single regret." His words were fierce and sharp.

My heart leaped before I leashed it again and pulled it back to Earth. There was no need to get ahead of myself. It was one night. A night he needed someone and it would probably mean nothing, but I could be here for him tonight.

I believed him, but now it was my turn to take care of him. I set down my mug and stood.

"What are you doing?"

"We're going to bed."

29

HUNTER

"Sabrina..." As much as I wanted her with me... as much as I needed her with me...

"It's okay." She held her hand out to me.

My throat tightened, Adam's apple bobbing with an iron strike of panic. I stared at her outstretched hand, wanting to take it and curl up behind her with my arms wrapped tight around her chest and my nose buried in her hair, but I couldn't. "I don't want to freak out with you beside me."

"I'm tough. I can handle it." She let her hand fall and turned, pulling the shades down, blocking out the sun slowly emerging through the three windows beside our chairs.

I cleared my throat. "Sabrina..."

"Don't even try it. I'm here, so you're going to have to deal with it." She grabbed my hand and pulled me forward out of the chair.

Without another word, I let her lead, walking on stilted, numb legs. My body was stiff, and I was teetering on the edge of a full-on freak out.

She pushed back the freshly made sheets and scooted

into the bed, never breaking eye contact, like she was afraid I'd bolt into the bathroom again and lock the door. The thought had entered my mind.

Rising up onto her knees, she looped her arms around my neck and pulled me down with her until we were both flat and my head rested against her shoulder.

Her breath ruffled my hair. "Are you comfy?"

Trying to calm myself, I inhaled deeply, breathing every molecule of her scent I could. "I am, but I still don't think—"

"Don't think at all. Just rest." She ran her fingers through my hair from the crown of my head to the nape of my neck. "It'll all feel better once you've gotten some solid sleep."

She stared into my eyes. Her expression was filled with concern and resolve.

I licked my dry lips. "You don't have to do this." This was a weakness I hadn't wanted to share with her. I'd hoped I could handle it all on my own.

Her face softened. "I want to. Let me be here for you. If you start to have another nightmare, I'll wake you up."

A ghost of a laugh escaped my lips. "How are you going to do that if you're asleep too?"

She brushed my hair back from my forehead. "I already got enough sleep. Just close your eyes and we can talk about it all in the morning."

My heart hammered so hard it felt like it was rocking my whole body. Slipping my arms around her, I tightened them around her waist. A war was raging inside of me. I was Hunter fucking Saxton. I didn't need anything from anyone. I was the guy who made things happen for other people. I was the one everyone turned to.

Showing this side of me was like sawing open my chest and giving her a look at the ugly insides. But the comfort in her arms and hearing the steady drum of her heart helped calm me.

She was too close, but trying to step away would be like hacking off a limb. She was who I'd been fighting this whole time, because I'd known how easy this would be. How easy it would be to fall for her completely and never stop falling.

I sighed and relaxed my muscles one by one. "Thank you, Sabrina."

All rigidness in her body was wiped away with those three words. I didn't want to be alone anymore. My resistance had fallen. The wall I'd erected between us, already slowly crumbling, disappeared.

"Don't mention it." She brushed her fingers through my hair.

I closed my eyes and let the sleep that had been stolen from me for the past four months drag me under, only I wasn't scared of what lurked beneath the surface for the first time, because she was here with me. The drumbeat of her heart would help me find my way back.

I woke, not in a puddle of my own sweat or feeling like my heart was punching like a speed bag against my ribs, but to the gentle rhythm of snores that didn't belong to me.

Sitting beside her was my copy of *The Order of the Phoenix*. My throat tightened, and I leaned over her and picked up the book, running my fingers over the front cover.

Her eyes shot open, and she sucked in a sharp breath before her gaze focused on me. Relaxing back against the pillows, she stretched. "Sorry, I fell asleep."

I pushed myself up farther in the bed. "So did I."

"Yeah, but you were supposed to sleep." Her muscles stiffened. "How was it?" Concern rippled through her words.

Taking her hand in mine, I lifted it to my lips and pressed them against the smooth skin, while tickling her palm with my fingers. "It was perfect. The best night's sleep I've had in a long time."

Her smile was megawatt wide. "That's great."

I looked down at our intertwined hands and ran my fingers from the inside of her elbow down to her wrist. "You know what this means, right?" I glanced over at her.

"What? You think now I'm going to sleep in your bed every night?" She smiled and picked up a pillow with her free hand and whacked me with it. "That I'll just sprawl under the sheets with you night after night?"

I was torn between that fantasy of spending every night with her and the hint of sadness behind her smile that I knew I'd put there. I blocked her second hit. "I know after what—"

She stopped me with a kiss. Her hands were on the sides of my face and she interlaced her fingers around the back of my neck and pulled me down on top of her. Her lips were magic, like a balm and an accelerant all at once. The fire was stoked with each brush and nibble of her lips, with every flick of her tongue.

I don't know how I'd gone days without kissing these lips. I thought I'd blown my shot or was too broken to feel their salvation again, but she was liquid desire being poured straight down my throat.

Breaking the connection, she stared into my eyes, her own wide and wanting. "I could be persuaded."

Grinning, I brushed her hair out of her face, trailing my fingers from her cheek over the shell of her ear and down the side of her neck. "How exactly might I be able to persuade you?"

She shuddered and her lips quirked up. "You're Hunter Saxton, the man who can get anyone anything. I think you can figure it out."

Bracing myself on my arms above her, I settled my hips between her parted legs. The fabric of both our bottoms got in the way. I'd never hated sweats more than I did at this moment. "You tell me when I've figured it out well enough." Slipping below the blankets, I tugged her sweats down. My knuckles brushed against the soft plushness of her thighs. It made my mouth water.

Skimming my fingers along the insides of her thighs, I ripped my sweats off and threw them across the room.

She shoved back the blankets.

Cool air washed over me.

The air in the room crackled with a covetous craving. Mine for her and, from the way her lips parted and her nostrils flared, hers for me.

Parting her folds, I delved into my afternoon delight, not wanting to stop until she'd screamed my name more than once.

Her fingers threaded through my hair, gripping it tight right along with her thighs against my ears.

Lapping at her, I basked in the taste, smell, and feel of her. Her moans, gasps, and cries guided me. My dick throbbed, pressed hard against the bed, my hips jerking with each call of my name. Using my thumb, I began in large circles around her clit before concentrating more on the swollen bundle of nerves.

"Hunter!" Her back bowed off the bed, and her thighs provided close-to-crushing ear protection. Every muscle locked up, and I kept going, urging her higher.

Her heels dug into my back before she pressed on my forehead and scooted up the bed panting, "That was..." She swallowed. "Quite a way to wake up."

I crawled up the bed and kissed her. Pride radiated in my chest at the flushed, flustered, and stunning vision beneath me. "Are you ready for more?"

Her legs latched around my hips. My cock brushed against the curls at the top of her sex, and I shuddered, trying to rein myself in. I didn't want this to end before I even got inside her.

"Whatever you're dishing out, I can handle." The combative playfulness was back, and it revved me into overdrive.

I snagged a condom out of my nightstand and raised up, poised at her entrance, trying to figure out how I'd leave this bed without losing my heart to her and trying to decide if I wanted to keep it at all.

Sinking into her, I kept my eyes from rolling back in my head, not wanting to miss a thing. She was hot and wet, gripping my cock so tightly I gritted my teeth as the pleasure demanded release, to sprint for the finish line.

She rolled her hips, meeting my thrusts with her hands on the side of my neck. "Let go, Hunter."

In three words she peeled back the edges of my soul and slipped in, slamming it closed right behind her.

I powered into her, not wanting this to end, but knowing I couldn't hold back for much longer. She came apart beneath me with my name a strangled whisper on her lips.

My jaw locked, and the heady rush of pleasure sprinted down my spine. Light-headedness overtook me as I spilled into the latex between us.

Collapsing, careful not to crush her, I stared down at her once I had control of my body again.

Breathless with orgasm-glazed eyes, she looked up at me, making me feel like anything in the world was possible. And I knew unequivocally, there was nothing I could do to stop the invasion. She'd overrun my heart in a blink, and I was blinded by her beauty.

30

SABRINA

Had I mentioned Hunter being the worst roommate ever? Talk about an Uno reverse card he'd laid on me with that one. However terrible he was as a roommate made him a thousand times better as whatever it was we were now. Life didn't change that night from what it had been before other than the dinners out once a week, no more loud music late at night—oh, and the sex. A new, not-to-be-underestimated perk to living under the same roof as Hunter.

I turned off the water and stuck the last of the dishes into the dishwasher. Hunter had handled all the heavy lifting with scrubbing the pots, the least I could do was clean the dishes, although there was a certain someone who hadn't left the kitchen yet, who was making it increasingly difficult to focus on rinsing and loading.

I was no longer woken by a spiraling drum solo; instead it might be his lips on my neck, fingers trailing over my stomach, or insistent nudge of his shaft against my butt.

"Fine, I'll let you go for Thanksgiving, but only because I'm getting you for Christmas." The back of Hunter's hand pressed against the small of my back, knuckles scraping my skin and fingers tickling the gap in my jeans, which never fit my waist as they should and right now I wasn't the least bit mad about it. With his hand anchored where it was, I couldn't move away. Not that I wanted to.

I laughed. "How magnanimous of you. Will the apartment car service take me to the airport or should I call a taxi or take the train?" Still no word from Harper Linens, so the bank account was close to cobweb levels.

He made a disgruntled noise. "I'll take you. Of course I'll take you." His other hand trailed up and down my arm.

The skimming sent a flush racing through my veins.

"I'm surprised my parents had the money to spring for this ticket, so I think our Christmas together will be a guarantee." I tilted my head and rested it on his shoulder, not wanting his teasing to stop just yet.

His lips brushed against the back of my neck. "I can't wait."

Knowing there wouldn't be a good time to do this, I went for it while Hunter seemed to be distracted.

His hands drifted from my back and wrapped around me, fingers dipping below the waistband of my jeans.

"What will you be doing for Thanksgiving?"

"Most likely going to Jameson's. Although we might all go over to Leo's instead. August gets back the day of since the wedding he's working on in Madrid is on Thanksgiving Eve, so he won't want to cook. And Everest will probably spend the whole day in his car in the parking garage of his building, determined not to give in to his family's demands to see him. He'll show up just in time for the turkey and won't have to cook anything."

"What if you hosted it?" I raised my arm and raked my fingers along his scalp. "You could cook."

His chest rumbled against my back, and his laughter tickled my ear. "I can order like a pro, but I don't think anyone would want me cooking for them on Thanksgiving. We might as well have it in a hospital waiting room while we prepare for the food poisoning." His fingers dipped lower, palm pressing against me now under my belly button.

The flutter in my stomach was almost to the point of distraction when he kissed right below my ear.

Refocusing, I turned in the circle of his arms, and he groaned like I was ending all the fun. I ran my palms over his chest. The solid, ridged, and rippled one I'd rested my head against for almost a few weeks now.

"But if you had it here, maybe you could invite Ryder." I lifted my gaze, hoping he'd have come around some over the past few months. Maybe he'd agree to eating with Ryder; it would help them both. Anytime I got a text from Ryder after checking in on him, he always seemed so alone, and I knew how that had felt growing up. Eighteen was a hard enough time, but adding in rejection from his only brother probably wasn't helping.

His hands dropped from around me, and he stepped back. "Why would I want to do that?"

The coldness in the room wasn't just from the loss of his touch. He was shutting down. Light and playfulness were no longer in his eyes. They were reserved like a wall had shot up between us. "He wasn't going to have anywhere to go, and I thought…"

"You've been talking to him? I can't believe you've been talking to him." He whipped back around to me. "Did he put you up to this?"

"What? No. Of course not. He's not a Machiavellian mastermind, Hunter. He's an eighteen-year-old looking for someone to turn to." I hated how hard he was fighting even having a conversation with Ryder. Sure, I'd wished I had siblings growing up and knew from Cat that having one didn't mean you had a new best friend in the world, but what harm could talking to Ryder do?

"That's not going to be me."

"Why can't it be?" I reached for him.

He backed away, slamming his head into the overhead cabinets and grimacing. "Why do you think I'm in any shape to be that for him? The only reason I'm not waking up with nightmares is because I am sleeping beside you. Should we invite him into my bed too?"

Irritation rippled through me. "Hunter, I'm being serious."

"Me too. I don't owe him anything. And he's got no right to ask for it from me."

This would probably backfire on me. It would probably burn down whatever easygoingness we'd had over the past month, but I had to try. The guilt had been gnawing at me that I'd waited this long to try. "Then how about me? Can I ask you to do this? Even if you don't have dinner, maybe just meet with him. Give him some food. It would mean a lot to him." I peered up. "It would mean a lot to me."

His gaze bored into mine.

"It's the holidays. Everyone should have someone during the holidays, and I don't think he has anyone."

His jaw clenched, the muscles pulling and bunching. "Welcome to the club."

A rush of anger joined with aggravation. The victim card had to be nothing more than a singed corner of paper at this point. "You have plenty of people in your life. You have Barbara, you have Leo, Everest, Jameson, August, you've got hundreds of people all over this city, probably the continent who'd open their doors to you in a heartbeat if you had no place to go.

"He doesn't have that. I'm not saying you have to sign up to coach Little League with him or bind yourself to him for the rest of your lives. I'm asking you to do the decent thing I *know* you'd do for anyone else." My lips twisted together, and I left him alone in the kitchen.

This was getting too heated. I'd try again when we had more time, but I couldn't miss my flight. And right now I didn't want to spend Thanksgiving with him after being so damn selfish.

The silence mounted with each step. Maybe it was a step too far, but I needed to say it.

Halfway through packing my bag, the front door slammed shut. I dropped my head and slid to the floor with my back against the bed. A sound caught in my throat, which already felt raw from how tight it was closed. My eyes filled, but I squeezed my lids shut. No, I wasn't going to cry. If this ended because of me feeling like I needed to tell him something important, that meant a lot to me, then so be it. It was fun while it lasted, but damn, this hurt. My chest was being hollowed out with a soup spoon. Keeping my mouth shut would've been advisable, but I couldn't help myself. Taking a few deep, shaky breaths, I got back to packing.

Maybe over the long weekend I'd start looking for a new place for after the New Year. I'd start working on a plan where my life wasn't a hair's breadth from toppling off a cliff, where I was an adult who made smart decisions.

Maybe if I pretended that was me for long enough, I'd start feeling that way for real.

Just as I zipped up my carry-on filled with a couple changes of clothes and sheets for my parents, Ian called back to let me know their cars were all reserved, but he could call in a limo service for me, I'd told him thanks for checking, but I'd find another way. There were times I forgot I lived in a building where some people spent the money I made on one project on a nice dinner.

If I didn't want to miss my flight, I'd have to leave soon. I could take SEPTA, the city metro, and be thankful I only had a carry-on.

Sliding the bag off my bed, I grabbed my purse and left my room. Leaving without talking to Hunter wasn't what I wanted to do, but it looked like he wasn't giving me a choice.

He knew I had a flight to catch.

This wouldn't be my first time breaking up with someone and leaving without another word. Would I come back to all my stuff in the package room behind the concierge desk in neatly organized and labeled boxes?

In the hallway, I was joined by Millie, who was pulling a small carry-on of her own.

I took a deep breath and smiled—or at least my best approximation of one—trying to act natural. "Hey, Millie."

"Hello, Sabrina. Are you headed to visit your family?"

"I am. What about you?"

"My children have rented a house in Aspen. I'm headed there until after the new year."

"New Year's? That's a long trip. All you have is that bag?" I pressed the down arrow on the elevator.

She laughed. "Oh no, this is all my last-minute things. Ian took down the rest of my luggage earlier. Is Hunter going with you? There's certainly been a change in him over the past few weeks."

My heart skipped a beat, dread balling up tight in the pit of my stomach.

She'd always been so sure we'd get together from the day I moved in, but now we were... whatever the hell we were... and I didn't want to have to burst her bubble. "No, he's not going with me. I'm taking the train to the airport."

She waved her hand and laughed like I'd said I'd decided to take a hot air balloon there. "Don't be silly. Do you want to share my car to the airport? You can tell me all about how things are going between you two."

A few minutes ago that had seemed like the perfect idea, but the questions about Hunter wouldn't stop and I wasn't exactly sure how to answer them.

"No, I'm fine. I was going to meet a friend first for lunch and then head to the airport."

In the lobby Millie turned to me and cupped my arm, giving it a gentle squeeze. "Have a wonderful Thanksgiving, Sabrina, and stay safe." She smelled like the perfume counter at a store way too expensive for me to even set foot in.

"Thanks, Millie." I hugged her back.

She squeezed my arm and walked over to the concierge to stand beside the trolley filled with a wardrobe's worth of matching luggage that probably cost more than all my clothes, electronics, and camera equipment put together. Whenever I spoke to her, it was easy to forget that she probably had multiple bank accounts with two commas when I was lucky to have one account with one comma before it slowly dwindled to cobwebs and mothballs.

A doorman opened the door, and I popped out into the city street. The sun hadn't set yet, and I pulled the zipper up even higher on my coat, tucked my scarf into the gap at my neck.

I turned to walk toward the train stop when a car horn honked. It didn't feel like the normal city traffic, and I spun around, expecting an angry taxi driver shouting at a biker.

Hunter ducked his body out of the open passenger-side

window of a shiny black car, which wasn't the one I'd seen him drive before. He'd reached inside to honk the horn to get my attention. He'd been waiting—for me.

I froze, not sure if I wanted to be in the car with him right now, but feeling some of the heaviness lift knowing I wouldn't be leaving town without even a goodbye.

He'd left after our fight—our first official fight as more than roommates—and I wasn't sure how I was feeling about what had happened back in the apartment, let alone him.

The decision on whether I was going with him was made for me when he crossed the sidewalk and took my bag from my hand.

"What are you doing here?"

He stopped and looked at me over his shoulder like I was the one being weird. "Taking you to the airport."

"I thought..." I straightened my back. "I thought you'd left."

"There was a last-minute issue with a vendor I needed to sort out, but I knew I could make it back in time. Come on." He held out his hand to me.

Trying to sift through the emotions welling in my chest, I wasn't sure if I wanted to believe him or actually believed him. He was acting like we hadn't had an argument an hour ago. But I'd take this over leaving thinking he was still angry with me and me pretending I was okay with that. I took his hand and let him lead me to the car. "Whose car is this?"

"An acquaintance."

"Only you have acquaintances who'd let you borrow cars like this from them. Cat's my friend, and if she had a car like this, I don't think she'd let me drive it, let alone borrow it."

He popped open the passenger-side door and held it open for me. "Everyone's got an angle. Once you figure it out, getting what you want isn't that hard."

I slipped into the car, letting those words roll around in my head. What exactly did he want from me? Was there some angle he was working to get what he wanted that I couldn't see? Sometimes it felt like there had to be. For the first time in a long time, I went to the place of why the hell had he chosen me? I aggravated him, irritated him, pushed him, and it was hard to make sense of why he wanted to be my guy.

The trunk slammed shut, and he opened the driver's side door and slid into the car like he'd been driving it for years.

"I'm sorry I snapped at you." His gaze cut to mine. Remorse and uncertainty filled his tone and his eyes.

Some of the tension coiling in my belly loosened. "I'm sorry I pushed you. I know it's not easy for you, Hunter." I ran my hand over the back of his, gripping the gear stick. Tracing my fingers over his knuckles, I tried to find the right words to keep this from boiling over again. Licking my lips, I took a breath and kept my gaze trained on his hand.

"If you'd spend just a few minutes with him, it would really mean a lot to me."

At the red light, he dropped his head back to the headrest and closed his eyes. With his chin tilted toward the roof of the car, he nodded. "Fine, I'll get him some food and talk to him. Maybe he'll lay off if I let him get whatever he wants to get off his chest."

Euphoria engulfed me. I was floored, completely caught off guard by how easily he threw that out after fighting against even speaking to Ryder for months. The two of them would finally have a chance to talk to each other. Maybe Hunter would see that Ryder wasn't the boogeyman, and Ryder would finally get a little of the connection he'd been craving for who knows how long.

Pulling against my seat belt, I grabbed his neck and hugged him as tightly as I could. "Thank you."

Rolling his head to the side, he brushed the back of his fingers against my cheek. "Don't mention it."

The trip to the airport was short. Too short for me. As much as I wanted to see my parents, I wanted to be with Hunter. But maybe I was falling back into the old patterns I'd had with Seth, jumping in too quickly. We'd already skipped ahead to the moving-in part, although we'd done it in reverse, so the long weekend apart would be a good thing.

It would help keep me from falling too hard and too deep.

Instead of pulling up to the curb, he drove into the parking garage and found a spot.

"You don't have to take me in."

He leaned back into his seat. "I know, but I want to."

What was it I was saying about falling hard and deep? Damn it.

Walking hand in hand, Hunter pulled my bag and stayed with me through check-in, where wouldn't you know it, he knew someone behind the counter. With my newly upgraded ticket, we hopped onto the escalator to take me up to security.

He wrapped his arms around me tightly, burying his nose in my hair and inhaling like he was trying to imprint my scent on his nasal passages.

"Will you be good while I'm gone?"

We'd been sleeping in his bed since the night I found out why he'd been kicking me out. Other than a few cover-kicking incidents, he hadn't had any more nightmares.

"I'll be okay. The bed still smells like you." His fingers brushed against my chin.

It was three days. Seventy-two hours and I'd be back in

his arms again. "I should go." I jerked my thumb over my shoulder to the rapidly growing security line.

"You should." But he didn't seem like he wanted to let me go any more than I wanted to go.

My arms shot out almost involuntarily for another quick hug, and I rushed off, not trusting myself not to miss my plane while standing here with him.

I checked back over my shoulder once I hit the metal detectors and waved to Hunter. He waved back. Once I'd gathered my bags and turned the corner, I peeked back. Only then did I see his head disappear back down the escalator taking him to ground level.

So many things had changed in such a short period of time. Living together heightened every interaction and emotion. In three days I'd be back and the welcome home felt like it would change us both.

31

HUNTER

Ryder looked up at me from one of the lobby chairs. His elbows rested on his legs, and his knee bounced up and down, shaking his whole body. "Sabrina put you up to this, didn't she?"

My jaw clenched and I nodded. I'd instantly regretted finally calling him, but I'd do it for Sabrina. The look on her face when she'd left the kitchen before getting on her flight had been so full of profound disappointment, I hadn't been able to stomach it for long. And then the way she put me in a choke-hold hug when I'd said I'd agree to meet with him had cemented my decision, although I'd wished it hadn't.

He shot up from his seat with a look of total disgust and walked toward the door. "I should've known."

I hooked his arm, not expecting him to care that much as long as he finally got what he wanted. The temptation to let him go was crowded out by how upset Sabrina would be at hearing what had happened, and I had no doubt he wouldn't keep his mouth shut. The disloyalty from our father's side ran though his veins—and mine. "What does it matter?" I bit out, irritated that he was making this more difficult than it had to be.

He stopped and glanced over his shoulder. "Sabrina will be pissed if she finds out you didn't do it, won't she?"

The muscles in my neck tightened. I bristled at how dead on he was. Was I that transparent when it came to her? "Do you want food or not?"

"Is that how you invite all guests into your apartment?" He turned and folded his arms over his chest, self-satisfied that he now had the upper hand.

My breath fumed in my throat. Close to boiling, I grimaced. "Would you like to come up for some Thanksgiving leftovers?"

"That was better, but—"

"Fuck it, do whatever the hell you want." I spun around and stormed toward the elevators, having not even a hint of the reserves necessary to deal with his bullshit.

"Wait." He rushed after me. His sneakers squeaked on the marble floor. "No, I'll come up." Falling in step beside me, he followed me into the elevator in silence.

Maybe it wouldn't be so bad if he didn't talk. I could give him the food, and he could be on his way. I should've made up a container of food and shoved it into his hands the second he stood from the chair downstairs.

The doors opened to my floor. And I trudged to the apartment. It would be ten minutes, tops. I'd spent longer periods of time with much worse people. Like the time I'd had to sit through a three-hour monologue about a big shot's polo days up in Connecticut and how much he missed riding, all to get access to the grounds of his former stables for an outdoor private concert.

Ryder and I would talk, or, hell, maybe we wouldn't. We'd talked already, maybe that would be enough for

Sabrina—but deep down I knew it wouldn't. Fine, we'd keep it light. Conversations about school, the weather, nothing about our families or father. Boring, banal, basic information only.

Ryder came inside and kept his coat on. Good, maybe he was thinking the same thing I'd been. We'd get this over with and forget about it and never have to see each other again.

"Does this mean Sabrina's your girlfriend now?"

I walked into the kitchen and pulled out all the trays and containers filled with leftover food from the fridge. One perk of working with so many food vendors was that catering trays of delicious food were always being offered up. What was in my fridge was less than a fifth of what was left at Jameson's house. Taking a load of utensils out, I tried to keep my anger in check and set them on the counter. "Sabrina and I are none of your business."

He leaned against the counter and smirked. "When she invited me up last time, she said you weren't, but after that kiss, it seems like things have changed. Even if you don't spill, she'll tell me." Shrugging, he looked around the kitchen with his arms still folded.

"If you don't know already, then Sabrina's decided that too." I took a sliver of petty satisfaction at his gloomy expression.

I took a clean, empty container and lid out and slammed it on the counter. The lid flew out of the plastic container and flopped down beside it, spinning and whirring until it dropped flat. Silence filled the space, tension thickening by the second. "There. Take as much as you want."

"Did you have Thanksgiving with your friends?"

"Yeah." Although this very interaction had been buzzing in the back of my head like a bee I couldn't swat the whole time. Other than that, we'd had fun together. Our family of friends had enjoyed the day of quiet in our otherwise break-neck lives.

"What did you do all day?" Probably avoiding the kitchen and talking to friends online. At least that was what I'd done growing up. My mom had taken over the kitchen, and it was a no man's land from sunrise until we ate. I'd sneak in to steal whatever scraps I could before she marched me out.

"Played video games and ate cereal." He shrugged again. It felt less done to irk me and more like a teenage attribute to give everything a nonchalant or insignificant vibe, even if that wasn't what he was feeling.

Against my better judgment and prying my locked jaw free, I asked the question that would roll around in my head all night if I didn't. "What about your mom?" I barely managed to keep my lips over my bared teeth.

His statuesque mom who'd leaned against the car in her sunglasses with bright red lipstick and a smirk on her lips while my dad slid the last of his boxes into the trunk of his car.

Another shrug. "Somewhere. Probably with her new boyfriend. I don't know."

"She's got a new boyfriend already." Our dad had only been dead for six months. I mean at least she'd waited until he was actually in the ground. He hadn't given my mom the same courtesy.

"It's been six months. I guess she figured it was enough time."

All the rage and burning feelings coursed through my veins at hearing about my dad or the woman he'd left my mom for. I hated that she was still running around having her fun while my mom wasn't here.

"But it's cool having the house to myself. Loads of free-dom." A sheepish look and a ducked head before he continued. "It's part of the reason why I've been able to come visit you so much, so it's not without its downsides."

Our parallels were hard to ignore. GiGi had looked after me after my mom died, but she also had my grandfather to look after. She hadn't wanted to uproot me afterward so I'd stayed in the house. She stayed there with me, but also spent a lot of time in the hospital or rehab facilities and then hospice, so I had a lot of time by myself too, but I never felt alone.

I'd used the stretches of hours and what felt like days on my own lifting weights, studying to make sure GiGi didn't get any calls from school about my grades failing when she had enough on her plate, and hanging out with friends. Interspersed in there were my moments of deal-making infamy in my high school that created a legend I'd ridden to this day. Securing party locations, security at the door if needed, kegs and whatever anyone else needed while never having a whiff of trouble around me. The veneer of the straight-laced, smart kid had served me well in more ways than one.

"Throwing parties?"

He laughed and grabbed the container, scooped out a heap of mashed potatoes into it. Next, came over half the turkey I'd brought home, a football-sized amount of stuffing. He skimped on the green beans and Brussel sprouts. A few biscuits were tucked into the gap on the side of the mound, and he ladled out a fist-sized ball of gelatinous gravy.

"Do you think you have enough?"

A beet-red, splotchy pattern glowed on the back of his neck.

"Sorry, I can put some back."

I sighed, and the balloon of anger pressing against my lungs slowly deflated. This was part of the reason I'd tried to stay away from Ryder. It was easier to hold onto the anger in short bursts, flashes that didn't need to be sustained. After any length of time it would dissipate, which was why I needed to get him out of the house. "Forget I said anything. Take as much as you want. Sabrina's not back until Sunday, so it's not like I can eat it all."

"Cool, thanks." He shoveled even more food into the container so that he needed his full weight resting against the lid to close it. Gravy globs and mashed potatoes shot out between the lid and the bottom and dropped onto the counter. "Sorry."

I grabbed some paper towels and mopped up the mess and chucked it into the trash can. "There you go. You got your food, and I talked to you. What I told Sabrina I'd do, I've done."

"Did you guys finish the puzzle?" Instead of taking the blatant cue from me, he walked past me with the container in hand into the dining room.

What had I been saying about my anger lessening? I'd spoken too soon. "We finished it a while ago."

His shoulders dropped a little. "Oh, I wanted to see it all finished."

"I can show you the picture on the box. It's the same thing just with tiny lines all over it."

Ryder half turned and looked at me with his eyes barely visible above his shoulder. "Why do you hate me so much?" The words were barely a whisper. His eyes were filled with confusion and sadness. He looked at me like I'd betrayed him.

The balloon popped, snapping against my insides. I

dragged my fingers through my hair and leaned against the wall. My fingers tapped against the chair rail. "I don't hate you, Ryder. I'm just not the big brother you're looking for. We don't know each other. We didn't grow up together. My dad left my family to start a new one with yours. After cheating on my mom, who was dying of cancer, with your mom. Can you understand why seeing you and being around you would bring up bad memories?"

My mom had tried to hide her tears. She'd cry behind closed doors, but she'd been dealing with so much and I'd been helping her along with the nurses' aides and doctors—she couldn't keep anything from me for long. The red, puffy eyes, the full boxes of tissues in the trash. I'd hated my dad for putting her through the revelations of his cheating during her last months of life. When she should've been focusing on getting better or at least having all the peace and joy she could soak up, he was ramming a divorce down her throat and ripping her heart out.

Even giving Ryder the food and talking with him for this long felt like I was forgiving a wrong I'd never planned on forgiving. *Don't worry, Dad, I'll be there for your kid after you left Mom and me high and dry.*

Ryder's head dropped. "Yeah, I can see how I'd be a reminder of all the shitty stuff our dad did. And it seems like you've got nice friends and a great place to live." His fingers tightened on the container. "I'll go now."

He rushed out of the dining room.

I followed behind him, both relieved and guilty. Every reason I'd resisted meeting with him was all rolled up into one, and these complicated feelings were only tangled up even worse by spending time with Ryder.

Accepting him wasn't possible. The guilt would eat me alive. Like all the things I'd never said to my dad were all forgiven just because he was gone. All the things I'd been too much of a coward to say to his face. Staring at Ryder was a mirror and a portal, and I couldn't go back there again. But the look on his face and the defeat in his voice, it was a tire spike to my chest.

Without putting his coat on, he gathered it up in his arms and rushed out the door, letting it slam behind him.

I'd done what I said I'd do, and now he was gone. It was for the best.

Twenty minutes after her flight popped up on the cell phone lot board, I got out and leaned against the car, waiting for her to come out the doors.

The cops were patrolling, barking at anyone there for more than ten minutes. Just when I was worried I'd need to do a lap of the airport, she raced out.

Her eyes twinkled with happiness and excitement.

I couldn't stop watching her, and she rushed forward, slamming into me. The car kept us both from toppling to the ground.

Cupping my hand to the back of her head, I held her close. "Happy to see me."

"Always." She kissed me: more than a peck, less than how I wanted to kiss her.

I laughed. "I don't know if that was always the case. I feel like there were a couple of months where you'd rather not have seen me."

"You've always been pretty to look at. It was more the shitty attitude and obsession with loud music throughout the night that I hated."

"Point taken." I reached back into the car and grabbed

the bundle I'd picked up along the way. "I got these for you." Maneuvering it out of the car, I held it up beside us.

Her eyes widened, and she looked from me to the orange, pink and yellow flowers.

"Seriously?"

A few people walking across the sidewalk with their bags turned to look at us.

The tips of my ears burned. "Seriously." I kissed her and took the carry-on bag from her. "You take these and hop in. I'll throw this in the back."

She took the bouquet and stared at them like I'd shown up with the crown jewels or Hope Diamond.

I stuck the bag in the trunk and got into the driver's side. At the same time, she settled into her seat.

Her fingers reverently brushed across the petals of the pink and yellow roses. "No one's ever gotten me flowers before."

Pulling out into traffic, I glanced at her. "Never?"

She shook her head. "No, never."

"What about the last guy you dated?"

Her body stiffened, and I felt like a dick for bringing him up, but also wanted to know more about who she'd been with before she met me. I wasn't exactly practiced when it came to relationships. How'd they stack up? How'd I compare?

"No, he wasn't great at treating people the way they deserved to be treated." Her smile faded.

I hated him without meeting him for however he'd treated her. "Is that why you left?"

"Something like that. It was time to move on, and I found out he wasn't who I'd thought he was."

"I'm sorry you had to go through that. Did he cheat?" A boulder solidified in my throat, the only thing bottling up the burn of anger in my chest that a guy might even think to betray her like that. I'd made a promise to myself to never do it and hadn't even put myself in a position where it would be possible by never even having someone I'd consider exclusive—a girlfriend—until her. Never being like my dad was on the top of my list and would continue to be when it came to how I'd live my life.

Her gaze shot to mine. "In a way."

"I don't get people like that. It destroys lives. I'll never understand or be able to forgive people who do it. And I can't believe there are people out there who'll look at a relationship or family and say, 'Yeah, I'm cool with breaking it apart.'" I shook my head.

"Maybe they don't always know," she whispered, her face nearly buried in the flowers.

I thought back to Ryder's mom sitting outside our house. "They know."

Silence descended on the rest of the ride. Sabrina stared out the window. When we pulled into the garage, I rested my hand on her leg just above the knee. "What's up?"

She turned to me with a weak smile. "Nothing, just tired."

"How was it seeing your parents?"

"Good. A lot of the usual. The couch is lumpier than ever, but it was nice to see them. My dad nearly set the house on fire deep-frying the turkey under the carport. Mom and I watched it from the kitchen window with fire extinguishers ready. If we'd been outside, I'd probably have to draw my eyebrows on for the next few months." She brushed her fingers over them as if double-checking that they were still in place.

"But the turkey was delicious. We went to the movies the next day. It was pretty relaxing. Oh!" Bouncing in her seat, she patted my arm like she didn't have my undivided attention.

Not that I minded anytime she touched me.

"And I won another job. The e-mail came in right before I took off, so I forgot to tell you. Between this and the expo in a few weeks, I might have enough work to get me through the next few months."

She worked hard. Day and night, it felt like she was working on her pictures, pitching clients, endless scrolling to find the perfect image out of the hundreds or thousands she took, and then editing even more than required to go above and beyond for her clients.

I was proud of all the work she put in and getting some recognition for how she kept up her relentless pace.

"Then we should celebrate your win. Let's get upstairs."

Celebrating turned out to mean interrupting Sabrina's unpacking with a bit of distraction on my part. Something about her putting away her things in a place I'd thought of as mine made me want to show her how much I'd missed her. Most of her clothes that hadn't made it into the drawers were shoved off the bed and spread all over my floor, which made them feel even more at home there.

"We don't need to order food. We can just eat leftovers." She opened the fridge and picked up a container of mashed potatoes with half a spoonful left. "You were really hungry, huh?"

I took it from her and set it out on the counter and took this as my opening to tell her about my visitor. I'd gone through it and the place hadn't burst into flames, so I deserved at least the slightest pat on the back. "I had Ryder over, and that kid can eat."

Her whole posture brightened, and her eyes were wide

with awe. "You did it?" She grabbed my arm and shook it, grinning.

"I said I would."

"That's great. What did you two talk about? Did you eat together?"

"No, he came up, packed up some food, and left." Which was probably not how she wanted our meet up to go, but I'd done as she'd asked. I'd leave out the part about Ryder running out of the apartment, and hopefully he'd leave that part out too.

"Oh." Her shoulders sagged, her disappointment wafting off her.

"Sabrina, don't. I can't do more than that with him." How not-angry I was with him after only a few minutes was reason enough to stay away. It felt like a betrayal down to the depths of my bones to spend any time with him. Like I was somehow excusing what my dad had done. *All water under the bridge, old man. Let me just welcome your other kid from your other family into what remains of mine.*

The guilt was sharp in the center of my chest, like someone was driving a spike straight into my sternum.

"I know you two don't really get along, but, he's a really great—"

"Stop."

Her mouth snapped shut and she nodded. "Sorry."

"I need to deal with this my way." And my way was not dealing with it. "Can you let me do that?"

She nodded. "Sure, I can do that."

32

SABRINA

"D**o you want to grab some food?" Zara looped her arm through mine and stalked us toward the food court without me responding.

I laughed, trying to keep up. "I take it you're hungry?"

"Do you remember the hyenas at the end of *The Lion King*? Like that, but hungrier. That croissant sandwich this morning was not enough."

"Seems like you've been busy."

"Waverly Hotels has acquired a new chain of boutique hotels in Vienna and Tuscany. Their design teams are here, and I wanted to be in the mix while everyone worked to learn as much as I could." She held up a notebook with colorful sticky tabs jutting out. "They'll be back at it in forty-five minutes, so this'll be the only chance I get to eat until after seven. How's it been for you?" She glanced over as we hustled past all the other attendees wandering through the convention space.

"All my samples have been claimed. And the QR code idea you suggested has already gotten thirty views." I was scared to believe it was all coming together. Arriving at the expo, I'd expected an unmitigated disaster, but this might work. After all the work I'd put in and the years of rejection, this might finally be the moment, and I was scared to hope it might be possible.

"That's amazing! I'm so happy you were able to come."

"Thank you for getting me the ticket. It hasn't hurt having the Waverly name on my badge when I try to strike up conversations with the buyers."

"No thanks required. The ticket was going to go to waste. Anytime I can help out, just let me know and I'll see if I can." She craned her neck, scoping out the food options. "How averse are you to the cold?"

I followed her gaze to the food trucks lining the street outside the convention center doors.

"This food truck is supposed to be so good, and according to their social media, we've got ten minutes before they leave. I told Leo he needs to add them to his catering list, so technically this is recon work and not me wanting to stuff my face with delicious seafood."

"You don't have to ask me twice. I'm game."

Outside, I shoved my hands into my sleeves and ducked my head, following after Zara. My breath hung in the air in front of my face, and my cheeks stung from the cold. Going from a hot, stuffy convention center to the December afternoon wind blast chilled the sweat that had gathered on my skin. I'd be shaking ice cubes out of my bra once we got back inside.

Zara glanced over her shoulder. "Are you using me to block the wind?"

I held onto the back of her blazer. "You're the one who wanted to come outside."

The two of us huddled up in front of the trucks, thankful there wasn't a line.

At the food truck serving lobster rolls, I ordered the hot buttered lobster on a warm toasted bun and their special seasoning, a side of chips, and a pickle. My stomach rumbled for some seafood goodness.

By the time they called our number, I was no longer able to feel my fingers.

We rushed back inside and found a recently vacated table.

The tender buttered meat melted in my mouth. "Okay, this was worth it."

Zara finished before I did, dragging her pickle though the leftover butter in the bottom of her platter, which made me feel less self-conscious about doing it myself.

"Will they be here tomorrow?"

"God, I hope so." She stared out the doors where the food truck had been parked but was now gone. "I'll check their social to see if they've posted their route for tomorrow. I swear, I could eat five of those."

"That butter sauce was creamy and tangy at the same time."

"Right? I want to drink it."

She was my kind of dinner date.

The overhead speakers that hadn't been used all day clicked on.

"Excuse me, sorry for the interruption, but we have a lost child at the information desk." It was a deep male voice.

Everyone around us looked up at the speakers broadcasting the announcement.

"A lost child belonging to Sabrina Mason. If Sabrina Mason could come to the Information Desk immediately."

Zara's head whipped around toward me, her eyes bigger than they had been when she spied the lobster roll truck.

"You have a kid?"

"No." I threw down my napkin into the empty plastic clamshell container. "Maybe it's a different Sabrina Mason?"

"Sabrina Mason from Flagstaff, Arizona."

I scrambled to grab my empty containers and rushed from the table, throwing my trash away. There was only one person who could cause this kind of mayhem in my life with a single announcement. I was giddy and also the tiniest bit afraid of what she had in store for me.

"Wait up."

I didn't stop for Zara. God knew what other information would come booming over the loudspeaker next.

Resisting the urge to hide my face with my hand, I made a beeline toward the Information Desk sign hanging high above the booths laid out in a grid across the convention center floor.

The sweat that had cooled outside was back, and my feet slid in my shoes. I rounded the end of the row of booths and raced for the desk.

Perched on the edge of it with a dopey-eyed security guard between her legs was the one person I never knew if I wanted to strangle or hug. Sometimes it was both.

"Cat!"

She dropped her head back and peered over her shoulder. "There she is." Leaning back, she fan-kicked her legs from around the security guard and spun on the desk like she'd done it a million times.

"You're finally here!" She rushed forward and plowed into me, nearly knocking my feet off the ground. Her arms wrapped around me, squeezing tight and rocking us back and forth. Whether we'd been apart for a day or a year, her hugs were always the same, and always showed how much she cared.

Shaking my head, I hugged her back. "I thought we were meeting at six."

She let go. "I finished early, so I thought I'd swing by and check out the legendary expo."

"And the announcement." I pointed to the desk and guard, who still had the lovestruck look in his eyes. The poor guy didn't stand a chance. Whether she gave him her number or not, brought him back to the hotel room or not, guys always looked at her the same way no matter how much time they got with her, because that time always came to an end.

"You know I love to make an entrance." She raised her hands and froze in a model pose with her gaze lifted to the exposed-girder ceiling in a perfect silhouette. "Plus, I didn't feel like tracking you down in this place." Her eyes glittered with mischievousness.

I waved my phone in front of her. "That's what texting is for."

She made a dismissive sound. "Boring." Turning, she extended her hand toward Zara, who I hadn't even realized had been following me. "Hi, you must be Zara. I'm—"

"Cat." Zara finished for her with a wide smile. "I've heard a lot about you."

"Sabrina told me all about you too." Cat opened her arms wide and flung them around Zara's neck. "Thank you for helping her get here. I'm just happy she's got someone around her she's not too stubborn to ask for a favor, so thank you for going to bat for her."

Zara let out a slightly shocked laugh and hugged her back. "No problem. I'm glad I could help."

The two of them looked to me, and my heart squeezed. I'd forgotten what it felt like to have friends close by. I'd forgotten how much I missed Cat and how good it felt to let new people in. For so long I'd let myself fall into the safety of my relationship with Seth and hiding out in the apartment with Hunter. I finally felt like I was more of *me*, more of the Sabrina I'd been before taking one too many knocks and dings from life.

"The happy hour we're heading to isn't for another few hours, so I'm game to follow you guys around until it's time."

"You don't have to. Zara, is it okay if Cat goes up to the room to hang out?"

"I don't—"

"I've been trapped in conference rooms and hotel suites for forever. Let me mingle. I swear I'll be good." Cat stepped back and folded her shoulders in a bit and ducked her head, attempting to make her oversize personality seem more contained. "You won't even know I'm here."

After all this time, I knew when to argue with Cat and when it was a losing proposition. "Not a word."

She zipped her lips, took the imaginary key, and stuck it into my front pocket, which was only big enough to hold an imaginary key.

We roamed the aisles of booths, and I made introductions, offering anyone who requested samples of my work postcards with my QR codes on them. I even had a chance to speak with members of the Waverly Hotels Group Zara worked with.

Cat wandered around, immediately breaking her zippered-lip pact and began talking me up in a way only she could, never mentioning that she knew me, but talking about how she'd snagged one of the last of my cards although I had a stack in my bag.

She was a one-woman hype machine, and as much as it heated my cheeks, I loved her for it.

Dead on my feet with a cheek-aching grin, I finally felt like maybe I was getting somewhere.

We reconvened back in the hotel room a few hours later.

I collapsed into the chair and set my bag down on the desk. Kicking off my shoes, I curled and uncurled my toes and leaned my head against the seat back.

Cat sat on the couch and smiled back at me.

I tilted my head, looking at her down the bridge of my nose. "What?"

"Nothing." Her smile widened.

"Now you have to tell me. What is it?"

"It's good to see you so happy doing your thing."

I chuckled. "Running around like a demented chicken trying to get people to look at my work?"

"No, sharing what you're good at. Not being afraid to show them your passion." Her head dipped, and she folded her hands, resting her forearms on her thighs. "For a long time I wondered if you'd get it back."

"I went into hibernation mode for a while there, huh?"

She leaned back with her arms stretched over the back of the sofa. "You did. But I get it. When you keep getting doors slammed in your face, it's hard to gather up the courage to knock again."

The years between college and Seth had been one nonstop rejection-fest. It wasn't until right now that I saw how much it had made me retreat into myself and how much I believed that all the bad being visited on me was because of wrong choices in my past.

The Siren Song event and what had happened with Trevor—Old Sabrina would've never blamed herself for that. I would have immediately kicked him in the balls and cursed him the hell out.

I sat up straighter in the chair. "It feels good."

"It looks good on you." She glanced at her watch. "If we want to make the happy hour, we need to leave soon. Did you want to send Zara a message?"

The lock beeped, and the door opened. Zara walked in and dumped her stuff on the couch beside Cat.

"Zara, are you up for happy hour?"

She groaned and collapsed beside Cat and nodded.

"That noise and the head nod don't exactly match."

"I know, but I do want to go out. Give me ten minutes to mentally throat punch a few people and call Leo, and I'm in." She stood back up, grabbed her phone, and walked into the bedroom of the suite.

"What exactly are you planning for us tonight?"

"Nothing big. Don't worry. It'll be a lot of fun, and I'll have you both home by eight. Trust me."

The taxi pulled off, leaving the three of us standing outside the building. It was at the end of a driveway lined with red flags with white crosses in the center flapping in the sharp December air.

I regretted this decision immediately.

Cat walked up to the security guard standing outside with an earpiece and clipboard like we were trying to get into the hottest new club, not a glass-fronted building complete with metal detectors, K9 units and armed guards.

Zara and I exchanged a look. Hers was a face of abject terror. Oh right, I'd been through years of exposure therapy to Cat's antics, but even I was a little wary of what exactly she was getting us into. I rushed forward and grabbed Cat's arm.

"You said this was a happy hour with killer drinks," I

hissed, my gaze darting to the security guard with the closely cropped hair and unamused look, and trying to maintain a smile.

She glanced over her shoulder and smirked. "Oh, it is. Have you ever had a Nordic Mule?"

"This is the Danish Embassy!" I hissed through clenched teeth.

"Exactly." She winked and turned back to the guard with rapid-fire words.

He threw his head back and laughed before nodding, opening the door, and ushering us inside.

The guard corralled Zara and I forward through the bag scanner and metal detectors. My heart was doing an Olympic gold medal gymnastics routine in my chest.

Cat waltzed through the detector, winking at the security officer, who pulled her aside for a wanding behind a security screen.

She came back out with her patented smirk that told me she didn't think she was even the slightest bit in over her head. With her own flair, she spoke to all the other embassy staff, who laughed and smiled like us popping by to Danish sovereign ground was no big deal. After handing over our licenses and signing in, we were joined by others and walked toward a room filled with music, laughter, and animated chatter.

Cat walked into the room like she did this every day. With her line of work, maybe she did. Now more than ever, I wanted to grab her, lock us in a room together, and go over exactly what she did for the Ivans with a fine-tooth comb.

"Catherine!" A voice boomed from across the room. Heads turned in our direction. A large man with a broad chest, impeccable suit, and twinkling eyes burst through the circle of people who surrounded him and strode across the room. He held both her arms and bent to kiss her on both cheeks.

Zara grabbed my arm and leaned in, whispering, "Who is he?"

"I have no idea."

Cat introduced us to the man, who we found out was the ambassador to the US, and the two switched back and forth between Danish and English. We were also provided with a steady flow of Nordic Mules, which were as fantastic as Cat raved about and a hell of a lot stronger than most drinks normally served at any happy hour I'd been to. The rye bread and smoked salmon open-faced sandwiches helped soak up a lot of the alcohol, but not enough, which could have been the reason that when she waltzed out of the embassy arm in arm with me and Zara, we didn't demand to go back to the hotel.

Instead the European tour continued.

In the Italian Embassy, sipping a mandarin-and-Prosecco Puccini that tickled my nose, Zara and I sat in awe of the ease with which Cat roamed from one group to another, seeming to know everyone.

"She must've been a hell of a lot of fun in college."

"Once she came out of her shell, there was no stopping her."

"I can't imagine her in a shell—ever."

"As crazy as it might seem, she was. I used to be the outgoing one."

"Wow." Zara stared at Cat like she was seeing her with new eyes before turning back to me. "I know what you said earlier about you and Hunter not being a thing."

The heat of the cocktails went straight to my cheeks. Not a thing went out the window a few weeks ago, but we hadn't broadcast that to anyone yet. Something to do with being cooped up in the apartment and only coming up for air for work and necessities that couldn't be delivered.

"But I'm happy you're in the apartment with him. He's so good at being present, while always keeping people at a little bit of a distance. At least we all know he's got someone close by."

Close didn't begin to describe it. Even the weekend away down here had felt like there was a continent between us. I had less than three weeks left before my intended move-out date. Neither of us had broached the topic. I didn't want to skip things ahead and put undue pressure on the newness between us, but the idea of moving out hit me harder than it should have.

But knowing Zara had given me her stamp of approval took some of the weight off my shoulders. The worries about what his friends would think after all the denials about anything going on between us weren't as scary now.

"I'm glad to be there too." I drained the last of my drink.

Vowing to spend the night enjoying the little bit of time I had with Cat and to not let the Hunter situation monopolize my every thought, I shifted back to Cat, who beckoned me forward from the dance floor. Knowing she'd drag me out, I grabbed Zara's hand and pulled her out with me.

Romania. Estonia. Lithuania. Poland. Each only a minutes-long taxi ride from the next, where magically we were welcomed for invite-only parties where we didn't have invites.

I wished I'd brought my passport for the European tour. At every party, Cat knew someone. They'd call her by name and order us a few rounds of drinks. Zara and I, at least, had one another when the conversations crackled with heated laughter in the language of choice, which Cat flitted to like it was second nature. In her line of work, I guess it was.

We crawled into the hotel room at the ass crack of dawn. So much for our nine p.m. bedtime.

I collapsed into my bed, facedown.

Zara did the same, groaning. "I'm never drinking again."

Cat nudged me to scoot over.

I moaned and moved an inch to my right. "You're a bad influence," I grumbled, trying to gather my strength to get out of the bed and wash my face, get into pajamas, and pass out until noon tomorrow.

She flopped into the bed beside me. "If life was all good influences, it would be no fun at all. How you doing, Zara?"

"This is going to hurt tomorrow."

"Let me get you two lightweights a cold washcloth."

She disappeared into the bathroom. The running faucet was enough to send my parched mouth into overdrive.

"I've got water and ibuprofen for both of you." She handed each of us a glass and two tablets. "There's a bottle of water on your nightstands. Anyone want help getting into pajamas, or are you two party girls okay going to sleep in your clothes?"

Zara's soft snores answered that question.

I lifted my head. "How are you still so coherent?"

She shrugged with a smile. "I've been drinking with Russians for the past two years. If I hadn't built up a tolerance by now, I'd have never made it this far."

My head dropped back onto the bed. "I don't think I can move. Are you getting in?" I patted the empty space in my bed.

"I would, but I got a text from Ivan the Terrible. I need to head out."

I shot up and immediately regretted it. The room spun around me. "What?"

"Duty calls."

"No, you were supposed to have a whole day off."

"You know how it goes." She set the washcloth on my forehead. "Get some rest and kick some ass at the expo tomorrow. I'll put in a breakfast order for extra carbs and bacon for the two of you."

I peeled my eyes open. "I thought we'd have more time."

A sad smile creased her lips. "I know, but I'm happy we got to hang. I missed you." She bent and hugged me as tight as my revolting stomach would allow. "Night, Sabrina."

She clicked off the light, and the room was bathed in darkness.

A flash of light from the hotel room door and she was gone.

As much as my life kept me confined to my apartment and chained to my desk, Cat seemed to be living a life in spurts and gasps of time she could call her own. Our paths had diverged after college, but it was funny how we were both living lives that weren't our own. But I was determined to grab my life by the reins and not let any more time to do what I truly wanted slip through my fingers.

33

SABRINA

Zara and I had said bye at 30th Street Station, still nursing the tail end of the hangovers that had made the last day of the expo a nightmare I didn't want to repeat anytime soon. Damn embassies and their copious amounts of alcohol.

Cat had made good on the promise of room service. The poor bellhop was probably afraid he'd been called to a room filled with groaning zombies after how I answered the door, but after a near IV drip of coffee and carbs, I showered and Zara and I dragged our butts down to the expo floor.

With all my samples and QR code postcards gone, I got a chance to roam. While a lot of the floor was filled with industrial, utility-style works, there were corners of exciting, creative work. Intriguing pieces drew inspiration from great works of art, artistic periods, and cities around the world I hoped to one day visit.

It wasn't often I got to geek out over textile design—hell, I almost never got to geek out over it—but being in a place buzzing with the appreciation and excitement over the same things I loved made it one of the best days of my life.

And it was made even better by being able to come home to Hunter.

I opened the door to the apartment. Bags and boxes lined the hallway leading to the living room. The gentle melody of Christmas pop music drifted from farther in the apartment.

A thump and growling curse spurred me ahead.

In the living room, against the windows, Hunter looked like he'd become part man, part tree. He kicked a quarter of a tree on the floor and pressed his thumb against his lips.

"What happened? Are you okay?" I rushed across the room.

He spun around, and his eyes widened. "You're back early." His smile warmed me from the inside out. Standing in front of the glow of the lights strewn all over the floor in the comfy T-shirt I knew he only wore at home—at home with me—he made me want things I hadn't thought I'd want again for a long time.

"We got an earlier train out of DC after Cat may or may not have gotten us all added to an Interpol list."

His head jerked back with furrowed brows, and he dropped the tree pieces he'd been holding. "Do I want to know?"

"No, you do not. I don't want you added to the list right alongside me."

Wrapping his arms around me, he pressed his palms against my lower back. "I wouldn't mind being anywhere as long as I'm with you."

"Remember that when Cat gets us all shipped to Siberia." I rested my palms against his chest, running my fingers over the threadbare fabric, so thin I felt like I could see his skin through the cotton.

He dropped his head, nudging my head up with his forehead and resting his against mine. "I missed you." His eyes were full of an open vulnerability I'd have never thought he'd show me.

I trusted that he did. I trusted him to at least be one hundred percent real with me, even if he wore the facade outside of these apartment walls. I dragged my fingers along his stubbly chin. The sharp facial fuzz scraped across my skin, sending tingles dancing down my spine. "I missed you too."

His lips were on mine, hungry but savoring all at the same time like I'd come back from a month away, not less than forty-eight hours.

The kiss left me light-headed and wobbly and wanting. I ran my hands along the bottom of his shirt and up to his stomach, squeezing them between us.

He broke the connection and looked down at me with a glimmer in his eyes. "Ah-ah-ah, no fun until we get this tree up. Then I can give you a proper welcome home."

We worked together, cranking up the Christmas music, popping popcorn on the stove to string for the tree, and getting tangled up in lights, which wasn't all that bad when I was tangled up with Hunter.

I was happy. From head to toe, everything finally felt like the tide had changed.

Perched on top of the stepladder with Hunter's hands on the backs of my thighs for "balance," I set the star on top of the tree and handed him the plug. The metal star with smaller star and sparkle cutouts came alive, lighting up the top of the tree, and covered me with geometric designs.

"We did it." I looked down at him, feeling keenly aware of how perfect this moment was. It was a moment I'd stamp on my heart and recall by just closing my eyes and being wrapped up in these feelings all over again. Staring into his eyes, I said a thing I'd been afraid to say for fear it would all evaporate, going up in a poof right from my in-box. "I have a contract sitting in my e-mail from a company that wants to buy one of my designs."

His eyes widened, crinkling with the creases of a smile. "You did it!" He grabbed me off the ladder.

I yelped and tried to grab onto the stepladder.

With strong arms wrapped around me, he took me down to the couch like I'd told him I'd won a Nobel Prize, falling on top of me. "I knew you could do it."

My stomach fluttered and flipped, exhilaration flushing my body. "That makes one of us."

"Two." He spoke in between kisses peppering my face and lips. "Cat's solidly on board the Sabrina-will-kick-some-design-ass team, isn't she?"

"Yeah."

"Did you tell her already?"

"No." I dropped my gaze, feeling silly. "You were the first person I wanted to tell." For some reason I'd held out until now, wanting to share it with him, like that would make it feel even more real.

He stilled on top of me. "Thank you for letting me be your first." He said it so earnestly and innocently I couldn't hold back my laugh.

The bright, shiny feeling in my chest rivaled the tree light. It rivaled the sunrise. "Thank you for being in my corner."

"Always."

Overwhelmed with emotions welling and cresting, I pulled his face down and captured his lips with mine.

We were naked in record time, clothes discarded in a pile on the living room floor.

Hunter focused his attention on me. "How'd I get so lucky as to be here with you tonight?"

"No idea. Have you been stealing birthday wishes again?"

His laugh was deep and rich, husky and weighty.

Sprawled out in front of him, I welcomed his gaze without a hint of doubt or self-consciousness. I wanted him to see me. I wanted to give him what he wanted, and that was more of me.

The path of his eyes set my skin on fire, making it tingle with anticipation.

My legs were locked around his waist, holding on throughout each thrust. The couch burn on my back was soothed by the cold sheets on Hunter's bed.

His whispers against my neck added to the pleasure coursing through my body, shooting me straight to the precipice of carnal bliss.

"Do you know what you do to me?"

"No." I moaned. My fingers sank into his back, losing myself to the overwhelming feelings. The sizzling turned to sparks tearing their way down my spine, tightening every muscle, all centered around the sensations streaking across my skin.

"You make me crazy. You make it hard for me to remember what my life was like before you were in it."

My heart was full to bursting. "You make me crazy too." In so many different, terrible, wondrous ways he'd made me every kind of crazy.

His hips snapped, pounding into me in a way that left me clawing at the sheets and feeling like I was coming out of my body. White-hot currents of sensation swamped my nerve endings, turning me into a writhing mess under Hunter as he unleashed his restraint.

"God, Sabrina."

I wanted to respond, but a shift of his hips above mine and I was shot off the mountain peak into the stratosphere. My vision darkened, filled with stars like the twinkling lights on the Christmas tree. My present had come early, and it was wrapped in the most beautiful man who looked at me like he was lucky to have found me.

Hunter stiffened above me, his angle changed, driving across my G-spot and triggering another spasm inside, leaving me clamping and convulsing against his expanding shaft.

My core overly soaked and sated, I collapsed with my limbs heavy and sluggish.

Breathless, sweaty, and with a chuckle, he dropped down on top of me, kissing my neck.

"Was that a proper enough welcome home for you?" He pushed back the sweaty streaks of hair stuck to the side of my face.

"I'll need to leave more often if that's what I get to come back to."

"I hate it when you go." He pecked me on the lips before hesitating and then pressing up and pulling out of me.

I groaned at the loss of him between my legs and his warmth blanketing me. The nakedness of his words had nothing on the nakedness of our bodies. I hated going, too.

We headed to his bathroom for a thorough bath that went on long enough for my fingers to prune and had a lot less to do with getting clean than it did with making up for lost time, which required a shower after.

In Hunter's bed, I rested my cheek against his chest,

listening to his heart beating strong and steady. I traced my finger up and down the peaks and valleys of his muscled body, still not quite believing I was here with him.

"The whole 'me leaving and coming back' thing will probably be easier next month." Swallowing, I burrowed a little deeper against him. "I need to sign the lease for my new place." I'd started searching over Thanksgiving and finally found a place.

He shot up, his arm tightening around me. "What new place?"

"My new apartment. I contacted them when they had a sale with two months free, which would keep it in my price range with the new work I have coming in. I snagged the last one at the price, so it's perfect. And with the invoices that were finally paid, I have money for the security deposit."

He stared at me with confusion filling his gaze. "Why would you be looking for a new apartment?"

I ran my hands over the sheets covering my lap. "Because I always said this was temporary. I told you from the beginning I'd move out after New Year's. I didn't want to just assume." I peeked up at him before dropping my gaze back to the navy sheets.

He grasped my chin, turned my head, then threaded his fingers into my hair.

My heartbeat skipped, my skin flooding with heat at the tender look in his eyes.

"Then I'll make it official. Will you move in with me, Sabrina?"

A small gasp sneaked past my lips, and I broke out into a wide grin, shaking his fingers loose from mine and flinging my arms around his neck, squeezing him tight enough to pull a grunt and laugh from him.

"Well, what do you say?"

34

HUNTER

I t was official. Sabrina and I were living together and together-together. It was both scarier and less scary than I'd expected.

Things continued on just as they had before. I cleared out drawers and closet space for her.

She moved her clothes and toiletries into my bedroom. While she could've kept using her bedroom, I liked having her in my space. I liked making it our space.

Her former bedroom became her full-time studio.

"How many contracts have you gotten so far?"

She worked her fingers through her hair, smoothing it out and working it into two braids. "At least five for product photography, but I have three meetings for my design work. I had to turn down a few of the photography jobs."

Pride filled my chest.

She'd take the world by storm, no matter what she did. "That means your rates are too affordable and you need to raise them." It was what we'd had to do once the ninety-hour work weeks started wrecking everyone at SWANK.

"Then I'll lose clients."

I tapped my finger on the end of her nose. "Exactly, but the ones you get will be even more profitable, especially if you want to clear more time for design work."

Her nose scrunched up as she put the finishing touches on her braids. "You're infuriatingly right." Her gaze narrowed playfully.

I tugged on the braids, drawing her closer. "I know. Get used to it."

Laughing, she grabbed her coat and slipped her boots on.

Inside the closet, our coats hung together and our shoes were side by side on the floor. It was everything I'd sworn I'd never do, but with Sabrina it had happened naturally. We'd flowed from reluctant roommates to friends to two people who couldn't get enough of each other. My late nights at work were more of an annoyance than fun. I went for as long as I needed to, and wanted to talk to the guys about transitioning my work to different events. Maybe concert series like the New Year's Eve gig. It was still at night, but not every night. Bigger events, maybe a music festival like Coachella or Bonnaroo. More risk, more reward, and a hell of a lot more nights with Sabrina curled up beside me on the couch.

We walked out of the building. Snow fell from the sky, dancing through the air, and landed on her knit hat and cheeks before melting. She waved to the doorman, and I couldn't stop looking at her.

My chest clenched, squeezing my lungs so tightly the puffs of air seemed to trail off into nothing.

Tucking her scarf into the opening at the top of her coat, she glanced up at me. Her head tilted, and she reached out to me. "What's up? Are you okay?" Concern flooded her words.

"I love you." It scared me how easy it had been. How naturally the words had left my mouth without a second thought. I was struck by what it meant and how deeply I felt it.

Her hand rubbing down my arm stilled and her eyes shot open and her lips parted before curving. "I love you too." She slipped her arm through mine. "That was a nice early Christmas present." Her skin glowed under the snow and streetlights.

The words had rocked me to my core much more strongly than they seemed to have rocked her, like it had seemed inevitable to Sabrina, and I was the idiot for only realizing it now. I had been. I'd thought what we had could continue on as it was, that she hadn't become sewn into the very fabric of the life I'd envisioned for myself, of the only life I thought I'd live. "You've been the present I didn't know I needed."

And again the words tumbled out without me being able to hold them back.

She beamed at me and pressed her lips against mine in a chaste kiss, nothing like the ones I'd laid on her earlier today and would again once we got back to the apartment. Whose idea was this date-night dinner again?

"I know. I'm awesome like that." She winked and laughed. "How many blocks is this place? It's freezing." She gripped my arm even tighter when her feet slipped on a little ice patch.

"Three blocks. Can you make it, or do I need to go get some ice skates?"

"How are you not having any trouble walking on this?"

She held on tighter, and I didn't hate how it felt to be the one to keep her steady.

"There's a crazy thing called boots."

"You're trying to blame me for the bullshit differences in industry standards for men's and women's winter footwear?"

"I'm not complaining if it means I get to have you on my arm when it's snowy out."

"Bravo, Mr. Saxton. You sure know how to take the wind out of a woman's indignant sails with lines like those."

My grin widened. The winter wind battered my skin, but she made me feel like we were walking on a sandy beach somewhere. "It's true."

"Stop before I make you turn around and go back upstairs." It was her tease every week when I took her out for date night.

I didn't mind butting heads with her, especially when I knew how it would all turn out when we got back home. This would be a solid two hours of foreplay over a great meal, even better drinks, and the perfect company.

"Not happening. You're not getting out of our date night."

"Fine." She moped with a smile twitching on her lips.

The sidewalks weren't busy, but there were enough people out finishing up their Christmas shopping that it felt lively. Despite the freezing winter air and wind, I wanted to walk with Sabrina like this all night, talking, laughing, teasing, her holding tight to me.

She stood with her back to the street and pushed the crosswalk button.

I dropped a few dollars into the red bucket in front of the bell-ringing Santa and laughed at her dance to the Christmas music pouring from the stores lining the street. The snow was coming down a little harder now. Flakes dropped onto the side of my hand before melting and rolling down over my skin.

A flash of headlights caught my attention.

Over her shoulder, a car rocketed out of a parking spot to make the still-green light and skidded. The sound sent my stomach plummeting—the sound of loss of control and the desperate wheel-turning to try to gain it back. Only it wasn't possible, not with how quickly the road had become blanketed.

I bolted across the sidewalk, fear propelling me faster than I'd ever moved before.

Her eyes widened as I rushed toward her, and I jerked her away from the curb. Inside my head, the volume increased, drowning out every other sound and sight except for ones that signaled the direction for our escape.

Darting to my right, I pushed her against the painted metal of a bus shelter and locked my body around hers, bracing for impact.

A sickening screech and splintering of glass split the jovial night air. A bang rumbled the ground at my feet. Screams, a revving engine, and twisting metal roared in my ears along with the pounding of my heart and Sabrina's sharp, panicked breaths. A shower of glass hit my back and tinkled, bouncing off the metal we were braced against.

But there was no pain, no breaks or bumps. I opened my eyes and stared into her wide, frightened ones.

Unlocking my muscles like they'd been cemented in place, I pulled myself away from her and looked over my shoulder.

Bystanders rushed to the driver of the car. The pole Sabrina had been standing in front of had been ripped from the concrete and lay on the ground a couple feet behind me.

Sabrina took in the scene at the same time I did, her

fingers gripping my arms even tighter. "Are you okay?" Her hands searched my body and flicked at my hair. Pieces of glass fell to my shoulders.

I pulled a single cut cube of glass from her hair. "I'm okay." My throat tightened, nearly choking me. "Are you okay?" My body was numb as if I had taken the hit and my nerves hadn't registered the pain yet.

She nodded, swallowed, and sucked in a shaky breath. "A little freaked out, but I'm not hurt. You saved me." Her gaze darted from the wreckage where the driver was walking and talking and being tended to.

"Let's go back home." I grabbed her hand, just wanting to get us back between our four walls where I could calm down and stop feeling the crazy whirling vortex in my mind threatening to drag me under.

She swallowed again and held onto me, not letting me walk back toward the apartment. "No, we're both okay. Let's go to dinner. I could use a glass of wine after that."

"We have wine back in the apartment."

"No, let's—I don't want this to ruin our night."

"You could've died." My voice boomed in the post-accident commotion.

Heads turned in our direction, but I wasn't focused on them, I was focused on her like my life depended on keeping my gaze locked onto her.

She held onto my arm, stopping my attempt to drag her back to the apartment and wrap her in bubble wrap. "But I'm perfectly fine. You grabbed me and the pole stopped the car."

It had all flashed in front of my eyes. All the time we'd had together and what it could stretch into in the future, right along with an end that would destroy my world. "How are you being so casual about this?"

All the planning I'd been doing without a thought of where this could go, of what this would mean to me and how easily my world could be shattered all over again with a random diagnosis, car accident—hell, anything. My lungs must have been working at a quarter capacity, based on how hard it was to drag air into them.

"I'm not being casual. Sitting in the apartment isn't going to help keep your mind off this."

"You were the one who wanted to go back a few minutes ago."

"And now I want to go to dinner." Her facade of pretending she wanted to go back home was dropped now that I was finally on her side.

The insistence didn't make any sense—she could've been killed. Was she in shock? Did I need to call Dr. Sean to check her over? Panic flooded my limbs.

"From the way you're looking at me, it might be my last chance to ever leave the apartment again."

At least her quips were back. The ground swell of unease ebbed away a little. "Are my feelings that transparent?"

She slipped her glove off and locked our fingers together. "Let's not let what happened ruin our night. Can you do that for me?" Maybe she needed the distraction of other people and a good meal to keep her mind off what had almost happened. If it was what she needed, then as much as I wanted to throw her over my shoulder and carry her back to the apartment, I'd deal.

I tucked more of her hair into her hat with my other hand, which shook. "I can try."

"It's all I ask." She lifted my arm over her head and draped it over her shoulder, holding on tight like she still didn't trust me to throw her into a taxi and go back to the building.

And a reason for that insistence sat right inside the entrance to Parc.

Ryder stood from the padded benches in the vestibule in front of the hostess station, smoothing out his tie and standing up like he was showing up for a job interview—nervous but still wearing a smile. I had a feeling he wasn't here for an interview.

Thunderbolts felt like they were raining down around me. I was trapped. I'd been trapped, and the spring had been sprung.

I shot a look to Sabrina, who evaded my eyes. "What a crazy coincidence."

The insistence on coming and not putting up nearly the fight she normally did on date night made so much more sense now. My adrenaline was still running high, speeding through my veins.

She'd lied to me, hadn't said a word, knowing how I'd feel about this—and after I'd spoken to him after Thanksgiving just like I promised I would. Now, after asking her to let me do this my way, she went behind my back and invited him out on our date night.

My anger simmered, primed for flaring.

"Hey, Sabrina. Hey, Hunter." Ryder waved to us both like Christmas had come early.

She pulled my arm down from her shoulder and held onto my hand and with the other arm, hugged Ryder. "It's almost Christmas, and I thought it would be nice for us all to eat together."

Pulling her closer, I spoke into her ear, trying to keep the fire of my fury out of my voice. "I thought you agreed to let me handle this my way."

She tipped her chin. "Your way seemed to be not handling it at all. Let's head inside."

Ryder held out his hand, but I ignored it, instead kept my gaze on her retreating figure.

The feelings I'd had outside were morphing and melding into new feelings of betrayal by the time we handed off our coats and were seated at our table. She'd overstepped.

Sabrina and Ryder were chatting like old friends, and at this point, she seemed to know him better than I did, which was entirely intentional.

The two of them talked across the table with me on my end where an ominous cloud of dread felt like it was rolling in from the horizon. Everything felt out of control, like the car on black ice on a winter's evening. Somehow, the night had turned from a routine night out with Sabrina to one where the weight of everything I'd been holding at bay for the past five months was coming to a head.

Sitting next to Ryder, who looked so much like our dad and all the reminders that brought up, was exactly what I'd been trying to avoid. And then there was Sabrina's brush with death. What had I told myself? Getting close to people brought about the kinds of entanglements and expectations I couldn't handle.

Then the dread was pushed aside by a much easier feeling to grab onto. Anger. Anger that she'd gone behind my back to set up this meeting with me and Ryder. Anger that everyone else couldn't just respect my damn choices, and anger at myself that I hadn't been strong enough to avoid this head-on.

It had been so easy to fall for her. It had felt like I'd been fighting it from the second she caught me in my sweats, and now here I was with her and Ryder in a packed restaurant where they traded pleasantries and all I wanted to do was be anywhere that wasn't here.

"Hunter?"

My head shot up. My menu knocked into the water glass sitting to my right, spilling some out onto the tablecloth.

"Are you all right?"

35

SABRINA

N o, he wasn't all right at all. Hunter had been quiet the whole meal. Quiet was too loud a word. He'd been almost silent throughout the entire time other than when someone he knew walked over to say hi, but even those interactions were shorter and more abrupt than I'd seen him have in the past, with no introductions for Ryder—or me. It was like he was at a meal all alone. No, it was worse; it was like he was at a meal with two people he didn't want to be around.

Normally on our date nights, I felt like I was out with a mayoral candidate or celebrity, but tonight he was as hospitable as a rabid raccoon. To say the evening hadn't gone the way I'd hoped was an understatement—from the car crash to how shaken he'd been after to his reaction to Ryder, it wasn't shaping up to be any type of bonding time.

When Ryder had mentioned his mom was headed out to Colorado to ski without him through the holidays, I had to do something. Sure, he was eighteen, but he'd be alone. I knew how that felt and hated that he wouldn't have anyone.

Ryder and I had talked throughout dinner. He'd gotten

his acceptance to Fulton U, which had gotten a whiff of Hunter's attention, but not enough to spur him into conversation.

"When do you have to decide?" Our plates were sat in front of us. Seared scallops for me, a steak for Hunter, and Ryder had gone with the cheeseburger, which was exactly the type of fancy I'd have expected from this place, served with frites, not fries.

"A few weeks. I'm waiting for the financial aid letters to come in, but I'll get some of the insurance money. A few of Dad's accounts had my name on them as a beneficiary, so I'll have access to that too."

Hunter dropped his fork. It clattered against the plate and bounced off the base of his wineglass so hard I jumped.

"How nice he made sure you were looked after."

My lips slammed shut. "If Ryder can use it for school, I think that's pretty nice." My attempt to turn his comment wasn't helping from the way Ryder pushed his food around his plate.

I glared at Hunter and kicked his foot under the table.

He swung his gaze to mine with flat eyes.

"Hunter, can I talk to you for a second?" Without letting him say a word, I grabbed his sleeve and pulled him toward the bathrooms.

After checking over my shoulder, I whipped back around to him. "Could you at least pretend to be conversational?"

"Why would I do that?"

I clenched my hands at my sides and breathed through the fire that felt like it was burning in the top of my head. Resetting, I took a deep breath and tried to speak calmly. "You do it all the time. You've done it with everyone who's stopped by the table, but you can't do it with your own brother."

"I told you to let me handle it." He wasn't even looking at me. His gaze was trained on the empty space where his plate had been before it was cleared.

"And you haven't contacted him since Thanksgiving. It's been nearly a month and Christmas is only a few days away."

"It's my choice." His head whipped in my direction, and there was fire in his eyes. I still wasn't sure if this was better or worse than numb Hunter. "Why are you trying to force this? Why do you think you can just show up and make these big decisions in my life? You come in and you're trying to disrupt everything and make me feel things I don't want to feel."

My stomach knotted, then plummeted off the edge of the cliff. The words hit me in a different way, it felt like there was a lot more to this than Ryder, but this was not the same Hunter who'd held onto me out on the slippery slush outside our apartment. Maybe I should've let him take me back, but Ryder had already arrived.

"All I'm trying to do is give a lonely kid a little connection and show him there are people who care about him."

"Are we talking about Ryder or am I your little pet project?" There were barbs in his words. Hidden and unexpected.

They wedged in between my ribs and sliced at the soft tissue.

"I'm going to head back. It would be nice if you joined us."

I left him in the hallway and walked back to our table. Scanning the restaurant, I hoped our voices hadn't carried and we hadn't been too loud. Halfway to the table, I spotted a familiar face—two, in fact, although I'd only ever seen one in person.

Pain radiated through my hip. I slammed into one of the tables along my path. My hand shot out, and I grabbed the wineglass before it toppled, and ducked my head, getting low, not wanting to draw any more attention to myself. The panic was nearly suffocating. I should've definitely let Hunter take me back to the apartment.

"Are you okay?" The concerned couple at the table looked up at me, the stranger who'd knocked into their table and almost ruined their meal.

My throat was like a collapsed stray. "I'm fine." It came out in a wheezy whisper.

I chanced a glance and felt light-headed and nauseated all at once. My heart slammed into my ribs. My heart rate spiked like I'd just raced up the stairs from the lobby to our apartment. My skin felt prickly, like I'd become aware of every square inch of it. With my head down, I slid back into the chair I'd left. The folded napkin I'd slid off my lap was refolded beside my plate. I chugged the glass of wine in front of me and took Hunter's as well. My hands shook so badly, the wine sloshed onto my hands, but both glasses were drained in seconds.

"Sabrina, are you good?" Ryder stared at me across the gathered water and wineglasses.

I nodded, trying to get my bearings because it felt like I was on the deck of a boat in the middle of a hurricane. My finger shot up to get a waiter's attention, and I ordered another couple glasses of wine. I refused to look over my shoulder, but I felt the weight of their presence like someone was sitting on my chest.

Seth was here. He was in the same restaurant I was.

After nearly five months, since the day I moved out, I was seeing him—and his wife.

I'd never hyperventilated in my life, but I felt close.

Hunter rejoined the table adding another layer of grim to the evening, and Ryder looked at both of us like we were insane. Maybe we were. An even more stilted and awkward conversation sputtered across our table.

The waiter stopped by with our desserts, chocolate lava cakes.

Ryder wolfed it down in record time. "I'm going to head back to the train. I don't want to miss the last one."

I wasn't far behind him, wanting to get out of the restaurant just as quickly. Although getting up from the seat I felt locked into would take more courage gathering. But I needed to leave. We needed to go before things got any worse, although at this point, I didn't know how they could.

He had more than enough time before the final train, but I couldn't blame him for wanting to escape the cluster of this dinner. Reaching into his pocket, he suddenly seemed one-hundred percent an awkward teenage boy completely unsure of himself.

Standing, he set a box down and slid it across the table to Hunter. "I got this for you. And I wanted to say, Merry Christmas. Thanks for the dinner. I really appreciate it. See you, Sabrina. Bye, Hunter." It felt final, like he'd given up on ever having any type of relationship with Hunter and at that moment, I couldn't blame him.

My emotions were all over the place. The last lingering guilt after seeing Seth and knowing what he had made me a part of, anger at him as well as with Hunter who couldn't even bring himself to talk, which had turned the evening to shit long before Seth and his wife had burst onto the scene.

There was less than a week until Christmas, and at this point all I wanted was a little calm in my life.

Once my head wasn't buzzing like it had been filled with a thousand bees, I'd call Ryder and...I didn't even know what I could say. Defeat weighted me down. This hadn't gone at all how I'd planned.

In a moment of clarity, not tinged by my abject fear and wine buzz, I reached out. "Merry Christmas, Ryder." I cupped both of my hands around his. "Let me know if you need anything."

His gaze flicked to Hunter before focusing back on me. He nodded and then he was gone.

"Was it everything you'd hoped it would be and more?" Hunter dropped his napkin down on top of his untouched chocolate cake.

Instead of responding, I grabbed my glass of wine and drained it. "Let's go." As terribly as I'd imagined the evening going, this kicked it in the freaking teeth. Standing, all the wine finally got to me, and the pressure on my bladder was toe-turning. "I'm going to go to the bathroom."

"I'll get the check."

I was gone before he finished the sentence. A walk back to the apartment like this would've ended up with me getting cited for public urination, so as much as I wanted to bolt for the front doors and never look back, the bathroom beckoned.

After finishing up, I stared at myself in the mirror, trying to pep talk my way out of this, but maybe I was too tipsy for my brain to function properly, because it was failing miserably.

Hunter and I could sleep this off and have a real conversation tomorrow, when I was less inebriated and he was less angry. Whatever was going on with him...I didn't even know how to describe it, but it didn't feel good.

I pushed out of the bathroom.

A man stood outside the women's room in the ambient lighted hallway. A man who'd once been someone I'd loved. I'd given over pieces of myself to him in fear of losing him, and had lost parts of myself in the process.

I stormed out of the restroom, trying to put as much space between us as I could.

"Sabrina." My whispered name sent a shudder of revulsion through me.

I refused to turn and look at him and kept walking down the hallway leading to the dining room.

"I miss you."

I clenched my hands at my sides and kept going. My blood hammered at my eardrums like I'd walked into one of Hunter's club openings.

"I'm leaving her for you." He blared it, like he was so proud of himself for making the choice.

A gasp was wrenched from my throat. My back went ramrod straight, and I spun on my heel, the narrow space swaying a little. Emotions rushed through me, flushing my skin, making it so hot it felt like it should be sizzling. "Don't you dare make this about me," I hissed, glancing behind me.

He creeped closer with a look in his eyes of *how could I not know?* "Of course it's about you." The triumphant tilt to his words turned my stomach.

The evening's bottle of wine tickled at the back of my throat, threatening to make a reappearance. "It's not. It's about you and your selfishness which apparently knows no bounds." My hiss vibrated my gritted teeth. To think I'd ever thought I was in love with him. My stupidity also knew no bounds.

His gaze flicked over my shoulder. "You've got a new guy now and you don't care about me anymore."

"I stopped caring about you the minute I found out you were married. The minute I found out you'd made me the other woman." My stomach lurched. All the wine had been a mistake.

He pitched forward and gripped my arm, just above my elbow. "I won't be married for much longer."

"Good for your wife. Why would you think I'd want anything to do with you? My silence should've been all the answer you needed. We haven't spoken in five months. In case you need me to say it again, goodbye, Seth, and I never want to see you again. Let go of me." The words banged against my clenched teeth.

"I love—"

"Don't you dare pervert those words by saying them to me again." The same words Hunter had said to me hours ago. I struggled to get free from his hold. What was it with entitled assholes lately and putting their hands on me? All I knew was I was sick of it. "Go fuck yourself! I don't want to ever see you again, you selfish asshole. Let go." My teeth ached, I had them clenched so tightly.

"Seth?" A woman's voice came from over my shoulder. The voice of the woman I'd tried not to think about since I left my old life behind.

Her heels clicked on the tile floor.

I jerked my arm free from his hold and spun around.

The woman's gaze jumped from me to the spot on my arm where Seth had touched me and back to Seth. Her smile slid off her face with each dart of her focus until it settled back on me with a glowering that made my skin blister.

My stomach knotted, threatening to bring up the little

bit of food I'd choked down from the minute they'd sat down.

Her eyes burned with venom and unshed tears. "You're Sabrina, aren't you?"

My lungs burned, unable to bring in any more air. My mouth opened and closed, and the need to escape flooded my body. The flight instinct became harder to ignore.

"You're nothing like I thought you'd be." Her scrutinizing gaze raked up and down my body, every flaw probed and prodded by her eyes.

"If you'll excuse me." I ducked my head and tried to walk around her.

"Stay away from my husband."

My lips tightened, and my gaze shot to hers. "Gladly. Now, please let me go." I wouldn't let my voice waver, although the panicked breaths I'd been able to draw in were barely enough to keep me on my feet, let alone forcefully speak.

I rushed around the corner and slammed into a solid chest.

He steadied me, holding onto both my arms. "I paid the check and got your coat and purse." Motioning to my coat draped over his arm, he wrapped the other around my shoulder. The earlier granite stare softened the longer he stared at me.

I must've looked like a wreck and clung to his hand resting on my shoulder.

Some of the cold stiffness that had been there throughout the dinner faded, and worry filled his gaze. "What's wrong?" He glanced behind me. "Are you okay?"

I squeezed his hand and nodded, croaking out, "I'm fine. Let's go." Trying to be nonchalant and failing miserably, I speed walked through the tables, almost dragging him along.

"You don't look okay."

Glancing over my shoulder, some of the panic eased. They hadn't emerged from the bathroom hallway. If I was lucky, they'd spend the next ten minutes fighting and we'd make a clean escape. "Maybe the accident is finally getting to me." Yes, I'd lean on that sorry excuse if it meant getting out of here faster.

Near the restaurant entrance, Hunter released me and held out my coat.

Before I could slip my arms into the sleeves, a male voice interrupted our escape. "Hunter Saxton!"

Hunter spun around, and his lips spread into an approximation of a smile, the closest he'd sported since we'd arrived at the restaurant. He draped my coat back over his arm.

My dread grew.

We were so close to getting out—to getting away. Frustration brimmed higher, almost spilling over the edge at this whole situation and Hunter saying more in three minutes to this person than he had since we'd arrived for dinner.

"How are George and Gregg?"

"They're great, high school seniors now."

The two of them slipped into easy, casual conversation.

He seemed more interested in these other high school seniors than his own brother, but I could only deal with one disaster at a time and right now one would be solved by escaping this restaurant. "Hunter, I'll meet you outside."

His hand shot out. "It's freezing out there and you don't have your coat on. Mark, this is Sabrina. Sabrina, this is Mark." Of all the times for him wanting to make up for being an asshole tonight, it was right at this moment.

"So nice to meet you." I shook the man's hand with way too much vigor. "Can I have my coat, so I can go?"

He helped me into my coat while talking and moving at exactly the twentieth of the speed I needed him to move at.

I checked over my shoulder.

Seth and his wife emerged from the bathroom hallway, and my stomach was seconds away from staging a revolt.

Keeping my gaze averted, I tracked them out of my peripheral vision.

They walked to their table, and some of the strain loosened, just enough for me to button my coat with trembling fingers.

"Hunter, I need some fresh air." I tapped his elbow.

He looked over at me and nodded. "Sure, let's go." Saying goodbye and slipping his arms into his coat, he took his time.

I turned to the front doors. A pair of couples walked in, laughing and chattering, and blocked my escape.

Hunter's presence behind me at least felt like a shield from the view of the restaurant.

"You'd better watch out." The voice hit me even harder than the cold blast from the door on the other side of the vestibule. Her words boomed throughout the restaurant. "You should know your little girlfriend likes to try and steal other women's husbands."

36

HUNTER

The words dumped on me like the icy, stinging spray of slushy snow from a passing car. They shot down my spine like daggers.

Sabrina turned with her eyes wide like she'd been hit with the same sheet of ice water. "Hunter, let's go."

"Who are you?" I turned to the woman who'd approached us out of nowhere.

She wasn't familiar.

Names and faces came easily to me, but I hadn't met her before and strangers didn't normally approach me with such a stormy expression. The guy wasn't one I recognized, although it was hard to get a good look at his face.

Behind her, a man with a sheepish look kept his gaze trained on the floor like he was a second from getting a smack on the nose with a newspaper.

"I'm the wife of the man your girlfriend tried to steal away."

"Hunter, please, let's go." Sabrina pulled on my arm so hard I stumbled back.

"You know this guy?" I looked from her back to the man. *This* was her ex.

My first instinct was to tell the woman she was wrong and there had been a mistake. I glanced over at Sabrina, and she looked up at me with imploring eyes, begging me.

"I'll tell you everything once we're home. Please can we go?"

The woman seemed to have said what she needed to say and didn't elaborate. I let Sabrina tug me out the doors and into the biting, cold air. My stomach didn't feel like I'd had a full meal. It felt hollow, the numbness clawing at it, trying to deprive me of all feeling.

Instead of walking back to the apartment, I got us a taxi. Normally this would've been because I wanted to get her naked in record time, but this time it was because I didn't want to delay the conversation. I shoved away the feeling trying to blanket me with quiet. I needed answers.

My thoughts whipped by like I was racing on a test track. With each pass the speed increased, and it felt like my grip on the wheel was slipping.

We sat in the cab with the middle hump between us like strangers sharing a ride. Her hands fidgeted in her lap.

She hadn't corrected the woman. She hadn't said she had the wrong person and she'd never even met that man.

The thud in my stomach came in intervals, ticking—like a bomb waiting for the clock to hit zero.

"Ask me whatever you want to ask me." She peered over at me with a pained look.

Maybe she didn't think I'd make it to the apartment or thought I might jump out of the taxi at the next light, if she didn't tell me everything.

But I didn't want to have this conversation here. I couldn't. The platform I'd been walking on had shrunk to a plank throughout dinner, and now I was standing at the top of Liberty One on a tightrope. I looked to the driver and back to her. "When we get back to the apartment."

We didn't speak for the six-block trip, but it wasn't the quiet comfort I felt when we lay in bed together with her head resting against my chest. Instead, this was a stifling, suffocating silence.

The situation sank in deeper—bone-deep. She had known him. She'd dated him. And she'd cheated with him.

My body worked on autopilot and I fought to get the control back, but I didn't know if I'd be plowing straight into a brick wall.

In the apartment, I walked straight to the living room without even taking off my coat. Sabrina did the same.

I paced, unable to sit or stand. "Tell me everything."

She perched on the arm of the couch with her shoulders rolled in. Her arms were crossed over her chest before she swiped them down the skirt of her dress. Her discomfort rolled off her in waves, although it was only the two of us here—in our apartment. "I met Seth two years ago. He seemed like a nice guy. We went on a few dates and after a few months, we moved in with each other. Things were good. He met my parents in Arizona. We spent most holidays together. And—" She dropped her gaze to her fingers, which she'd locked together. "And then, a couple days before I moved in with you, I found out he was married."

The floor tilted and I was knocked off my pacing path like I'd been punched in the gut. All the food I'd choked down during the disaster of a dinner shot to the back of my throat. "He was married."

She lifted her chin and met my gaze, not wavering, but the flickers of guilt were there. "I found out he was married."

"You cheated with a married man." My stomach knotted

and a watery feeling coated my mouth. Everything buzzed with an unseen energy, racking my muscles with tremors.

There was a flare of fire in her eyes. "I didn't know." She caught my arm as I tried to walk away. "As soon as I found out, I broke it off with him. I left."

I needed to walk away. The icy spikes down my spine were now heated metal. "How could you not know, Sabrina?"

"It's not my normal course of action to ask a guy I've moved in with whether or not he's married." She flung her arms out to her sides.

"You lied to me about him."

"I never lied to you. I said we wanted different things."

"Like he wanted to be with his family."

She shot up from her seat. "No! I broke things off the second I found out. He didn't want to be with his family. He cornered me in the bathroom to say he was leaving her for me, and do you know what I told him?"

My skin tingled, muscles locked and straining. Was she going to go back to him?

"I told him to go fuck himself. I told him I didn't want to see him again, and he was a selfish asshole. I'd never go after a married man."

"You're not that stupid. He had a wife and probably kids and you just never noticed?"

She gasped and her eyes filled with furious tears.

It twisted my gut to think I'd lain beside her at night and never thought she could be the type of woman who'd do that.

She wiped at her cheeks. They were so red it felt like the dampness should sizzle against her skin. "He's a pilot. He was always coming and going."

"I'm sure he was."

She glared. "I have never been anything but honest with you, and it's been the same for every person I've ever dated."

"You cheated with a married man."

"I didn't know!" Her voice echoed, booming off the walls, and she stepped in closer.

"At least I know who you are now." Bitterness seeped from the words.

Her cheeks were flushed and her gaze furious. "No, I'm not going to let you pile onto me. I beat myself up about this enough, and now I can finally say, it's not my fault. You're not going to twist this because of your past."

"Don't drag me into your mistakes. I don't even know who you are."

She jabbed her finger in my direction, inches from the center of my chest. "I could say the same for you. This isn't the same as what happened with your mom and dad; it's not. And you pretend that only cheaters are liars. What about you?"

"Don't try to turn this around on me."

"No, fuck that. You want to pretend I'm the bad guy when I'm not, then you're not without fault either. How about how you've been with Ryder?"

His name fanned the flames of the fire scorching its way under my skin, burning and blistering a path straight to my head. "This has nothing to do with him. I told you I'd handle it in my own way, and you decided to go behind my back to have him show up tonight. Lying about it." I dragged out the words.

"I did. Because he's someone trying to reach out to you. He's trying to connect with you."

"I don't want to connect with him. Every time I look at him, all I can think about is my dad walking out. He walked out and left us alone. Why would anyone want that reminder? Why would anyone invite even more pain into their lives?" Was that what I was doing by being with her? I'd opened myself up for a huge new gaping wound that cleaved right through my chest and straight into my heart.

"Then now he knows, because the way he said goodbye tonight, I don't think he'll be bothering you again."

"Good." The single word was sharp and final.

Sabrina looked at me like she was seeing me with new eyes and shook her head. "It's been a long night. I've had too much wine and need some rest. We've said some things maybe we shouldn't have. And we've all made some mistakes."

"None of my mistakes have broken up a happy family." The words were out before I could stop them. It was like a blister I kept prodding. I wanted to keep poking and prodding to cause a reaction, a bigger one, even though I was screaming inside to leave it alone. But embracing this pain in the moment felt easier than waiting for the ticking time bomb to explode in the future at an unknown time for maximum anxiety and dread.

"Neither did mine!" The muscles in her neck strained. "What Seth did was wrong, completely and totally, but I trusted him. Maybe too blindly or maybe I had stars in my eyes about what the relationship was. I trusted him not to lie to my face and make me the other woman. Trusting a person I thought cared about me was my only mistake."

"How can I trust you? How am I supposed to trust you?" It was inevitable. I'd lose her no matter what. The thought struck a spike of fear into the center of my chest, but maybe it was better this way. The devastation wouldn't be so sharp after only a few months. Tonight had proved so many things to me and made running away feel less like a cop-out and more like a necessity. I needed to keep my sanity and heart intact, although right at this moment it felt like it was being scooped out of my chest.

"I didn't tell you because I knew you'd react this way. You're so busy pushing away people who want to be close to you, if they're not in the tightly defined box your friends are already in. It seems like they snuck in under the wire before you slammed the lid closed."

She brushed past me and stormed down the hallway.

I followed her, bristling that she was once again trying to shift the blame.

She wasn't going to turn this around on me. This was about her and what *she'd* done.

"The way I live my life has nothing to do with you."

"You're right, it doesn't." She walked into the closet and came back out with a bag.

"What are you doing?"

Her head tilted, and her gaze zeroed in on me. "What do you think I'm doing? Do you think I'm going to stay here and let you berate me and try to make me feel like I'm a terrible person for who knows how long? I'm leaving."

The last two words were launched into the air like an errant missile. "To go where?" The fiery boulders we'd been lobbing at one another cooled in a split second.

She couldn't just leave.

She jerked open drawers and grabbed handfuls of clothes, shoving them into the bag. "I don't know, but not here."

"And you say I run from people."

She shoved the bag to the floor and held her arms out wide at her sides. "I'd have thought you'd be happy—relieved even. It's like that night I left your bed. I'm doing this myself. What do you want from me, Hunter? You're staring at me like I'm gum on the bottom of your Italian loafers, but then you don't want me to leave? We're back to the push-and-pull situation? There were red flags with Seth that maybe I missed, but I'm not setting myself up for even more disappointment again. So I'm getting in front of all the flag waving with you right now."

My muscles locked, and I couldn't move. She was leaving. All the fears I had when it came to her and she was taking care of them in one fell swoop. She was leaving, not because something horrific had happened or because she was being ripped away—she was just walking out on me. Just like my dad had done. If it wasn't one thing, it was the other. The fire in my chest was being stoked, more coal poured on top to increase the dirty, gritty burn of it all.

"Just...we'll talk about this in the morning."

Clothes fell out onto the floor as Sabrina jammed even more into her bag. She kept going like I wasn't there.

There were so many things I wanted to say, words I wished I could take back, but tonight drove home that we were never going to work. Nothing lasts forever. I'd been taught that early and often.

"Sabrina—"

"I'll come get my stuff sometime later." She paused at the door. Her fingers gripped the wood so tightly the color leached from her knuckles. Her lips twisted and pinched, and she stalked toward me. With a sharp breath, she leaned in and kissed me, hard and powerful—there were so many unsaid words in that kiss.

I raised my arms to hold her, but she was gone and I gripped nothing but the air.

"Bye, Hunter."

The front door slammed, and once again I was alone in my apartment. The silence roared louder than any of my nightmare screams.

I sat on the edge of the bed and stared at her dropped clothes dotting the floor. She wasn't coming back.

This was supposed to be for the best. It was supposed to make things easier. So why did I feel like I'd just taken a knife to the chest?

37
_____

SABRINA

I staggered out of the elevator into the garage level and fell into my car. The interior light didn't turn on. No, no, no. I turned the key in the ignition and a choked, whining greeted me. Slamming my hands against the steering wheel, I dropped my head against it and took deep breaths. This time, I didn't even have my former escape route.

Back in the elevator, I went up to the lobby.

The doorman on duty looked at me.

I winced at the wide-eyed gaze radiating concern and pity. He was one of the night guys I generally only saw on date nights and didn't know his name.

"Sabrina, are you okay?"

But he knew mine. Damn full-service, way-too-fancy apartment building. "Yes, I'm okay. I just need to go." I rushed out the door before anyone else could ask me more questions.

I wasn't okay, and I didn't know where I was going. My options were limited and I doubted Barbara had another apartment here in the city I could stay in and I didn't want to worry my grandmother with another last-minute move where I once again need a place to stay. For a split second I'd thought to ask Millie, but she was in Colorado with her family.

Ian wasn't an option after he'd moved in with his girl-friend a couple months ago. The last thing I needed was another woman thinking I was trying to break her relation-ship apart. Staring at my phone, I pulled up my pitiful contacts list. There was only one option.

I waited in a coffee shop a block away from the building, nursing my coffee.

Zara rushed in, her head whipping around until she spotted me.

"I'm sorry I called you so late. I didn't have anyone else." The tears I thought were finished were back again.

"Of course." She grabbed my bag and shepherded me out of the coffee shop with an arm around my shoulder.

Inside the car, I sat in my seat and barely remembered to buckle.

Zara dropped my bag into the back seat and slid into her seat looking at me the whole time like she thought I might evaporate in front of her. Her mouth thinned into a severe line, but her eyes were soft, sympathetic.

"You don't have to tell me what happened." She pulled off into the empty street. "I figured you might not want to stay with me and Leo, so I got you a room."

Panic gripped me. I didn't have money for a hotel room.

"Don't worry, it's comped. I have a ton of nights in the hotels that I never use."

I nodded, fearing my voice would give out and didn't have the strength to put up a fight when I had no other options.

"Whatever happened, I want you to know I'm here for you, Sabrina."

And those were the words that broke me. My eyes hurt, the tears poured down my face so hard. Those were the words I'd wanted to hear, just not from her. Everything came spilling out. The whole horrible truth of why I'd left my apartment with Seth and moved in with Hunter in the first place. What happened tonight from the car crash to the disaster of a dinner, and then the Seth bomb at the end and our fight. I word vomited it all, filling the car with my hysteria in between nose-blowings and eye-wipings.

"Wow." It was all she said. Her face was set and determined, and I hoped I hadn't just talked myself out of the one person in the city I felt I could talk to.

Staring back at my reflection, I could see why Zara had looked at me like she had when she walked into the coffee shop.

My eyes were red and puffy. My face was splotchy, and it felt like my skin was brittle, crackable in the brutal cold. I wished I was numb though. That would make it all so much easier. Instead there was only raw, piercing, searing pain.

I'd thought I'd be immune to it by now, but this was so much worse. At my humorless laugh, Zara shot me a look. "We're almost there." Her fingers tightened on the steering wheel.

"I thought finding out about Seth's wife was hard. I thought that was the worst I could ever feel, but the joke was on me all along. I'd take that over what I'm feeling right now."

"Honey, once everyone cools down, maybe he'll be willing to listen."

"I don't think I want him to. He didn't trust me. The

things he said to me..." I clapped my hands over my ears like I could block out the words reverberating inside my head.

Her hand touched my back, rubbed it, trying to bring me comfort. "We're here. I'll grab your bag from the back. Just head inside."

I let Zara handle everything, not that I'd have been useful—I was feeling nearly catatonic.

She guided me, and I followed, trying to make sense of how the world kept going like nothing had changed.

Inside the room her footsteps were absorbed by the plush carpet and hotel soundproofing. The door quietly closed behind me.

"You have a tab for breakfast, lunch, and dinner for as long as you need."

"You don't have to do that." I wiped at my face with my sleeve.

"Trust me, it's not a problem. I've been where you are, Sabrina, and I know there's not much I can say right now to make it better." Her expression was so calm and quiet like she didn't want to spook me, but I saw the truth in her words, even though I couldn't imagine Leo and her ever going through what Hunter and I had.

My mind switched into survival mode. Making plans would save me from feeling like quicksand would come pouring into my mouth and fill my lungs if I didn't move fast enough. "I need to call the property manager for the apartment I gave up. Maybe they'll be nice and give me the discount. Or maybe I'll go somewhere else. Cat's always offered up her couch and she'd let me stay with her for a while. If my freelance work picks up, then I could float myself for a bit longer."

Zara brushed her hands along my arms like she needed to warm me up. "You don't have to do anything right now except get some rest. It's the weekend and then everything's going to be closed for Christmas."

My stomach twisted. A Christmas I was supposed to spend with my new boyfriend opening the presents I'd gotten for him and finally getting to see what he'd gotten me. "You're right." I nodded and climbed onto the bed, getting under the covers still wearing my clothes. My energy was zapped, and there wouldn't be much I could do until after the holiday.

She was still in the room, but I stared off into the distance. Snow began to fall again. It stuck to the windows before melting against the glass and dripping down in streaks. Some gathered at the corners, piling up.

"I'm going to order you some soup and a sandwich. Why don't you take a shower and get into your pajamas? You're still in your clothes from tonight."

Snapping myself out of it a little, I lifted the sheets and stared down at the hunter-green dress I'd put on for our big Christmas date night. Had I chosen the color because of him or because Christmas was right around the corner? Either way, I needed it off. I dragged myself out of the bed and grabbed my bag.

Opening it, I stared at the contents I'd shoved inside. Perfect, I had ten pairs of underwear, three t-shirts, one sweater, a pair of pajama pants, and a pair of jeans I'd been meaning to get rid of because the muffin top was getting out of control. At least I had enough for me to figure out where I went next. In a moment of clarity before I'd left I'd rushed into my room to get my laptop.

Taking a t-shirt and pajama pants, I went into the bathroom and closed myself in the floor-to-ceiling glass shower. It was a lot like the one in our—no, his bathroom. Working like I'd forgotten how to use my limbs, I stepped under the spray and let the water roll down my body, trying to warm up.

This would be the perfect time for a bath in the deep tub on the other side of the bathroom, but I didn't have the energy and would probably fall asleep inside it.

However long I was in there, it was long enough for Zara to knock on the door and announce the food had arrived.

My fingers were waterlogged and wrinkled. I dried off and dressed, not wanting to see my reflection. If it was anywhere near as rough as I felt, I didn't need the visual.

In the room, Zara had the food set up on the desk and stood beside it while I sat, like a babysitter expecting me to dump it all over my head.

Chicken noodle soup and a ham and cheese on a crusty roll. Basic and beautiful comfort food. After barely eating my dinner, I was hungrier than I'd expected. Maybe my body was trying to fill the hollowness in my chest.

"It's a big sandwich." I offered Zara half of the monster-sized meat and bread combo.

She took it and nibbled on it, probably only taking it to make me feel better.

We both ate in silence. The warm broth and chicken chunks helped settle my stomach, trying to undo some of the damage from too much wine and my boyfriend accusing me of being a homewrecker.

The tears welled back up in my eyes, blurring the food in front of me. I set the spoon down.

"I'm finished."

I climbed back into bed, curled up into a ball, and pulled the blankets up to my chin.

Zara clicked off the lights. The bed dipped beneath me, and her hand ran up and down my back. "I'll be here tomorrow."

I flipped over. "Zara, no." Even though I'd just had half a bowl of soup, my voice sounded croaky and on the verge of being lost. "There are only a few days left until Christmas. I'll be fine by myself."

"The room's in my name and it's not like you can stop me from visiting." A small, sad smile lifted the corner of her lips. "You might not want to talk about it, but I want you to know you're not alone, okay? Just because I'm Hunter's friend—although I'm thoroughly reconsidering that right now—it doesn't mean you're on your own, okay?"

My throat tightened. "Thank you for everything, Zara. I swear I'll pay you back. The next check I get—"

"Nope. I don't want to hear about it. It's not costing me anything other than my time, and you could use it. We've been through the Cat Embassy Pub Crawl trenches, we've got to stick together, right?" She leaned over and hugged me tight.

That happier, insanity-filled night felt like it had happened in another lifetime. Then, I'd felt like my design career had finally had a big break. I'd been spending a night out on the town with my oldest friend and a new one, and my reunion with Hunter awaited me less than twenty-four hours later.

"I'll put the tray outside so it doesn't smell up the room, and you'll have breakfast delivered in seven hours. Get some rest, Sabrina."

I looked at the clock on the nightstand: 12:01a.m. The day felt like it had been a week long.

"Tomorrow. I'll see you tomorrow afternoon."

I nodded, knowing if I tried to speak, I'd burst into tears again.

Zara left and the whoosh of the heater and distant sounds in the hallway made me feel like I'd never been more alone. For once, I wished for the pounding drum solos coming from Hunter's room. But his room was across town in the apartment I used to call my own. And now I was here with my head throbbing, trying to figure out what came next.

38

HUNTER

I nstead of spending Christmas morning with Sabrina, watching her open the presents I'd gotten her, I'd sat in the armchair in the living room, staring at the twinkling lights that only a few days ago had felt so magical.

I ripped the plug out of the wall and sat with the darkened tree while I finished the last of my not-tar-like coffee. The kind that sent caffeine blazing through my veins and made me feel like I could lift a truck. The kind I'd gotten used to when Sabrina got to the coffeepot first. The kind I missed.

Sabrina hadn't come back to the apartment. I'd sent her a message, but she hadn't responded and my phone calls went unanswered. It was all for the best, right?

Less than a week ago. It felt so long ago, but it had been fewer than four days since she'd walked out.

The numbness was better. Her handwriting was scrawled on little notes sticking out from the tops of the boxes under the tree, although we were the only ones with presents down there.

Where had she gone when she left? Was she safe?

Maybe it was best she hadn't responded to my calls or messages. What exactly was I supposed to say to her?

But I needed to know she was safe and sent another message.

Me: Just let me know you're okay

The bubble popped up and disappeared a few times but no response came through.

She hadn't come for her things yet, which gave me hope, but did I even want it? This was why I had stayed away from entanglements and relationships. The worry. The fear. The desire to change things that were immutable facts of life. The endings.

I shook my head, trying to push those thoughts aside. I needed to bury them deep down, and soon I wouldn't worry about her. I wouldn't want to know what she was doing, wouldn't want to hear her laugh again. I wouldn't want to sleep beside her at night.

Although my sheets still smelled like her, I'd tossed and turned all night. It hadn't been the nightmares from my past; this was something different that I was scared to put a name to.

My days before Christmas had been filled with work on the concert. All the pieces were set in place, and other than paying through the nose for the gear to replace Trevor's, it was running much smoother than I'd anticipated. For some reason, although one part of my life lay in fiery rubble, the rest was smooth sailing.

On Christmas Day, instead of throwing myself headlong into another fourteen-hour day, I'd been forced to be social, although I'd had the rest of the guys turn it into a meeting. It hadn't been too hard since the concert was a week away.

We were meeting in Leo's apartment. It didn't count as work if we didn't go into the office, right? Other than Jameson, who always complained about Teresa waking him up at five in the morning to open presents, it was like any other day for the rest of us. A day meant for food and family. GiGi had invited me down to visit her, but I'd told her I needed a rain check due to the concert. And due to her questions about Sabrina, which had gotten more pointed.

Since she hadn't ripped me a new one, it seemed like Sabrina hadn't mentioned it to her or her grandmother either. So GiGi was at her Widow's Weekend in the Virgin Islands with the ladies who were on their own, keeping everyone in line.

And here I was ready to iron out all the final details for the blow-out of the year, and feeling like my chest had been caved in.

I knocked on Leo's door. The voices of everyone else drifted into the hallway.

The door swung open, and Zara's smile fell. "You have the nerve to show your face?" She glared, eyes burning with a fury I'd only ever seen directed at Leo.

"Why wouldn't I? Am I too early?" I checked the time again.

"You're lucky I even answered the door." Her words were clipped and cutting. "Who do you think Sabrina called after your fight?"

The blood drained from my head, making me woozy. But I clung to the fact that she was at least safe. "You."

"Bingo. She was a wreck, Hunter."

Steeling myself, I grabbed onto my anger with both hands, needing it to pad my landing or I'd come crashing straight back down to earth all over again. "This is between her and me."

Her eyes narrowed, and she flicked her wrist to close the door. "And you think treating her how you did is okay?"

I wedged my booted foot in the rapidly closing space and stopped it from slamming shut and leaving me out in the hallway. "She lied to me. She lied to me, and she cheated with a married man."

Zara pushed harder on the door, trying to close it in my face. Thankfully the winter boots held up against the combo of her body weight and the solid oak slab. "You know she'd never do that. She didn't know. And the second she found out, she left, which explains how she ended up in your grandma's apartment in the first place."

Her words nudged at the part of me that knew it was true, but I grabbed a chest and some chains, and padlocked that part up. This was inevitable, and all I was doing was getting in front of the eventual end to spare us both. "It's done. What happened doesn't matter anymore."

She let go of the door so quickly I pitched forward, stumbling into the apartment.

"Doesn't matter?" Her voice pitched higher.

Everyone stared at us. Their faces morphed from surprise to happiness to confusion at Zara's sharp tone.

"You think crushing someone doesn't matter? That kicking them out of where they're living only days before Christmas doesn't matter?"

"I didn't kick her out. She left."

"Because you called her a cheating whore."

My spine stiffened. "I never said those words," I volleyed back at her. "I'd never call her something like that."

"Did you even have to? She was a mess when I picked her up. She couldn't stop crying."

My stomach knotted, twisting and churning at hearing about how she'd been after she walked out the apartment door. She'd looked closer to punching me than she had breaking down in tears when she said goodbye to me. That goodbye had hit with a finality I still didn't want to face. But I wouldn't let Zara burn me with this, so I ground out again, "I didn't kick her out. She left."

Zara folded her arms over her chest. "Was she supposed to stay under the same roof with you after you showed her exactly how little she meant to you?"

How little she meant to me? Would someone I didn't care about set my soul on fire like she had? Bring me to the precipice of saying the words and making the commitments I'd promised myself I'd never make? No, she didn't mean too little to me. She meant too much. More than I could risk. "I love her. That's how I feel about her. But she lied to me."

Her face softened, and her arms dropped to her side. When she met my eyes again, it wasn't with the skin-peeling anger from before, but with pity. She shook her head. "You can't keep doing this, Hunter."

My eyebrows pinched together. "Doing what? How is it my fault she lied to me about her ex?"

Leo walked behind Zara and ran his hand up and down her arm. The small show of solidarity sawed at my chest, pouring salt in the gaping wound that was still raw and would be for a long time. His lips pinched together in a grim line. "She got too close, didn't she?" His gaze focused on me, unyielding and unwavering.

"This has nothing to do with how things were between me and her. It's about her cheating and her lies." I clung to the reason, but it felt more and more like an excuse each time I said it out loud and as it rolled through my head.

Jameson sighed and cleaned his glasses with the hem of his shirt. "This is what you do, Hunter. We're lucky we met you before those walls were cemented completely, because it feels like if we hadn't met you back in college, you'd never have let anyone else in."

My hands clenched at my sides, and I looked over Zara's shoulder to everyone else who seemed perfectly fine to gawk and level their judgment at me. "Are we working or not? This is bullshit."

Everest and August stood from their spots on the couches and walked toward me like this was an intervention.

"You're ganging up on me? Last one in, first one out?" My heart slammed against my tonsils.

No one responded to my jab.

Everest stepped forward. "She had you twisted up in knots from the beginning. We could all see it." Our conversation one of the first nights she'd moved in and how much I'd tried to avoid her came rushing back.

Jameson circled to my right. "I've never seen you look at anyone like you looked at her at Teresa's birthday."

"Because he's never let anyone get close enough to look at them like that." August leaned against the wall, looking not entirely on board with what was going down. At least there was one person on my side. "Trust me, I get it. Falling for someone and having them punch your heart out of your chest isn't easy. In fact, it fucking sucks. But Sabrina seemed nice." He shrugged.

"Oh, you're the relationship guru now? The wedding planner who was left at the altar? How many dates have you gone on in the seven years since Carrie left you?"

The second the words escaped, I wanted to claw them back.

There was a collective gasp and stillness that only came when a line had been crossed.

I stepped forward. "August—"

He pushed off the wall and stalked over to me. "If you want to bring this shit to all of us and lash out because you're scared, that's on you. But don't be surprised when you keep doing this and end up alone—really alone. I'm sure everyone else can handle whatever you need for New Year's Eve, but I'm out of here." He snatched his coat off the back of the chair closest to the door and barged past me.

The door slammed, shaking the whole wall and large overhead lights.

Everyone else stared at me like I was a stranger who'd broken in. I wanted to curl up and hide my shame, not only at what I'd done here but what I'd said and done with Sabrina.

"She could've died on the way to dinner that night." I stared at my clenched fists jammed against the tops of my legs and tried to shove down the overwhelming panic filling my lungs with terror.

"How? She looked fine—I mean, other than the sobbing and splotchy face." Zara's voice broke through the rising tide.

Wincing, I thought of the tears burning in her eyes and how she'd kept her head up high, not wanting me to see her crack. Just like I hadn't wanted to open myself to her—not fully.

"We were walking to Parc, and a car skidded out of control. I saw it careening toward us and grabbed her. I put myself between her and the car and waited for the hit. But it didn't come. Luckily the streetlight pole saved us both. The whole time I just kept thinking she could've been gone in less than a second." I blinked back the liquid welling in my eyes.

"My life flashed before my eyes—our life flashed before my eyes—and all I could think was she'd be snatched away."

"So instead of talking that over with her and being calm and reasonable about it, you jumped straight to 'you're a cheater' and kicked her out?" Jameson sounded honestly confused about why calm and reasonable hadn't entered the equation when it came to her.

My head shot up. "I didn't kick her out. And the fight was later. We went to the restaurant. She was insistent we go even though she'd almost died, and when we showed up, Ryder was there. It was a setup to get us together before Christmas after I said I'd handle it my own way."

"Which means you'd never have contacted him again. Okay, I think we need to know the deal with Ryder. Sure, it's probably annoying to have a teenage tagalong, but why do you hate that kid so much?"

"I don't hate him." Suddenly standing felt like too much. I leaned against the wall and slid down it until my ass hit the floor.

Leo, Zara, Everest, and Jameson exchanged looks before joining me on the floor like this was story time.

"What happened?" Zara almost whispered, wedged under Leo's arm.

It hurt to look at them.

I wrapped my arms around my legs and locked my hand around my wrist. My legs bounced like they were trying to break the circle of my arms and shook my upper body. "I only saw my dad twice after he left.

"I was thirteen. My mom was sick. The treatments were wreaking havoc on her body. GiGi was a world away, flying in whenever she could. We had a nurse most of the time, but a lot fell on my shoulders. My mom didn't want to burden GiGi with how bad things were because she knew how hard it was for her to be away. And my mom never asked, but I couldn't not help. She was my mom. I'd have done anything for her."

I stared at the blank space on the wall between Leo's and

Everest's heads.

"Then one Saturday out of the blue, my dad pulls up into the driveway. My mom had been trying to get me to go to my friend's house all afternoon, but I didn't want to go. When I saw his car, I jumped up and was gone before she could call me back.

"He kept promising he was coming back, but it had been a couple months at this point. But it didn't matter. I flung the front door open and raced out, jumping on him like he was a hero returning from war. I was so excited. I was so happy." The lump grew in my throat and throbbed like it had a heartbeat of its own. "I was so relieved. He was back and he'd take care of things. I could go back to video games and just fucking around. I wouldn't have to deal with all the pressure anymore." The guilt twisted in my stomach like a knife. "I was all wide smiles and excitement that I wouldn't have to take care of my mom by myself anymore." The serrated edge dug even deeper.

"I turned around, holding onto him and feeling like things would be okay. And my mom was in the doorway. She had on her big sweater that looked like it was swallowing her up whole and had a look I didn't understand at the time. She didn't look happy to see him at all."

"Thanks for being so understanding about all this." He held a manila envelope out to her.

She looked to it and back to him and then to me before she stepped back inside. Her eyes had so much pain in them, and I didn't get it then.

"I hovered in the hallway. The only sound in the other room was a pen scribble and the flicking of paper. He walked out of the living room, ruffled my hair in the hallway, said he'd see me later, and left. They were divorce papers. He'd come by to get her to sign divorce papers, and I'd been so happy to see him. I betrayed my mom, one-hundred percent relieved and excited that he was back. But it was finally the end. The real end.

"And my mom's eyes said it all in the doorway when she first saw us. She tried to comfort me and console me, but..." I squeezed the back of my neck, embarrassed and burning with rage that I'd wanted him back in my life at all. "It was a bad few days for the both of us. After that, I only saw him at the funeral, where I told him exactly how little I cared about him and never wanted to see him again. He took it to heart, and I didn't. But I'll never forget the disappointment in her eyes."

Zara scooted forward. "Hunter—and maybe I'm totally out of line, but I've met your grandma and I can only imagine how awesome your mom was—but I don't think it was disappointment in you that you were seeing. I think she was disappointed about how your dad was letting you down. She was sad for you. She was hurting for you because she knew what was coming. And it seems like she was trying to protect you." Her hand wrapped around my bouncing knee.

Jameson scooted beside me, his shoulder right against mine. "Getting close to Ryder isn't betraying her, Hunter. I never met her either, but I don't think she'd want you to carry this burden. She knows you loved her, and spending time with Ryder isn't you accepting what your dad did or forgiving it. All it's doing is being kind to him and maybe letting him into this ragtag family situation we've got going on in here." He pointed between the five of us. "And August."

"I need to apologize to him."

"You do, but don't worry. He knows you and he'll forgive you because he'll know you mean it and because he's family."

Tears burned in my eyes.

Dropping my head to my knees, I dragged sharp breaths into my lungs. "I need to fix this."

Jameson's arm wrapped around my shoulder. "You will. Just take it one piece at a time."

We didn't get any work done. I left Leo's not too long after that and sent August a text asking him to call me back or tell me when I could call him. I went to the apartment to grab a lone package under the tree and my next stop took me across the bridge to New Jersey, twenty minutes from where Jameson lived.

Sitting in my car on the suburban street, I stared up at the house that looked a lot like mine had growing up. I rubbed my fist at the center of my chest, trying to alleviate the ache that had been there since Sabrina walked out. Since I'd driven her out.

Now or never. I opened the door, grabbed the box from the back seat, and walked up the slush-covered walkway to the front door and knocked.

I gripped the edges of the box, crinkling the wrapping paper, and waited. The breath clouds gathered in front of my face before drifting off into the sharp post-Christmas air.

The lock jingled, and the door swung open.

Ryder stared back at me with shock-wide eyes.

"Hey, Ryder."

"Hunter. What are you doing here?" He shook his head like he was trying to wake himself up, although after how I'd treated him, I must have felt more like a nightmare than a dream. "I mean, come in." He pushed the door open wider and held his arm out, trying to usher me in.

My stomach clenched. The house where my dad had lived. The house where he'd lived with his whole other family. "Do you mind if we walk instead?"

"Sure. Give me two minutes." He ducked back into the house and let the door partially close behind him.

Against my better judgment, I peered inside. Framed pictures of Ryder hung on the walls. A few family portraits with the three of them on the mantle in the living room. Then Ryder blocked my view, joining me outside.

"This is from Sabrina." It had sat under the tree along with the other unopened presents. I couldn't bring myself to shred the paper on the last gifts she might ever give me.

His eyes jumped from the box to me. There was a hint of disappointment in his gaze before he brightened and reached for it.

I held onto the box for a second before releasing it to him. It almost felt like I was giving away a piece of her. One more thing she'd touched that I wouldn't get back.

Excitedly, he ripped into the paper and shoved his hands into the box, pulling out what she'd gotten for him. A plush knight came out first, stuffed into a mug. Dangling from his hand was a personalized key chain. The mug had the Fulton U seal on it. Ryder grabbed the note attached to the handle and read it aloud. "'To start off your collection for next year. Sabrina.'"

I rubbed my knuckles at the center of my chest, banging them against the buttons of my coat.

"That was really nice of her." He stared at the bundle and ducked back inside, dropping it off.

When he reemerged, I led the way, although I had no idea where I was going.

He fell in step beside me, peering over at me every few steps, mouth opening and closing like he wanted to start whatever conversation I finally wanted to have, but unsure how.

The ground was slick and slippery. Patches of snow and

ice were dumped onto the lawns and patches of grass between the curb and sidewalk, but encroached onto the walkway.

I shoved my gloved hands deeper into my jacket pockets. "I owe you an apology."

He sucked in a sharp breath but didn't say anything.

"What happened between my mom, your mom, and our dad had nothing to do with you. It was never your fault, but it was hard for me to admit that."

"Why?"

"Part of me felt like I'd be letting my mom down. Like I'd be forgiving some of the betrayal if I got close to you. How could you exist if he hadn't cheated? And embracing anything that came from what he did felt wrong."

He shoved his hands deeper into his pockets. "And now?"

I stopped and turned to him. "And now I'm finished letting what our dad did dictate how I live my life."

His breath came out in a rush, the cloud escaping from his mouth, and his whole body relaxed. "When I found out, it made me feel bad for a long time. I looked at them both in a whole new light. It was—rough."

"I can imagine." For the first time I truly could. How he'd made a mistake that had nothing to do with him, where none of it was his fault. The same way Sabrina probably treated herself when it came to her ex. I'd kept trying to assign the guilt I saw in her eyes to her being complicit, but now I saw what it was. A good person who'd taken on the burden of someone else's mistake when it had nothing to do with them.

We walked around the neighborhood and talked, covering his college plans, what he wanted to major in, how excited he was to get out of the house.

"They'll love you at Fulton U, if that's where you're still planning on going."

He tugged on the zipper to his coat. "I am still trying to decide."

"Don't not go just because of me, and don't go because of me. Go because that's where you want to be, but I'll tell you, I made some of the best friends I could've ever hoped for at that place."

He snorted. His nose was bright red.

"It's cold. We should head back."

We approached his house, which no longer felt like a looming beacon of bad memories and betrayal, but just a house. "I'm sure Sabrina will want to hear all about our talk when you get back to the apartment."

It felt like an icicle had been speared through my chest. "No, she won't."

"Why not? I figured you were here because she bugged you enough to get you to come talk to me."

Staring off into the distance, I'd rather have my heart carved out than have her look at me like she had the day the door closed between us. "No, she didn't."

"Did you guys have a good Christmas? Hold on, one sec." He ran back through the front door. The whole house seemed to shake with his thudding steps. A few seconds later he popped back outside. In his hands was a poorly wrapped box. "Can you give this to her? It hadn't gotten here before our dinner, so I couldn't give it to her then." His chin dropped, and he shoved the box toward me.

And then it hit me with a blinding, brilliant light.

"Why don't you give it to her?"

He tilted his head and looked at me.

"What are you doing for New Year's Eve?"

39

SABRINA

More snow had fallen since I'd arrived at the hotel. It slowed everything in the city to a crawl. No one was especially motivated to do much during Christmas week, and many people took it as an extended break. Not that I'd been outside.

Hunter's calls and texts still glowed in my notifications, but I couldn't talk to him. I didn't even know what I could say at this point. We'd both said everything we needed to. And he was not going to let me in. I wouldn't put myself in a position to be hurt again. This time there was no blissful ignorance.

He'd shown me how hard it was for him to open up to others. He'd shown me how scared he was to let me close to him. And he'd shown me exactly what he thought of me.

It took two days to get myself out of bed. Zara had visited and brought me a phone charger the following day like she'd promised. She stopped by every day, even though she had her own life.

The last time she'd been here, she'd tried to get me to

come to her place for Christmas, but the chances of a Hunter run-in were too high for that.

"You're going to turn into a mummy in this room."

"I'm moving and haven't been ingesting any pine needles or whatever it is those monks eat for self-mummification, so I think I'll be fine."

"When was the last time you left the room?"

I opened my mouth.

"Not to put a tray outside."

And snapped it shut. "I've answered my emails and have five client meetings set up for the second week in January. That gives me two weeks to get my life together, figure out where the hell I'll be living, and find a work space." There was also the semi-important issue of how to retrieve all my equipment from Hunter's. I didn't care about my things, but my work gear I'd need—soon. And that made me tired, weary to my bones, which made me think maybe self-mummification wouldn't be such a terrible thing after all.

The clouds would part and I'd have to get over this eventually. I'd been knocked down before, but this time, dragging myself back up felt like standing at the base of a craggy, jagged mountain in bare feet.

"What about Cat? Will she be back in town soon?"

"I don't think so. She's in Australia or Austria. The connection was bad last time we spoke."

I'd kept my texts to Cat brief and vague. It was the holidays and she might have a whole day off at some point, she didn't need to be worrying about me half a world away.

Plus, I had everything I needed.

Meals arrived three times a day even though I didn't do more than pick at the food that came up. Was this the thing where people talked about being so upset they could barely eat? Apparently, I'd never really experienced this type of hurt before. Normally I'd grab a pint of ice cream or box of cinnamon rolls to make it all feel better, but this was different.

Housekeeping and I had come to an agreement and I'd handled most of the cleaning, mainly so I didn't have to leave the room.

But today was quieter than normal. The hallways were quiet. The streets were deserted. The whole city felt like it had slept in for the day.

Zara left not long after and I couldn't blame her, not one bit.

"Merry Christmas to me." I stared at the room service tray with my plastic-wrap-covered container of gravy. It had been delivered hours ago. The top of the gravy had congealed. The smells had turned from appetizing to awful.

My stomach rumbled, and I placated it with a bit of turkey and some gravy Jell-O while watching the gentle dusting of snow on the ledges of the buildings across from my window.

A knock on the door pulled me from my stare-athon at the white-light-lined building across from me. I'd turned off the lights to see it—and also so I wouldn't have to see my reflection sitting at the desk beside the window.

I opened the door without checking to see who it was and gasped, not sure I wasn't hallucinating.

"Jesus. If your face were any puffier, I'd think you'd been attacked by bees." Cat stood in the hallway, complete with a red and white Santa hat. "But I'd still like a kiss." She held a sprig of mistletoe above our heads.

Instead of serving back a biting retort, I burst into tears.

Her face fell. "Shit." She wrapped her arms around me

and hugged me so tightly it was hard to breathe—or maybe my lungs had just given up. "Don't do that; I'm sorry. I know I'm a total asshole. I wasn't sure what level of breakup you were at." Her Cat-hug magic worked, and she rocked me. "I can see how you're still in the chest-bursting tears phase." She shhed and rubbed my back. Her arms were warm and tight around my shoulders.

My cries turned to hiccups, and I lifted my head from her tear-soaked coat. I jolted when I saw the hotel room door hadn't closed.

There was a man in the hallway with his hand splayed against the door, keeping it from closing.

Fear gripped my chest. Had he been here the whole time? Who the hell was he?

I held onto Cat tighter and whispered to her, "There's a guy behind you."

She waved her hand like it was a mild annoyance that a large, scowling man had his gaze locked onto both of us. "Don't mind him." A look of irritation flashed on her face, and she glanced over her shoulder. "You asked and now you can see. You can leave now."

His lips pursed. The severe look didn't seem like one he could ever take off. It was etched in the strong lines of his face and would've probably sent most people diving for cover. Cat spoke to him like an overly large nuisance.

"When will you be back?" The thickly rich accent spilled from his lips, not overly harsh or severe like his look. As I'd suspected, this was one of the Ivans. Or maybe it was one of the other two.

"I'll see you on the second. I haven't used a single vacation day in three years. I'd say I deserve it."

"We're going to Washington for New Year's Day."

"Have fun." She stared at me, not even sparing him a glance anymore.

"I'll need you for the meeting at one p.m. that day."

A seething sound escaped from her pinched lips. "Fine, then I'll be there for the meeting at one. If I smell like a bar exploded on me, that'll be your job to explain it to the clients."

The muscle in his neck tensed, and a vein on his forehead bulged. "Try to be at least half-sober."

"I'll be as sober as you are. You can close the door now." Dismissiveness shot through her words like barbs like he wasn't one of the people signing her check. It must be nice to have that much job security—or balls.

His gaze lit with a fire that didn't seem like it was all anger. There was an undercurrent I couldn't put my finger on, but from how tense Cat was, I wasn't sure she believed she'd be able to get rid of him this easily.

Instead his gaze jumped to mine. "It is nice to meet you, Cat's friend Sabrina."

Wow, he knew who I was.

On a hunch, I threw out the most likely name. "Nice to meet you too, Ivan?"

He nodded. "The car will be here at nine a.m. to pick you up on the first."

"I can't wait. Bye." She tilted half her body backward rather than turning around, and flicked her fingers toward the hallway.

The muscles on his jaw were getting a work out. The tension in his face coupled with those cheekbones—how anyone stopped staring at him was beyond me. "I will see you soon, Cat."

The door slammed closed behind him, and her shoulders dropped. Tension escaped her like a breath she'd been holding.

"What was that?"

"Don't worry about him. I'm here for you. For the next few days, we're doing nothing but watching terrible TV, ordering room service, and lying in bed. How's that sound?"

"That sounds a lot like what I've been doing already."

Her nose scrunched up at the abandoned tray sitting on the room service trolley. "Not so much the eating part."

She placed an order for a pizza, two slices of double chocolate cake, and glasses of cold milk.

"Minibar prices are such a rip-off. I'll be right back." After bundling up, she ducked out to stop by a liquor store she'd seen a couple blocks away.

When she got back, it turned out that vodka cranberries were the perfect pizza-eating drink. I wasn't going to turn down a little oblivion at this point.

Cat being beside me under the blankets, watching trash TV helped keep my mind from the places it drifted to in the quiet of the hotel room on my own. I'd begun making plans for what would happen next, but it had to be outside the city. Crossing the bridge into Philly hadn't been far enough to keep from running into Seth, but I could deal with Seth. Adding Hunter to the mix would rip my heart out and stomp on it. My job was portable. Maybe I would take Cat up on her offer to crash on her couch for a bit. It wasn't like she was in her apartment much anyway. As long as I had a solid internet connection, a corner of a room, and my computer, I could do my work.

A fresh start in a new city sounded like a better idea all the time.

This could be my chance to mend my heart in a new place without the reminders of our time together. Maybe then I'd forget how much it hurt. Right now, it felt like the pain had been stitched deep into my heart, and I wasn't sure how long it would take to heal.

I wasn't sure if I wanted to have my time with Hunter become vague, distant memories of a place I'd left behind. But I didn't know what other choice I had.

40

SABRINA

Sabrina - Zara (getting ready/going to NYE event)

The New Year's Eve festivities were in full swing all over the country and city. Fireworks had been going off outside my hotel window since dusk. There was an electric air of anticipation and promise blanketing the city streets, but it hadn't reached me. New Year's Eve always felt like a letdown, like being packed into Times Square for one night of your life and ending up peeing into a Gatorade bottle while people barfed into KFC buckets, all while penned in for eight hours with a hundred other people in below-freezing temperatures.

I'd stay in my hotel room tonight, thank you very much.

The door burst open, and Cat walked in with a garment bag.

My stomach dropped, and I was shaking my head before she even held out the bag.

I waved my hands in front of me. "No."

Her lips curled into that should-be-trademarked smile. "Yes."

"Not tonight, Cat. Let's hang here, order room service, and watch TV." The whine was clear even to me.

"Oh, you mean the thing we've been doing for the past week? I'm antsy, Sabrina." She rocked up onto her toes, which was impressive in those heels, and shook her shoulders like an impatient five-year-old. "This is the longest I've been in one place for years."

"Shouldn't that be a nice change of pace?"

"No, it's making me feel like I'm going to burst out of my skin. Please, just go out with me. There are parties all over the city."

I flopped back on the bed. "Thank you for thinking of me and trying to cheer me up, but I'm not in the mood tonight."

Cat tugged on my arm. "Which is exactly why you need to go out. Shake off the post-Christmas blues for a few hours to get dressed up, dance, and drink with your friends."

The door opened again. Damn key cards. Next time they left, I was flipping the door lock.

Zara rushed in, smiling wide. "Did she say yes?"

"Not yet."

They both looked at me.

"Why don't you two go together? You'll have a lot of fun and be much better company for each other." Turns out Cat aggressively giving out her phone number to anyone she felt might be a new friend had come in handy when Zara had called Cat after picking me up that night at the coffee shop.

"We want to go with you." Zara sat on the edge of the desk.

"But—"

"I will burn this hotel to the ground if that's what it takes to get you out of this room."

Zara's head snapped in Cat's direction.

"See what you've unleashed?" I flung my hand in Cat's direction. "You brought her here, not me."

I pulled the pillow over my head. "I don't want to go anywhere. I don't even have anything to wear. All my things are still at Hunter's. Any word on when I might be able to go over there, Zara?"

She grabbed for the pillow. "No, sorry. He's been getting ready for the New Year's Eve concert, so it's been hard to track him down. But he's probably so busy he's not even in the apartment. I'm sure you could get them to let you up."

I turned my face to the side so I didn't smother myself, and peeked out. "I'm not willing to take that chance. I need to know he won't be there. I can go pick up all my stuff and be out in a few hours." Lugging all my equipment out would be a pain in the ass, but Ian or one of the other doormen would help. That would make moving out suck a lot less than it had moving out of my last place. Although my heart was broken in a different way this time.

Zara rubbed her hand on my leg and looked to Cat. "It'll all be okay, but let's put everything with you and Hunter on the back burner tonight. Let's go out and have some fun."

"Shouldn't you be with Leo?"

"He understands. I've got a friend down, and I'm not leaving her behind tonight."

I flipped the blankets over my head and shouted to them. "You and Cat go. Just let me stay here and watch the street-level fireworks display."

"Sabrina, don't make me come in there after you," Cat chimed in.

"I don't even have anything to wear."

A heavy weight dropped across my chest and stomach.

I pushed the blankets back and peered down at the black garment bag draped across me.

"Don't worry about the clothes. I've got you covered."

"What the hell is it with people feeling like they need to dress me? Am I unable to dress myself?"

Cat shrugged. "At the moment, yeah. Be happy you're getting choices. There are three dresses in there. Get into the bathroom and try them on."

"You're both actually going to make me do this?" I looked between them.

"If everyone plays nice, Sabrina puts on the dress, and we leave here with no more argument, I can leave the Duraflame logs and matches behind."

Cat was madness wrapped in chaos, wearing Louboutins. She unzipped the garment bag and pulled three other dry-clean bags from inside without breaking her gaze. "You say I'm dramatic. I'm not asking you to drink Drano in a suicide pact. All I'm asking is for you to let us take you out tonight." She crossed her arms over her chest. "If I have to shove you into that dress myself, I will. I'm not letting up until you come with us."

Glaring at them both, I swung my legs off the side of the bed and snatched up the hangers. "How do you know I won't lock myself in the bathroom until midnight?"

With a sigh, Cat took the dresses from my hand and led me toward the open bathroom door. "Because you're ready for the distraction just as much as we want to distract you. Tomorrow you can go back to wallowing. Let's spend tonight getting drunk, dancing, and pretending that everything will be okay in the morning. I've got one night of freedom, Sabrina. Please?"

Man, I was a shitty friend. Cat finally had some time off and she'd kept my company with mild grumbling.

Tomorrow was the first, and I'd vowed to start getting my life together beginning then. Might as well get a jump on it and be ready at the stroke of midnight. I let out a long, overly loud breath. "Where are we going?"

Cat leaned in. "We're taking you, that's all you need to know."

"I don't get to know where?"

"A New Year's Eve party. Let's leave it at that."

There was no joke in her tone, no mischief, only her showing me how much she wanted to do this for me. She held out the hangers.

Stepping into the bathroom, I took them from her hand and closed the door. I was being a stubborn, colossal asshole. All they were trying to do was help. "Thanks, Cat."

"You'd do the same for me. Get dressed and we'll figure out hair and makeup once we know which dress you're choosing," she shouted. I could tell her mouth was pressed right against the wood with her hands cupped around it.

I ripped the plastic off the first dress. It was a bright red mini halter dress that looked like it doubled as a bikini. I wasn't in the mood for an eleventh-hour asshole-bleaching to wear this. I also didn't feel like freezing my ass off.

The second was a backless number that would most definitely show off my butt crack if I breathed too deeply.

Readying myself up for this evening to get even harder, I sent up a prayer to the god of crazy friends that the previous two had been a colossal joke.

Peeking through one eye, I tore into the final bag. Both eyes popped open. Inside was a shimmering emerald dress with three-quarter-length sleeves. The sequins that didn't catch the light were shaded and looked dark green, like a Hunter green. This was a disco-ball version of the dress I'd worn the night Hunter broke up with me—or had I broken up with him?

Either way, it was the only option and flattered me,

which was always a double plus in my book. I slipped the dress on and was contorting myself to finish with the zipper.

"Are you wearing the red one?" Cat knocked and shouted.

"How'd you know?" I looked at myself in the mirror for the first time in days. My skin no longer looked like I was having an allergic reaction to the air, but the bags under my eyes were dark and deep. They'd need a truckload of makeup to smooth it all out.

"Do I need to come in there after you?"

"I swear, you're the pushiest, most annoying person I've ever met." I jerked the door open.

The two of them were perched on the edge of the bed.

"Ohhh, turn, I love it." Zara clapped then circled her finger in the air.

I put my arms out wide like I was preparing for a pat down and spun for them.

"It's gorgeous. We've got all the supplies and not much time, so let's get to it." She grabbed my shoulders and sat me down at the desk where her spread of makeup was neatly laid out.

"Not much time for what?"

Cat picked up a brush and flicked the soft brown bristles against my cheeks. "Before the ball drops. We'll need to get you nice and loosened up by then. Tonight's excursion is sponsored by the Ivans. Town car, open bar wherever we go."

"Such generous bosses."

She rolled her eyes. "It's all a ploy to make sure I'm there tomorrow. The driver will spirit me back home at a *respectable* time. but don't think I won't take advantage of all they're offering. My gift horses don't get looked in the mouth, they get saddled and ridden." Lifting one arm, she whipped it overhead, waving her imaginary lasso.

Zara picked up a powder foundation and brush and started on my overly shiny forehead.

"Do you know what you're getting into?" I whispered to Zara loud enough for Cat to hear.

She laughed and nodded. "It'll be fun. Who doesn't want to spend a night out on the town with their girlfriends?"

Ones with boyfriends. I stopped myself from saying it. She should be out with Leo, dancing with him in a restaurant with a spectacular view of the fireworks where they'd toast champagne at the stroke of midnight and kiss under a volley of bright and bombastic glitter in the sky. Instead she was stuck here with me, although she didn't look stuck. Neither of them had made me feel like I was a burden.

"Thanks for tonight. I needed a kick in the ass."

They exchanged a look and responded in unison. "We know."

So the night began. The life I'd thought I'd been building with Hunter was gone, and I was back to the foundation. It hurt. The ache was there, insistent and always right behind my sternum.

Cat and Zara had put in a lot of work, and I wouldn't spoil it. I'd take the first step out of my self-imposed seclusion and onward to my future—alone.

41

HUNTER

"Thank you guys again for doing this." I shook Camden's hand in the backstage greenroom where the rest of the guys had been hanging throughout the show.

He sat on the worn and sagging brown leather couch that looked like it had been through more debauchery than either of us could imagine.

"Don't mention it. You're helping with the Maddy situation; it's the least we could do. Plus, I can't say I don't get wanting to make a total fool of yourself for someone you care about." His tone was light, but there was an undercurrent that told me he got this on a deeper level than he was letting on.

"Thanks for the vote of confidence." I laughed; it felt brittle in my chest. So far there hadn't been any word from Leo or Zara about Sabrina.

Maybe Zara had told her what was going on and she'd said screw that and refused to leave her hotel room. I couldn't blame her. If she didn't show up tonight, I'd have to figure out another option. Funny how after all her work to get me to talk to Ryder, the last person I'd wanted to talk to, here I was needing to convince her to talk to me. It felt like an apt part of the punishment I'd already been visiting on myself.

"You forget, I was there for sound check." Camden stuck his finger in his ear like it was still ringing.

"It wasn't that bad."

He grabbed my shoulder. "Whatever you say, man, but thank you from the bottom of my heart. After you're out there singing, my voice will sound even better, so you're doing me a favor."

"Happy to help."

He grinned, the blue in his eyes catching all the light in the room before bursting into laughter. "I'm just kidding, man. I think it's cool what you're doing, and I hope she loves it."

"She might hate it, if she even shows up. I'm pretty sure she hates me after what I did." I reached for the glass of water on the table and fumbled it. It pitched to the industrial-carpeted floor, the contents creating a pool in front of me. "Shit."

I'd been a mess all day. It was a surprise I'd even been able to dress myself. My stomach had been a roiling mess for days. I couldn't sit still, and focusing on anything beyond what was right in front of my face was almost impossible. The guys had taken on a lot of extra work and backed me up at every turn.

"Don't worry about it. It's not beer, and I don't think that's the worst thing that's ended up on these carpets. About what you're trying to pull off tonight? Women can be mysterious creatures. One second you think you're giving them exactly what they want, and the next you wake up in bed alone."

"I'm sure that's not a problem for you. We had to hire extra female security guards who wouldn't be swayed by just how convincing your female fans can be."

He laughed again and scrubbed his hand over his closely shorn hair. "They can be persistent, but those days are long behind us. We were never the 'party until we're puking up blood' kind of guys. Even Lockwood doesn't go the groupie route. At least not when he's sober." He grimaced. "Anyway, you'll kill it out there, and if your girl doesn't come around, I'm sure there are plenty of women who'll be throwing themselves at you after the show."

"Dressed like this?" I got up and held my arms out at my sides. From the second I'd left the apartment like this, I'd felt like I was wandering around naked. The looks from people who knew me confirmed just how different I looked. I hadn't felt like I had a shield up to everyone, but even Everest, Leo, Jameson, and August had done double takes when they had first seen me. Maybe I was better at hiding parts of myself in plain sight than I'd realized.

Sabrina's words came flooding back to me, and it solidified my resolve to not chicken out. I had a lot to prove, and I might only have this one shot.

"You're going out onstage looking like that? I thought these were your pre-show clothes because you'd be helping the roadies or doing mechanic work during our set."

"Ha-ha, very funny. No, this is what I'm going out there in."

"Balls of steel. I mean, we don't exactly have a glam-rock look or anything, but—I'm pretty sure I can see your pits through that hole."

"Yup."

With a look of uncertainty and pity, Camden nodded. "If

she's got you going out there like this, Mr. Impeccable, then you must really care about her."

"More than care." I loved her. In a way that made me crazy, because as much as I should want to run from it, being away from her hurt so much more than all the imagined scenarios that had run through my head since Christmas Eve night.

I walked down the painted cinderblock hallways to the stage. The music vibrated the floor and got louder with each step.

More than a few people shot me looks as I passed by, and if I hadn't had the all-access laminate dangling from my neck, there would probably have been a few people trying to stop me along the way. My suits were my armor. They deflected most uncomfortable situations and got me into places I wouldn't otherwise have been able to go.

Right now, I wouldn't be able to talk my way into a Wendy's drive-through.

The music thudded in my chest when I got to the side of the stage. Fans screamed, probably a decibel from having their eardrums ruptured, but they stared up at the stage, entranced by the performance.

Onstage, Noah Ellis finished up his set. The lights cut out, and he rushed off to the wings, sweating and grinning. Glow sticks and flashlights lit his way.

The crowd didn't quiet down. They were chanting his name. Even though Without Grey was coming up next, there was a vocal portion of the audience screaming his name.

He turned back toward the stage. "Can I?" He looked to the tech running the soundboard and then to me.

"Go for it."

There was a flurry of chatter between all the backstage crew.

The tech checked Noah's in-ear monitor battery. "You're good to go."

He rushed over and shook my hand again. "Thanks, Hunter, for this chance. You guys were always so nice to me whenever I played at The Griffin."

"Don't worry about it. In a year I won't even be able to get you on the phone."

He laughed, swung his guitar back in front of him and jogged out onto the stage.

The encore might've been another chance for me to stall what was coming. My stomach churned like I'd eaten bad takeout. It wasn't the thought of walking out there—it was knowing I might walk out there and it wouldn't matter one bit. That I might've ruined the best thing I'd ever had in my life because I was afraid of losing it.

Turned out pushing her away had hurt me more than I had thought possible.

Not waking up next to her had made me feel like my chest had been hollowed out. I'd stare up at the ceiling, straining to hear her bumping around in the house, although I knew she was gone. I slept in total silence so I'd hear even the jingle of the door handle. Instead there was only the beating of my own heart and the blanket of quiet in the apartment.

"You sure you're up for this?" Everest stepped up beside me with his arms crossed over his chest. The suit he was in made him look like he was running the show tonight, not me.

"What are you doing here?" I hadn't expected him to come, not knowing Maddy would be in the same building.

"It's your big night. Why wouldn't I be here?" Every

muscle in his body was rigid and set like he was a wrong move from shattering.

"You know why." I tilted my head to check behind me. Maddy hadn't been in the greenroom, so she was probably somewhere around here.

"She's in the other wing."

That explained why he was over here when the backstage party area was set up over there. "Have you seen her?"

"We saw each other."

And most likely fled in the opposite direction.

"She didn't seem like she was looking for closure. She looked straight through me."

Even over the booming music and rising guitar crescendo Noah built to on the stage, I could hear the heartache in his voice.

"She's working. She takes her job very seriously."

"It's the most important thing in her life, right? Makes sense. I need a drink." The front was slipping—before it had been easy to skate over the way Maddy affected him, but it was getting closer to the surface. He walked to the unattended bar setup and poured two shots.

Camden had been right. There was so much anguish and suffering between them both. They'd have a chance to air it all and finally figure out what they were to each other once everything was set up for their meeting in the new year.

I knew all about regrets, and didn't want to spend years on that path like the pair of them.

Tonight I'd have my answer. I'd know if there was a chance I could repair what I'd broken, or if she was finished with me.

Checking across the wings of the stage, I spotted Leo.

He nodded. She was here.

I swiped the drink from Everest. The sharp bite shot down my throat. Lifting my hand, I went to adjust a tie that wasn't there. Instead it was the t-shirt Sabrina had seen me in the first night we met.

One of the audio guys handed me a mic. I wiped my sweaty palms on my pants. It was now or never.

I walked across the stage. Behind the giant curtain, whispered voices got to work finishing up the setup for the big reveal.

"Almost Happy New Year, everyone."

The crowd screamed and shouted with drinks liberally flowing for hours now. Chants of "Without Grey" popped up from various corners of the arena.

Standing out here in front of everyone, I felt exposed in a whole new way, but it would be worth it. God, I hoped it would be worth it. Although abject humiliation after what I'd done would be at least part of my just desserts.

"I know you're all ready to see the big band of the evening. They'll be out in a few minutes, but there's one announcement I need to make to everyone here first."

The crowd hushed as much as an arena of ten thousand people could.

My palms were sweaty and the mic felt like it would slip from my grasp. "There's a very special person here tonight that I owe an apology to. And I'm going to need your help. Are you up for it?"

42

SABRINA

"You lying assholes!" I shouted in the wings of the stage.

A bunch of people *shh*ed us, but I didn't care. I tried to pull away from Cat who had me in a bear hug from behind. Holy hell, she was freakishly strong. Or maybe I needed to go back to the gym.

She did have nearly a foot on me, but even so, all that work with the Russians had turned her into the Hulk.

"You need to see this."

"I don't want to be here." But hadn't I known? As much as I wanted to pretend I'd been oblivious, when we'd pulled up to the back of the stadium, it hadn't been hard to piece together where we were going. Now my feet were beyond cold; they were ice blocks, never to thaw, and I wanted to get out of here.

"Whether you want to be here or not, you need to hear him out."

"I don't need to do anything. You weren't there." I broke her hold and spun around. I had no illusions that she hadn't let me break free.

"No, I wasn't. But I also know I've never heard you happier than when you were with him. He got you to go out. He had you sounding like the old Sabrina. You know I'm not one for second chances, but I think you should at least listen to what he has to say."

Behind me, the people out in the stadium erupted in cheers, which petered out to confusion. A live mic turned on, and the voice I'd grown to know so well against my ear night after night boomed in the arena.

"And I'm going to need your help. Are you up for it?"

Standing in the wings of the stage, I was locked, unable to move from the first note. Everyone around me stood in stark stillness staring at the man on the stage.

The words were drowned out by the roaring sea swelling between my ears. It had been over a week since I'd seen him. A week since he'd given me no choice but to leave. And now he'd had me brought here. There wasn't a doubt in my mind that he'd orchestrated this whole thing for some reason, but I didn't know what had changed. What he thought could've changed between now and then.

If nails down a chalkboard and a knife in a garbage disposal had a baby, it would have had a better singing voice than Hunter.

He stood under the spotlights from the non-Trevor provided lighting rigs in his ratty t-shirt and sweats combo I'd only seen the day I moved in with a mic up to his lips. The crowd seemed just as confused as me, but everyone in the wings seemed to know exactly what was happening, which was probably why he hadn't been tackled from the stage.

Sweat glistened on his skin and his horrible, terrible voice wavered, but he pushed on.

Hands pushed against my back, guiding me closer to the

edge of the wings, where I was blocked from the audience by the rigging.

My heart leapt into my throat and my mouth was sandpaper dry.

I tried to dig in my heels and run away, but I was surrounded by a horseshoe of people. Cat, Zara, Leo, Jameson, August made up a human wall to block my retreat, but I was rocked when my gaze landed on a not-so-usual suspect. Ryder?

He grinned wide and stepped forward for a quick hug before taking up his spot as part of the blockage. "I think he's got some things to tell you." With a lift of his chin, he directed my gaze back to the stage.

Seeing Ryder here and with a smile on his face brought tears to my eyes. I pressed my hand to my mouth before letting my gaze return to the stage.

Hunter was giving it his all and had the crowd in the palm of his hand even though we'd probably all need a hearing test when this was over. But he turned, and his eyes locked with mine.

The words finally filtered through. It was a beat and rhythm I knew. He had the arena singing along with him about how much I light up his life and didn't seem to know how beautiful I was. These were all words I'd heard before and sung a thousand times, but hearing them so nakedly and pitchily from Hunter as he stood in front of a sea of thousands of faces, they hit me differently.

He was exposing a part of himself he'd never showed anyone, not even the people closest to him, in front of strangers, and eviscerating the One Direction hit line by line.

"You all know this song, so how about you sing along while I bring my special guest out here."

I shook my head and he walked toward me.

Still in the shadow of the wings, he reached for me and I jerked my hands back.

The fans behind him took over, singing the words like a giant choir.

"Sabrina, I was the biggest asshole known to man. I was scared of how you made me feel and scared of what it would mean to lose you. I've never loved a woman like I've loved you, and without you in my life, I've felt like a little piece of me was dying every day."

Tears brimmed in my eyes and my heart raced in my chest at a gallop.

"I've missed you so much and I wanted you to know and I wanted everyone else here to know that. I love you unapologetically and without question. But now I have a question for you..."

The crowd died down and that's when I realized everything he'd said had been on mic.

He pulled me forward.

My legs stumbled and hitched like a newly born calf and I was in the spotlight along with him.

"Can you ever forgive me? If you can, I promise I'll spend the rest of my life proving to you how much I love you."

The arena was filled with lights from people's phones. Silence blanketed the massive space and all eyes were on us.

This was certainly the opposite of hiding me away. He'd brought me up on stage in front of thousands of people to torture them with his voice and profess his love to me, a love he didn't know if I could still return, and more than all that, he'd gone to Ryder. He'd brought Ryder here, and from the looks of it, he'd won him over after the kid had given up hope.

I ached to be near him, deep down I'd known I'd never just get over him.

He brushed a tear from my cheek and his gaze was watery too. "I love you, Sabrina, and I'd rather spend the next thousand years cherishing every moment we have together rather than worrying over losing you. I've felt what that's like, and I'd rather soak up every ounce of you for as long as you'll let me than know you're out there in the world and you're not mine. You have my heart, and you always will."

Unable to stop myself and not wanting to, I flung myself at him and let him lift me.

The mic thudded to the floor setting off some terrible feedback, but I didn't care.

Hunter's arms were around me and he spun me around on stage. Our lips met, bringing the electric charge rushing through me out the tips of my fingers. I hoped there wasn't a grounding issue with the equipment all over the stage.

He kissed me hungrily and I savored his taste right back.

Setting me down on the floor, he cupped the side of my face. "Is that a yes?"

Loosening my arms from around his neck, I looked around us and spotted the mic. I let go and grabbed it. "What does everyone say, should I forgive him?"

The cheers from the smiling faces in the crowd were deafening. The stage rumbled under my feet.

"I think the people have spoken." I handed him back the mic.

"Thank you everyone." He threaded his fingers through mine. "And to show you my thanks, I've prepared another song."

Everyone in attendance started shaking their heads and screaming 'no' at the same time.

"Hunter, that's really not necessary." I tried to tug him away.

"No, I've got to do it."

The beginning notes of As Long as You Love Me by the Backstreet Boys began. Hairs on the back of my neck stood up as he earnestly began the ballad and held onto my hand. I tried to keep a straight face.

Before I could say another word the curtain that had been stretched behind us dropped and all of Without Grey joined in on the accompaniment. The crowd switched from horror to screaming delirious happiness.

Camden strolled forward with his own mic, and I blessed the sound engineer who swapped the levels so his voice overpowered Hunter's.

I loved the man, but he couldn't sing to save his life. I couldn't stop grinning, the kind of grin that made the spot behind my ears ache. I'd thought tonight had been shaping up to be a new chapter in my life, a dreary one, one I trudged through while piecing myself back together.

The song ended to cheers and Camden talked into his mic thanking everyone for being here tonight. "And I want you all to know you've got ten seconds left until midnight, so grab someone you love and show them as we count this thing down."

Hunter walked me into the wings and held my face in his hands. His thumbs brushed along the corners of my mouth. "I'm really happy they got you to come."

"If they'd told me why, I never would have." My chest tightened at what might've happened to us if I hadn't.

"I know."

"One!" Camden's voice boomed in the arena. Glittering confetti rained down from cannons shooting it into the air.

"Happy New Year, Sabrina." His breath brushed against my lips.

"Happy New Year, Hunter." My lips parted, and that was all the opening he needed. Another hungry kiss met my own. I held onto him and he wrapped his arms around me, keeping me close.

The band on stage played Auld Lang Syne. The confetti drifted through the air and sprinkled over us, twirling and reflecting the stage lights.

Staring into Hunter's eyes, I had no doubt that this would be a New Year's Eve to remember.

EPILOGUE

HUNTER

I lay beside her with my head propped up on my arm.

Her chest rose and fell beneath the blankets in our bed. It still didn't feel real, and there were times I jerked awake only to be calmed by the gentle sounds she made in her sleep.

Months had gone by since the New Year's Eve concert, but I still found myself grateful every day I woke up beside her and not alone.

The nightmares had been washed away and the sleeplessness was a thing of the past, but midnight admirations weren't the worst way to wake up. Folding her up in my arms, I inhaled deeply.

She snuggled deeper against me, her ass brushing against the front of my boxers and her hands curled around my arms.

Even in sleep, she could drive me wild, but I'd save that until the morning. I closed my eyes, letting myself drift back to sleep.

"Why does it feel like you're trying to trap me here?" Everest's voice rang with the suspicion of a person who had a feeling they'd been set up—mainly because he'd totally been set up.

"Trap-schmap. You're being a bit dramatic." Camden and I had worked together to orchestrate the perfect scenario to finally bring these two together. One week of island isolation where the only way out was a propeller plane or some strong rowing skills.

I hated sending Everest in blind to the whole Maddy not knowing he was coming thing, but Camden had assured me that Maddy would without a doubt paddle the 190 miles to get to the mainland after she'd throat punched all of them, and he needed his voice.

Tapping my phone against my chin, I hoped Camden knew Maddy well enough to pull this off, and I hoped we all made it out of this with our throats intact.

Sabrina's footsteps padded down the hallway.

"Where have you been hiding these?" She walked into the dining room and lifted the four brightly wrapped boxes high into the air.

My stomach clenched seeing the presents I'd tucked away in the closet after Christmas. I hadn't been able to bring myself to look at them again, and then, in the aftermath of New Year's Eve, I'd forgotten all about them.

She slid into her seat beside me and shook the box with her name on the tag. "At first I thought you were super prepared for Christmas already, but then I saw this one I'd gotten you and realized they were from last year." The paper glided across the table to me. "You didn't open mine." There was a tinge of sadness to her words.

My name was in bold blue ink on a small tag with one of Sabrina's designs on the back that she'd done in marker and pen. I traced my fingers along the intricate lines. The striking interlocking design reminded me of a sunrise.

I met her gaze and covered her hand with mine. "If it was the last present you ever gave me, I didn't want to open it. I didn't want it to be over."

She brought my hand up to her lips and kissed it. "Who knew when I first moved in you were such a softie? You hid it well."

I chuckled. "I wanted you too much from that first moment, and I was good at hiding it."

It was her turn to laugh now. "You definitely did. This one is yours." She drummed her fingers on the one box, sliding it to me and stared at the others in front of her. "And these three all mine?"

I nodded and watched her tear into the paper.

Her head snapped up when she opened the first box. Inside lay a necklace using one of the designs I'd snapped a picture of on her tablet before taking it to a jeweler. The same jeweler I'd visited not long ago.

With wide eyes, she cupped the platinum in her hands and stared at me with shocked surprise. Just the look I'd been going for. "You—I can't believe this is one of mine."

I popped up and pecked her on her open mouth. "There's more of that coming." Her design work had been getting recognized more and more, and the rates she charged kept creeping up, especially with the addition of her custom design work to August's wedding client portfolios.

"I love it." The other gifts, a new stylus for her tablet and a new tablet for that stylus were met with even more kisses peppering my face.

"You didn't open yours yet." She nodded toward the one sitting in front of me.

Ducking my head, I peeled back the wrapping paper off the thick package on my lap. Gingerly lifting the tape away, so I didn't ruin it, my eyebrows dipped when I saw the blue cover I was so familiar with. The one I'd thought was still on my shelf or had been misplaced in the apartment.

I glanced up at Sabrina and she fidgeted with her fingers.

"I found the pages, the ones that were ripped out."

My chest tightened. The pages where Harry lost Sirus. The ones that had been next for me to read to my mom while she lay in the hospital bed in the room we'd converted to a bedroom for her when the stairs had gotten to be too much.

I flipped to the spot where there had been a gap, a missing chunk of the story that I couldn't bring myself to read again after losing so much as a scared little kid.

"After some YouTube channel searches and a little trial and error, I thought I'd put them back." She lurched forward. "I know I should've asked, but I—I wanted it to be a surprise."

My chair scraped across the floor and I wrapped my arms around her and stood, holding her close. Tears burned in my eyes and my throat was vise-grip tight. I wasn't sure if I was still breathing. "Thank you." I squeezed her tightly.

Her arms were locked around my back. "You're welcome. I know it was important to you and your mom, and I wanted to try to restore a little bit of that if I could."

I buried my face in her hair and breathed deeply, trying to rein in the emotions that threatened to get away from me. "I can't tell you how much it means to me." Releasing her, I captured her face between my hands and kissed her. This woman had driven me absolutely crazy from day one and would keep my heart in the palm of her hand for as long as I lived.

There was a time that would've scared me, would've sent me running as far and as fast as I could, but now I wanted to let her know how true it was, and that I knew she'd keep my heart safe.

I gave her another peck. "I'll be right back." Sprinting down the hallway, I expected nerves or sweaty palms to creep up, but I didn't feel a thing. I felt lighter than ever. Inside my closet, I grabbed the box I'd tucked away a month ago.

Back in the dining room, standing over our puzzle and slotting in a new piece, Sabrina turned to me. "There's one more present I thought you might like."

"Hunter, you already got me too much."

"Maybe, but this is a gift for me and for you."

Her eyes lit up with mischief. "I don't know why you buy me that stuff, it doesn't stay on for very long." She stepped forward and dragged her finger down the center of my chest.

Ripples of desire flooded my veins, but not just for that. For more—for forever. "More can certainly be arranged, but this I'd want you to wear all the time."

With my gaze locked onto hers, I lowered myself to the floor on one knee.

Her eyes widened and she gasped. "What—"

From behind my back, I palmed the black velvet ring box and flipped it open. The platinum band with inset pavé diamonds and a solitary diamond at the center that I'd had to have special ordered catching the light from the windows —it all paled in comparison to her.

Her hands flew to her mouth and her gaze darted from

me back to the ring.

"I measured for it using a piece of string while you were sleeping. I chose it after that Say Yes to the Dress marathon we had a couple months ago. It was as close as I could get to the one you said you'd wear."

She was stark still, like the cardboard One Direction cut out resting between the dining room windows.

"Without you, my life isn't anywhere near as full of joy or love as it is when I'm with you. I need to know: will you do me the honor of being my wife?"

The fridge hummed in the kitchen, my heart shifted into overdrive, pounding in my ears, and Sabrina's darting gaze felt louder than anything else in the apartment.

My smile dipped a little and the worries I'd put aside began to creep back in. Was this too soon? Had I read the signs wrong? "Sabrina?"

Instead of nodding or answering with the only word I needed, she flung herself at me in a full-body collision. "Are you serious?" Her voice was shrill and filled with wonder, the kind that opened my chest and injected that awe straight into my heart.

We were on the floor now, with Sabrina on top of me.

"I've never been more serious about anything in my life."

She unlocked her arms from beneath me and pressed her palms against my chest. "Really?"

"Really." I nodded and laughed.

"But...but we're..."

I tucked her hair behind her ear and rested my palm against her cheek. "In love. I love you, Sabrina, from here until forever. I love you and I'll never stop loving you."

Tears welled in her eyes and she sat up more. "I love you too, Hunter. Sometimes it scares me how much and how well things have been going. I just—" There was a flicker of doubt that hit me like a fist to the ribs, but it was quickly replaced by peace. Her face brightened, and I knew she could feel it too. The fear and apprehension melted away, and it was just us. "Yes." She touched her own lips like she couldn't believe she'd said it. "Yes." Louder this time. Then she lifted her chin toward the ceiling and screamed at the top of her lungs, "Absolutely, one hundred percent yes!"

Grinning wide, she looked at me and kissed me. It was full of everything I loved about her and every single bit of love I shared with her.

I slipped the ring on her finger and she stared at it like I'd given her a star from the night sky. If I could have, I would. We sat at the table with our fingers laced together, our music playing in the background, working on a new puzzle. Sometimes life was messy and chaotic, and sometimes it felt like things would never slow down, but then there were these quiet moments alone together where I knew there was never any other place I'd rather be than here with the future Mrs. Hunter Saxton.

Thank you for spending some time with Hunter and Sabrina! It was so fun to revisit these guys and the wonderful world of SWANK once again. I do have an extra scene you as a treat! If you want to grab it, you can click here.

Next up will be Everest and Maddy! I do love a bit of enemies to lovers and a second chance, so I can't wait for you to read their book in The Second Chance Set Up. I've had a few questions about the rest of the guys as well. They will all get their own books, hopefully early next year!

If you're looking for your next book to escape into, you

can check out my newest series, The Falling Trilogy. This is a spin off of the Fulton U series where there will be some surprises for you!

The Art of Falling for You

"Are you stalking me?"

"We live right next door to each other, New Girl."

Bay Bishop aka The New Girl is my new neighbor. Glasses, stage crew black clothes and a knack for fading into the background.

I catch her singing with a voice unlike any I've heard before that taps into feelings I shouldn't have for the girl who avoids me at all costs. I need to know why she hates me.

With three months until graduation, the final play is on. Only it's not for more points. It's for Bay.

Unlike my success on the field, this win is anything but assured. But I can't stop myself from taking the risk.

The countdown clock is ticking. The only thing scarier than finding my first love will be losing her.

Grab your copy of The Art of Falling for You!

ACKNOWLEDGMENTS

Thank you for being here! I also want to thank my editing team: Dawn Alexander, Sarah Kremen-Hicks and Sarah Plocher, you're the best and I this story wouldn't be half as amazing without your help and guidance.

I can't wait to bring you even more sweet and steamy stories in the future.

Thank you for taking the time to get to know Hunter and Sabrina and the rest of the SWANK guys :-D

Until your next read!

Maya xx

ALSO BY MAYA HUGHES

Fulton U

The Perfect First - First Time Romance

The Second We Met - Enemies to Lovers

The Third Best Thing - Secret Admirer

Falling Trilogy

The Art of Falling for You

The Sin of Kissing You

The Hate of Loving You

Kings of Rittenhouse

Kings of Rittenhouse - FREE

Shameless King - Enemies to Lovers

Reckless King - Off Limits Lover

Ruthless King - Second Chance

Fearless King - Brother's Best Friend

Heartless King - Friends to Enemies to Lovers

CONNECT WITH MAYA

Sign up for my newsletter to get exclusive bonus content, ARC opportunities, sneak peeks, new release alerts and to find out just what I'm books are coming up next.

Join my reader group for teasers, giveaways and more!

Follow my Amazon author page for new release alerts!

Follow me on Instagram, where I try and fail to take pretty pictures!

Follow me on Twitter, just because :)

I'd love to hear from you! Drop me a line anytime :)
https://www.mayahughes.com/
maya@mayahughes.com

facebook.com/mayahugheswrites
twitter.com/mhugheswrites
instagram.com/mayahugheswrites

Made in the USA
Middletown, DE
07 August 2021